W9-CDD-532

A CURIOUS LAND

Stories from Home

SUSAN MUADDI DARRAJ

University of Massachusetts Press
Amherst and Boston

This book is the winner of the 2014 Grace Paley Prize in Short Fiction. The Association of Writers & Writing Programs, which sponsors the award, is a national nonprofit organization dedicated to serving American letters, writers, and programs of writing. Its headquarters are at George Mason University, Fairfax, Virginia, and its website is www.awpwriter.org.

Printed in the United States of America

ISBN 978-1-62534-187-7 (cloth)

Designed by Sally Nichols
Set in Monotype Centaur Std

Printed and bound by Sheridan Books, Inc.

Library of Congress Cataloging-in-Publication Data

Darraj, Susan Muaddi.
[Short stories. Selections]
A curious land : stories from home / Susan Muaddi Darraj.
pages ; cm
ISBN 978-1-62534-187-7 (hardcover : acid-free paper)
I. Title.
PS3604.A75A6 2015
813′.6—dc23

2015024889

British Library Cataloguing-in-Publication Data
A catalogue record for this book is available from the British Library.

The Grace Paley Prize in Short Fiction is made possible
by the generous support of Amazon.com.

For Elias, always,
& our children, Mariam, George and Gabriel

"Stop, oh my friends, and let us weep over the remembrance of the beloved and the home."

—Imru' al Qays, *Mu'allaqah*

"How curious a land is this, —how full of untold story, of tragedy and laughter, and the rich legacy of human life; shadowed with a tragic past, and big with future promise!"

—W. E. B. Du Bois, *The Souls of Black Folk*

CONTENTS

A
CURIOUS
LAND

THE JOURNEY HOME

1916

When Rabab lowered the wall of the tent and clapped-clapped to the well in her mother's too-big slippers, the stone jar digging into her shoulder, she didn't, at first, see the body. The morning sun glazed everything around her—the cement homes, the iron rails along one wall, the bars on the windows, the stones around the well—and made her squint her itchy eyes.

She was hungry. That was all.

They'd arrived here only last night, stopping as soon as Awwad and the men were sure the army had moved south. It must have been the third time in just a few weeks—collapse the tents, load the mules, disappear into the hills. She hoped this war would end soon, and she didn't really care who won, as long as it *ended* because they hadn't eaten well in two years. In the past few months, her mother had sold all her gold, except for her bracelet made of liras. It was the only thing left, and she was holding onto it, and Rabab realized, so were they all; she imagined that the day it was sold, when her mother's wrist was bare, would signal that they were at the end.

This village, as they had approached it, had looked strange. Not the homes, really—they were simple and squat, but sturdy, their stones large and gray. It was really like every other village, a cluster of houses, on the side of a hill, organized around this well like a band of admirers, hoping for a bride. Rabab had heard her father say that they were now past the Galilee, into Lebanon. They had left Jordan so long ago, it seemed like years, and been awakened too many times at night by the sound of gunfire and shouting. Rabab felt like her nerves would scatter at any moment, like grains of sand caught in a brisk wind. Even this village, emptied and ghostly quiet, frightened her. It felt like a sad mother, abandoned by her brood, her speech paralyzed by the loss. Nothing moved—no sound emerged, as if a *jinn* had cast a spell and turned the people into stones. They'd come across places like this before, but here she felt frightened, as though someone may jump out from behind a door or a tree and snatch her away.

As she filled the jar with water, she glanced up suspiciously at one house, the one directly opposite the well. Who had lived there? Its small windows looked like seashells, built by alternating dark and pale stones. The door was slightly ajar, and she knew it could swing open easily if she wanted to go inside. That made her feel worse—had the people walked out alive from their own front door, she reasoned, they would surely have bolted it behind them. People who had solid walls, who owned doors, would lock them. Their well was full, the water cold and crisp. She cupped her hand into her jar and sipped it, then used the last few drops to freshen her face.

Only when she looked up, using her scarf to wipe her eyes, only then did she finally see it, where it lay on the other side of the well. It looked like a sack, and at first her hunger made her imagine that it was a hastily abandoned sack of rice or grain. But then, there it was—a dirty foot jutting out from under one side, and she recoiled, screaming for help. Her mother ran out of the tent and her father and two brothers scurried out from their side, the younger one wielding his knife. Rabab had pushed the full jar out in front of her, not knowing what else to use in her defense.

But of course, they all understood quickly, there was no need to fear. The black hair on the large toe and the size of the foot told them that it was a man, and his stillness told them that he was dead.

"He didn't move, not a hair," Rabab said over and over, as if to prove that he was indeed no longer living. Her younger brother squeezed her arm protectively and her mother muttered prayers in her ear, to frighten away the evil eye.

"No," said her father suddenly, bent over the bundle of dark cloth, "no, he's breathing." He motioned excitedly to his sons, who scrambled around to carry the long bundle into their side of the tent, struggling under his weight. All Rabab could see was a scabbed wrist, then two dusty feet, their toenails broken and blackened. One of his sandals, ripped at the buckle, slipped off his foot as he bobbed up and down, and flopped into a pile of fresh dung and dust. "*Maskeen*," she thought, hoping that whatever he'd suffered, he wasn't conscious of his pain. She brought some of the water and poured it into a leather satchel, then passed this, along with a clean cloth, to her brother inside the tent.

For the next two days, she helped her mother mix pastes and medicines for their unexpected guest. She was sure he would die before the first sunset, but he defied all their expectations and was alive two sunrises later. He'd been, her brother reported, stabbed deeply in his shoulder, and not by a sharp blade, but by something rusty and unfairly jagged. "The wound is old," she said, "and your father thinks he must have been walking for a long time and bleeding."

"How does he know?"

"The blood is all over his *abaya*, dried and brown."

The middle-aged Imm Yacoub, whose two sons had starved to death last winter, was summoned to stitch the wound. Her eyes were steady, despite the tears they had wept in the last year. She'd been so desperate to feed her boys in those last days that she'd ventured off alone into al-Salt when they'd passed it, gone for a whole day, and come back with a heap of rice folded in her dress, some bread and some overripe apples. Nobody asked. But it had been too late for her sons—they'd been drying out for many days, and once they'd started vomiting, everyone had accepted that it was over.

The fact was that they had all been starving for two years now. Rabab felt that she existed in a constant state of hunger, alleviated only twice a day by a small ration that she received. It happened in waves—sometimes her stomach felt at peace, dry but settled, then a headache would sweep over her, followed by a gnawing pain. She often suppressed the pains by drinking more water. Last year, she'd eaten snake meat for the first time, a large one caught by her brother, and they'd skinned it, roasted it, and satiated their appetites. Awwad, who had been married to their cousin and who had four children, all girls, was also quite good at capturing small animals in the desert. He also had a superb instinct for the journey, knowing which way to turn, where to find water, how to bargain with Arab villagers and farmers, and even with the foreign soldiers to secure more supplies.

Awwad came now to their tent, several times a day, to check on the guest, and whenever he did, Rabab and her mother stayed in the *maharam.* In the old days, they would have busily prepared coffee for him, but now there was nothing to serve, except tins of cold water. Rabab felt the rough cloth that separated the two sides of the tent, and wondered what it was that made it feel like an insurmountable wall. It was awkward to be on that side of the tent; there were so many things she had to pretend she didn't hear: Awwad's conversations with her father, the feeble voice of the nearly dead man she'd discovered, the murmurs of worry from her brothers. For years now, she'd been perfecting the art of seeming unaware. At night, when her brothers were taking their rounds outside the tent on guard, she sometimes heard the whispered summons to her mother, who would rise quietly from her mat and slip under the cloth, and a few moments later, the hushed grunts of her father. Rabab often tried to inhale through her nose to steady her breathing, to slow it down so that her mother would suspect nothing as she slipped back across and lay next to her afterwards. If she were brave, or foolish, she thought, she would taunt her brothers, ask them if, while watching the sands shift at night, listening to the wind slide over the rocky hills like a groaning lover, if while surveying the horizon for bandits or soldiers or quickly moving storms, they were alert to what was happening in the tent right behind them.

⁂

It was not until the fourth day that Rabab finally saw the stranger, and that was only because they had received the alert from Awwad that they should move. They worried, again, that they would starve on the journey. A summit among the men was quickly convened in Awwad's tent, to settle the question of whether they should enter the abandoned houses to take as many supplies as they could.

She pretended not to hear, but she was outside, dusting and packing the rugs, and listened intently. "The question is, are these people returning?" she heard Awwad's voice ask. "If not, then we should take what we can." Rabab wanted to tell them what she knew: that the day before, while at the well, she'd seen a bony cat amble over to the slightly open metal door, sniff the ground before the entrance, trail its nose along the doorjamb, then slowly enter. A second later, it dashed out again, looking stricken, running faster than she'd imagined it had the strength to do.

"Better us than the Turks," agreed a voice she could not distinguish.

"Whether they come back or not, we are stealing." That was unmistakably her father, and his voice was weary but firm.

"Ask the stranger," someone suggested. "Maybe he is from this village and knows."

"He does not. He is from the south, as best I can tell. A Jerusalemite, probably."

Awwad presented an idea: that they should only take supplies from houses that seemed well stocked, and that they should leave some goods behind in exchange. He had some good leather he could leave, and each of the other men agreed to this plan. They left the tent and entered the largest house off the center of the village. Awwad pushed open the door, which swung away as if it feared him. He looked back at the other men, who shrugged, and then they all walked in. Rabab's younger brothers hurriedly exited again, but she couldn't see their faces, and several minutes later, the others also emerged, their faces grim. They carried jars, several small sacks of rice, a barrel of oil, boxes of matches, a tin of benzene. "Do not enter the other homes," ordered Awwad, looking angry. "We have all we need here."

"What?" whispered Rabab to her brother, whose face betrayed a sense of shock, of having seen something that would hound him in his dreams.

"Nothing."

"Tell me."

He jerked his head towards the house. "They're all inside." He peered at her, and she put on her steadiest expression—people never trusted you unless they thought you could handle it. She tried not to look like a child. He finished: "It's a family. They're cut up like . . . like lambs," and she felt for sure that, right here, outside the caravan, she would vomit, that all the agony and frustration would erupt from her mouth, but her brother gripped the edge of her scarf. "Bandits or probably the *frangi* soldiers. Hold yourself in one piece. We need to get out of here. We've been in a cemetery all week."

Within an hour, they were slowly winding out of the village, the mules heaped with rounded packages, pulling their supplies. Most of them walked, but Rabab saw him then—the stranger riding one of the mules, wincing every once in a while. His head was wrapped and his body huddled inside her brother's *abaya,* but she was startled by his face: such a smooth face, so much so that he looked like a baby. And wide, soft brown eyes, with long lashes that curled upward towards his thick eyebrows. She'd imagined him as an older man, someone her father's age, but he was probably only in his third decade, close to her mother's age.

"Where?" she murmured to her mother as they walked, their feet sinking into the soft dirt, the pebbles in the road digging into the worn soles of their shoes.

"To the west," she replied, sighing. Her mother seemed relieved for now, not worried as usual. Perhaps knowing that they had some supplies alleviated her worry. "It's too long, this war. The worst one I have seen."

Her mother spoke like she was an old woman, and yes, Rabab thought, she looked like an old woman, despite her thirty-five years. Her hands—her hands revealed all, in their bloody knuckles, the broken and dirty nails, the wrinkled palms. Still, her mother's energy was unstoppable; she rarely lay still, hardly sat except to weave a rug or crush grains or some other task that required the hands, but not the feet, to move. Sleep was for the lazy, she regularly chided, although Rabab often saw her head droop on her chest while she was sitting in the shade when the sun had risen high.

"We should have buried those people." Her mother's voice was soft, sad.

"How could we do that?"

"It's not right. Nobody should be abandoned like that."

"So, what's the story of this stranger?" Rabab asked, trying to change her mother's mood. "Do we know anything?"

"He's from the south. He may have run away from the army, so your father doesn't want to ask too many questions."

"He will live, at least?"

"*Inshallah.* There has been too much suffering. We saved one soul, and God smiles upon that surely."

"Does he want to go home?"

"I'm sure he does. Those who have a home always long to return."

Within three days, they reached the Bekaa Valley. Their supplies were dwindling, as the sixty people in their caravan devoured the supplies they'd pilfered, and so her father and Awwad and the other men decided they would settle here for some time and try to glean some food from the land. "Spring is here, so we should see some flowering on the trees soon," she heard them say. "The fields are full of grain."

When they established their base, Rabab's job was assigned to her: to go out with her younger brother in search of scraps—pieces of wire, metal, iron. These could be melted down and used to repair other items or bent into rough spoons and knives. It was the worst job to get when they arrived in a new location, but one that allowed her to explore the new surroundings. Being outside of the tent, in the sun, for any reason, was like a small gift.

The camp was quiet when they returned, and so she assumed everyone was out looking for food. Only her brother and Awwad sat at the center of the camp, and with them was the stranger. Her younger brother joined them, and Rabab slowly moved to her tent. She looked back to try to glimpse the stranger's face again, to see how he looked, but instead she noticed Awwad watching her closely, studying her. It was a strange look, and it made her feel nervous. She glanced away and ducked into the *maharam.*

She tried to avoid Awwad after that. His glance had been revealing. She wondered if he was looking for a new wife. His first wife, her cousin, had died while birthing her baby, when Rabab hadn't even finished a decade, and his second wife had already given him three more children. She decided to ask her mother about it.

"You have only fifteen years. Don't think of such things."

"I'm not thinking about it. But I wanted to tell you what I observed in him."

"Try not to make eye contact. I wouldn't want you to go to Awwad anyway." Her mother was cleaning the scrap metal Rabab and her brother had retrieved.

"Isn't he a good husband?"

Her mother squinted her eyes at her and grunted. "I thought you were clever—maybe you're not."

Rabab sniffed. "Is he a good husband or isn't he?"

"Why are you asking?"

"Why not? I want to know."

Her mother shook her head, annoyed. "Ahh . . . Your father is good with me, so that is why you are naïve."

"I don't think I am naïve."

"Naïve people never think they are so." She packed up her supplies, but before exiting the tent, she said, "Do you think he was kind to your cousin, God rest her soul? Look at his wife's arms, her wrists, if you can. Learn to observe things, to understand people."

Rabab found her chance the next day, in the fields, when Awwad's wife was bending down vigorously, yanking the wheat stalks from their roots, causing her sleeves to pull up almost to her elbow. Rabab slowly moved to where the other woman worked, and chatted with her as they both dug and pulled. She was polite, but quiet as usual. Rabab's stomach roiled when she saw the blue marks:

small, circular burns on the woman's wrists and forearms, like those made by a cigarette.

As she worked, she chatted less, trying to comprehend the meaning of it. When she looked up from her work, she noticed Awwad approaching, as if to speak to his wife. He had his rifle over his shoulder, and his knife in his belt, ready for the hunt. Selfishly, she forgot his wife's scars and thought about food: what would they bring back—perhaps some rabbits, some small birds? She wished they would find something good. They'd been without meat for so long. Rabab recalled a wedding just five or six years ago, when they'd actually served lamb—the only time she'd ever eaten lamb in her life, so tender and juicy. But of course, she realized with a start, it must have been Awwad's wedding to this woman. He'd waited only a few months after her cousin had died to remarry.

She kept her head down, half-dreaming, half-listening to their conversation. He was acting gentle, reminding her to grind the coffee and informing her that he planned to have the men eat in his tent that evening. "I'll bring you the meat at noon, if I can find it," he said, then grew quiet. Rabab didn't want to look up, hoping he wasn't watching her. But soon, she heard his voice, above her, "You're working hard, little Rabab."

She nodded, still not looking up.

"You're quite strong, aren't you?"

"Yes." She saw, from the very edge of her vision, his wife pick up her basket and shuffle away, and then Awwad knelt down in front of her.

"How old are you now? Surely you're not little anymore, although I call you that."

"Fifteen."

"A flower! How the girls of our tribe blossom so quickly," he said. Seeing that he had no effect on her expression, he chuckled and wished her a good day.

She picked up her own basket and moved back a few yards to where she had been working previously, on a patch that was filled with tall, brown stalks. Suddenly she noticed the stranger beside her, bending slowly, pulling and piling into his own basket. Had he overheard her conversation with Awwad? There was no one else on this side of the field.

He was tall, and his face soft and handsome. Those thick lashes! She wondered how he looked while sleeping, at night, if those lashes settled like feathers over his high cheekbones. His hands were strong and large, his little finger as thick as her thumb.

Where was his home? she wondered, startled by a flash of hope that he'd never return to it, that he'd stay with them, join them in their wanderings. He wouldn't be the first to have done so—rumor had it that Awwad's grandfather had been a refugee from his own people, and her own grandmother had been a slave captured in a battle from far away, the land of the *frangis.* She'd been known for her pale, pale skin, like fluffy, fine flour. Rabab remembered her doughy cheeks, and her lolling accent, how every Arabic word sounded like a poem dropped from her tongue. Yes, this man should stay—it would be easier for him than it had been for her grandmother. No new language to learn. And he was a man—everything was easier when you were a man. The sun rose in the sky, it seemed, because it was a woman and men commanded her to shine.

Let him stay. Then almost immediately, she felt guilty—he probably was worried about his people. Did he fear for them, wonder if they'd been attacked like the people in the last village?

"Are you well enough to work?" she asked him, delighted at her own boldness. Something about the way Awwad had addressed her made her feel daring and grown-up.

"Not quite, my sister."

"Then why do you work?"

He glanced warily at her, then around to see if anyone were listening. Quietly, he replied, "Because I cannot keep imposing on your hospitality."

"Where are you from?"

"The village of Tel al-Hilou, near Ramallah."

"So far!" She had never been to Ramallah, but she knew where it was, not far from where they had been in Jordan, but on the other side of the river.

"How long has it been for you?"

"Since I've seen my home?"

"Yes."

"Almost a year." His voice was sad. "I hope I will see it again. Sometimes I don't know." His somberness threatened her mood, her desire to be new with this stranger, and she tried to change the topic.

"We have traveled north and now west, and perhaps we will travel south too," she said brightly. "Maybe we will see your village."

"I don't think it is safe for you to go south," he said quietly, pausing in his work to catch his breath. She noticed how he'd been pulling with only his right arm, protecting his left, which hung stiffly from his shoulder. "I've spoken to your father, although it seems that brother Awwad holds a lot of . . . authority with your clan. The south is dangerous."

"The armies?"

"The Turks are bad enough. But the *frangis* are coming too, for sure. We don't know anything about them, and they will come from the south."

"Can they be as bad as the Turks?"

"One never knows."

"Are they—are they very bad? The Turks?"

"Vicious." He sounded angry, resentful, and she remembered that his wound was real, that someone had struck him, cut into his shoulder barbarically and tried to kill him.

She wanted to ask him more, but she noticed her older brother walking towards them. She huddled down close to her basket and focused on stacking the shafts neatly, to allow for more space.

Her brother came with a jug of water for her. "Drink up. One more day of collecting."

She drank, and some droplets spilled down her chin and into the bodice of her *thowb.* Was he watching her, seeing the water slip under her dress? Surely not—her brother was right there, and he didn't seem like a fool. She felt annoyed with herself as she passed the jug back to her brother, who promptly handed it to the stranger. "Here Jamal, refresh yourself, brother."

Jamal. At last, a name. She watched how the ball in his throat bounced up and down with each swallow, how he held the jug carefully in his large right hand, using his left forearm simply to balance and steady it but not leaning the weight of the vessel on it.

"God bless your hands, brother," Jamal told him, and then bent down again.

Her brother stood there for a few minutes, alternately watching them and glancing up at the sky.

"It might rain soon," he said. "Come back to the camp."

"I will," she said. "I have some more room in the basket still. Aren't you on the hunt?"

"It's over! Awwad—he's amazing. He caught four rabbits, alone, within the hour."

He walked away. Rabab and Jamal continued their work, but silently, for she noticed her brother observing from a distance. Within half an hour, she picked up her basket, dusted off her dress, and walked back to the camp. She noticed that Jamal stayed much longer in the field, coming back shortly after twilight, but his basket was filled to the top.

The next day, he moved next to her as they worked in the field again. "Your mother made me a wonderful poultice for my shoulder last night," he said.

"Yes, my mother learned healing from her mother. My grandmother knew all these things. They say she was a Roma."

"What was in it? The poultice? Do you know?"

"Chamomile. My mother carries it with her everywhere we go." Rabab spoke easily, happily. "If we find a field of it, she collects it and dries as much as she can."

"Yes, of course, it did actually smell like chamomile."

"Yes."

A silence emerged between them, but Rabab felt comfortable. She did not feel compelled to either speak or to move away from him. She was aware of his body the entire time, bending down, straightening up, kneeling by the basket, gasps of breath, short blunt exhales of air as he yanked at an especially stubborn root. He knew what he was doing, clearly. When her father passed by them on a mule, he paused and explained to her father that they needed a large cloth to cover the grains that they would grind tomorrow.

"Why?"

"There is not much of a wind, my uncle. We should grind it all up, then cover it, and when a wind kicks up, that is when we toss it up to separate it."

"You know this work, young man."

"Yes, uncle. We are farmers in my village."

"I hope you will see it again, and your family, when you have tired of us."

"Uncle, I owe everything to your hospitality. You will want to be rid of me long before I ever think of leaving."

"You are among family here." Her father looked at both of them pointedly, then moved on, guiding his horse carefully. Rabab flushed, refusing to look at Jamal, and as far as she could tell, he avoided glancing in her direction as well. How dare her father make such an insinuation? she thought. Between this and Awwad's recent attention, she felt like a new saddle or a pair of shoes on display, for sale. The sun blazed down on her head, her shoulders. "You're a bitch," she railed at the sun in her own mind. "A stupid bitch. With all your power, you still obey. So what am I to do?" She left that day without saying goodbye to Jamal.

A week later, the grain was spread out on a stone floor, covered carefully with several cloths, just as Jamal had instructed. Large stones held down the corners of the cloths, unnecessarily so, it seemed to Rabab, since there was not the slightest breeze.

"What do we do now?" her father asked Jamal, as several of the men and women looked expectantly, awaiting instructions.

Jamal surveyed the large expanse of cloth, then lifted his dark eyes to focus on the dozen adults before him. His eyes paused on Rabab's before moving on, then he broke into a wide smile. It was the first time she'd seen a happy expression on his face.

"Now, we wait!"

They did just as he suggested, awaiting the breeze, which might come at any moment over the hills. In the meantime, old Abu Ali and his son brought a *tabla* and a *rabab*, to pass the time. Jamal knew several songs that the rest of Rabab's tribe had never heard, about his village and its orange groves, about the way the girls swayed when they walked, and how the men stamped their feet in the *dabke* line. They listened eagerly, learning the new words and *ooof*-ing their appreciation of the lyrics, singing about his village as if it were their own, as if they knew what it was to settle down and love the land as they would love a woman.

Rabab sat behind her mother, who took a turn thrumming the *tabla*, and imagined, without knowing why, that when Jamal sang about the wind's whisper of love and longing, he was singing to her. She was glad when dusk fell, and nobody could see her face, for then she felt free to gaze more directly at him. She liked his face—it was marked by straight lines: a long nose, long eyebrows that reached almost to the edge of his hairline, a wide, narrow mouth, a mustache like thick wings on a bird. Because he was so tall, his wrists stretched out beyond the sleeves of her brother's *qamis.* Once, someone gave him the *tabla,* and though he played for a few minutes before passing it on politely, she could see that his shoulder pained him when he smacked his palm on the leather.

And that was good. Selfish, selfish, but it meant he would be with them for a while longer, relying on her mother's poultices.

Her thoughts and their music were interrupted by a shout from the ever-alert Awwad—a breeze was stirring.

"Hurry, lift the cloth!" Jamal shouted, pulling back the section on which he'd been seated. As the wind came, he dug his spade deep into a pile of brown grains, and tossed it up—the chaff spread like glitter through the twilight sky, and floated away. The heavier wheat hung suspended for a moment, gleeful at its gasp of freedom, then sank back down to the cold ground.

The summer came, Rabab turned sixteen, although only her mother and brother remembered, and they remained in camp. There was only once when they thought that soldiers were approaching in their direction, when they packed and headed for the caves in the hills—but the news that the battalion had rolled its tanks in a different direction, had headed east instead, made them all exhale with the relief of a desert wanderer, close to death, who has finally found water and shade.

The dampness of the caves, during the four days they stayed there, made Jamal's shoulder cramp, and she huddled by him as her mother applied poultices as well as she could. He sat in the deepest corner of the cave, away from the opening and his forehead on his knees, his *abaya* pulled down to reveal rough, brown skin, matted with dark hair. Rabab watched as her mother pressed a piece of cloth cut from a sack, wrapped around chamomile leaves soaked in tea, to his skin. Was it the heat of the cloth, or the wetness, that soothed his skin? Maybe the aroma of the chamomile that calmed his muscles, his senses? Rabab watched the side of his face, as his lips pressed together and his face folded into a tense, pained smile.

"God bless your hands, my aunt," he said to Rabab's mother. "I am in your debt."

"I just wish this war would end, so you can find your family," she told him. "Your mother surely misses you."

"She surely assumes I am dead," he said, and Rabab felt touched, stirred, by the sadness in his voice. The night before, to keep the wolves away, he had played a melody on a flute, a hardened reed into which he had hollowed out four holes. A sorrowful tune was all that could be played on it, whispering its way huskily into the crisp dark night, echoing in the walls of the cave, sending her to sleep with mournful images of desolate villages, of starving people and emaciated animals, their ribs pushing through their skin. She'd awakened in the middle of the night, tucked next to her mother, whose arm was thrown around Rabab's body. She'd lain there, listening, sure that she heard someone sighing across the cave, sure that it must be Jamal.

She looked at him now, still wincing under her mother's rough fingers, and wondered about him. He'd never spoken of his injury, of the jagged, blackened line behind his collar bone that looked like an animal had sunk its teeth into him and pulled. It had healed badly, and the bubbles on its edges, according to her mother, meant it was dirty, the skin was dying, so she kept applying her poultices. The chamomile cleans and heals, she insisted, and it seemed to be working, although slowly.

"If we can find some alcohol," she muttered now, "I will apply that also. *Inshallah.*"

"I am indebted," he repeated.

Her mother's hands stopped moving, the poultice slipped a bit, as she seemed to ponder. Then she turned to Rabab: "Go see if your father needs you."

Startled, Rabab hesitated, but her mother's arched brows made her snap her mouth shut and stand. "Yes, of course," she said, and moved away, deeply annoyed with her mother, for dismissing her like a child, especially in front of Jamal.

They returned to the valley a few days later, scuttling carefully down the rough hillside, the mules and horses picking their way on patches of wiry grass, as if they knew it was safer than putting their weight on pebbles and stones. Rabab walked, carrying two sacks on her back and pulling one of the smaller mules by the reins.

"Can I take some of the load from you, little Rabab?"

Rabab hoped it was Jamal, but instead saw Awwad beside her, and the disappointment beat down on her like the sun on her head. He easily carried four sacks, two over each shoulder. His neck was thick, and she saw, despite his heavy beard, long veins snake into his collar, slithering down into his *qamis.* He was strong, and the weight he carried didn't seem to affect his stride. In fact, he was slowing down to keep pace with her.

"I'm fine, thank you," she replied, refocusing her eyes on the ground. Awwad was so . . . masculine, like a lion that prowled around in search of prey. She'd never noticed before, or viewed him in this way until he'd started paying her more attention. Her mother had warned her several times now to stay away from Awwad, but how could she do so when he seemed to seek her out at every opportunity? She suddenly imagined herself a rabbit that he easily hunted, scampering away from him as he aimed a rifle at her head.

He strode beside her silently, which made the heat feel more oppressive and the breath escape more painfully from her lungs than it should. She tried to signal her mother with her eyes, but she was not looking in Rabab's direction, helping instead to pull one of the frightened horses. She did sense that someone else was watching her, however, and when she dared turn her head, her glance skittered and then settled on Jamal. His gaze was reflective, suspicious, alert, flickering to Awwad, then back to her. Somehow she sensed that she must not let her gaze waver from his, must help him clear the black fog drifting across his imagination.

She had to be bright, like the moon.

He nodded. Once.

And then he looked away, moving towards her mother, and Rabab was astounded by her own power.

Two weeks after they returned to the camp, the wheat was finally baked. The women and children spent the day collecting the cakes of dried mule droppings they had scattered in a corner of the fields to dry in the sun, and when they'd built a small pile of them, the men ringed them with flat rocks. Then they set them on fire, stoking it while the women kneaded the flour. They stayed up late in the camp, the smell of baking bread wafting over the tents, the animals, the shorn fields.

Later, as Rabab stacked the warm loaves in a basket, she felt Jamal brush past her and whisper something in her ear.

"What?" she asked, her voice almost inaudible. Somehow, her hands knew to keep moving, to continue stacking, re-arranging.

"My sister? I need to speak with you."

"Yes."

"By the horses. Follow me in a minute."

She nodded, her throat feeling suddenly dry.

"Trust me."

"I do," she wanted to say.

Two nights later, what he had said came to pass.

Awwad entered her father's tent and her mother was called to bring coffee. And it was done, the date set for one week later.

"Why did my father agree?" Rabab demanded angrily of her mother. She'd stayed in the tent all day, rather than face anyone's congratulations or Awwad's company. A man hadn't taken a second wife in years, but Awwad dictated his own rules, and no one could match him anymore.

"Awwad will be the sheikh after your father dies," replied her mother, sounding shocked, her voice dull. "That must be why. It would be good for us to be part of his family."

"That is not a good reason." Rabab sat on the rug, her stomach clenched, not touching the dough her mother was kneading. A few minutes later, she saw a shadow, her father's limped walk, pass by the tent, and so she repeated, loudly, "That is not a good reason!" until her mother smacked her leg to hush.

Rabab quieted, but looked at the spot on her calf where her mother's fingers had stung her. She wondered what the legs of Awwad's wife looked like. Were they pocked as badly as her wrists? Why did he hurt her? Because he didn't yet have a son? If she tried, Rabab could squeeze a drop of sympathy for Awwad. It did seem strange that such a virile man, after two wives, had only daughters. But then she pictured his wife, her ribs jutting through her skin, biting her fist to keep quiet while he pushed the cigarette into her other arm, weeping silently so that nobody else in the surrounding tents would hear her, and the rivulet of sympathy she'd begun to feel for Awwad dried up. No, she realized, feeling nauseous. No. No one has ever heard the poor woman screaming.

Her brother put his face between the tent folds. "*Ya aroos,*" he said to his sister, grinning, and she pitied his stupidity. Neither of her brothers knew the truth about Awwad. Probably her father didn't know either. Was it just the women who saw and recognized the wicked shadows that lurked in people's eyes, the evil they encouraged in the privacy of their sealed tents?

Her mother shooed away her younger son, who laughed and said, "What a demure *aroos* we have!"

One more day to endure. Jamal had promised, when the moon was full, and that would not happen until tomorrow. One more day to go out, to appear normal, her usual self, to pretend to be shy when the other women and girls asked her about Awwad, to keep her eyes averted from those of his wife, who seemed stunned and walked around as if in a daze, quieter than ever. One more day to avoid the *arees* himself, who seemed bolder, eager, and who followed her everywhere. Two days ago, behind the olive grove, he'd crept up on her, smiling. Then he'd grabbed her wrist and leaned forward, licking her neck in one long stroke before he nipped the soft skin with his wolfish teeth. Even though she'd been startled, and it hurt, she hadn't screamed. Not one whimper, one gasp—the dryness of her throat shocked her. As she ducked under his arm and ran back to the camp, she knew that she had to do it.

She spent the day with her brother in the fields, her hands covered with rags, picking up the dung of the horses and mules, collecting it in a tin bucket. Then they walked together, chatting about the heat and the beauty of the valley, as they spread the moist brown piles out on the ground, in line with the sun. When they dried in a few days, they would return to collect it, using them as bricks of fuel.

"This is the longest we've ever been in one place," her brother said. "I wish we could stay."

"I bet it would be cold in the winter here," she said, realizing that she would never see another winter with her family, would never huddle under blankets with her mother, hugging her body for warmth, never again feel her strong arms secure around her.

"Awwad says no. He says it would be fine, the weather would be mild."

"How does he know?"

Her brother gave her a sharp glance. "He knows a lot."

She refrained from answering, knowing that her brother wanted her to respect Awwad, that her brother was probably very happy Awwad would be his relation now. Rabab felt like the chain that connected the wagon to the mule's saddle; it was the most worn piece of their equipment, always needing repair. Nobody actually cared about it, unless it snapped.

The next night, when the full moon gleamed in the sky, Rabab was ready.

She waited till everyone was asleep in her tent, then grabbed her already packed satchel and crept out. Before she lowered the flap of the tent, she took a final glance at her mother, who lay still. She couldn't see her well, which disappointed Rabab, but she could hear her breathing deeply. She had to be satisfied with that, she thought, as she ducked down and left. Abandoning her mother, betraying her like this, would be the worst thing she would ever do in her life.

Jamal was waiting by the horses. "We'll take one horse only," he whispered.

"Yes."

"Are you sure about this?"

"I have no choice," she said, her tone bitter and anxious.

"I will keep you safe," he promised.

"*Inshallah.*"

As he led the mare away from the camp, she kept stuffing its mouth with wheat stalks to keep it from neighing. When they were far enough, Jamal mounted, then pulled her up behind him with his good arm.

"Can you find your way to Jerusalem?" she hissed in his ear as the mare heaved beneath them, rocking them back and forth as she galloped.

"Blindfolded, my sister."

By the morning, they had reached a sizeable village, and Jamal told her this was a village of mostly Christians. Suddenly, as Rabab was leading the horse to a well and making sure it drank sufficiently, it struck her that Jamal himself must be a Christian. She watched him, several yards away, as he spoke to a street vendor about some sandals—his own were dusty, torn, re-stitched—and marveled at how she hadn't realized it before. He didn't look different, of course, but still he was the first Christian she'd ever met. Her mother had once told her a farm they had passed in Jordan was owned by Christians, because of the cross etched in the stone above the door of the main house, but they hadn't interacted with any of them.

Her poor mother must be awake now, in the camp, frantically looking for her. The whole camp must be alerted and worried, and surely they would think Jamal had kidnapped her. Even worse, she thought, her face flushing hotly, they might think that she willingly left. Poor mother, who would now have to forget her, to pretend she was dead . . .

"Tell me *mabrouk,*" Jamal joked, displaying his sandals on his feet.

"*Mabrouk,*" she mumbled shakily.

"Sister? What is it?"

"Just worried about everyone—the whole camp must know by now."

"No, it's all been arranged. Your mother said she would wait till noon to alert anyone."

Shock ricocheted through Rabab's slim frame, and her breath came out ragged. "What?"

Jamal inclined his head towards her, his expression grave but tender. His eyes watched her carefully, and so she gave him her practiced look, looking as grown-up as she could. Forced her voice to sound calm and tried again. "My mother knows?"

"She is the one who begged me to take you away."

They sat on the edge of the well, looking for all the world like a brother and sister stopping to rest on a journey home. She didn't know what would become of her, what he could do for her, but she was assured that the camp would head deeper into Lebanon, guided by her mother. "She'll tell them I planned to head up north," he said, "and they cannot keep looking for long. There is still a war going on, and while a caravan cannot elude a battalion of soldiers, two people can slip through, with God's grace."

"They will forget me." She said it calmly, matter-of-factly, though the simplicity of it should have made her reel. "All of them." She felt tears threaten the back of her eyes, creep up her throat, and she busied herself by opening her satchel for the first time, digging through it for the food she had brought. She handed him a hunk of bread, and broke off another small piece for herself, while he dipped his leather canister into the well's bucket.

"It's just as well," she continued. "I cannot go back to them anyway. Awwad would have me thrown in a well just like this one."

"Your father would protect you."

"My father is weak," she said angrily. "He gave me away over a cup of coffee."

"No, no. It's the war."

She knew it was partially true, that her father loved her, that some of her happiest moments had been spent sitting beside him—even now, she was starting to think of him in the past sense—listening to him tell stories, pray, or just sit quietly, watching the world through their triangle view from inside the tent, a house made of flappable, thick skins, not a house of stones, but still she'd been content. Until this war, she'd been almost happy.

"He knows everything is so . . . random in this life," Jamal added, sounding earnest.

"Don't you worry too? You never seem to be afraid," she told him bluntly. She would never have spoken to him like this normally, but then again, she would never have imagined running away from her people on the back of a horse with a stranger either.

"I leave it all to God. When the Turks came to my village, when they took me . . . I despaired. But then I decided to let God handle it. And I was not disappointed. I am alive," he added, as if she would miss the point.

Rabab turned away to look at a group of children walking together on the road, kicking a stone between their feet. After several kicks, one boy launched it against the side of the well, and it burst into several shards. A sliver landed near her and she bent down to snatch it, fingering the newly hewn, knife-like edges.

Jamal remained quiet, and she relaxed. She had always felt relaxed around him, since the beginning. Was it because, when she'd first seen him, he'd been helpless and unconscious on the ground, so vulnerable? He'd lost the chance to look strong at the first, but now, she could see the toughness in him, despite the wince when he raised his arm.

She dug in her bag again, looking for her own canister to fill, and found a lump of cheese, which startled her. She'd seen this cheese in the tent, made the week before by her mother, preserved in a jar of salt water, and she'd deliberately not taken it when packing her satchel. Then her fingers touched something hard and cold, and she yanked out a deep-yellow bracelet of linked coins; it was heavy in her palm, the liras like big stones. Her mother had always kept it close, because she didn't trust some of the women, tucking it into her bosom when she was working in the field or with the animals. She looked up to find Jamal watching her grimly. "Hide it," he urged, so she slipped it into the front of her *thowb* close to her heart.

As they rode again, she sitting behind him, hands tucked into the leather belt on his waist, she was lulled into conversation by the slow, rhythmic rocking, the way her cheek settled comfortably on his good shoulder. Before long, the sun began to sink in the sky and the air around them turned smoky and gray.

"Where will you take me? To your village?"

"I cannot explain your presence in my village," he answered, the breeze carrying his deep voice back to her.

"Then, where?"

"I have friends in Jenin."

She didn't press him, felt that he was still working out the details in his mind, and she trusted him to settle her somewhere safe. But she had to know, had to ask. The sharp metal of the bracelet, hard and cold between her breasts, made her feel daring, bold. "Will I be able to see you?"

"I'm not sure."

"Surely, I . . . I can? I will owe you my life now."

She could tell by the way his back stiffened, by the exhalation that she heard through his rib cage, that he understood her subtle implication. He pulled on the reins and the horse whinnied in protest, having enjoyed its leisurely gallop, and Rabab's heart thudded as she worried that now she'd pressed Jamal too far, had said something truly stupid in her desperation to sound so mature.

He finally stopped the reluctant horse and turned in the saddle, using his good arm to grip her hand. She twisted forward as well, so they could see one another's faces, both half-turned as they were.

"I call you my sister," he said slowly, "because that is how it must be."

She didn't reply, just lowered her eyes, feeling slapped with shame. His words cut her more painfully than Awwad's teeth on her neck.

"It must be like that, because I am already promised to someone, who has been waiting for me these many months." He stopped, then said fiercely, "If I were free, I would have found the closest church, had you baptized and already made you my bride."

She still refused to look at him, until he said, nearly shouting, "Do you believe me?" Rabab nodded. He kissed her once, on her forehead, then turned again in the saddle. She settled her cheek again on his shoulder, her fingers anchored in his belt, and, guided by the arrival of the moon, they flew silently into the safety of the night.

ABU SUFAYAN

1936

When the men filed out of the church—their feet, clad in shoes usually reserved for Sundays, scraping over its marble threshold—the signal finally came from young Imm Fareed. They had been waiting for it, watching her since the priest had made his final sign of the cross over the small, white coffin. Tall and majestic in her best *thowb,* black with blue embroidery, she paused outside the church's thick wooden doors, pockmarked by bullet holes from the last troubles with the British soldiers. "Honor is everything," she'd spent the entire mass whispering to others, and now, at the front door, she tipped her head back and ululated from the depths of her heavy throat.

And then they all charged forward.

Abu Sufayan was one of the few who did not. Instead, he stood staring at the white statue of the Virgin Mary on top of the dome, the Blessed Mother who watched over the village of Tel al-Hilou, and offered a quick, silent prayer that the day would end peacefully. He glanced back at the women filing out of the church and caught his wife's eyes—red and swollen, but such fine eyes nonetheless. Green, as no other woman's eyes in the entire village, or in any of the surrounding countryside, for that matter. He'd known, when they'd promised him a Galilean bride, that its women were famous for this. A handsome Crusader who'd fallen in love with a beautiful Arab girl and settled down, no doubt—at least, that was the joke he'd heard since childhood. His bride had arrived on horseback, naïve and innocent, to marry her older, battle-scarred husband, and her eyes and her beauty had made him the envy of the other *shebab*. The years had toughened her too: she was still slim and lovely, but so hard now, not soft like before, no longer eager to slip into his mat at night. He missed her soft gasps in his ear more than he missed the feel of her body.

She caught up to him, pulling their granddaughter, behind her. "Jamal! Jamal! Where is your son?" she demanded, pulling her scarf more snugly around her hairline. Her skin glowed moon-white in the dimming light. Her parents had named her well—"Hilwa." Beautiful—so simple, a declaration, a wish that she'd fulfilled.

"He went with the men," Abu Sufayan replied, shivering. Such a strange air tonight—a fierce wind suddenly kicked up, blowing Hilwa's scarf and *thowb* and shaking Salma's braids. "I wish he hadn't."

"He had to," Hilwa snapped. "That's where all the men from our family have gone."

"You think I should be with them?" he asked, trembling with a sudden anger at her brazen attack.

"You are the father of Sufayan. Shouldn't you be with him now?" She tucked Salma's hand inside her *thowb*'s wide fabric belt. "Let's check on your mother, little one," she said, heading up the hill toward their home in the east end, her scarf flapping back behind her as the wind increased in strength.

Abu Sufayan suddenly found himself surrounded by women—huddled in small circles, their children playing and running toward the white stone plaza outside the church entrance. Three adolescent boys huddled angrily behind one of the etched white pillars, looking resentfully at their mothers, no doubt having been restricted from going. Walid Boulos' grandson—eleven or twelve years old, such a tall boy for his age—climbed up the adjoining convent's ragged stone wall, taunted by his cousins below, until his mother's shrill yell sent him scuttling down, like a spider that's just spied a large shadow above him.

Demetri's son had been just such a boy—small frame, sun-polished skin, and shiny black eyes. At last Sunday's mass, he'd been the altar boy, swinging the perfumed censer and offering the bread. After he'd received communion, then solemnly crossed himself, Abu Sufayan had plucked a small square of bread from the proffered basket, tugging the boy's ear and winking. A boy who would have grown up to be a handsome man, an intelligent and devout man.

Though, with the strike on, it may have all been a waste anyway. Everything felt so muddled these days. Abu Sufayan set out up the hill after his wife, leaning more heavily than usual on his cane. Al-Husseini was leading this strike, in Jerusalem, but all the cities and towns soon joined. It had been weeks now, and the British soldiers who regularly patrolled the village were growing uneasy. When they passed on their horses, their tight uniforms brass-buttoned up to their necks, they avoided looking into the eyes of the villagers. No doubt they felt the hostility creeping up again, even though things had been peaceful for over a year now. Abu Sufayan never acknowledged them.

Maybe this quiet village would explode, he'd thought recently. Everyone was angry, tense. Even the women were marching—he'd told Hilwa she could go to Jerusalem the following week for the women's solidarity demonstration, and she'd been re-stitching her shoes to get ready, at least until yesterday. Now he wasn't sure what would happen.

In the distance to the west, he heard a surge of cries and shouts, too faint to discern the words; but the only thing out that far was

Abu Radwan's farmhouse. The crowd had reached its target. Abu Sufayan wrapped his *abaya* more tightly around his shoulders. The air was too strange, bitingly cold, like ice crackling through the marrow of his bones.

Their village was designed around a central square, and his house was in the northern end, in the Christian neighborhood. There were only about a hundred Christian families, their houses clustered around the Orthodox Church on the east side of the hill. He arrived at his home, the white stone façade as sturdy and strong as when his great-grandfather had built it. The three stories, each crowned by its own long balcony across the house's length, had survived the Ottomans, now the British. What was the next test? he wondered. The Jews? Could al-Husseini be correct after all? His friend David in Jerusalem, who bought his oil—would David become his enemy? Impossible. Maybe these blond ones, these foreign ones arriving every day, but not David and his family.

And yet . . . yes, even David had disappointed him. Last year, a group of the European Jews had seized some of the land on the opposite hilltop—some of it, the mid-range down to the valley, belonged to him. The rest belonged to two other families. When they'd sent a delegation, including the *mukhtar,* they'd been greeted with guns and sent away. "File a complaint with the British," David had told him. "I want you to come with me, to talk to them," Abu Sufayan said. But David had shaken his head miserably, looking mortified. "They don't even speak Hebrew. I cannot talk to them. I'd be of no help to you." The British had written up their report, but nothing had happened, which still stunned Abu Sufayan. Was he really naïve, as his wife claimed? Why? Is wrong so difficult to correct? Wrong is wrong. Now a long fence encircled the hilltop, and, six months ago, a low flat building had been constructed. And the strike had prevented Abu Sufayan from going to Jerusalem to see David again.

"You will always be disappointed, if you continue to believe in everyone's best," Hilwa shouted once, when he'd allowed Abu Talat another rent-free month. "And you gave him a barrel of olives on top of that!"

"He has six children, and no work," he'd yelled back. "Give thanks to God, woman—praise Him! We are content by His mercy alone." Of course, the monthly checks from his two youngest sons in Guatemala helped as well, but he didn't mention this. She knew it anyway—Raed and Suleiman, operating a tailor shop among *frangis* for two years now, when they should be home in their own country. Hilwa itched to find them wives, decent girls, as she'd done for Sufayan, to see them settled on the third story. She would probably move him into the cellar to make room if necessary. By God, but she'd become so cold.

He pushed open the metal door leading to the stairwell, and headed to his room on the second story. A light was on in Sufayan's rooms on the first floor—his daughter-in-law would deliver this baby before the week was out, Hilwa had whispered the night before. "A boy this time, *inshallah*," she had said, and he'd returned "*Inshallah*," although he'd welcome another gazelle like Salma.

Pausing at the door, he heard a small boom, then crackling in the night, and saw lights to the west. Startled—it was already beginning—he leaned forward on the balcony's rail, peering into the distance, past the steeple of the church, but the light was too dim and he saw nothing.

"*Sulha*," he'd told them. "*Sulha* is best." But the other men had protested—Abu Radwan's son had spilled blood—the blood of a child. His blood must be spilled in return. That was the way they settled it. During the meeting, Abu Sufayan had studied Demetri's face carefully. Demetri's father was his second cousin. Blood ties, of course. He knew that. But this had been an accident, not a murder. And the old ways were not always the best ways.

He heard the wails begin in the other room. Demetri's home was small—the walls trembled from the force of the women's cries. They'd washed the child's tiny body and were wrapping it now, hurrying before the sun set, cleaning the hole in his skinny chest. Demetri had six children, but this had been his first son, and his wife's wails were among the most shrill, her moans the deepest and most wrenching. He also heard Hilwa's voice, not shrill like the rest, but level and strong. She'd be furious if she realized he was in here now, calling for *sulha* instead of retribution.

"Abu Radwan's family—the whole clan—have been our friends since this village was founded. They are heartbroken. Their son didn't see the child playing in the field."

"How does one shoot a child by accident, *ya* Abu Sufayan?" one of his cousins asked almost reproachfully. Heads nodded around the room, beards were stroked grimly.

"The grass is tall, and they were hunting for rabbits. How could they have seen him? Why would they have killed him intentionally? It cannot be."

They all looked at him, the men lined around the room, some sitting on old benches, some squatting on the cement floor. They glanced from Abu Sufayan's face to the ashen one of Demetri.

"An accident, my family. An accident, my brothers." He paused for effect, while he looked at the other men, who seemed suddenly like strangers to him. "An accident calls for *sulha,* not the spilling of blood. This village has not spilled blood since I was a child! Let's remember our ways, our laws. We have them, despite what these British soldiers in their decorated uniforms think of us," he added bitterly.

The room was silent for several long seconds, as they waited for Demetri to speak. Abu Sufayan looked at his own son, seated beside

Demetri. His own blood, Sufayan, his eldest son, who had his mother's green eyes. But Sufayan would not return his father's look; he kept his head down, and his father knew he was ashamed.

Demetri finally spoke quietly. "It is up to you, my fathers and my brothers," he began softly. In the half-second during which he paused, nobody in the cramped room seemed to draw a breath, to exhale. All were waiting. "You can decide what my son's life is worth," he finished, and his words were greeted by a low hum of approval.

The women's voices continued to boom through the wall behind him, threatening to crumble it to ashes, and Abu Sufayan knew, not for the first time, the misery of his own helplessness.

Below him, Salma emerged from her parents' room and headed to the stairwell. "*Whayn?*" he called down to her. Startled, she looked up and then grinned at him.

"Teta told me to go ask what is happening—I was going to run down to the—"

"No, stay here with me, darling."

"But Teta told me—"

"I forbid it," he shouted at her. Good God, what a strange night. When had he ever raised his voice at this child? "Go tell your grandmother you need to help me with my shoulder instead."

She obeyed, scampering back inside the room. He went into the kitchen and heated some oil in the burner. In Guatemala, his sons wrote in their letters, they had large machines with doors and eyes on top for cooking their food, and carts that propelled themselves, without the need for horses. They boasted of water that flowed inside the house, rather than being hauled from a well, like the one in the family's courtyard. He often felt that they must be humoring him, or worse, that it was all true—that the vast world was flying forward, and he was being left behind in a whirl of dust, alone to serve as a companion to the past. The past—everyone seemed to hate the old ways, but to him they were usually a comfort. Sometimes he passed the entire day on his balcony, drinking tea and remembering his childhood, reliving memories of his mother's voice, singing to him at night, hunting with his father, working in the fields. It had been a good life. He murmured snippets of old conversations, sometimes loudly enough to be heard by Hilwa, who would watch him worriedly. "Take his mind and body at once, heavenly Father," he could imagine her thinking. "Don't take his mind and leave his body behind. I don't deserve that." If only she could see how his mind churned, how deeply he pondered even the smallest things; the sight of the nest in the tree, built painstakingly, one twig—he once saw a bird carrying a sliver of metal, and it looked like a key—one rubber shred at a time, until it was a home.

In his room, Salma helped him remove the *abaya* as he straddled a low stool, then pulled down the left side of his *qamis,* exposing his bare left shoulder.

"Teta said that if I can't go outside to see what is happening, then I have to at least go down to the cellar and kill the mouse down there. She said he's been noisy ever since we came home and Mama can't sleep."

"I'll get him later. Girls shouldn't be chasing after mice. Or gossip."

Giggling, she worked the oil into his skin. "Tell me again, Sedo."

"About what, my gazelle?" he replied, pretending not to know.

"You know!" she entreated, tracing the deep scar line with her strong thumbs.

"I don't like to talk of such times, child," he teased, but pretended to finally give in. And he told her once again how the Ottomans had pulled all the young men into the war, conscripted them against their wills—that was the single memory he usually avoided thinking about when he was alone on his balcony, but he enjoyed discussing it with Salma. The solders had hammered on the door that night, demanding entrance, and his mother had urged him into the pantry, pulling a curtain over him, as if she'd known all along and been ready. But he'd heard their voices, roughly demanding that they give up any *shebab* and money they had. The voices of his father and mother had risen steadily until Jamal heard them shouting that they had money but no young men—and then a sudden hush. When his father moved the curtain and pulled him out, Jamal saw why: a rifle jammed against his mother's temple. Her lips moving in prayer: *Al-salaam alayki, ya Mariam . . .* His father handed him over miserably, his mother screamed as the soldiers looped a rope around his wrists. Outside he saw a train of the other *shebab* in the village—ibn Nasim, ibn Hanna, ibn Wael—all strung together and attached to a lead horse. Nobody spoke, and only the cries of guilty mothers echoed in their ears as they were dragged from Tel al-Hilou, down into the valley and up the next hill, toward someone else's war.

He told Salma how they'd walked for a week, and were made to drink from the same water as the horses. He'd tried to escape once they reached Syria, when he realized the soldiers meant to send them in as easy targets on the front lines. That was when it had happened, the slashing from the sword of a commander, a brutal fellow with a beard so long he braided it. "His beard wasn't all one length, so he had three or four uneven little braids that jutted out, like a cactus," he described, taking his time. "He wanted to cut off my arm, but I ran and ran, then hid out with some Bedouins near Lebanon. They did some of their magic and repaired my shoulder."

"How long did you stay with them?"

"About three or four months. Until my shoulder healed," he lied smoothly. He had never, in his life, told anyone the truth about the slender Bedouin girl he'd stolen away. He remembered so clearly, so crisply, the day he'd left her with his friends in Jenin, the elderly Sawwaf sisters, who'd constructed a neat story—she was their niece, orphaned in a Turkish attack, and with clothes they gave her, the girl with the markings on her face, an aluminum stud in her nose, the thick brows and long lashes, was transformed from a beautiful gypsy to a polished Jenin teenager. Years later, he'd heard that she'd married and had children. He'd often wondered and worried about her, recalling the desperate pleas of her mother to take her daughter away, the complete trust that woman had in him, to marry her or find someone who would, the pain in her eyes, the necessity of the thing coursing through the hard hands that massaged his aching shoulder. And those two nights—filled with fear, but also contentment: Rabab's slim body behind his on a stolen horse, his good shoulder pillowing her cheek, his free hand gripping both of hers to his waist when he suspected that she'd fallen asleep. How he longed to take her to a church, to offer his horse, her bracelet, anything, to a priest to marry them, to hush it up, in any possible way, to trade an unknown future with a Galilean woman for a simple one with this strong girl, who'd found him dead by a well and resurrected him.

But there was Hilwa, already promised to him, waiting. She'd turned down others to wait for him, and he knew, even when the Turks came into the village that day, that she would wait to see what became of him, if he'd ever return. They'd stood before a priest, before God, to be betrothed, and he could not have denied that. He hadn't been a coward, he reassured himself time and again. Rabab would not have been happy in his village, and thus two women would have been upset by a rash decision.

"And then?" came Salma's voice, interrupting his reverie.

"And then the war was over anyway, and I came home."

"Teta says you should have stayed to fight."

"Your grandmother doesn't know what she says, child." He closed his eyes and sighed. "Why stay? To die? I would have died like the rest, from the war, from starvation. And then there would have been no Sufayan, and—how awful—there would be no Salma to help me with my old shoulder."

She was quiet, thoughtful, and so he added, "And tell your grandmother she might have ended up marrying an old troll instead of a handsome, tall man like me. I'm still the tallest man in Tel al-Hilou. Remind her of that fact."

Salma remained quiet, then blurted out, "Why won't you go tonight?"

He patted her hands, and taking the signal, she stopped working and used the edge of her *thowb* to wipe the excess oil from his skin. "Save the oil that's left. Your grandmother can use it in the lamps."

"Does it feel better?"

"Yes—you must be a gypsy yourself." He pulled one of her braids. "Go check on your mother, child. And reassure your grandmother that I am still useful. I'm off to kill a mouse."

After pulling his *qamis* back over his shoulder, Abu Sufayan walked to the far side of the kitchen and pulled back the latch on the steel door leading to the cellar. He folded his torso down over his thighs, moving in a squat, to ease down the narrow, circuitous tunnel. His great-grandfather had probably built this as a hiding place in case of thieves, but for the new generation of inhabitants, who owned guns, it became merely a shortcut.

He stopped at the bottom stair, and reached up in the darkness to the small shelf for the oil lamp. The window shutters remained drawn on this small room, because the darkness sealed in the freshness of the wheat and rice they stored here. The well lay in the ground just outside, also keeping the ground cool and dry.

The mouse was being quiet. He struck a match several times before it would light, then held it to the lamp. The flame flickered, then assumed a strength that made the room glow. Abu Sufayan glanced up and nearly dropped the lamp. Across the room, a pair of desperate eyes—then two, then four—stared back at him.

"God keep us from evil!" he muttered, thrusting his cane before him like a sword. "Show yourself."

"Please!" And in that cry, he recognized the fearful voice of his friend, who stepped forward from behind the barrels.

And then Abu Radwan's family emerged nervously from the shadows: his unmarried sister, his wife, their three sons, including the eldest, Radwan himself, who'd misfired yesterday and thrust the village into such disaster.

"I left my daughters-in-law and the grandchildren with their own families, and then we fled."

"Yes." Abu Sufayan tried to calm his nerves. Outside, the wind rattled the windows. "They are safer with their families. And it's good that you left."

"I took your advice," Abu Radwan said bluntly.

"I think they are burning the house," Abu Sufayan said, then immediately regretted it, as the women began weeping in shudders.

"Strength, mother," Radwan chided. "Your voice."

"Only my wife and daughter-in-law are home," Abu Sufayan told them. He knew they understood that his son was out with the others. "How long have you been here?"

"Since last night. Nobody saw us."

"We're sorry to bring our troubles to you," said Radwan, his voice raspy. "But we didn't know who else to trust."

"They will look for Radwan everywhere," whispered his father. Abu Radwan's dour face looked yellow in the lamp's glow. They'd raced horses and worked in the olive groves together as children, and stood as witnesses for one another's weddings. Now, his friend, whose roaring laugh could infect everyone around, suddenly looked like a dead man, ready to be wrapped and dropped into the grave. "We had no options."

"I thought you might not."

"God help us. This has not happened in sixty years. I thought those days were finished, with our parents' generation."

Abu Sufayan turned toward the steps. "Stay as quiet as you can. I'll send my granddaughter down with some food and drink. You're my guests, after all."

Upstairs, Salma was delighted to be part of her grandfather's secret. She disappeared down the tunnel nimbly, her braids flapping on her back as she descended with a jug of water and a basket of bread and cheese. They would be gone by early morning, huddling back to the charred stones of their home, but for tonight, the boy was safe. Later, they would find a way to get him out. Maybe, Abu Sufayan thought, he'd write to his sons in Guatemala.

The crowd would purge its anger, though it would not draw blood. In a month or so, a *sulha* would be held, gold would exchange hands, cheeks would be kissed grudgingly. In a year or so, the families would resume civility, and in fifty years, even, perhaps Salma's children would think nothing of marrying into Radwan's family. But that was the future. For tonight at least, he was a traitor, keeping secrets with a child, for he knew not what else could be done. And these were strange times.

THE WELL

1966

She would do it eventually, Amira told herself, watching Father Alexander make the sign of the cross over the communion cup. *Bi'sm al-ab, w'al-ibn . . .* Next year, she'd be twenty-one, and her already-worried father would be in a full panic. No husband yet, not even the hint of flirtation on the horizon, no exchanged looks that could be watered and nurtured with an invitation to the boy's father to visit the *qahwah.* Amira knew the game well by now. Since her first embarrassment, when a smile at a wedding turned into a sudden, horrible new family friendship, she'd learned to keep her eyes, at a wedding, fixed on the bride and groom, and at a funeral, on the coffin. She had higher ambitions.

The Theotokos Orthodox Church was one of the oldest in the West Bank. King Abdallah had visited here once, and Major Allenby had taken communion here, the villagers said. It was small, the inside painted yellow, the color of the sun, with thirty-six pews in its oval-shaped interior. It had tall windows, six on each side for the twelve apostles, each shaped like a teardrop, the glass so old it was permanently fogged. The exterior was marble, and two majestic pillars rose to the roof like stalwart sentries guarding the queen: a white statue of the Theotokos, the mother of God, graced the top of the dome, like a bride on the top of the wedding cake. The Virgin gleamed in the sun, polished once a year on the feast of the Annunciation by a teenager who scrambled to the top with a cloth to wipe away twelve months' accumulation of dust. In the small village, with its dirt roads and squat stone houses, with their old wells, the church looked like a fat pearl accidentally dropped onto the hillside by a passing *jinn.*

The first row on the other side of pews was, every Sunday, filled with serene nuns, the black veils of their habits flowing elegantly down their backs, only a thick white stripe framing their faces. Most of them were old, their heavy glasses slipping down their noses, deep lines etched between their brows, knotted veins like rosaries criss-crossing the backs of hands that were folded in prayer. But there were young ones too—at least three of them, including Sister Barbara, the Greek nun. Hands slimmer, cheeks more plump, eyes still strong. Amira loved them, as a general scans the line of his soldiers dressed in their regalia and feels a swelling of fatherly pride.

Amira watched as they all stood uniformly, filing together to receive communion. Always first. Father Alexander depended on them—they ran the school, the orphanage, the church itself—and so the honor every Sunday was theirs. "The brides of Christ," that was what he'd said of them once, at the dinner table before he blessed Amira's family home. Her mother had stuffed squash all day, Amira and her sisters had polished every inch of the tiled floor, of the impractical glass table. Her father, whose job it was to ride over to fetch the priest, had even shined the saddle, pushing his rag into the leather grooves, the rag pulling away black with dust.

"The body of Christ," Father Alexander murmured now, holding the communion before each bride, pausing before spooning the bread, soaked in wine, into her mouth. When they'd all returned to their pew, the rest of the congregation stood. In the first pew across,

Amira's family was next. Standing behind her father, Amira crossed herself, pulling in her breath slowly. Her heart raced as usual—she was not worthy, and yet would still receive. Father Alexander lifted the bread before her, and placed it in her mouth. She let it melt—one did not chew the body of Christ, after all—and shuffled back to her seat.

She looked over at the pew, those black veils falling demurely over hunched shoulders. In the gaps between processing bodies, she watched them—eyes closed in fervent prayer. How wonderful to know where you belonged, to understand your mission. The last of the bread dissolved, slipping down her dry throat like a drop of water.

The rug weighed almost as much as she did, so she called her sister Huda to help. Together they tugged and dragged it across the tiles to the balcony, and then the real labor—draping it over the stone ledge. "Don't crush me, girls!" their father yelled from the courtyard below. A sunny day, perfect for beating the rugs, for fixing the rusted well bolt, as Baba was doing, bent over, his *hatta* on the ground beside him. Too warm even for that, the very thing supposed to keep the sun from baking your neck and shoulders. Amira lifted the heavy wooden cane and brought it down awkwardly, thudding it against the side of the rug. Her grandmother, God rest her soul, used to walk with this cane, used to creep slowly around the rooms of the house, her other hand clutching her rosary beads, her lips muttering prayers.

"What are you praying for?" Amira had once asked her.

"For your salvation, child," she'd responded. Then she'd looked more closely, her eyes trying to focus. "Which one are you?"

Three girls—no wonder her grandmother always confused them. But her memory had grown worse since the war twenty years ago, when she'd moved in with them. Amira hadn't known at first; how could she when nobody liked to speak of it? "It was the disaster that caused it," she'd heard a cousin whisper at the funeral. Her first clue. She'd asked Baba about the disaster, what it was and what it had caused, but he'd hushed her. "Don't speak of it, little one, especially to your mother," he'd made her promise. She'd kept it—always did, but figured it out on her own. The disaster, so many years past, the house in Haifa gone. Grandfather gone. Whose mind wouldn't have started to unravel?

"Uncle!" Muneer's deep voice bellowed from below, followed by her father's enthused welcome. Amira peeked between the gap in the stones of the balcony. Her father's second cousin always looked polished, gentlemanly, more like a nobleman than the village's actual *mukhtar*, Imm Fareed's stocky, short husband. For all that Imm Fareed ranted about honor, her husband always looked disheveled, the stray hairs on his head stood up as if to say hello, his collar crumpled, his boots rimmed with baked-on dirt. But Muneer was . . . together. Even now, his *hatta* was in place, crisp whiteness draped over one sloping shoulder, his horse's tail arched, whipping side to side. He dismounted, pulled a sack from the saddle.

"Thank you, *ya* Muneer." Baba lifted a heavy wrench from the sack. "It will save me hours. My well's almost dry. I need some rain. Some rain, *ya rab!*" he shouted at the sky for emphasis. She hated it when he joked like that, using God's name.

"Don't we all?" Muneer tied his horse to one of the posts against the wall. He glanced up at her and waved.

"*Ahlan wa sahlan,* Muneer," she called down.

"*Uncle* Muneer," her father corrected her jokingly. "He's your elder, after all."

"God forgive you." Muneer clapped his hands to his head in mock protest and laughed, his mustache stretching out to umbrella his smile. "I'm five years younger than you—don't make me an old man!"

"So I'm old, then?"

"Yes, if you must know."

They both laughed and Muneer called out to her again. "We will have Adlah's communion this Sunday—will you come to the house early, to help Lydia get them all ready?"

"Yes, of course." Muneer had four children, all of them a year apart. Adlah, the oldest, only seven years old, was already receiving communion. She'd been taking the Eucharist since her baptism, of course, but Father Alexander formalized it when children became older and able to understand its importance. Last year, she'd asked Amira to help her prepare, doing the New Testament readings, learning the prayers she would have to recite. It had been a pleasure, sitting with her, guiding her. During their sessions, Amira imagined herself in a black veil, before a room filled with eager students, helping them to learn God's word, like this, for the rest of her life.

Lydia, Muneer's wife, was always scrambling, chasing or feeding or bathing one of the others. "Thank you, Amira," she always said. "God knows I can't handle one more thing!" Her hair was golden brown, her skin milky white, and her eyes large and upturned at the ends. Her nickname in the village was "Little Chinese," even though none of them had ever actually seen a Chinese person (and of course, nobody dared say it in front of Muneer). Sister Barbara, who'd been to Taiwan as a younger missionary, had said emphatically that Lydia looked nothing like the Chinese, but the name stuck anyway. Only eighteen when she married Muneer, and now she looked like a woman in her mid-life.

Maybe marriage did that to you, Amira thought, raising the cane again and again, the dull whacks ringing throughout the upper level of the house, the rug shivering, dust clouding around her. She'd once seen her mother standing in her shift before the mirror, clutching the rolls of skin at her waist. "I used to be slim as a reed!" she'd wailed, then slipped on her *thowb*, cinching the belt tightly, pulling hard at the cords.

She thought of black veils falling over shoulders, large gold rings—the crucifix wrapped around a finger, knuckle to knuckle, as her own bare hands beat at the repentant rug. When she looked up later, she saw that Muneer had ridden off, his horse already climbing the west road.

The water in the aluminum tub was still warm, even after her sister Rhanda's bath, so Amira shut the door quickly and undressed. She hated sharing the bathwater, but the well was still dry. The heavy sponge in hand, she lathered with the square bar of soap she and mother had caked from last year's olive oil. The scrubber felt rough—good—on the skin of her arms, shoulders, the flatness of her belly. "It will always remain flat," she realized, with pleasure. Her breasts would always remain this full, not sag from the weight of milk, the nipples would remain soft and pink and not pucker and darken from the hard work of nursing a baby. She washed her hair and rebraided it quickly. Huda, who was on her cycle and had to bathe last, would soon start banging on the metal door, eager to have her turn before the water cooled.

Amira toweled herself dry, rubbing especially the cracked skin of her feet. Back in the bedroom, she massaged a few drops of olive oil into the scratchy heels and backs of her toes, then pulled on her pair of thick socks knit from old yarn. Quiet in the house tonight—Mama and her sisters were awaiting the arrival of Raed, who was in love with Rhanda. Baba was waiting for the regiment to pass by, back to their stupid barracks in the north end, before he switched the radio on. She knelt by her mother's bed in the corner, rosary in hand. On Sunday nights, like this, when the skies were only just darkening, now, like this, when the taste of the communion still in her mouth (she never ate after Mass), and her skin clean and dry, only now did she feel calm.

She prized this quiet. Who knew when it would return? The

radio blared news of invasion—the Egyptians and the Syrians, united, would save them. Last week, a meeting of the men of Tel al-Hilou was called in the home of Abu Fareed the *mukhtar,* to discuss what would happen if the war did erupt. Her father attended and reported to "his women," as he called them, that indeed every man had been there—old, young, Muslim, Christian, farmers and teachers. "We have enough guns for our own militia," he said, and every man needed to keep his weapon hidden from the Jordanian soldiers who patrolled the village, but loaded and ready. Amira had watched her father that very night clean and load bullets into his old rifle, the slide it into a tall barrel of dried hummus beans. "Put it under your mattress," she'd said. "No," he'd said. "If they raid, that's the first place they'll look," and he'd sighed that sigh that said that a son of his would have surely known that. But Amira hadn't been worried about his tone—no, she was used to that. That night, his words had terrified her, had made it all real, even though she'd been unsure who "they" were. The Zionists? The Jordanians? She hadn't asked any more questions, but had prayed the rosary twice.

The solitude, the security of being the middle of three sisters—the anchor between their extremes—threatened now by Raed, the shop owner's oldest son, who wanted to marry Rhanda. He'd fallen into the trap of being treated to coffee at the *qahwah* and had been visiting Baba in the evenings, to listen to the radio. Her mother and Rhanda whispered late at night, Mama from her bed and Rhanda from her spot on the floor mats. "His mother is a nice woman, thank God. You'd live with them, above the store, but who doesn't have to live with their in-laws these days? But their apartment has a new kitchen, I've heard. That's good."

The tinkle of glass (her mother soaping the dishes), the scraping of footsteps outside (Baba pacing the balcony, watching), light chatter (Rhanda and Huda, nervously waiting for Raed)—these sounds comforted her, a routine that lulled her sense of panic, which arose every now and then. Clutching the tenth bead in the decade of the rosary, she recited the final "Hail, Mary": *Al-salaam alayki, ya Mariam . . .*

She was granted a few more minutes until the gentle knocking of hoofbeats on the street, then the squeaking of the outer metal gate (the immediate hush of voices in the next room) signaled Raed's arrival. Then the usual noises—was she really hearing them or just imagining it, her memory filling in the sound at the appropriate time and moment?—the squeaky turn of the metal key in the front door, the slow scrape of the shutters closing on the windows, and then Baba calling her name. "Amira, where is your sister?"

Rhanda was permitted to stay inside to help her mother in the kitchen, all for Raed's benefit, so he could see that she had mastered all the essentials of cooking and housework. Outside on the balcony, ready for their duty, Amira and Huda sat on stools and leaned their heads against the smooth stone walls of the house; her stomach was pained by now, but she ignored its sinful rumbles. She would tame it. Ignoring this hunger was a small sacrifice—how had Christ suffered, thrashed and bleeding on the cross, roasted by the sun? She put her hand in her belt and found her rosary, thinking briefly about Adlah, whom she'd taught to recite the decades expertly.

"Rhanda is lucky," Huda said, taking the bench, tucking her legs under her hips. She pulled her crochet hook out of the belt of her *thowb* and a ball of red yarn out of the basket she kept on the ledge.

"Because she gets to stay inside?"

Huda quickly looped a ring of red yarn and then began inserting stitches to form a square. "Because she'll be getting married."

"*Inshallah*," Amira replied, her fingers moving quickly along the path on her rosary beads. The shutters and the stone walls formed a seal on the sounds inside, but she knew Rhanda was probably boiling water for coffee while Baba and Raed sat hunched before the radio. In a few minutes, if not already, Nasser's voice would crackle out of the small gray box that Baba worshipped almost as an icon. He'd traded so much to get it, even putting up three barrels of olives to make up the difference when he didn't have enough. "But it made his eyes shine again," her mother reminded them. For days after a broadcast of Nasser's speeches, Baba would recite the Egyptian president's words from memory, sharing them with the men at the *qahwah* who were not so lucky as to own a radio themselves. Amira wondered if he took notes while he listened, since he seemed to pay more attention to Nasser than to the sermon or the Gospel readings at church. She didn't know, since she always had to be out here, watching.

"What are you making now?" she asked her younger sister.

Huda shrugged and paused in her stitching to yawn deeply, stretching her arm above her head. "I don't know yet. If we hear good news officially, maybe a shawl for Rhanda."

"And if not?"

"God forbid. Don't jinx it." Huda yawned again. "I hope our sister brings us some of that coffee. It smells good." The red square quickly expanded to another level, growing larger and wider, the crochet hook dipping in and out swiftly.

Amira's fingers finished a decade and moved on to the next. Her ability to pray and carry on a conversation pleased her—she could pray while doing almost anything, in fact—soaping dishes, cleaning the floors, stitching socks, although it was always better if she could hold the rosary in her hand. The beads helped her focus, her fingers gripping one at a time. The prayers churned slowly, steadily in her mind's bottom layer, almost without her noticing it until an "Our Father" concluded abruptly with an "Amen" and startled her back to consciousness.

From the street below came the lazy clack of a horse's hooves and the hushed sound of men's voices. Voices approached, at least as close as the neighbor's courtyard. Amira reached up and rapped twice on the metal door. The sudden silence surprised her—she hadn't noticed the vague hum of the radio inside, the voices. They'd all seemed like part of the quiet, the stillness of the night.

The horses passed the two large trees in front of Abu Iyad's courtyard, and then they saw them. Two soldiers, in the dark uniforms of the Jordanian army. Huda put her head down and worked intently on her square of red yarn, but Amira peered into the night air down at the street. One soldier glanced up, started to raise his hand, then lowered it. Two girls—he would not acknowledge them, would not want to seem disrespectful. "At least the Jordanians know our ways," she'd once heard Abu Iyad tell her father. Baba had shaken his head angrily. "Don't be lulled into thinking it's better with them. They are colonizing us, just like the British did, and like the Zionists wish they could." But they wouldn't, he'd often say, because Nasser's forces in Egypt would protect Palestine, and the Arabs would rise again.

When the soldiers had disappeared and the sisters could no longer hear the sounds of hooves or voices, Huda nodded at Amira, who rapped again—once this time. The hum resumed and Baba opened the door. "How many?"

"Two. They came from the south side."

"Okay. One more hour." And he ducked inside, anxious not to miss a word.

"This gets so tiring," Huda complained. "If I could, I would kill Nasser's speechwriters. Or give them a page limit."

"He gives people hope. Why would you limit that?"

"Hope?" Huda clucked her tongue reprovingly. "We're always so scared of everything. The soldiers, the Jews, another war. We're all stiff from fear."

"They heard old Sufayan listening to Nasser's speech a couple of months ago, remember?" Amira cracked her knuckles and resumed the decade. "Six nights, that poor old man sat in jail. Miss Salma said he looked like a skeleton when he came home."

"God help us, sister," Huda muttered. "I wish one of these Arab boys from America would come home and marry me. I'd get on a boat or a plane with him and never come back." Not hearing a response, she looked up at Amira's startled face. "I'm sorry. I didn't mean it."

"That's terrible!"

"Don't you get . . . *tired*?" Huda asked, stabbing the air with the hook. "Am I the only one?"

"Tired of what?"

"Tired of wha—? Of *this*!" She spread her arms out, taking in the closed door and shutters, the quiet street, the empty well below, its door gaping open in hope of rain, the quarter moon above in the inky sky.

Amira remained silent, not wanting to agitate her sister further. She was only sixteen, still young. Amira was twenty, but she often felt much older, more settled. She had a traitorous plan of her own, to serve God, not a husband, not marry Raed or an Arab from America as so many of the girls had done. There were hardly any young men left in Tel al-Hilou, it seemed. They'd all gone off to Germany, Holland, America. The stock of eligible *shebab* was as dry as the wells, but even more reason for her to enter the convent soon and for her father to see the wisdom of it.

"I have a higher calling," she reminded herself as Huda resumed her crocheting. She finished the fifth decade, but suddenly craved a cup of dark coffee. Even her stomach was being childish.

Sister Barbara had an unforgettable face: long, almost man-like. A slim triangle of silver hair separated her forehead from the black veil of her habit. She was Greek, from a place called Mykonos, and her mission had assigned her to the parish in their small village. Amira adored this tall, straight woman who sped around the rough roads in her thick-soled black shoes, the full skirt of her habit flapping around her long legs. "Move quickly!" she'd often instructed Amira's high school class during a field trip. "The Almighty allows us a limited time in this life."

The boys in Amira's class, usually boisterous with the female teachers, obeyed Sister Barbara like docile lambs. She stood taller than most of them, taller even than their fathers. "That's why she became a nun," Iyad her neighbor had once whispered in the back of the classroom. "What man would want to marry her?"

But Amira didn't think so. Sister Barbara—when you really looked at her—was lovely in a serene, powerful way, like the statue of the Virgin on top of the church. Men could have loved Sister Barbara easily, but she loved Jesus more than any of them. Lust was easy. Common. Pure love was rare, simple devotion, Amira understood intuitively. But sometimes she did wonder if it was enough, a life in a foreign country, far from your family, where people spoke of reclaiming the homeland in a foreign language, where soldiers patrolled the streets and censors filtered the newspapers and textbooks.

"Do you miss your family?" Amira had asked her once during a bus ride to Nablus. The church had called for volunteers to help out at the refugee camps, and Sister Barbara had organized the effort from their village. At first, her father had refused to allow Amira to go: "You're an unmarried girl." Amira had fled to the convent to complain to Sister Barbara, who'd stopped by their house and spoken to Baba. "As long as she stays by you every second," Baba had said, amending his statement, trying to look gallant. Sister Barbara had simply nodded, as if she'd assumed he'd never say no to her. Nobody ever did.

As the bus's engine rumbled to a start, and the driver bumped his way out of Tel al-Hilou, Sister showed that smile. The one that made her blue eyes go soft, that made Amira feel secure. "My earthly family—yes, of course I miss them," she replied in her stilted Arabic. "But I married into the church, and that is my spiritual family. So I am home wherever there is God, and that is everywhere." She peered at Amira, who fingered the golden pendant of the Virgin around her neck.

"I see, but are you happy?"

"Of course!" Sister held up her hand, showing her crucifix ring. "I'm serving the Lord, doing His will. Nothing could bring me more happiness." They glanced out the window, watching the tall brown slopes of the rocky hills slide by them, seeing the roads curled around one hilltop, the Israeli settlement on another, which had expanded this year. More buildings. Higher fences. People had grumbled lately that the water from the Jordan was being diverted, by secret pipes, to this Zionist city that rivaled Tel al-Hilou.

Maybe that had been when Amira had decided, her final doubts overcome, overpowered by the stillness, the satisfaction that glowed in Sister Barbara's eyes, that crackled in her voice. She desperately wanted that same inner peace, the peace that held you still when everything around you trembled.

Adlah, Muneer's eldest girl, came over the night before her communion to practice her prayers. "I have to stand up in front of everyone and do it," she pouted. "Why doesn't God allow us to read? Why do we have to memorize everything?"

"God wants to know that you remember your prayers even when you have nothing else," Amira replied, adding her favorite line, one she planned to use with her future students. "And you remember your prayers with your heart, not your head."

They sat in the kitchen, the prayer booklet open before them. They recited together, Amira prompting Adlah over and over, for an hour, cracking almonds that sat in a bowl before them. As the hour faded, shells piled into a small dome between them.

"Thirsty?" Amira poured two glasses of water from the pitcher on the counter.

"Thank you," Adlah replied. Her hair was shiny black and long, held back from her face by a metal barrette. "My father said the wells in the village have no more water. How did you get some?"

"We have enough to drink. We just have to be careful not to waste it."

"I don't mind the dry spell. We get to drink as much juice as we want now," Adlah replied impishly. "Will you braid my hair?"

Amira's father entered the kitchen just as she finished weaving the long strands of Adlah's hair in a tight, sleek braid, using the barrette to secure the end. "Hello, Miss Adlah," he said, pulling gently on the braid. "How did we get so lucky to have you in our humble home?"

She giggled. "Practicing the 'Our Father'."

"Will you say it for me now?" he asked, folding his arms across his chest expectantly. "If you do, I'll take you home myself on my horse."

As she recited it, stumbling only twice, Amira felt proud. As she helped lift the little girl up into the saddle, into her father's waiting arms, Amira blew her a good night kiss, and Adlah blew one back.

A few weeks later, Amira listened from the kitchen while her sister's life and future were being decided by the men sitting in the salon. Raed sat between his father and brothers, gulping while his eldest uncle spoke grandly of the friendship between their families. At last, the older man ventured an offer on behalf of the jittery Raed: "We want the hand of your daughter Rhanda as a wife for our son Raed." Sitting between Baba and Muneer, Amira's great-uncle accepted, and then they all stood, kissed one another's cheeks and drank the coffee that Amira had started to serve. When the last man had his small cup,

Amira hurried out of the salon, dropped the tray on the kitchen table and sped into the bedroom to report to her mother and sisters.

"We'll miss you, my sister," she announced. "But *mabrouk.*"

Gasps of delight, then almost immediate chatter of wedding gowns and ceremonies and gold. "I'll embroider the gown myself," Huda promised. "You'll wear the bracelets your grandmother gave me on my wedding day," their mother said.

The chatter continued to simmer later that night, but Amira found herself slowly pulling away, her mind carving out another, quieter place.

"Is Amira asleep?" her mother asked eventually.

"I think so," Huda replied, and Amira kept silent. They lowered their voices, but continued talking of earthly parties and gifts and dowries.

She was pleased for Rhanda because she knew her sister wanted this, but she couldn't be as happy as they were—to exclaim over the details of the wedding gown, the guest list, whether Imm Tha'er or Imm Hanna could be recruited to style her hair. And yet, she was happy for a more selfish reason: a wedding now would make her own eventual announcement—whenever she dared to make it—more palatable to her parents. Rhanda would given them a grandchild by then. Maybe even Huda would be married or on the road to a wedding.

Amira wondered what the sisters in their stone-walled convent whispered about at night. Did they notice and discuss what people wore, who smiled at whom, whose house was cleanest and who couldn't keep the dust off her floors, whose children were most polite and whose behaved like monkeys in a jungle? It all felt like a weight on her chest, crumpling her lungs till she would suffocate. No, no, she told herself. Surely they whisper about all the good they've done and then pray together and ask God to send peace to this lost world.

Muneer had built a glorious house, Amira thought later that spring as she sat on his couch and rubbed his wife's feet. Like a snatched fish, Lydia lay writhing on the low sofa, her swollen legs nestled in Amira's lap like one of the many loaves. "It's too much, too much, *ya* Amira, too much," she complained. Her soft, white skin, which everyone usually admired, was splotchy and red.

Amira *tsk*ed sympathetically, slipping her thumb into the arch of her foot and pressing firmly. In the excitement of Rhanda's wedding, she'd forgotten about Lydia, who was expecting yet another baby. Rhanda's wedding had been small, as weddings tended to be these days, but it had absorbed all her time. When you had a wedding, people still visited for days before and after, to offer congratulations. Every visit meant more cleaning, required more coffee, more serving, cooking. She was exhausted.

Just sitting in Muneer's home was relaxing. Lydia's kitchen had a new stove, a squat white box that didn't require a match to light. And an icebox! Amira's mother still salted and wrapped leftover meat in cloth, storing it in the bottom pantry, the coolest spot in the kitchen. But Muneer was making good money—the whole village knew he was the most industrious man in their midst. He had a stone-cutting business, and he provided stones for new houses, for graves, flooring. Some people whispered that he secretly cut stones for the Jews in the settlement on the next hill, which was why he had so much money, but Amira knew that was an ugly rumor. Humans were so frail—they immediately experienced jealousy when they witnessed someone else's good fortune. The popular bet among the men in the *qahwah*, she'd heard, was that he'd be the first in the village to own a car, like so many men in Ramallah did.

"He's industrious in more ways than one," she'd heard the neighbors whisper laughingly to her mother two months ago. Mama had hushed her and glanced at Amira, who pretended not to have heard. But she knew. She'd sat in the salon the week before as Lydia raced to the toilet, the retching noises echoing.

"It's worse this time," Lydia moaned, holding up her hands. Her fingers were swollen, the skin puffed up around her thick gold wedding band. "I can't even get this thing off. Or this." A thick, gold bracelet, a circlet made of old yellow lira coins, seemed clamped around her fat wrist.

"Your face is swelling too," Amira said gently. "You must get some rest." She wondered if Rhanda would get pregnant soon—she'd been married for almost a month. How hard it was on the body—to be used like that, to have a life depend so completely on you, to feed on you, draining your body to sustain its own. Lydia's toes, in her lap, looked like thick slugs.

Lydia continued to examine the bracelet. "Did you know my grandmother was rumored to be a gypsy? She was always so mysterious. Lots of people said she'd run away from her tribe."

"Oh, I don't like rumors."

"I don't know sometimes." Lydia ignored the gentle protest. "She gave me this bracelet a long time ago, when she was sick, before I even knew Muneer . . . hmmm, like a present. She told me it was to bring me luck in my marriage." Lydia suddenly giggled. "I wonder if she meant I'd have lots of babies? I must find a way to take this thing off."

They laughed and then sat contentedly, until a wail from the next room alerted them. Amira shifted Lydia's legs onto a couch cushion. "I'll get him." In the bedroom, she found Khalil indeed fully awake, his black eyes focusing on Amira as he gnawed on his hand. Only two years old, and soon he'd have a sibling to keep him company, to fragment his mother's attention. Amira picked him up gently and wrapped him more securely in his blanket. In the living room, she said cheerily, "Khalil is awake, and he looks hungry."

She handed him to Lydia, who grunted as she lifted herself up on the cushions, and helped her unclasp her brassiere. "Can you imagine—in a few months, I'll be nursing two children?" she muttered. "I'm going to turn into a pile of dust."

"Give him the milk!"

"Maybe I should. I kept nursing because they told me you can't get pregnant if you do. Liars."

"The other children will be home from school soon. I'm going to get some milk from Abu Raed's store." Amira slipped on her shoes. "I'll hurry back and start cooking dinner."

"God bless your hands, Amira," Lydia said, offering a tired smile. "How could I do all this alone?"

"Don't let it concern you," Amira replied, opening the front door. "And if he sleeps again, make sure to get some rest too."

The weather was just as she preferred; sunny but cold, the breeze blowing south, slipping under her braids and cooling her neck as she walked to the store. The vegetable seller from the next village, an old man with only a couple of brown teeth left in his mouth, passed her, his mule slumping under the heavy canvas sacks of dusty carrots and potatoes. At least its owner walked beside it, rather than adding his own weight to the poor beast's burden, but Amira still felt a sharp twinge of pity for the animal. The village road from this point north was all uphill.

Several men sat in front of the *qahwah,* sipping out of tiny cups and playing backgammon intently, tossing yellowed dice and moving stone chips whose ornate carvings were thumbed clean. Her father sat towards the back, close to the wall, and she waved quickly to him. He nodded in return and annoyingly resumed his game. This was his church, where he was a devoted attendee, a believer in the holy trinity of gambling, coffee, and politics.

Abu Raed's store was like a narrow box, with only a few shelves nailed in one wall and canvas sacks of lentils, chick peas, flour and sugar lined up against the opposite wall. Still, it was better than waiting for Muneer to go to Ramallah. Going to the city these days was dangerous, when demonstrations erupted and the soldiers had stopped being meek about firing their guns.

"*Asalaam aleikum,*" she said to Abu Raed, a slim man with a leathery face. Behind his narrow counter, he looked like part of the wall—cracked and brown. He leaned forward, hands under his chin, listening to his radio.

"*Ahlan wa sahlan,* your Majesty," he returned in his deep voice, smiling. Amira hated that her name meant "princess"—it prompted jokes like that from everyone. How poorly her parents had chosen for her. "Your sister sends her greetings," he added

Amira wondered whether she should ask to go upstairs to see Rhanda, who was surely home at this time of day. But her own mother had told her and Huda to leave Rhanda alone for a while after the wedding. "We don't want to appear intrusive." This kind of shyness and formality was one of the few things that angered Amira—why should they pretend that her sister was no longer a member of the family? That she was suddenly a stranger, instead of the girl with whom Amira had used to share chores, meals, a bed, even bath water? Amira missed hearing Rhanda's voice at night, seeing her face at breakfast, sipping tea on the balcony in the afternoon sun. "How is she doing?"

"She's lit up our home," he replied automatically, then checked his watch and adjusted the radio dial. "King Hussein's speech is beginning," he explained. "Let's see what smoke he tries to blind us with this time."

Amira did not pick up the can of powdered milk right away, lingering at the shelves as long as she could, even though she'd promised Lydia to hurry. Would Rhanda come down, perhaps to tell her father-in-law lunch was ready? Or maybe to pick up some sugar for her mother-in-law?

She fingered each can of *tahini* and jar of olives, each bag of cumin and sumac, until she'd dusted everything in the store with the pads of her fingers. King Hussein's voice boomed from the radio speakers. Amira wondered if he really was as short as everyone claimed, because his voice did not seem to belong to a little man. And all the pictures of him in her old school textbooks depicted a strong man, in full military regalia, gold emblems decorating a broad chest and broad shoulders.

"We know you're in bed with the Israelis," Abu Raed muttered, arguing with the drone of the king's voice.

Just when she thought she couldn't procrastinate any longer, when the speech seemed to wind down but then charged mightily into a new point, a shadow darkened the doorway and a deep voice called her name. "Hello, cousin!"

"Quiet, Muneer—please," Abu Raed hushed him.

"Ah, the great king speaks and all his subjects must heed his words," Muneer retorted, though in a quieter voice, directed at Amira since Abu Raed had already gone back to ignoring them both. "If only King Hussein knew we all wished for Cairo to move a little closer to Jerusalem."

"Or better, that Jerusalem stands by itself," Amira returned. She could tell from the nod of his head, the half smile, that her answer pleased him. "I came to pick up milk for Khalil."

"Thank you for all your help," he said, sighing. "Lydia is really tired all the time. I wish I didn't have to work, but it's the season."

Amira shook her head dismissively. "I'm happy to help you. Lydia's family lives too far away, after all." She didn't add, "And your sister has her own troubles, and your mother is too busy gossiping about everyone else . . ." She knew, from the way Muneer avoided mention of his mother, how he'd turned red at the communion dinner to see his mother and sister seated like the other guests, waiting to be served—he knew what they were. She didn't like to remind him of embarrassing facts.

He took the can of powdered milk from her, and his fingers—they were surprisingly warm—closed accidentally over hers. She pulled them away, her face suddenly flushed, and waited while he picked a few other items from the shelves—nails, a leather polisher—and thought about her cousin's troubles over the past few years. The death of his father in '56 had nearly devastated him. She was only ten years old then, at the funeral, and saw his body, wrapped in white muslin and draped in a flag, carried through the street in a wooden casket on the shoulders of several young men. Muneer had been twenty-one, sweat dripping from his forehead, arms high above his head as he held up his father's body in a wooden box. Then he'd moved to Jenin to find work: he'd returned only a few years ago, with money, a wife and two babies.

He turned to her, dropped a few coins onto the counter. Abu Raed remained transfixed, listening intently to the radio. "The children will be home soon?"

"Yes," she said, taking the can from him. "You're heading back to the factory?"

He nodded, and they parted at the door, he straddling his horse, she hurrying back along the road. Behind her, the king's voice echoed against stone walls.

The morning of Rhanda's *frad* brought the first rain of the season, and her father rushed out into the courtyard. Soon she heard the scraping yawn of the well's metal door opening wide. "Thank God," she said, and offered a rapid "Hail Mary" before soaking her rag in a shallow basin of olive oil and lemon. She turned first to the small wooden table and began polishing its legs and top, rubbing the oil into the grooves until the wood shone. She heard Huda in the kitchen helping their mother wash the rice. It would take an hour to soak and then more time to boil. In the meantime, Baba would have brought home the lamb from the butcher. It was rare to eat *mansaff;* lately her mother had even made it with beans or even slabs of eggplant, but Rhanda would only have one *frad.* "Either we serve lamb or have the whole village laugh at us," Baba had insisted. And that was it.

After she'd finished the other tables and all the furniture, she seized the tub of yesterday's dishwater and used it to scrub the tile floor. She leaned heavily into each swipe, feeling the muscles in her back and shoulders stretch and contract. All for Rhanda, and her good news.

They'd heard from Rhanda's mother-in-law, Imm Raed, when she'd come to have a cup of tea one afternoon, her gold bracelets clinking on her wrist and an ornate, gold crucifix around her neck. The makeup on her eyes alerted Amira that she'd planned this visit, that she hadn't simply passed by on her way to visit her friend. "Rhanda is such a wonderful girl," she gushed, holding her cup elegantly, her little finger arced up and away. "I haven't cooked a single meal since she married my son. She treats us all very well."

"We are blessed to have united our families, Imm Raed," their mother answered, nodding at Huda to refill her teacup.

"And now, thank the Almighty, our family will grow larger," Imm Raed said, watching their faces. A slight smile pulled at the corners of her lips.

"*Inshallah,*" their mother answered carefully.

"Indeed, it's true."

Their mother gasped loudly, and Imm Raed instinctively jumped up to embrace her. Her mother was too stunned to stand, so Imm Raed bent down to wrap her arms around her shoulders and kiss her cheeks. Then she kissed Amira and Huda, and they all murmured, "*Mabrouk.*"

"We'll wait to tell your father," Mama said as they started washing the windows. "Let's have this *frad* first. She will show soon enough."

"I wonder if she'll have a boy or a girl," Amira said aloud, looking over the balcony to see if Baba was on his way home yet from the butcher.

"A boy, *inshallah,*" Mama muttered as she wiped the panes with a dry cloth. Of course her mother wanted a boy for Rhanda. A boy first, so the village would say, "Finally, a boy to that family." Amira knew people felt sorry for her father, a man whose wife had produced only three girls.

"Girls are a blessing," he always said. "If God loves a man, He gives him a daughter to take care of him when he gets old." Then he'd smile before the punchline of his running joke. "So I am apparently one of God's favorites." But Amira often wondered, in his weak moments, in those bleak times that every marriage must endure, whether or not he berated her mother for this disappointment.

"Is your father on his way?" Mama asked. "I need to start boiling the meat. Does he think this only takes half an hour to prepare?"

"I'm sure he's on his way," Huda said soothingly. "I'm so excited for Rhanda. Whatever it is." Her voice assumed a dreamy tone, wistful.

Sister Barbara had two nieces and three nephews. Their pictures sat in tiny brass frames on her desk in the convent. "I love them like my own children," she'd said once. Amira didn't ask if she'd ever wished for her own—she wasn't sure she'd like the answer. Or that she'd believe it.

As she looked out, thinking of Sister Barbara, and her five brass frames, the rain coming down in a steady drizzle, she saw Muneer riding past at a frenzied gallop, headed north on the road, his *abaya* pulled over his head.

"That's Muneer," she said aloud. Huda had come outside at the sound of hoofbeats. "I wonder where he's going."

It wasn't until they'd all finished their meal, Rhanda, in a black dress, looking demurely down at her lap, Raed beaming beside her, everyone sipping coffee and picking on biscuits and fresh slices of cantaloupe, that Imm Fareed appeared in their doorway. "*Ahlan*," her father began reluctantly, unable to hide his annoyance.

"Lydia! Haven't you heard?" she said, choked up, cutting him off before he could continue. "I came to tell you right away. It's very bad." She was looking directly at Amira, who put down the tray of coffee too quickly, spilling the sugar bowl on the table. They all stampeded out the door after her, except Rhanda. When Amira looked back, she saw her sister fixed in her seat, her expression stricken. She must have known somehow, have sensed it, Amira thought later.

It seemed that the whole village was trickling south towards Muneer's home, like small streams compounding into a great river. Everyone whispered the news: Muneer had ridden hard to Ramallah for the doctor, who'd delivered the baby safely, though it was early. But poor Lydia. Poor Lydia. Amira slipped around to the back door, as was her habit, and entered into the kitchen, where she found Adlah, holding little Khalil, and the others.

"Where is the baby?" she asked gently, taking the toddler from his sister's arms.

"I don't know," she said, her voice high-pitched.

"Did they tell you anything, my darling?"

"I don't know anything. Someone said they will bring . . . her . . . they will bring our mother later tonight. In a car." Her voice became hoarse and deep. Amira peeked into the salon, and saw Muneer sitting in a chair, surrounded, being kissed, consoled. She tried to get his attention, to let him know the children were with her, but there was no way to lock eyes with him. It was like a wide chasm had opened in the hard earth between them.

Then she heard the wailing of the women begin, and, making a rapid decision, she ushered the three children out the back door and down the road to her own house. She found Rhanda still there, cleaning the kitchen.

"Is she—?"

"Yes."

They prepared some sandwiches—cheese and wheat bread—and put out a plate of olives for the children. Amira poured glasses of juice. Nobody asked her anything—they just ate and drank quietly, looking intently at their plates, their hands, their feet.

Before long, the sound of a hospital car came from the street, and Amira asked Rhanda to stay with the children. She hurried back to Muneer's house, and saw the body being carried in, wrapped in a white sheet. The sounds of wailing, of crying were louder and louder, threatening to explode in her ears. She kept pushing through the crowds of people until she saw it: a small bundle, wrapped in a purple blanket, lying on the lap of Muneer's mother. She approached the woman and took the baby, and not a word or sound of protest was uttered. The older woman just nodded. Amira felt a manic possessiveness as she held the baby to her chest and left the house again.

Almost tripping once on a shifting patch of dirt, Amira scurried to the house of Amal, her friend who had just delivered a baby two months earlier. Amal absorbed the news and gave her a can of baby formula and a bottle. "I'll have my husband go to Ramallah tomorrow morning and get you some more supplies."

"Thank you."

"Boil the water first."

"Yes, of course."

They buried Lydia the next night. Amira stayed home with the children, and refused to allow them to attend, not even Adlah. She kept them in a happy cave, sealed off from the outside, where they played games and ate and talked and giggled. Only Adlah came to her later, put her head in Amira's lap, and sobbed quietly.

Muneer came the morning after. The children ran to him, crying, and Amira placed the infant in his arms. He stood stiffly, looking down at the dozing bundle.

"What is it?"

"You don't know?"

"I never asked."

"A boy." When he remained silent, she asked, "What will you name him?"

His eyes were red, and his expression stony. "I will not name him." And he handed him back.

Amira named him Issa. Sister Barbara suggested it during one of her visits. "To be named after the Messiah—well, it's a beautiful thing," she had said. Amira agreed. Adlah and the other children returned home with Muneer, but Issa stayed with Amira. She claimed the bed, and he slept in it with her, against the wall, while her mother and Huda took the floor mats. They did not question her, nobody did, in her care of the infant. They seemed to accept that he was somehow hers, that she was responsible for him in all matters, from his food to his sleep to his bath.

"I wish Muneer would at least come to see him," Amira confided one day to Sister Barbara. Issa sucked hungrily on a bottle in her lap. "Lydia has been buried for almost two weeks."

"Many people have a difficult time coping," Sister Barbara replied in her broken Arabic. The triangle of silver hair at her forehead gleamed in the afternoon sunlight. "You're very good to help him like this."

"What good am I doing?" Amira asked, shaking her head. "It's not right, this situation."

"I worry about the other children." Sister Barbara picked up both empty teacups and put them on the kitchen table. "I only see Adlah, the eldest, in school. She has grown so quiet."

"His sister usually watches the younger ones. But Muneer stays home most of the day with them."

"And his work?"

"My father says he hasn't gone to his factory since it happened. And he really does not keep his house clean or organized. His plants are overgrown, his well is dry."

"He's distracted—his grief makes him so."

"But he must continue—he has five children. The two youngest are babies!"

There was a pause, then Sister added, "And I haven't seen you at Mass."

"I know."

"We used to see you three times a week."

"How can I come?" Amira replied, laying Issa on his stomach across her lap and patting his back. "Who else will take care of this child? His sister is overwhelmed, my mother is busy helping Rhanda prepare for her baby, and Huda . . . well, Huda is too young to worry about these things."

"His mother?"

Amira snorted. "It's unkind of me, I'm sorry. But we cannot count on her."

"I don't know what to tell you," Sister replied. "Sometimes we must act because others won't."

Amira thought carefully about her words over the next few days. That Sunday, she wrapped the baby tightly and carried him to church, early in the morning, walking carefully over the half mile of road. The weather was dry and hot, and she felt the sweat trickling along her hairline by the time she arrived. Father Alexander was still in his office, preparing his sermon, his head bent over his pile of ruled paper.

"Father," she said quietly, standing just outside his door.

He glanced up, then jumped out of his chair. "*Ahlan wa sahlan.*" He nodded at the baby. "Muneer's son?"

"Yes. His name is Issa."

He took her free hand and pulled her in, settling her into a chair across the desk from his own. She sank into the soft cushions and relaxed her stiff shoulders.

"They say Nasser might move his army into Sinai," he said, slumping back into his chair and crossing his left leg over his right knee. She felt the energy in the room, emanating from him, his fingers twitching, his ankle bobbing his foot nervously up and down. "I'm trying to craft this sermon."

"So there *will* be war?"

"It looks that way." His eyes closed for a few seconds, and he spoke with them shut. "God forgive me, but it will liberate us from these Israelis. They've been encroaching on our land, and the Jordanians cannot protect us."

"Some people say they can, but will not."

"I'm not sure," he murmured. "The settlement on the hill looks like a fortress. They just added a medical clinic and a mechanic shop. I'm sure they are armed better than Hussein's army."

She wondered if her father had heard the news. Issa twisted in her arms, and war didn't matter anymore.

"Father," she began, "this baby is forty days old now. I'd like for him to be churched today. And perhaps to be baptized next month."

"Yes, of course. His father is not here?"

She shook her head, and Father simply nodded. "I've heard," he said simply. He picked up his pen again. "Wait in the foyer until I am ready to church him. I'll do it after the Gospel."

She wished she'd asked to wait in his office. Everyone who trudged into the church stopped to kiss her and ask after Muneer, then shake their heads sadly. Several pushed a few dinars into her hand, or into the baby's fists, like she was a beggar, and she knew her father would be angry when he heard. Nothing stayed hidden for long in Tel al-Hilou.

Finally, she heard the chanting of the choir. The Mass had started and soon Father Alexander would beckon her inside.

The door creaked open slowly, and she looked to see who was entering late. A small foot in a dirty sandal, and then Muneer's eldest stepped inside. She was alone, standing in a maroon dress with a wrinkled collar. Her hair was brushed but looked like it hadn't been washed in days, the strands limp and greasy.

"Adlah!"

She took Amira's extended hand and sat quietly beside her. "Is this my brother?" she asked, peeking at Issa, her fingers pulling at his wrapping to see his face. Her fingernails were long and ragged, with lines of black dirt underneath.

"Why haven't you come to see him?" Amira chided her.

"I have to help Auntie Jihan with the others," she replied quietly.

"Are they giving her trouble?"

"Khalil gets into everything. He broke her vase yesterday. She was really mad and yelled at all of us."

"Does she yell a lot?" Amira asked quietly.

The girl shrugged her thin shoulders.

"Is she coming with you?"

"No. I came alone. Bringing us all to church gives her a headache."

When Father motioned for Amira to enter the church with the baby, she took Adlah with her, holding the girl's hand firmly in hers, the baby in her left arm while Father prayed over him.

Later that evening, she went to Jihan's and asked if the children could spend a few nights with them. She saw the way Adlah's face perked up, the way Jihan served her hasty tea, with the water barely boiled. "Of course! They would love to spend time with you," Jihan said gladly, then jumped up when one of her own children cried out in the next room. "I need to feed my daughter—just take them with you when you leave."

The four children slept anywhere they could find a space for their small bodies: on the floor, on the divan. They were cramped but cheerful, giggling as they cuddled together. Khalil tucked himself securely under his eldest sister's arm. When they'd finally dozed, Amira fed Issa a bottle, but he fidgeted and whimpered. For the first time in two weeks, Amira's mind veered in wild directions, longing for quiet and calm. "Take him for a walk," her mother suggested, as she wiped up the kitchen table. Amira did, heading to the convent with Issa, hoping the walk would lull him to sleep. The air was clear, clean, no breeze to stir up dust on the road. She kept the infant held tightly to her chest, though he felt lighter than he had this morning. Father Alexander agreed to baptize him the next month, sooner if a war did break out. "Though you shouldn't worry," he'd chided. "Nasser and al-Assad's armies will topple Israel. We'll feel nothing here." She couldn't explain to him, though he'd always spoken openly to her—he'd baptized *her* after all and both her sisters—that she worried about the baby's salvation more than his physical life.

She knocked on Sister Barbara's door, and it opened quickly. "I had a feeling I'd be seeing you tonight," she said. "I saw you in church, but you left so quickly after the mass."

Amira felt her eyes itch, and tears threatened to fall. Why was she feeling so confused, nervous? "I'm not sure why I came," she said, feeling the itch travel to her throat.

Sister Barbara took Issa from her arms, and she felt herself, for the second time that day, being pulled into a warm, safe room. "My child," she said, "my ears belong to you. Tell me."

A month later, it rained again, surprising everyone. Amira's father opened the well door and ran back in, watching the sleeting water stream into the well as though he were supervising its descent. He checked the smooth rocks in the drains that filtered the ground water as it slipped into the well. Amira sat inside the salon, rocking Issa to sleep. He sat placidly in her arms, his eyes closing slowly. The scrape of her father's footstep outside jolted him, and he stretched fully in her arms before finally allowing himself to fall into a slumber. She looked down at his peaceful face, noticing the hair on his crown was growing in thicker, and how his cheeks were more plump than they'd been last week. The yellow in his skin had yielded to a healthy red color.

Her father walked by the window again, peeked in and waved gently. He pointed to the sky, as if to say, "See? What luck!" She knew he would come in soon and try to speak to her again. Yesterday when she'd returned from Sister Barbara's, he'd waited for her.

"I heard you were in the church today with the baby and Adlah."

"He needed to be churched."

"That was a good idea. You have been very good to our poor cousin." He'd paused briefly, then took out his cigarette case from his pocket. Pulled one slowly from the slim, aluminum case, took his time lighting it. He then waited, it seemed, for her to speak, but she'd stayed silent, mentally willing him to keep quiet. There was always noise, too much noise, dislodging her center.

Now, as the rain fell steadily behind him, he looked in the window again, and she beckoned him inside. He stepped in quietly, lifting the door slightly by the handle as he closed it to prevent the old hinges from squeaking.

"He sleeps so well. I hardly ever hear him at night," he said. "What a beautiful boy."

She had imagined this conversation so differently, imagined her anxiety would be greater than it was, perhaps because of the end result. She gazed at her father, his smiling face, looking down so softly, but strangely, at the baby, like there was a puzzle before him.

"Baba," she began. "This baby has been with us two months now." How shallow, how silly her words seemed now, though they had been more weighty last night as she'd thought of what to say.

His lips folded down into a frown. "But Muneer will come for him. Your cousin will come. And God knows you'll be rewarded in heaven for all you have done for him. His mother and sister should be ashamed! Those bitches." He eased himself down into the armchair beside her.

"Muneer will not come, Baba."

"A man will not abandon his family, his own child," her father continued. "And this war will begin any day now. Any minute. Nasser's forces are ready to strike, and the Israelis are frantic." He peered at her. "Can't you feel it? Liberation, *habibti.* It's coming."

"*Inshallah.*"

"Imagine it, Amira." His hands shook with excitement, spread open before him. "Maybe once the coast is liberated, I'll take your mother back to Haifa, to reclaim her father's land. She has the deed hidden away somewhere. She hasn't been there since she was a teenager."

"Baba."

"Yes, my darling?"

"Muneer will not come for the baby. I think . . . I think I need to go to him. As his wife."

The rest of the conversation devolved into screaming, until Amira simply left the room. She had never dared walk out on her father before, but she couldn't abide his childish ranting, although she still heard his voice throughout the house. "Have I raised a sacrificial lamb?" he raged to her mother. The stone walls, despite their thickness, could not keep out the anger that rippled throughout his tone. "I love Muneer, but his tragedy is not ours."

And her mother's soothing voice, only murmurs through the wall. She would betray that later, when she came into the bedroom. Her mother's fury made that of her father seem harmless. "Have you lost your mind?" she said, her voice terse, clipped. "How long have you both been planning this?"

"He doesn't know anything. I have not spoken to him."

A blow landed on Amira's cheek. Strangely she welcomed it, felt the pain spread across her face as she watched her mother address the ceiling. "Madness! She's asked her father for her own hand? Have we lost our honor?"

"I think it's the right thing to do," she replied quietly.

"Have we ever made you feel like a burden? Never! Why would you do this?" She muttered about how Amira had always been the easy one, the steady one, and Amira began to understand that, while she'd always craved those compliments, she'd done herself a great wrong in being so subdued. So content with everything that happened. She should have been more like Huda, she mused. Watching her mother rage, she felt more and more detached from the display of anger before her. Drama wasn't her goal—other girls were better suited for that—but this was hardly her fault. It was as if God had placed a task in her arms and bid her to accept it. This was the only way. Sister Barbara had agreed.

"Someone has cast the eye on you. I just know it," her mother said suddenly, looking genuinely frightened. "We must undo this . . ."

Amira shook her head, trying not to laugh. "I've not been stricken with the eye. And Muneer knows nothing."

But her mother had already rushed out to report the ridiculous news to Baba, to declare her diagnosis.

"You're crazy," Huda hissed at her from the mattress on the floor. "He'll marry again, probably a widow. The kids will be fine."

Amira pulled Issa more closely to her chest. She did not trust herself to speak calmly.

"What girl dreams of her prince already burdened with children, and a wife's ghost?"

The rain was too heavy now, she thought, but this afternoon, if it slowed a little bit she would go to Muneer. She'd put the baby in his arms, open all the windows, let the fresh air, cleaned by the rain, blow in and freshen all the rooms. She would tell him that she would stay with him, that Father Alexander could marry them in a small ceremony. She'd care for his children, keep their nails trimmed, their bellies full, their hair washed. And she'd be sure they attended Mass on Sundays. Sister had explained that sometimes you can be called in another way, to serve in another shape. That sometimes you must act when others cannot, or will not.

She prayed furiously for the next few days until the house had settled. When Baba returned to the fields, after the ground had dried, she wrapped Issa and left for Muneer's. The children were outside, supervised by a tired-looking Adlah, who perked up as Amira climbed the stone steps. They all ran over to see her and their brother. Khalil babbled happily, trying to convey something to her, using words only he understood. She knelt down and kissed his forehead.

"I can hold him," Adlah said importantly, holding out her arms for the baby.

"Not yet. When he's a bit older." Amira looked at the back, where the horse was tethered to the tall post. "Your father is where?"

"Inside. He's trying to cook dinner."

He was standing by the sink, a tall post in the midst of a vast, cold marble floor. Lentils soaked in a pot on the stove, and rice—overcooked in a mushy lump—sat in another. When he heard her behind him, he looked up swiftly from the onions he was chopping.

"Your majesty," he said, sighing. "Come to witness my helplessness?"

"You shouldn't say that. Not to me."

He turned at her sharp tone and shrugged apologetically. "You're right."

"What will happen, Muneer?" she asked, avoiding her real question.

"I'm not ready for him," he replied, missing her meaning. "I'm sorry. I know I have exploited your goodness." The knife dangled limply from his left hand.

"I'm baptizing him next week," she said. Then she decided to be firm, as Sister Barbara would be. "You will come, with the children. And the baby will go home with you." She noticed he was thinner and the bones of his cheeks jutted out. He looked wan and taut, but she also saw how lovely and deep his eyes were, like lakes of sadness.

"And I will go home with you too," she added nervously. "Father Alexander can marry us before the baptism. A brief ceremony." Still, he did not speak, and she wondered if her sister was right, that she really was crazy. The rosary felt heavy in her pocket, and, gripping Issa in her left arm, she reached in automatically with her right hand to finger the beads. But the words to the prayer—to every prayer she knew—drifted out of her head. She tried to grasp at them, but they were lifted away by a mental gust that left her empty. She suddenly felt strange, afraid of her own boldness. But, she realized, she was more afraid that he would reject the idea.

"It will be a simple thing. And it will be best for the children."

He put down the knife, stood silently before her, his eyebrows furrowed together, his shoulders slumped. And they stood quietly, the baby wriggling in her arms between them. At that moment, Khalil plodded in, nearly stumbling over the threshold. His older sister was chasing him, and he ran to Amira, grasping at her knees and giggling as he hid in her skirt. She almost fell as he pulled on her, but Muneer reached out and steadied her. She glanced up at him and knew he was going to say yes. And then the prayer, *Al-salaam alayki, ya Mariam,* flowed back into her head, and she knew it would be alright.

"I cannot . . . feel for you the things that you would deserve," he fumbled, his hand rubbing the surface of the table in a panicked motion.

"I will be content. Your children will love me."

"They already do," he said sadly. "Your father won't be pleased about this."

"It doesn't matter."

"Girl, you are wasting yourself on me."

"That's not for you to decide." She couldn't believe how clear-headed she felt. She didn't need his love. She didn't want his gratitude either, even though he knew that he needed her.

When it had been done, she decided right there, when the boy was baptized and their marriage blessed before the altar, she would set everything right. And the first thing she'd do would be to open the doors of the well and pray for the next rain.

ROCKY SOIL

1978

The day Eveline Rabah married Yacoub the *Amerkani* was blessed and exciting for all the people in Tel al-Hilou, save one. Decades later, in a different century and on a different continent, when Eveline's memorial photograph had been professionally framed and hung above his mantel, Emad thought back to that day, the one he'd formerly considered to be the worst of his life. He'd been, he remembered, weirdly obsessed with the weather: The week before the wedding, snow had fallen on the dreary hilltop—you know how rare that was, to wake up not to a brown, dusty earth but to a clean, white world. As his boots tramped on slick, crunchy ground, he prayed for one more storm to hit the village again on her wedding day, desperate for anything at all to stop it or at least lend it an ominous air, to make her parents rethink it all.

Of course, the Saturday of Eveline's wedding arrived anyway, and given his luck, not only did it refuse to snow, but the traitorous sun shone brightly in a clear February sky. Emad's sister went out to the grocer early in the morning and returned at eight o'clock, repeating the news: Eveline's mother and sisters were busily mopping the front steps and shining the walkway, while her brother was borrowing chairs from all the neighbors and lining them along the walls of the house. She'd also heard, she chatted to their mother as she thumped her satchel down on the kitchen table, that Eveline was already in Ramallah at the salon, getting coiffed and made up and *waxed,* she whispered. They both giggled, until Emad coughed to let them know he was in the bedroom and within hearing distance, and they moved to the other room.

He lay there, in bed, his regrets souring his throat, angry and frustrated that he couldn't let them explode, but his brother and the baby were on the other side of the room on their mats.

It was actually happening. Today.

Unwilling to get up, he lay still and imagined Eveline dolled up in a white puffy thing, her eyes streaked with blue cream, undergoing the same transformation that all girls do on their wedding days. He had always—since his sister married years ago—marveled at how you see a girl one day, wearing a denim skirt, a knock-off Levi's t-shirt, maybe she's sitting next to you in class or riding beside you in a *servees,* eating *kunafeh* at the Alexandria Café with her girlfriends, and then one Saturday or Sunday in the spring, in the flurry of post-Easter weddings, after the church service, you find yourself walking in a stream of people to her father's house to marry her off, usually to some homegrown boy or maybe to someone from America who has been taught by his parents that you date American girls but marry Arab ones. Of this latter category, Emad's favorites were the ones who wanted to rediscover their "roots" and who spoke no Arabic and thought that eating hummus made them Palestinian.

Eveline's fiancé—it seemed odd to use the term, since she'd met him only a week earlier—was an *Amerkani,* with only his mother's connection to their village to recommend him. His father, so far as Emad had heard, was dead, but he had been a Jordanian, no specific village mentioned. Frustration. Given how much they excelled at spying, why hadn't her father, her uncles, her brothers shoveled through the gossip and unearthed all they could? Emad sensed that his suspicion was the child of his own disappointment, but he worried nonetheless that Eveline was leaving the continent with a man she—or anyone—barely knew.

Her family's attitude was proof that the *Amerkani*'s money impressed them. A rented Mercedes, a photo of a spacious home surrounded by lovely gardens in some American suburb erased all their doubts. They were people who hungered for money. Hadn't they thoroughly investigated Emad six months ago, asking him bluntly how much money he earned per month, how many *dunums* of land his father owned and what amount of savings he held? And still more. Two days after graduation, he'd visited his economics professor to pick up a job recommendation letter. The young professor had placed the sealed envelope in Emad's hand and shook his other hand, offering him luck and best wishes. "And a thousand congratulations also—I understand you are to be married soon?"

"Really?" Emad had answered in surprise. "I mean, I've made a proposal—to Eveline Rabah—she was in your 214 class with me, if you remember."

"Yes! Excellent."

"But how did you know this? I haven't been accepted yet."

The professor had explained that two men, her older brothers, had visited his office and asked detailed questions: What were Emad's grades? Was it true he was an Honors student? What were his likely job prospects with a degree in economics? "I answered every question positively and in your favor," he'd reassured Emad, and Emad had thanked him, apologizing for the trouble. "No, no, they are right to do that. A girl's future is like a delicate flower. It must be planted in good soil and not in rocky soil—they have an obligation to test it."

Yet, as Emad had walked out of the BS faculty building, his smile had dropped off his face. There was no anger, though he'd already assured her father of his grades and good standing at the university. Did they not believe him, a man from their own village? He and Eveline had been in school together since they were elementary students. They had studied for the *tawjihi* examination together for hours in Mr. Rabah's study, sitting with Mrs. Rabah in her kitchen during their breaks. Now they were digging through his profile, collecting recommendations, as though he were a stranger.

No, there was no anger—just a sense of loss because the answer, Emad knew instinctively, would be "no," and they were looking for a reason to justify it. He understood that this is what it had to be, and that knowledge was like a bulldozer forking down and pulling up his heart, tossing it aside, its leaves splayed on the dusty rocks, its stunned roots gasping for breath above ground.

When her older brothers approached their house a few days later, he disappeared into the back bedroom and let his father take the message, and when his father's sympathetic face appeared in the doorway a few minutes later, Emad begged him not to speak—"Just don't say it"—and sank onto the bed.

And now, here it was, six months later, and the sun shone in the clear sky, and not one cloud of doubt interfered. Emad rose and dressed reluctantly. As he arranged his tie, he felt that he'd been betrayed by everything and everyone, even the goddamned weather.

It was in 1965, when he was nine years old and his father had purchased a chicken coop with Eveline's father, when he saw her nearly every morning at the feed hatch, that Emad first loved her.

The coop was built from leftover scraps of sheet metal, pushed into old tires to stand them up, an odd hut, so lopsided and unsightly that the neighbors complained until Eveline's father agreed to have it moved behind his house, where a low stone wall hid it from passersby on the road. "Now we have all its ugliness to ourselves," Eveline told him her mother had complained, and they laughed because the beautiful Mrs. Rabah was known to love pretty, elegant things: a gold-foiled box of chocolates, an engraved bracelet, a Parisian-style loveseat. Eveline was lovely, like her mother, but she was not girlish, or soft—she was slim, like a rod of iron. He loved walking to her house every morning with his father, and as his father usually wanted to finish his cigarette, Emad would rap lightly on the side door of the Rabah home. Eveline's father emerged, sighing in the bluish light, and began cleaning the coop, yanking out any chickens who'd died in the night by their pimpled legs. Eveline often followed and would break off half of her *zaatar manouche* for him. "Offer them tea!" Mrs. Rabah would yell to her husband from the kitchen window, but Emad and his father always declined.

One morning, Emad and Eveline were given an important job: to place the baby chicks into the slotted crates, to pack them in carefully so they could be stacked and carried in a truck to be sold in Ramallah at the market. The crates were constructed roughly of wood that gave them both splinters and slots of wire mesh that poked and scratched them. They tenderly cared for each other's small wounds; once when a panicked chick bit Eveline on the fleshy lump between her thumb and her index finger, Emad soaked it in clean water and rubbed the triangular snip with water and soap. The soap stung her, and when she winced, he stroked her hand. When a fresh drop of blood squeezed itself out of the cut, he instinctively bent his head, as his mother sometimes did when he was hurt in the fields, and sucked it away. During quieter times, they drew pictures in the soil with sharp rocks, collected feathers, or just sat against the wall of the house, and she'd wind her fingers through his curly hair.

Two years later, the war came, the business dried up, and the morning work sessions stopped. Emad's father returned to his own sad farm. Mr. Rabah pretentiously opened a clothing store in Ramallah with his older brother, selling castoffs from Israeli warehouses to city people. While their families drifted apart slowly, Emad still saw Eveline in school, where they ate their snack together under the shade of the pillars in the church courtyard. Every day they shared what they had; sometimes they barely talked. He felt protective of her, even though she was his age. When they divided up boys and girls in the upper school, Eveline still always had a smile for him in the morning and afternoon line-ups, and during the religion lesson, which the two classes sat for together, learning about God and the Trinity and the Gospels from Father Alexander, who was losing his hair and who'd become so pale and tired since the occupation. In his sermons, he would compare the Israelis to the Romans—"They are the new Caesars," he would rail, but for Eveline and Emad, who were still only kids, politics and religion were both a matter of inconvenience.

⁂

During the wedding, he acted as he was expected to act—he attended the wedding in all its phases: the procession to the bride's house, the escorting of the bride to the church and all the singing on the way, the reception held in an open tent in the village square. Throughout the long day, he remained aware of his expression. It had to stay persuasively happy, not stupidly exuberant and not quietly pensive. Nobody could know or suspect his real feelings, especially Eveline and especially not her goddamned family. At one point during the reception though, when his *dabke* line paraded past the bridal table, he did accidentally catch her eye, and they both looked away quickly.

As his feet moved to the drumbeat in step, and as he laughed and joked with people around him, a new idea gnawed at him:

Could it be that Eveline herself had said no? Was she the one who'd turned him down and dispatched her family to handle the aftermath? He watched miserably as she was carried on a chair by a crowd of dancers, and as her husband was raised beside her. Someone put a sword in the *Amerkani*'s hand, and he waved it around to the beat, as everyone cheered. In her cloud of a dress, up in the air, she was so far from him. He had to get the hell out of there. After they cut the garish wedding cake, a tower of vomited flowers, Eveline leaning elegantly on his thick arm, guiding his movements, her white veil floating like a halo behind her head, after this last official feature of the wedding festivities was over, no one would notice if Emad slipped out of the reception, and no one did.

The next morning, while making breakfast, his sister and mother whispered in shock about the details: who wore what, how handsome, but really *burly* the groom was, why Eveline's brother was dancing with his fiancée's sister so much, and how *dare* Mrs. Rabah hang the blood-stained bridal sheet from her clothes line for all the people to see? "Imm Fareed approves, I'm sure," his mother groaned, then complained that it really was so old-fashioned: "My own mother had to pull the sheet from my hands to make me hand it over," she added, but his sister was vehement: "It's disgusting. I have less respect, not more, for their family for doing that." Listening from his mat in the bedroom, Emad wanted to just die.

On Sunday, the *frad* was held in her parents' home, and thankfully the sheet had been taken down by then. The whole dinner was rushed because Eveline was boarding a transcontinental flight on Monday. A small goodbye party assembled at her parents' home Monday morning to wish her well, then her suitcases were bundled on top of the *servees,* kisses exchanged as she and her husband left for America. It was a heartbreaking scene, as Emad's sister and mother reported it—her mother had gone back inside her home and fainted. Emad himself had missed the drama because he'd volunteered that morning to clean the storage unit and sort the grains for the month's meals, not a chore that had to be done that day but he would simply cry if he were made to go to the Rabah household.

For the rest of the month after Eveline's departure, he worked diligently for his father, cleaning, sorting, preparing for the upcoming planting; when his father handed him three hundred shekels as wages of sorts, he went to the bank in Ramallah and opened his first savings account.

Life in the village droned on, and it was busy in an everyday sense, but uneventful to people like Emad, who had changed since Eveline's wedding. Many times, he felt that he was indeed the only person in Tel al-Hilou who had changed at all. People worked, ate, napped. Some died, some married. A few babies were born; two of them died. Emad attended several funerals, weddings and baptisms, the triumvirate events of village life. At each gathering, he exhibited his new personality. He heard people remarking over how calm and quiet and *serious* he had become. His buddies complained that they rarely saw him at their Saturday night pool games, that he never appeared at their Friday afternoon backgammon games at the *qahwah.* Why did they no longer see his face at the church's young men's club room? How could Emad explain himself? How could he make them see that he'd had a vision of what his life would become in twenty years, had seen it in the wrinkled hands of the men at the *qahwah,* picking up their coffee cups, putting the hookah's hose to their cracked lips, sliding stone circles around the backgammon board. Did these men see the dirt on the floor, a floor that the owner bragged he swept but once a month as evidence of how busy he was, of how his business was thriving? Accumulations of caked-on donkey shit, cigarette ash, spit—all of it beneath their sandals. And his friends at the club room—how had he ever accepted the idea that a dingy room, behind Father Alexander's rectory, which had been the outhouse thirty years earlier, could be turned into a room for young men to gather, smoke, lift weights, and talk about girls? What went on there, besides listening to soccer matches on someone's static-ridden radio, with a rolled stick of foil as a replacement antenna, flailing their arms in pseudo- kung fu moves—this was not a club room. This was not a life. Ironically, the only people who would have probably understood him were the Rabahs, who had rejected him as one of the average dolts, who would not condemn their daughter to an average life, who'd put her on the first plane out.

The owner of the *qahwah,* rather than sweep and mop his stone floors, often spread straw on it if it seemed too dirty or perhaps smelled rotten or foul: it made Emad sad to pass by and glimpse the old man tossing fresh, wheat-colored shafts around, heaping it into the corners and under the small, round tables. Lift the tables, lift the chairs, he wanted to scream: scrub the floors, make them gleam, and your soul will be better for it.

Emad looked for a job in the months after Eveline left, and nine months after first hanging his diploma in the corner of his family's living room, right above the small table that displayed framed photos of the clan, he finally found a job in his discipline: he was the new research assistant for one of the college's professors, who was studying the Ottoman-era taxation system; he'd contacted Emad through a recommendation from his kind economics professor. Emad did most of his work in the campus library because there was no spare office space in the crowded faculty building. He didn't mind the library in the least, and he actually looked forward to his hours there because, like a winter *abaya,* it cloaked him in a quiet, solemn atmosphere that he could not enjoy at home. The hours—only twenty-five a week—were flexible, and he had to only present a weekly log of how he'd spent his time, as well as submit weekly reports of his research. Two months into the work, one of the librarians who'd befriended him mentioned that they needed help re-stocking and reshelving books in the evenings. She asked him to spread the word among the students, but Emad told her that he would take it himself. "Aren't you already busy?" she asked, but offered it to him anyway. So, he crafted a new schedule: four days a week in the library, and after a brief dinner break, he returned for more hours, until the building closed, pushing a small metal cart down the narrow aisles. He even calculated how much he could save by packing a lunch and dinner, rather than spending a few cents on a falafel sandwich, and decided it was worth it. The librarians allowed him to keep his sack in the small refrigerator in their work room. He only allowed himself to purchase a cup of hot tea with mint. Eventually, he even began to work through the dinner hour, satisfied and pleased with his frugality. Weeks later, he found that he could further save by catching a ride with Miss Salma, old man Sufayan's daughter, who owned her own car and drove into Ramallah three days a week.

He had become a machine, a churning press, and he felt liberated by the steadiness, the routine of it. Routine, work, scheduling, efficiency—all these qualities helped quell the nervous sadness that had threatened to swallow him. He could avoid thinking about Eveline almost completely by pushing his body, by not wasting spare minutes on reflection but by utilizing them to his advantage. His little bank account in Ramallah grew, and encouraged, he began to seek more ways to earn money. One night before falling asleep, he sketched out a weekly calendar and filled in the appropriate slots with his current schedule. He circled all the remaining empty slots and brainstormed ways to fill them. On Saturdays, he found work at the Dollar Grocery in Ramallah—stocking shelves, running the register, cleaning up. "Why does a college graduate want this work?"

asked Mrs. Sharif, the old woman who ran the store with her husband, both of them thick-waisted with drooping shoulders. "We are all enduring hard times, *ya tante,*" Emad offered sweetly, as an explanation, and he was hired. It did not pay much, but he got a sizeable discount on items he bought, which made his decision more palatable to his parents. "We paid for an expensive diploma and the boy works in a shop—as an hourly employee!" complained his father, and his mother had glared at him grumpily in the rare moments he was home, until he began to bring home loaves of bread, steel wool sponges, a matching dishtowel and potholder set, with an apple and pear design, for just a few coins. When the old woman offered him hours on Sunday too, he accepted, even though he'd be missing mass. The Sharifs were Muslim, and knowing Emad was Christian, they'd thought he would decline. But they were delighted because now they could, for the first time in decades, start visiting their daughter in Jericho on weekends, knowing that they didn't have to worry about the store. "Your work ethic changes when there are grandchildren to see," the old man joked with Emad. They both sweetly reassured Emad that he wouldn't have to worry about Christmas and Easter and other holidays.

His parents did care, however. It took them several arguments and tense Sunday mornings to finally accept this decision, though they didn't yet understand that he wasn't selling his soul for wages, that he hadn't felt, for a long time, that he benefited from attending mass. The sermons had simply stopped meaning anything to him, and he'd gotten more enjoyment from slamming the register closed after a sale, restocking a shelf that was empty, helping an elderly woman fill her basket. The shekel and the dinar and the dollar, all accepted in the West Bank, formed his new holy trinity. He put his faith in them.

While wading through the books aisles in the library, reading whenever he could, he felt at peace. How could he tell his parents, his sisters, that he'd devoured a book by a black American man, *Black Boy,* and spent days brooding over a shared sense of injustice? His new religion promised him that his saving and his labor would pay off, would set him apart from the rest, would validate his dreams that he not become a layer of dried dust on a dirty floor but something more, that he would never again be denied happiness because he was not good enough, that his life would have more value and meaning than anyone could possibly imagine.

Missing church meant that, rather than sit still, he could move, produce, fulfill a goal. It also meant that he would not have to see any member of the Rabah family, who always filled the first pews, sang louder than anyone, made a great show of touching Father's robe and kissing his hand.

But there were moments—those minutes before falling asleep, or before dawn when the muezzin's call from the north mosque woke him early, when he could not avoid thinking about Eveline. She floated into his mind against his will, and could only be pushed out if he was physically active. But he couldn't move every minute of the day—he was susceptible to moments of stillness. He realized, one afternoon, while waiting for a pot of water to warm on the stove so he could bathe, standing with his towel and clean underwear in his hand, that he was in mourning. He'd lost the one person who knew him best, had sensed his mounting frustration, who would not have been surprised at the emergence of his new personality.

He often thought of the days when they were in school together. During their study sessions, they'd talked frequently about life in the village, how stagnant it was. For their twelfth-year English class, they had been assigned to read Jane Eyre, a novel that their other classmates had hated. "I loved it," Eveline had said one day, as they sat together in assembly. She was in front of him, in the girls' row. Emad always made sure he was parallel to Eveline in the boys line; if she were the eighth in line, he would count off seven boys and bribe the eighth boy to swap with him—a few figs, a can of Israeli cola, or a stick of gum usually oiled the deal.

"I liked the end," Emad whispered. "I'm glad Rochester was humbled a bit."

"Me too," she agreed eagerly. "It fit into the whole theme of equality, right? He wasn't the dominant one anymore—he had to depend on her."

"But you always feel that she wouldn't take advantage of that."

"No. She's always fair, and honest."

They talked about other books in the same way: *Midaq Alley,* which the school would not assign, but which they borrowed from a friend of Emad's who was in college. For days, they debated the fate of Hamida. Was she really forced into selling her body? Was there no other option? Does poverty mitigate your moral obligation to live a decent life? God, how much they talked—how deeply they excavated topics. It was Eveline's complexity of thought that impressed Emad. Their discussions, though hushed, took on a formality that made it feel safe to say anything to her; he knew he could talk about a character's sexuality, desires, about moral issues in a novel that wouldn't make her blush or worry he was being too forward or inappropriate. "Mahfouz wants us to understand that Hamida's beauty and vitality opened doors that other girls didn't have. She would have had a happy life, but her downfall is that she lusted after material things," she said once.

"How is that a downfall?" Emad countered. "Everyone wants luxuries . . ."

"But are we willing to forgo them? Hamida lived in real poverty, which may have heightened her want for them."

"And don't we live in poverty?" he asked. They had begun speaking, of course, as everyone else their age had started to do, about The Situation. Father Alexander's complaints were becoming real, and Emad was seeing that the aftermath of the big war was not temporary. The occupation was not going to dissipate anytime soon. This was their new life. Whenever a new checkpoint was built, a new clash erupted in a nearby village, another house built in the settlement on the hill, a new speech made by the American president, Emad found himself wondering what Eveline thought of it all.

One evening, when they were both first year at the university, as he sat on his balcony with his family, receiving a visit from their neighbors, Emad became aware of a buzzing on the street—lots of doors being slammed, neighbors stepping out onto their front steps, clumps of young people hovering together, separating to then attach to other nearby clumps. And chatter, so much chatter. From where their balcony was positioned, on the second floor of the house above the street, Emad could see the village suddenly coming alive, being awakened in a panic.

"Something's wrong," he muttered, and their neighbor, old man Sufayan, shaky and mute at only sixty-five years old, nodded.

"Let's go see," said his daughter Miss Salma, patting Emad's shoulder to rise with her. Emad liked her—she was decades older than he, and like a mother in her actions and advice to everyone. He'd known her since he was a child, and had often wondered why she'd never married. She's a strange one, people said; she simply enjoyed her work and her books, and had even begun, they said, writing a book of her own.

They stood at the balcony entrance, then hurried down the steps to the street. "Fares!" Miss Salma called to one of the boys attached to a clump. The adolescent, his legs protruding gawkishly from the too-short hem of his pants, hurried over dutifully. The village had a new martyr—the sixteen-year-old son of the mechanic. He'd been in the demonstration in Ramallah, when the soldiers fired. A bullet pierced his shoulder, Fares explained in a hushed, shocked tone, and he bled to death. The mechanic had been fetched to go identify his son's body.

Several minutes later, new versions emerged: the bullet had pierced his heart and he'd died instantly. The rock he'd thrown had shattered the tank window—no, had given the soldier a concussion, god damn the son of a bitch. Yet another version claimed that the boy had been pulled from the crowd and executed, shot in the head—no, the neck, the neck! And the story grew, like a tree sprouting new branches, each producing a different, hybridized version of the same fruit. Emad felt frustrated and increasingly angry that he couldn't ascertain the truth.

The only thing that was clear, as Miss Salma said, was that there would be a funeral tomorrow.

"Not tonight?"

"Too late, and the family doesn't even have his body yet. It will be tomorrow," she repeated grimly. "And it will be awful."

She climbed the circular, stone stairway back to the balcony to inform her father and Emad's family, but Emad hurried back out into the streets. As he walked down the main road, he witnessed the panic and chaos rising; it seemed as though every living room had been abandoned. Nobody remained indoors, huddling instead before the grocery shop's windows, under the streetlamp at the *manarrah.* The *qahwah* suddenly opened for business again, and the men streamed there to smoke and talk in bitter, husky voices. Teenagers assembled in front of the rectory, in the church courtyard. As he walked, Emad paused at each crowd to glean the latest and to pass on what he'd heard, becoming a gust in the great sandstorm of information. Father Alexander had been summoned and had accompanied the boy's father to the hospital in Ramallah. The middle-aged owner of the grocery wanted everyone to know his nephew's taxi, though driven by someone else, had been the one to carry them. The martyr had been carried a full mile on the backs of his friends to the hospital, because an ambulance could not break through the police blockade. Six other boys, all from al-Bireh, had been killed, Emad heard, and later that number changed to eight and then to ten. Someone had heard that the boy had not been throwing rocks at all, but had been trying to extract himself from the clashes, but that version was quickly hushed by the others.

The sun was setting when Emad finally reached Eveline's house. She was waiting, sitting quietly on a small wooden bench on her father's porch, not doing anything, almost like she'd been waiting for him to arrive. She always enjoyed a few moments by herself, a respite from the family of four brothers and three sisters. One after the other they had arrived, which some people considered a blessing for her father, but others whispered was too much for her poor mother, whose looks were fading. By the time her baby brother had been born, seven years younger than herself, her hunched mother, who'd always fretted over her looks, her bones depleted, had started to truly suffer the effects of diabetes and could not see very well at all. She'd had to give up her precious embroidery, so Eveline had taken it up, which was fine and suited her as it allowed her a reason to sit quietly on the porch, to make use of the evening's last light.

But that night, she held nothing in her hands, although she fingered the pendant of the Blessed Mother around her neck, a habit of hers that he knew steadied her nerves. There was so much tension on the street below her, so many people hovering, some bursting into tears, other shouting their bravado, that she seemed nervous, and then like a quiet wave lapping to shore, Emad emerged from the throng. She quickly smiled, but straightened her lips again, as if reminding herself that people on the street would wonder why she was grinning when a boy from their village had been killed tonight. Emad didn't give himself a seat on the bench beside her, but as there were no other chairs, he sat on the top step, his back to the stone rail, so that he half-faced her and half-faced the street.

"Surely you know?" he began.

"Poor Jude," she replied. "I don't know the details."

Quickly, he recounted all he'd heard, in whichever variant details he'd heard them. "Miss Salma says the funeral will be tomorrow."

"*Allah yerhamo.*"

"*Allah yerhamo.*"

They were quiet for a while, and then, with that effort that people naturally exert to forge a connection with the dead, she asked, "Didn't he finish first levels with us? I remember him."

"Yes, he did. He took Miss Amal's geometry, remember? He dropped out to work with his father."

"He was clever, no?"

"I think he was. He dropped out in the winter, and I think it must have been a bad winter for his father's health. The asthma," he reminded her. "Jude's the oldest."

"Yes, of course."

Emad recalled how, when criticized over this decision, the mechanic had mocked schooling. Who needed a certificate when he could be making money in an established business? Why waste so many hours at a desk when one could be behind a cash register, under a car, filling oil, repairing an axle? The administrators could not convince Abu Jude that he was being short-sighted; he boasted that he knew what was best for his son, joking even—why learn math from the chalkboard when he could learn by making change, writing invoices, estimating volume, and counting wages?

"What was he doing in Ramallah on a Thursday, anyway?" Eveline wondered aloud.

"Meeting his fate. We all meet it, whenever it is written for us." Emad couldn't keep the gloominess out of his voice. He was so bitter. He didn't know Jude very well at all, had never befriended him in any real, bonding way, but he was a boy from the village, a son of Tel al-Hilou, and now he was no more. Emad began to feel an unfamiliar rise of desperation, because he knew that the version he'd heard—the one everyone hushed up—was most likely the accurate one, and it made the boy, his former classmate, more sympathetic to him than if he'd really been a willing martyr.

He stayed with Eveline for a while longer, but didn't want to stay long; if he did, one of her brothers or her mother would feel obligated to come out and sit with them, and Emad couldn't imagine making polite, small talk now, not when his emotions threatened to overwhelm him. He stood up, gripped Eveline's hand for a second, then headed to his usual hangout in those days, the church's club room behind the rectory. It was quiet, and looking inside, he saw his friends busily sketching posters of Jude's face, lettering slogans about the nation and martyrdom beneath his face, etched with strong lines. He pulled back, away from the door, and walked home.

The next night, after the funeral and all the songs and chanting, after the priest blessed the body and ordered them all to celebrate as though it were his wedding and not his funeral, after dozens and dozens of unsweetened cups of thick coffee had been served and drained, and washed and reserved to a new set of mourners, after all that, Eveline found him again, standing before the mechanic's house, on the *manarrah* near the village center.

"Not everything is written by fate," she said, returning abruptly to the conversation. It was late, and most of the older villagers were already home, but the younger ones like themselves were too restless and unwilling yet to say "enough." They were all dressed in black, like a flock of crows that had descended on the village, picking at every morsel of grief, holding it up for all to see and inspire new tears.

"It feels that way."

"I know."

"What are we doing here? We're not living."

She let him speak, remaining quiet, but kept a neutral look on her face in case anyone should be watching them. Even now, in the midst of mourning, people watched each other, absorbing and analyzing every glance, expression, and word.

"This is not a life," Emad continued, lowering his voice in volume but not intensity. "We're worried about passing a test or what *ibn*-who said about *bint*-whom. Small details. We are not really free—in this village, we think we are, but then in the real world, all our decisions are limited."

"Okay, *ya* professor," she chided.

"Listen. Jude—he worked. Probably in a few years he would've gotten married. He left school to learn the business—his choice, right? His family's decision and their matter. But it's not." His breath came in shudders now, panting. "It doesn't matter—these are all little things. They are so little. Because in the end, the only thing that matters for Jude is what the soldier thinks and wants, because he's holding a rifle."

Still she said nothing, but he was grateful that she moved in closer to him a little, and that she didn't glance around at everyone else to see who might be studying them. He was certain of the only thing that mattered, that she understand him.

"What should we do, Emad?" she finally said. "We're not the first people in the world to struggle."

"I know."

"So what should we do?" she persisted. "Swim to Egypt? Walk to Syria? Fly to Mexico and crawl into America?"

"I'd go to America if I had a chance," he burst out. "Even if I worked as a janitor in some shit-hole and died there."

She gasped and stared reproachfully at him, the first time he ever felt ashamed of something he'd said to her. Struggling to explain himself, he added, "I just don't want to live in a fake world, where I convince myself that I decide my own fate. When some soldier in a bad mood can just end it all for me."

Did she see? Just then, of course, her brothers passed by with suspicious looks and Eveline sighed, said good night and joined them. He felt terrible immediately, wanted to sprint after her and apologize, to ask her to stay with him a bit longer, on this, Jude's first night in the grave.

How easily she'd been stolen from him. That was the other thing he often thought about, when Eveline entered his thoughts.

Yacoub the *Amerkani*'s arrival in the village with his mother for the Christmas vacation was not remarked upon by many people. He was unremarkable himself, a tall, stocky man of thirty, already showing signs of baldness, his eyes always red and watery. Emad's mother initially sought an introduction to his mother, thinking there might be a chance for a match between him and Emad's older sister. "Why not?" she answered defensively at Emad's reprimanding look. "They say he's a businessman, that he owns a store in California." But Emad's sister wasn't very interested anyway, and as a dental assistant, wanted only to marry a professional man, which made her mother worry that she'd never find anyone. "Is the West Bank full of doctors and lawyers?" she often mumbled to herself, sure that her husband's years of spoiling their daughter and making her believe she was special, different, had only resulted in dooming her to a life alone. "You'll end up like Sufayan's daughter, everyone's aunt and nobody's mother."

When the man and his mother lingered in Tel al-Hilou, however, the storm began blowing. In fact, the village became grateful to the

American because he allowed them the same distraction during the winter holiday: Whom would he marry? Whose house had he recently been seen entering? In front of whose front door had he paused for a chat? With whose brother or father had he been seen playing *tawla* at the *qahwah*?

Emad paid little attention to it all. He was still, six months after graduation, looking for a job, still reeling from the rejection of his proposal. But when the talk zeroed in on Eveline, twelve days into *Amerkani*'s visit, he paid close, intense attention, as if he would be tested on the information. He listened, for the first time, it seemed to the idle chatter of his father, his mother, and sister as they sat in the evenings, sipping their coffee, warming their feet near the black metal *soaba.* "And wasn't he sitting in the taxi, next to her brother Jawad, on their way to Ramallah this morning?" said Emad's father, who was in the taxi with the two young men.

Perhaps he didn't believe at first that it was even possible. He knew Eveline better than anyone, he was sure, better even than her family. Surely, she was just waiting for him, to get a job, to prove himself to her family? One night, after listening to his family gossip over their empty coffee cups, telling and retelling the same piece of information until it swelled, bloated, right there in their room, into something unrecognizable, he went back to his bed, in the corner of the room he shared with the others. He used a thick goat skin mattress on a wooden box so that the cold tiles of the floor wouldn't seep into his bones. And a small set of drawers, broken and rickety, standing in one corner. That was his, too. A mirror lay on top of it, along with a comb and a small bowl, which he filled with cold water at night so that it was warmed enough by the morning to clean his teeth and wipe the sleep from his eyes.

In the bottom drawer, which he now pulled out, he searched until, in the dark, he found it: a slim gold ring, a gift his uncle had given him on his communion, encrusted with a small red stone that probably wasn't real. But the gold was real, heavy and dark yellow, despite its slimness. It was the most valuable thing he owned, and he'd offered it once to Eveline. The week before graduation, as they prepared for final examinations, he had waited until her mother left the kitchen and quickly pressed it into her palm.

"Will you wear it?" he asked her, his breath coming rapidly, in an answer to her surprised look.

"What does it mean?" she whispered, turning it gently in her fingers.

"Don't you know?" He touched her busy fingers with his index finger, tapped it gently, his ears attuned to the slightest sound outside the door, hoping they wouldn't be disturbed. Her wonder, her surprise, delighted him, and he imagined himself a poor beggar who'd dazzled the princess, willing to defy any mere social convention in order to win her pure love.

She didn't respond, but put the ring in the pocket of her red cardigan.

"I can see that it is dear to you," she said softly.

"Less dear than you."

They were quiet, his finger still touching, gently stroking the back of her hand, until he was obliged to withdraw it by the stomping of heavy feet in the hall, one of her brothers heading for the back door to the garden. And when he passed them, all he saw were two heads bent intently over thick textbooks and dense, curly writing in thin-lined notebooks.

Now, months later, Emad turned the ring over in his hand, examining such a puny thing—a yellow thread, it seemed. It had been returned to him in mid-July, a week after the refusal, delivered by her youngest brother into the hands of his mother, in an envelope.

The word came, a week later, through the neighbor Imm Fareed, who made the village news her devotion, that Yacoub Issa had been accepted by Eveline Rabah, and that they would honeymoon in Sharm el-Sheikh before returning to his home in Los Angeles, in California, in big, faraway America.

Two years after Eveline left the village—packed away like one of her many suitcases, filled with new dresses and sweaters bought on a hurricane-shopping spree in Ramallah, with her new mother-in-law, that the whole village heard about—after working several part-time jobs, Emad found full-time employment. Finally. And in his field, *al-hamdul-ilah.*

His interview at the American Colonial School in Ramallah went well, and he sat across from the director, a disheveled-looking woman with bushy gray hair and a baggy blue suit. She kept lifting her gold-rimmed glasses to wipe her eyes and forehead. Emad sat uncomfortably before her, barely able to see much amidst the stacks of paper piled on the desk, around the sides of the floor—in fact, he realized, the stacks were piled in such a way that a small pathway was carved from the doorway to the chair behind her desk. He felt awkward and hot, in his best suit, which was made of wool, but his cotton and linen suit didn't fit him as nicely. At least, it was dark so she wouldn't be able to see the patches of sweat growing under his arms.

The school was an old building, built in the mid-1800s by the American missionaries. This was said to him by the director, a friend of his professor, as if it were information he didn't already know, as if he hadn't spent his life living in the outskirts of Ramallah. "We provide schooling for girls as well as boys," she emphasized, peering at him again over those gold rims, as though she wanted credit for it, as if she had personally been alive and in charge at the time to implement that policy. He would be one of he people who handled the budget, recording and tracking tuition and expenses. She showed him to a desk in a corner, topped with an empty paper bin, a pencil box with two used pens in it, and an old calculator. "You can come on Saturday and set up things as you prefer. I will be here in the morning, until 1 p.m.," she said. And then she smiled at him, kindly, with confidence, and he felt suddenly relieved and eager again.

He set about his work diligently, making sure to arrive exactly at the correct time, knowing how Americans preferred punctuality. He spent his lunch hour eating at his desk and working as well, until he realized he wasn't being paid extra for it, that his salary was not by the hour. So he asked to cut his lunch break down to half an hour, and to leave half an hour early, so that he could arrive at the Dollar Grocery earlier. He had decided to keep the Dollar Shop job over the library job, because of the discounts and because his hourly salary there had increased. He spent two evenings a week there, and most of Saturdays and Sundays.

One evening a week, when he was not headed for the Dollar Grocery, he walked to the bank to deposit his week's earnings. It thrilled him to see the amount steadily grow, to see how little he had subtracted from his weekly earnings to spend on his own comfort. It became a competition, against himself, to see how little he could spend on himself and how much he could deposit every week: a good sum went to his father to help with the household expenses, a few shekels to Miss Salma for his daily ride into the city, a few shekels for tea, of which he consumed more than food, but not much else. He continued to pack food from home to eat for his lunch, and laughed to himself proudly to see his co-workers give the office boy several shekels a day, plus a tip, to run to the corner restaurant and pick up their meals. Their waste was his gain. Everyone was his competition now, an attitude that he honed well and thank god he did, because years later, when the beginning of life in America became difficult, he was an expert at saving and making do.

The work was not difficult, and he usually finished it quickly, sometimes before noon. But he tried to always look busy, so he kept reading material in the drawers of his desk. The director was never around; he only saw her in the mornings, when she dropped stacks of files and folders at his desk in his paper bin. Most of her afternoons were consumed by meetings. The other employees—Marwan, Joseph and Mustapha, and Eliot the Australian—certainly knew her schedule and benefited from it; they often pulled out newspapers, or tuned the small office television to a soccer match, or even left the building for a stroll. It was no longer in his nature to waste time however; every minute was an unopened chest, a still-buried jewel, a chance to either earn a shekel or to better himself, like the American Richard Wright, who ate canned pig meat with beans but devoured everything with his mind. The free time Emad had made him often regret that he had not kept the library job, because it meant walking to the public library branch for new material. He found himself reading some of the translations of American history, the lives of the American presidents and such. He had convinced himself that, since he was working for an American organization, he should know something of their country's history, and years later, it would help him to pass their citizenship test.

One day, while he was working, one of the teachers passed by his desk. She paused quietly above his desk, until he noticed her and looked up. "What are you reading?"

Because there was no chair to offer her, he stood up politely and showed her the cover.

"Richard Wright!"

"Yes. I like his work." He studied her without trying to look directly into her face—she was a Palestinian for sure, and he'd seen her a few times in the office, though she obviously spent most of her time in the adjacent school building.

"He's a black man?"

"Yes, an American black man. His writing is very, very good. At least I think so, from this translation."

"Great." She smiled, and without introducing herself, moved on. Feeling startled by the encounter, it took him a few minutes before he sat down again. He went back to reading only slowly, looking up instinctively whenever he heard a foot scraping on the floor, a door opening, but he didn't see her again that day.

But the next day, she strolled over to his desk again, ignoring the admiring stares of Joseph and Eliot the Australian, and asked him how the book was going. Her name was Manal, and she taught the second-level high school girls. Originally from Nablus, she'd been hired by the American school three years ago.

"Your family—they're all in Nablus?"

"Yes, I'm here in Ramallah all alone! Shocking, no?"

"No. Not at all," he replied. She was so sweet, so friendly. She looked him in the eyes when she spoke, and he liked it. They chatted regularly, and she'd come by every other day or so. When they spoke about books and politics, he even felt that perhaps he had met a mind similar to Eveline's. But he pushed that comparison out of his mind, ejected it, so he could focus instead on the vibrant Manal with the curly hair and slim legs.

Before long, he broke his own habit, and began occasionally taking an hour lunch break to eat with Manal at the corner restaurant. Her own lunch break at the school did not come until 1:30, by which time he was starving, but he forced himself to speak to her and not consume all his food like a ravenous animal. He paid every time, dipping into his funds more than he liked, but this was a lovely woman, who had begun to ease some of his disappointment just by her smile. He tried to get into her mind. She liked Albert Camus' books, and so he read them so that he could discuss them with her. She thought it was funny that an accountant enjoyed literature. He pointed out to her that she was a science teacher, not an English teacher, and she laughed. She knew Miss Salma, who came to the school occasionally to give lectures about local history, and she was also acquainted with some of the girls in his village, who attended the school.

"Your village sounds nice," she told him once.

"Not really."

"And why not?"

"It's stifling. The city is more liberating."

"Well, I grew up in a city, and it's not so liberating. In Nablus, my parents always worried about us going out, who we spoke to, who we walked home with. A village childhood sounds more pleasant."

She made him examine his life—he felt deeply that she was wrong, that living in the village, with so little, made one aggressive about finding a way out, about finding another path. He had done it by working hard, by filling his days and evenings with mental or physical work, trying to fund an exit strategy. Eveline, though he tried not to think about her much, had done it in the only way available to some girls. Living in the village limited a person's options. Manal complained about a protected childhood, but here she was, living in a big city, Ramallah, and her parents felt comfortable doing that, with letting go of her a little bit.

Eveline hadn't had those options, he thought one night with a flood of hot sympathy for the girl he'd loved so long.

And for the first time, in two years, he wished genuinely that she was happy, was living well and had a lot of friends and books to fill her time.

He took lunch with Manal at least once a week, and that hour always passed quickly. When he returned to his desk, Emad always felt restless, ready to pounce on something, to do something active rather than just sit. On days when he was scheduled at the Dollar Grocery, he walked, even though it was across town, rather than paying for a *servees.*

One day, the owners got in a new stock of British cologne, and after overhearing two young girls remark to one another that it smelled wonderful, Emad opened a bottle for himself. He did like the scent, and he told Mrs. Sharif to deduct the amount, including his discount, from his salary. The old woman smiled knowingly and refused his money. "It's a gift from me and your uncle," she said, insisting until he gave in and thanked her and her husband. His mother began to notice that he wore it, and his father occasionally looked at him expectantly when they found themselves alone, sipping their coffee or tea. Even Emad's office mates, with whom he rarely chatted, began to feel emboldened and to tease him about Manal, as if they enjoyed how seriously he insisted that they were just friends.

"Come on, my brother!" laughed the middle-aged Mustapha, who, everyone knew, was really still in love with his wife, who'd given him six children and still packed him a big lunch. "She is pretty! And educated like you. What's wrong with you? A man your age should start making plans."

~

One day, as they walked home from their lunch at the corner restaurant, a boy on a bicycle drove wildly toward them. The front of the bicycle was stacked high with wooden boxes, housing small yellow chicks, which peeked out from between the slats in their rough cages. The boy himself couldn't see above the stack, and he maneuvered his bicycle by peering around the side as well as he could, shouting as he went, "Please excuse me! Please forgive me!" When

Emad saw the circus-like show approaching, he instinctively grasped Manal by her elbow and pulled her into his embrace, against the window of a storefront. As they waited for the boy to pass on the narrow sidewalk, Manal shook her head, laughing and calling to the boy that the street was a safer avenue for his load. Emad breathed in the scent of her shiny curls, trembling below his chin, her narrow back pressed into his chest, and felt a strange ache in his stomach and a hardness in his groin.

Maybe he needed to speak to his father after all.

He worked late at the Dollar Grocery that day, but still managed to drive home with Miss Salma, who had told him she'd be at her office late. As he stepped into her aging red Corolla, he handed the older woman a box of felt-tipped pens. "These just came in. I know how you like to write with them," he offered with a smile.

"How kind of you! But let me pay you for them," she said, making a show of reaching for her large, cloth purse.

"No, Miss Salma! Never. I insist. It's a small thing, and you do so much for me!" he returned, closing his door.

"Well, thank you, Emad." She shifted the car into first gear. "Buckle up, young prince."

He laughed. She was probably the only driver in the West Bank who insisted on wearing a seat belt, but he did as he was told. He was in a jolly mood. He'd been paid his wages at the school, and he always looked forward to the next day, when he would deposit them in the bank.

"How's your book?"

"It's developing. Slowly." Miss Salma gripped the wheel firmly when she drove, and it seemed to him that she hardly blinked, as intensely as she stared at the road.

"Is there really so much to write about our village?" he asked casually.

"Oh yes! Of course there is. We're not just some quaint town, with pretty houses and farms. There are hundreds of stories." She was quiet for a while, then asked, "Don't you think so?"

"Not really," he replied. "I find it bothersome."

"Wait a few kilometers, and I will respond to that."

Confused by her answer, he waited quietly. After some minutes had passed, she nodded toward her side window. "Look at that."

In the distance, on the east side of the hill, he could see the familiar scattering of white buildings with new, orange-red roofs. It seemed to grow every year, meter by meter, like a puddle of white spreading as it slipped down the hillside. "Every year, since I've been a little girl, they add a new building," she said, her voice becoming clipped and almost fierce. "They want to push us out. And if they do it, how will we remember what we lost?"

Appreciating her dedication, he nevertheless felt annoyed by her lecture, and he sat without speaking much for the remainder of the way. He was in a happy mood, that wondrous ache still in his belly from the unexpected closeness to Manal, the feel of her back imprinted in his chest. He did not want to speak of politics, of occupation, of settlement—why must they always infringe on every corner of his life? Could he not steal away one happy, quiet day—a few moments of pure joy, unframed by occupation?

"See you in the morning," Miss Salma said cheerfully, stopping the car in front of his house.

He thanked her and got out. In the house, Emad saw his mother and fat Imm Fareed chatting earnestly, hunched together over piles of roasted pumpkin seeds at the kitchen table. They both seemed startled when they heard him walk in, his heavy shoes scraping over the threshold.

"Emad!" his mother said, getting up to stir a pot of broth simmering on the stove.

"Hello, *Tante,*" he greeted Imm Fareed, and reached into the refrigerator to pour himself a small glass of grapefruit juice. He couldn't wait to get into his room, stretch out on the mat, and think about Manal.

"I'm just telling your mother the news, so unbelievable."

"What is that, *ya tante*?"

"The Rabah girl. She's crawled back home—divorced, with a child."

Everyone declared it was a bigger scandal than when Radwan ibn Salim had killed Demetri's son so long ago, and then took off on a boat to America. The usual rumor press manufactured several reasons for her divorce. Emad heard them all from the lips of the members of his family and his neighbors: her husband had been unfaithful; Eveline had been unfaithful (in fact, the child was so dark, it might even be another man's); no, some said, she wasn't divorced at all, but had just returned home for a visit, or perhaps she and Yousef were fighting, which was okay and they would work it out after a brief separation.

He avoided the house of Eveline's family, but went instead to work every day as usual. He continued to pack a sandwich, except on days when he met Manal for lunch, and to walk to the bank once a week to deposit his savings. Over the next weeks, Eveline's tale began to release certain reliable facts: the child was a girl, less than a year old; Eveline was in Tel al-Hilou to stay, as her ticket was one-way; she had indeed become divorced; and she was rarely seen, as she was avoiding village parties, events and church services, as everyone expected a divorced woman to do. Other aspects of the story continued to wildly develop, and finally he made a conscious decision to leave the room whenever he heard someone talking about it, especially when the rumor emerged that Eveline's husband had been a drug addict and had beaten her regularly. That was not an image he could tolerate hearing, he realized, even knowing that it was probably false.

The Lenten mass arrived not long after Eveline's return, and Emad's mother insisted he attend. He wouldn't attend another mass until Easter, forty days later, so he agreed, letting Mrs. Sharif know he needed that day off. The Theotokos Orthodox Church was packed, and Emad saw, through the incense and the murmuring, Eveline's parents and brothers in the back pew, looking straight down at their feet. They barely moved, and he understood it right away; they were there just to show themselves, but not willing to talk about the disaster or interact with anyone. The wall was up, and it was high. Where was Eveline? he wondered. And the child? After mass, he avoided the coffee hour and left the church. The streets were empty, the only life emanating from the *qahwah,* where some of the men cared more about a game than about their souls. He was starting to understand them. He headed toward the Rabah house, walking quickly, as if his feet wanted to arrive before his mind forced him to alter the course. He slowed down as he saw its large porch, the white stone façade and the gold, damask curtains visible in the large windows. He didn't see Eveline at first, but then—there she was, sitting quietly on the bench as she always had. He'd stopped at the front gate, not uttering a sound, but after a few minutes she turned her head and saw him—he knew she did, by the way she sat up straight, like an umbrella that has snapped itself shut. She didn't speak, and neither did he. Part of him wanted to get close, to see her face again, to ask her so many questions, but when a baby cried inside, and she didn't move, Emad turned and walked away, back to his own house.

Then, one evening, she came to him. While he was closing up the Dollar Grocery at 7 p.m., he heard the brass bell above the doorjamb jingle. Sighing, he paused in counting the day's money. He hoped whoever it was would decide quickly, pay even more quickly and leave. It was his night to stop at the bank, because he'd missed going the day before, and his money was in his pocket for the deposit.

But when he looked up, it was a ghost of Eveline who hovered before him, a thinner, frailer version of the girl who'd once owned his heart—standing before the counter in a denim jacket, black pants and a black t-shirt, her eyes looking sad and tired. He had a sudden, crisp recall of that morning, so many years ago, before the war, when she'd been hurt by a nervous chick's sharp beak. Her eyes then, as his memory conjured up the image, bore that stunned and hurt look, and he remembered the startled giggle that had escaped her lips when he'd kissed her wound, sucked up the blood and the pain.

Before he understood what he was doing, he stuffed the money back in the drawer and walked around to her, and took her into his arms. She said not a word as he pulled her head into his chest and held her tightly, protectively. Her elbows tucked into him, her palms stretched across her own eyes, and she sighed once, deeply and audibly. Emad felt her breath expelled, penetrating his thin shirt.

"Where's your daughter?" he asked gently.

"With my mother. I'm supposed to be buying some things for the house." She shrugged. "They've decided to let me be seen once in a while, I guess."

"Did you know I work here?"

She gave him a slight smile. "I heard you made your parents angry by taking a job here. Big finance guy."

"Get what you need." Extricating her from his grasp, he grabbed a plastic sack and held it open. As he followed her, she filled it with a bottle of dish cleaner, a sack of infant diapers, a packet of baby wipes, a hair comb and bread.

"Which items are for your mother?" he asked brusquely. Confused, she pointed to the cleaner. "Just pay for that," he said, putting up his hand before she could protest. He didn't know why he felt so strongly about it, but he just knew he would never do anything kind or gentlemanly for her family members ever again. He put the baby items to the side and took the money from his own pocket, out of the roll intended for the bank deposit.

"There's no need," she said, her eyes downcast, her fingers gripping the handles of the bag.

"Let's go have a coffee."

He took her to the café near the university, where there was a small upper level. At a table in the back, he gave her the seat facing the wall, so that nobody else passing by would notice her and comment. He was already protecting her, he realized.

As if their earlier embrace hadn't happened, they asked polite, formal questions of each other while they waited for the coffee to arrive, in demitasse cups, sweet and hot. Once the waiter strolled away, Emad interrupted Eveline mid-sentence and asked, his voice shaking, because he couldn't stand it any longer, wanted things to go back to the way they'd been but for this huge wall in their path, "Just tell me why you've left him."

"What? Why do you want to know?"

"Because I do."

"You and all of Tel al-Hilou." Her eyes clouded over, and she didn't respond. He'd disappointed her, he saw, just like everyone else.

"Did he cheat on you? The other way around?" He knew he was goading her, but still she kept quiet.

"I have a right to know. You owe me that," he prompted her, his voice more angry that he intended to sound.

"I owe you *nothing.*" Her voice was fierce, her eyes large and round and blazing.

He took a sip of his drink, then leaned back in his chair, appraising her coolly. "You think not?"

She spoke slowly, as if it pained her. "Emad, you invited me for coffee. Can we drink it peacefully? I really want to do that."

"I would like an answer."

"I don't want to talk about it."

"So."

"So."

"Now what?" All he knew is that he wanted her to feel his pain, to know what he'd felt in the past two years.

"I don't know. Should I leave?" she asked.

"Maybe. You do have a talent for it."

They paused again, reaching an impasse, neither wanting to be the one to conclude it so badly. Finally, she made a move: her tired eyes filling with tears, she reached for her purse and her plastic bag.

"I don't blame you," she said.

"Damn!" His hand darted out and wrapped around her wrist.

"Emad?" She was poised in a half-crouch, unbalanced, looking not confused, just exhausted.

"Stay."

They sat for more than an hour, and he found himself telling her almost everything that had happened to him in the last two years: his work, his side jobs, what he'd read. He didn't ask her much, didn't want to push her, and while she didn't say anything about her marriage or about America, but she told him about her daughter. "Her name is Rawan," she explained, and she finally smiled.

Because Emad refused to visit her parents' house, and because she relied on limited reasons to leave and be seen in public, they saw each other rarely. That they *had* to see each other, however—that idea was never discussed, merely assumed and accepted. There was nowhere in Tel al-Hilou. Ramallah it had to be, and it took Emad a couple of weeks before he settled on the grocery store. One day, while stacking boxes of tissue paper that had been delivered into the back room, he stopped and looked around more carefully. The room was narrow, but long. And it had a door with a lock, and that key belonged to him, handed over trustingly by Mr. Sharif, who left at 4 p.m. as soon as Emad arrived.

The store closed the Sunday after for Easter, and Emad looked for Eveline at church. She stood in the pew carrying her daughter. It was the first time Emad saw this little girl, who looked perfect, like a miniature Eveline as he'd first known her, as a little girl sitting with her back to the chicken coop. But Rawan was much smaller, her hair not yet long, her legs not yet sturdy. She began to cry as the service droned on, and Eveline finally carried her out to the foyer. Emad followed them a few minutes later, ignoring his own mother's puzzled look as he shuffled over her legs and out of the pew. When the service ended, he and Eveline and a sleeping Rawan were sitting under the framed and gilded icon of the Virgin Mary. Two little girls, in matching pink dresses, sat on another bench, looking like a pair of wrapped chocolates, staring at them suspiciously. That was where Eveline's parents found them, and her father greeted Emad like the prodigal son. "Come have lunch with us today," he said, smiling broadly. "Remember the days when you'd come and study for the *tawjihi*, and your auntie would make you a *zaatar manouche*?"

"I have a fresh batch!" the older woman, wearing her trademark red lipstick and heavy gold necklace, gushed. She squinted at him through her filmy eyes. "I'll go home right now and warm them up—"

"No, thanks. I don't have time to come today. Goodbye." Her parents reddened at his bluntness, but Eveline smiled at him and he smiled back as he strolled away. During the coffee hour, his parents barely spoke to him, but at home they railed that he'd better not be thinking about that Rabah girl. His father stormed that he would never go ask for the hand of a divorced girl, a girl who was ruined, or consider a little bastard his own grandchild. Emad listened as if he were watching a movie, an Adel Imam comedy, and had to stop himself from laughing aloud—who was this man before him, dictating to him? Where did people get such silly rules from? Why did his mother think her tears would persuade him? He'd never felt more secure and safe and powerful in his life. Nothing could make him afraid.

When Eveline met him at the store that Monday night, arriving exactly at 7 p.m. as he'd instructed, it was inevitable that they would make love. He pulled her into the narrow room, and locked it, then kissed her deeply as she clung to his neck. "I need you," he whispered, wondering if she'd heard, too scared to repeat it. But then she nodded. His fingers shook as he undressed her, but she guided him patiently, sweetly, stroking his hair as he unbuttoned her shirt and kissed her warm, firm breasts. He pushed her back, more roughly than he wanted to, but he was just so nervous, and she understood, smiling as he slipped his hand into the elastic band of her skirt, then into her panties, stroking her. She was so hot, and she opened for him wider and wider, urging him on with her whispers, while he slid in another finger, then a third, still sucking on her nipple madly. "Please!" she gasped, and he practically tossed her onto the blanket he'd spread on the boxes. After fumbling with his zipper, he panicked suddenly, poised above her, and he tried to enter, so clumsy, and she winced under his jabbing then her hand reached out and wrapped around him, leading him, and he was finally, at last, inside her and pumping wildly until he felt her spasms and then his own, exploding far inside her, so far he knew only that he wanted never, ever to be away from this girl again.

They planned it all there, in that room, over the next two months. She would come twice a week at 7 p.m., and they'd always, always make love first, frantically and eagerly those first weeks, but then they learned to slow down, to linger and explore each other. On her fourth visit, he finally saw her scar, a hand's width below her belly button, as long as his finger, a line of pink on a sandy beach. And after they'd exhausted themselves, it was time to talk about how to do it: Eveline had a green card, so that made everything a little easier.

Father Alexander could help. Emad would eventually think to ask the American School director.

Eveline didn't care, she assured him, about just leaving her family again and that made him so happy. On her tenth visit, as she lay against his chest, running her fingers over his ribs, she admitted that she hadn't wanted to marry the bastard whom they both refused to name. That thrilled him. It would be years later, when they were safely living in a Boston suburb, having finally moved out of the stuffy, cramped downtown apartment, when they'd given Rawan a brother and a sister, that she'd told him about the drugs and the beatings, about how, when she'd once asked her mother-in-law for help, mumbling through bloody lips, that the older woman had sniffed and slammed the door in her face.

The only time Eveline balked, in those exciting two months of planning, was when she learned about Manal. "I heard about her," she said, in a ghost-like voice, when she appeared in the store one night. "Your father told my brother at the *qahwah*, he said he's waiting for you to give him the signal so they can arrange it." It took him some effort to convince her, but he saw—and it delighted him—that she was ready to sacrifice for him: "You *should* think of your future. You deserve someone who's not been used up like me." She was crying as she spoke, still crying and trying to convince him even as he was undressing her, pulling down her stockings over her knees and off her small feet. "You deserve better—everyone will say that."

Before they left, he wrote Manal a letter, as he promised Eveline he would do. He left it, four pages long, with the school director, who'd secured plane tickets for them. It was filled with apologies, explanations, and entreaties to think well of him, and after they'd been in Boston for a long month, both of them hunting for jobs—all the money Emad had saved only paid for the plane fare and the first month's rent and "security deposit," his first clue that Americans didn't trust anyone—a letter arrived from Manal herself. The director had given her their address: "I wish you luck and happiness," she wrote in her flowing Arabic script. After struggling to read English street signs and help wanted ads and rental contracts, the sight of Arabic automatically soothed him. "Thank you for your explanation," she wrote simply. "That was important to me. May your life together be long and filled with joy." He read and reread the letter that evening after a long shift at the factory, with Eveline in the living room, folding his clean socks in neat pairs, her hair snatched up in her big plastic clip. He put down the letter and watched her. She was tired already, but happy. Her eyes were no longer sad. She walked to the laundromat every week, and spent half a day cleaning and drying, and then had to walk back again to their apartment, down eight long blocks, so long and so far.

INTIFADA LOVE STORY

1988

When they came, they stayed on the rooftop for seven days. Nobody knew it would be that long, not at first. They came because of the demonstration in Ramallah, said Jamil's father. He'd been the one to see them from the salon window, as they'd trudged up the walkway, their backs loaded with olive green duffel bags, their shoulders embraced by the leather straps of dusty AK47s. Four *shebab* killed in that protest, including one of the boys from Jamil's history lecture class, and twenty arrested, they'd heard. All the villages were on lockdown.

The thumping of boots on the house's flat cement roof could be heard most clearly in the kitchen, despite the insistent humming of the old refrigerator and the loud coughing of the pipes. On the first day they were there, the heavy thuds shook loose bits of plaster from around the light fixture to the floor, like a light coat of snow that Jamil's mother sent him to sweep. Four, Jamil thought. There must be four of them up there. He counted their distinct footsteps and patterns of shuffling—one guy had a light, quick gait, while the another plodded like a giant with thick, flat feet—as he lazily swept the powdery plaster into a pile, then pushed the small hill into a dustpan. Since his last sister had gotten married, household chores had come down on his head. The usual bad luck of being the youngest, the last egg to be plucked from the coop.

He put the broom and the dustpan back in the pantry, then turned on the sink faucet to rinse his hands. The pipes groaned, then backfired sharply, and he smiled to realize that the footsteps above his head froze. He dropped the grin when his parents rushed into the kitchen.

"It's just the pipes," he calmed them. They knew that, of course; the pipes always made that horrible cracking. His father exhaled and sat down at the table.

"Go talk to them," Jamil's mother urged her husband, her hands picking on a hair of scratched wood on the table's surface. With her thumbnail, she pushed the line out at the sides, until it tore a sliver of wood of and chipped a crescent out of her polished, pink nail.

"And say what?" Her husband seemed annoyed, like someone who thought himself clever but was easily beaten at a game of cards or *tawla.*

"I'll go," Jamil offered.

"No! God forbid," his father replied, standing reluctantly, petulant at being pushed to the task. "This is my house."

Up he went, trudging up the cement steps off the balcony to the flat roof, calling, *"Salaam, salaam! Shalom, shalom!"* as he neared the top. Jamil and his mother sat down at the table to wait, interpreting the noises—the stomps, the scrapes—above their heads. No shots fired, no yelling. That was good, at least.

When his father returned, Jamil could see the anger in his face, and the sweat that made his hairline slick. He sat down and croaked, "Water," to his wife.

After he gulped down the small glass she filled for him, he told them, "Four or five days. They said it shouldn't be longer."

"Why our house?"

"It's the biggest on this side of the hill. They can see everything from up there."

Only later did he mention the rest of it. He admitted it nervously, like a confession wrenched from his guilty conscience by a priest. "They want us to stay inside."

"We *have* to?" asked his wife sharply.

"And if we leave?" Jamil muttered. "What? Will they shoot us?"

His father slammed his hand down on the rickety table, catapulting the glass to the floor, where it shattered like a spray of ice pellets. His mother rolled her eyes at Jamil—that was the first glass from a new set, sent by her sister in Michigan, to break. "They shot *four* boys in Ramallah!" his father shouted.

After his father trudged out of the room, Jamil started to sweep up the glass shards from the floor, but his mother took the broom from him. "My turn," she said. "And keep your mouth sealed. Let this glass be the only casualty this week."

⁂

They played backgammon for the first night, sitting on the grape-colored, velvet-upholstered sofas in the formal salon, where they never sat casually. Tonight, though, his mother seemed not to care when Jamil's father took out the J&B bottle, set a glass on the coffee table, settled on the largest sofa and opened the game board. Poor game board, Jamil thought, almost hysterically. Before tonight, its function had been to serve as a decoration in the room, its inlaid dark wood, in a geometric pattern, accenting the stuffy furniture. It had been set casually, like a movie prop, on the side table, to make it look like they played every day, to add to the aura of their perfect family: Father, a retired schoolteacher; Mother, a beauty in her day; and Son, a top student and soccer player—Tel al-Hilou's model unit.

The phone buzzed steadily that first night. Their friends and neighbors, the Ghanems, called first. "I can see them from my bedroom window," Mr. Ghanem reported. "Little kids with guns. These Israelis—what? Are they sending children to monitor us?" The old woman, Miss Salma, on the other side, could see them from her bathroom window: "Six rifles, but only four soldiers. They have a little stove, and they're taking water from your roof tank with a metal pitcher." She asked if she could bring them any food, but Jamil's mother said no. It was better to wait and not cause problems. "They're probably nervous, and a nervous boy with a gun is no good thing."

"They don't look nervous to me," Miss Salma replied before she hung up. "But let me know if you need anything. I'm not afraid."

For most of the morning of the second day, Jamil's father fretted that Miss Salma was implying that he *was.* "I carried her brother's body on my back when we buried him," he said angrily to nobody in particular. "She had better not be calling me a coward." Jamil's father lived his life worried about gossip, and as much as he claimed to despise old women with free time, he also feared their storytelling.

His wife soothed him, saying she'd only meant that they wouldn't bother an old woman. He reminded her of the girls who had been arrested in the demonstration three months ago, and the one who'd been released—pregnant—to her parents. "It's like the French in Algeria," he muttered. In his bedroom, Jamil listened, and while his annoyance with his father was blossoming, he was nevertheless sinking in the quicksand of his own worries. Being trapped in the house was upsetting his parents, who had to survive each other as well as the soldiers, but it threatened to suffocate a seventeen-year-old man.

The bedroom, large and square and white, had only become his when his last sister had gotten married. Years ago, he'd shared it with her and two other sisters: four children, crowded in one room, sharing the bathroom with their parents. When the house had been built eighty years ago, his father once told him, it didn't even have a bathroom. The third bedroom had become the bathroom when Jamil's parents had married. His mother—whose family had been the first to hold a wedding in the new hotel in Ramallah instead of in the church hall, like everyone else—had insisted. That left them with only two bedrooms, because she needed to keep a salon as well, to receive visitors properly.

Now it suddenly felt like the room, the whole house, didn't belong to him anymore, like the soldiers on the rooftop could come in and take this too. As he lay on his bed, listening to his parents' nervous chatter in the salon and the faint scrapes on the roof above his head, Jamil imagined that the soldiers would never leave. What if they stayed up there, nested, made the rooftop and the house their base, and Jamil stayed locked in this house forever? He'd never finish high school, never get married, never have children.

His thoughts spiraled like a hawk, seeking prey, until they centered and swooped down, as they inevitably did, on Muna, the Ghanems' daughter. She would be home from school in a few hours and he could see into her living room from his bedroom window. He hoped she would signal him, even call, perhaps, pretend she wanted to give him the homework assignments he'd missed the day before, just so he could hear her voice. And if he could glimpse her sheet of black hair, her eyes from the window, it would end this terrible day happily.

In the other room, his parents had started up another game of backgammon. Jamil napped, not knowing what else to do until dinner, but his thoughts were filled with Muna: Muna next to him in algebra class, Muna secretly holding his hand under their white robes during their confirmation ceremony, Muna being attacked in a jail cell by a soldier wearing thick black boots, Muna collapsing in his arms after he'd broken in, kung-fu style, to rescue her. He awoke in a sweat, noticing that it was four o'clock, hurried to the window. But all the drapes in the Ghanems' house were drawn. Of course they were. Jamil didn't blame her father. They had three daughters too, just like his parents, but he felt like a castaway nonetheless. There would be no communication today.

Dinner that night was meatless, since his mother hadn't been able to go to the butcher. Lentils and rice, a tomato-less salad since they couldn't even go out to their own garden. "The last of my cucumbers," his mother murmured like a mourner as they ate. "I suppose we can't even go to the shed to get some pickled jars from our shelves?" His father didn't reply, and she didn't raise the subject again. They ate as usual, in the formal style she always insisted upon—quiet, cloth napkin in the lap, salad first. She baked a tray of *haresia,* since all she needed was the sugar and the *tahine* and the wheat, and they ate it as their dessert.

In the middle of the night, in his bedroom, he heard laughter above his head, two loud stomps, and a man's explosive guffaw. He tried to fall back asleep, imagining his head so heavy that it sank into the thick pillow, but there was a pull, a tension in his neck that wouldn't relax. He gave up, instead switching on his lamp and pulling Muna's letters from his bedside drawer, where he kept them hidden under his old comic books. Every note she'd ever scribbled to him as they stood in line, had her younger sister discreetly palm to him—hastily written notes on napkins, plain notebook paper, on the pale blue sheets she'd used for half a year in tenth grade, all there in a bundle, organized from first to last from sixth grade, when their eyes first connected during Sunday mass, to two weeks ago, when she'd passed him a textbook in the library with a note tucked behind the table of contents. "All my love—*mim.*" Always signed with her initial, a simple circle— م —but the tail curliqued with a flourish, so secretly and lovingly. Whenever he saw a *mim,* in anything—a store sign, in the newspaper, in Mubarak's and Shamir's names, even—her face appeared, making the ugliness of it all more palatable. But her last letters were so insistent, and he hadn't answered them. Girls, he'd thought. Always needing confirmation, something official, some way to prove how he felt. Why? Why couldn't she accept the bare facts—she liked him, he liked her. Official things were in the distant future. He drifted off to sleep, wondering why Palestinian girls needed every little emotion clarified, every feeling uprooted.

He woke up in the morning, on the third day, startled, the letters under his chin, to the sound of yelling from the roof. An Israeli accent, speaking Arabic—"*Shai.* Bring *shai.* Four cups. Now." The voice was so close, and then he realized it was in the house.

His mother scuttled by in the hallway, glancing in anxiously as she passed. He shoved the letters back in the drawer and hurried out, pulling his robe over his shoulders and licking the sleep off his teeth. His mother had put her small teapot on the stove and was digging in her canister for peppermint. His father walked in off the balcony, cursing.

"Sons of dogs, may their mothers burn at their fathers' funerals—coming into my house! May the blackest plague swirl around them and kill them!" he fumed, his chest heaving even as he pulled four teacups from the pantry. "I should put some rat droppings in their *shai,* those bastards. Too bad you are too perfect of a homekeeper," he muttered, consoling his wife, and even Jamal could see his father had now exploded sufficiently, released his anger, and could focus on calming his wife's anxieties. That's how it was in their home: the privilege of emotional outbursts always were awarded to his father before the others could share it.

"The roof is one thing, but to come into the house!" his mother said shakily, steeping the tea leaves in the pot, pushing them down with a fork she pulled from the sink. It seemed to Jamil, standing in the doorway, leaning on the wall, that the water boiled languidly, slowly, and their nerves bounced like the leaves in the simmering pot. "They just walked in like they own it!"

"Sons of dogs," his father muttered again, pulling a tray from the rack. "Are we servants now, as well as prisoners?"

It was left to Jamil to carry the tray up to the roof. His mother had started to do it, only to be yelled at by her husband—"My wife is not a waitress for the Israeli army!"—but she wouldn't let him ascend either, because his temper would get them all killed. "Send Jamil," she finally said. And so up the cement steps he went.

He reached up above his head and knocked on the roof door, calling "*Shalom!*" as his father had instructed, listened for the mispronounced "*Idfa'!*" and walked through, pushing upwards, finally planting his feet on the cement roof and raising his eyes, to see a rifle pointed at his heart.

"You brought four cups?" asked a voice to the side, not owned by the curly-haired, rough-shaven teenager holding the rifle. The tray trembled in his hand and Jamil had the sense to steady it with the other.

"Yes," he answered the Voice, his eyes focusing for some reason on the fingernails of the soldier—lines of black tucked deep in the nailbed, the knuckles below caked and peeling as the fingertips playfully drummed the trigger.

"Put it down," instructed the Voice calmly. "Right at your feet."

He did, and looked to the right. The Voice's owner was younger than he thought, perhaps Jamil's own age, his face and neck browned by the sun. Eyebrows like even rectangles, separated by a slit of brown skin. A chipped front tooth.

"Get the fuck out of here. And tell your mother to make us sandwiches for lunch."

Jamil left, the gun still pointed at him, although he understood now that the initial splash of fear had dried off his body—they would laugh to themselves later, over and over, about his expression, imitate his reactions to pass the time.

His father roared, and his mother groaned, even as she began to pull the bread from the cabinet. When Jamil took it up to them, there was no gun now, only four pairs of eyes, four foreheads greasy and sweaty from the hot sun, four pairs of parched lips. They made Jamil break the corner off one sandwich and eat it, then the Voice took the small tray from him and they began devouring, not caring whether he'd descended or not, as they sat around the water tank.

Jamil stood awkwardly, feeling oddly like an intruder on their meal, despite the fact that they were gnawing on their hummus and pickle sandwiches while perching on his father's—his grandfather's—rooftop. He looked over the ledge, down into the courtyard, where the gate of the old chicken coop, long unused, swung lazily, unattached to the wall. Further up, he saw the metal doors of the old well, which they hardly used anymore.

The Voice licked his fingertips and picked up the fallen crumbs like a magnet attracting metal shavings, while the Gun paused, thumped his chest with a closed fist and burped. Jamil saw their guns leaning casually against the water tank, the large cylinder he'd helped his father install a few years ago. It caught the rainwater and stored it, a reserve right there on the roof, a modern development his father loved and was proud of, no longer depending on his well as many of their neighbors continued to do.

Across the street, in the window, a movement—small, quick—attracted his attention. A curtain pulled back at the Ghanems' house, then dropped hastily. He waited, wondering if Muna had seen him, but the curtain stayed in its place. He looked back at the four soldiers only to find the Voice staring at him.

The Voice handed him the tray, cracking, "You have pretty neighbors," in his rough Arabic. Jamil grabbed it as the others chuckled. He hurried down the steps, spent the rest of the day quietly reading and re-reading the three-day old newspaper, filled with turmoil that was meaningless in light of this moment. Riots in Jenin. A suicide in Lebanon, a girl jumped off her balcony. King

Hussein is feeling better, the Queen says in an interview with the New York paper.

That night he dreamed of himself in black ninja pants, his hands slicing through the air, breaking noses and cracking collar bones, defending his love. He woke up, sweating hard, his hands searching for the comfort of the bundle of Muna's letters.

On the fourth day, Jamil worried that he might scream at his mother, who was obsessively fretting over her inability to hang the laundry on the lines. Or at his father for his bluster, promising between TV viewing and snacking to slaughter the army with his bare hands. Jamil opted to be even more alone than he was: he spent most of the morning watching a crackly video tape of a kung-fu movie. It was in Chinese, as far as he knew, dubbed into Russian, or Polish, or something, but he didn't care. He could still follow the slow, angry glares, the face-offs, the jumps, kicks, and flips—the anger and its release. He knew every move by heart, had his favorite moments of the carefully choreographed fight scenes. But even that grew wearying, so he went into his room and spent the afternoon looking through his books. What were his classmates doing now? He lay on the floor in front of the low bookshelf. His sisters' old textbooks filled half of it, and all the family's other books—some inherited, some borrowed, the old Bible, some funeral memorial booklets of old people he didn't know, a couple of photograph albums—sat dutifully, side by side, like victims condemned and waiting at the gallows. He pulled a battered, creased literature textbook, his eldest sister's name scribbled in the front cover. *Literature of the Globe.* He opened it to the contents: "The Ancient World," "The European Middle Ages," "The Islamic Golden Era." He turned to this section: he read Moses Maimonides, scanning the biography: a Jew. Nobody had ever told him that. Back to the contents: "India and the Subcontinent." Tagore: he flipped to this section, and read "The Punishment," about a wronged girl who stubbornly accepts her unjust sentence without a fight. Picked up the old newspaper again: some stories he missed . . . Food riot in Thailand. George Bush elects his new cabinet. The girl in Lebanon again. Enough victimization. He felt confused, his world was not right. He skipped dinner and went to bed early.

On the fourth day, they ran out of bread. Jamil told the Voice, whose beard and mustache were thickening, that they were out of almost everything else too: milk, butter, eggs, vegetables.

"Tell one of your pretty neighbors to bring it," he replied gruffly. "And we need more tea."

"How long will you be staying?" Jamil asked boldly, but his only reply was a glare. Irritated by the casual reference to the Ghanems, Jamil repeated the question, regretting it instantly, feeling in that second that he had betrayed his father, his mother, his priest, Muna, including his own intelligence. The Voice rushed to his gun, reaching the tank in three strides, spun and pointed it at Jamil in one fluid motion, while one of his comrades watched casually. While the gun centered on him, Jamil still saw irrationally another soldier to the left, behind the Voice, picking his teeth with his fingernail.

"What did you ask me, you filthy dog?"

Jamil felt surprised by how smoothly the Voice cursed in Arabic. How did he learn it? This question circulated persistently in his head as he stared, for the second time in his seventeen years, at a gun aimed at his heart.

"What did you ask me?" the Voice was shouting now, and when Jamil still did not reply—did he learn it in the prisons?—the Voice lifted the gun skyward, perpendicular to the flat roof, and with a casual contraction of his index finger, punctured the cloudless blue sky with a single bullet. He just deflowered the sky, Jamil thought, and wanted to burst out laughing at his own insanity.

A small silence, and then Jamil sensed several things at once—a curtain pulled back, two sets of panicked footsteps below, his own heart pausing in its beats, a desert in his throat.

He moved to the steps to block his parents, to show them he was fine. His mother dragged him down by the hems of his pantlegs, then by the shirtsleeves, to the kitchen, ran back and locked the balcony door, and, despite his protests, searched every inch of his face, arms, and chest. "Are you sure? Are you hurt?" she muttered over and over, not listening for his responses and reassurances.

The phone rang and his father, his face gray, his tongue quieted for once, answered softly. "We are fine, thank God," he said robotically into the phone and hung up, but it rang again almost immediately. Six more phone calls followed.

That evening, Jamil sat on the couch, reading the newspaper yet again. The story of the girl in Lebanon startled him out of his reverie, as if he hadn't already scanned it ten times. Suspected rape, an uncle, fourteen floors, cement courtyard. The church wouldn't bury her because it was a suicide. Sadness flooded over his body again, and he stood abruptly, asked his father to play *tawla* out of sheer desperation to fill his mind.

After playing several rounds to soothe his father and himself and after eating every seed, nut and pastry his mother placed before him, after they'd all gone to bed, to empty his own heart, Jamil wrote a long letter to Muna.

The next morning, the fifth day, shortly after dawn, old Miss Salma hobbled over to their front door. Jamil's mother opened the door quickly and let her in. She carried two plastic sacks of her homemade bread, a jug of milk, and a block of cheese wrapped in cloth.

"God bless your hands, Miss Salma, and may God bless our lives with your presence for many more years," Jamil's mother said, accepting the sacks without the usual feigned reluctance and disappearing into her kitchen.

"Come here, Jamil," Miss Salma said, sitting down heavily on the velvet sofa, her thick ankles ballooning out under the hem of her blue dress. Her diabetes was worsening, he could tell. Her legs were like heavy slabs of meat, pushed into her shoes so tightly that the front bulged out against the leather tongue. Her mottled blue calves and shins looked like a world map. "Are you alright, young man?"

"I'm fine. They didn't touch me," he replied, putting a small side table next to her as his mother called from the kitchen that she was boiling tea. He walked to the kitchen and took from his mother a small dish of watermelon seeds and a glass of ice water.

"Those bastards stared at me as soon as I came out of my front door," she said, cracking the seeds expertly between her teeth and spitting out the shells into her palm. Jamil grabbed an ashtray and put it before her politely. "They leaned over the roof and watched me all the way until I got here and knocked on your door."

"Sons of dogs," Jamil's father grumbled from where he sat on the other sofa, his arms folded across his chest. "That other boy in Ramallah died yesterday. They couldn't find a kidney."

"They had one, but they couldn't get it in. And a new checkpoint around Ramallah, did you hear?" Miss Salma asked.

Jamil's father shrugged. "All I hear, my dear lady, is this news from you and sometimes whatever I can get on the radio. Our newspaper is a week old. The only thing playing on the TV are soap operas. We could have a full-out war, but Abu Ammar would find it only suitable to play Egyptian soap operas for us!"

"Sugar in your tea?" asked Jamil's mother, and Jamil wondered, ludicrous as it were, whether his polished mother would always fret over etiquette and appearances even in the midst of an apocalypse.

While the world burned around them, she might spend precious minutes wiping down the silverware or folding napkins. Yet, while it irritated him, this image also soothed him; there would always be order, as long as his mother was around. Women, he felt, brought stability, like Miss Salma who'd arrived and solved their problems with her bags of bread and cheese, like Madame Amira, the former nun who lived on the other end of the village, who threw herself on top of boys so the army didn't drag them away.

"Two spoons," Miss Salma said. "You know, they're closing the schools, no?"

"What?" Jamil asked, panicked into joining the adults' conversation.

"Oh yes, all the schools in Ramallah will shut down, starting tomorrow. Seven o'clock curfew."

"But not here in our village," Jamil clarified.

"Well, be prepared," she said, leaning forward conspiratorially. "Yesterday the principal of the middle school called and asked if they could use my cellar as a classroom if they need to. All the villages are making back-up plans."

During the rest of her visit, Jamil barely spoke, feeling fretful and anxious. As she prepared herself to leave, he suddenly decided on a course of action. He rushed to his room, grabbed the letter, and then returned, insisting on helping the widow at the door. Sure his parents were not listening, he pushed the letter into her bag, asking her quietly to give this to Muna, Mr. Ghanem's oldest daughter. Not Huda or Lena, but *Muna.*

"Miss Salma . . ." he stammered.

She smiled and whispered, "Trust me, young man. Nobody keeps secrets better than me." And with a wink she was gone.

Jamil sat in his bedroom window that evening, having just delivered bread and cheese to the roof. His parents watched the new Egyptian soap opera on the television, but he knew they weren't paying attention. His mother was knitting a sweater for him that he didn't need and his father leafed through one of Jamil's calculus textbooks, for lack of anything better. "If they need schoolteachers," he'd told Miss Salma, "I'll come out of retirement. They will need math teachers."

He thought back to Muna's last letter, which he'd memorized by heart—it seemed like she'd written it and slipped it into his satchel years ago and not just two weeks—and her insistence that something be made clear between them. She wanted an answer. Why had he interpreted it so badly? She was right—there was no time to be lost anymore.

It was nine o'clock, and he peered out the window. Across the alley, the curtain moved aside, although the room inside remained dark, as he'd instructed in his letter. A pause, then the curtain fell twice, and was still.

Yes.

"God bless you, Miss Salma!" he said to himself.

The soldiers left on Saturday night, the seventh day, while they were sleeping, slipping away in the dark, leaving crumpled napkins and dirty tea cups next to the water tank. Sunday morning, they woke up and realized they could attend Mass. He would see Muna, make plans. They could do a long engagement, marry when they'd finished college, lock it in now, rather than search for a bride later. Or maybe they'd just marry this summer, and attend classes together. Why waste time? There was no time anymore, and nothing was certain.

Jamil hurried into the bathroom to shave, scrubbing his face with a soapy rag. The water pipes creaked as the water flowed, and Jamil looked more closely at the water as it pooled in the white basin. A horrible thought came into his head at the same time that he heard his father cursing from the kitchen and footsteps stomping up to the roof.

His mother rushed into the bathroom, shrieking, "Don't use the water, Jamil! I think they—"

"I know. I thought as much." Jamil swabbed his face with rubbing alcohol, ignoring the sting and his watering eyes, then climbed up to the roof and stood over the water tank, staring down into it with his father. An empty bucket, which Jamil had never noticed before on the roof, lay on its side next to the tank. "They were using it," his father kicked the bucket, "as their bathroom, and then dumped it into our tank before they left."

Jamil stared down at the waste floating in their modern water tank, and suppressed the nausea creeping acidly up into his chest.

"Goddamn animals," he screamed. There, the anger did it. The anger quenched the nausea. His father was right to always vent.

He knew what to do. This week had made him into a man, with a man's problems and solutions. He walked down to the cellar and fetched a metal tin and a long rope, then strode down the courtyard steps to the well. He hadn't visited it in a long time, but he knew his father always opened it before a big rain. He pulled back the old, metal door, and he let the rope slide down its stone-blocked sides, the tin clanging, echoing, as it clunked down. The well was deep, deep, deep in the earth, and not as vulnerable as an open tank on the roof. The well was old, but could not be contaminated.

As he carried the bucket of icy, clear water to the house, he calculated how much it would cost to empty the roof tank, to sanitize it, and then how long it would take for the rains to refill it. He'd look for a job soon, start earning some money. Before he stepped through the doorway of the house, he glanced over at the Ghanems' window. He would see her today, no matter what, in church, would see, maybe touch, the black ribbon of her hair.

THE FALL

1990

Hell, yes, it was a bad winter: first, Riham's father gets sick with pneumonia. Two weeks at Greater Memorial, and they're talking about putting him on a ventilator before he finally looked at a bowl of gray oatmeal and said, "I'm hungry." Still another month to recover at home, and Riham was running over there all the time to check on him, and just when things are settling down, you know, everybody's calm and smiling again at Sunday night dinner—my mom falls down the stairs, rushing to open the door for the FedEx guy. Down fourteen steps to the marble tiles of the hallway, and I don't like to sound like a jerk, but I'd told my dad at least a hundred times: "Get carpeting," I said. "Carpet's cheap and safer." No, no, you know how he is. "In the old country, we had tiles everywhere," he argued. "It's so nice and clean. Like back home." And when he'd come to my house, he'd argue so much about how dirty rugs are, how they were hotels for filth and germs, that we finally took them all out. All my life he's wanted everything to be like back home, but the man has never gotten on a plane—I'm talking forty-three years—and actually gone home. He doesn't talk much, but he knows it's a life here.

No, my mom was fine. She's so tough. She always said, "Look, Sufi, when I was growing up in Guatemala, I used to tend the cattle with my papa, because he don't have no son. He always want a son, no luck. So I become a son." I can picture her sometimes, like a really rough nine-year-old tomboy, rounding them up. Except I keep getting cowboy images in my mind, and I know it wouldn't have been a rootin-tootin, down-on-the-ranch kind of life, not in Guatemala. No cactus in Guatemala, right, but it keeps popping up in my head anyway. There's always one in the foreground when I imagine my mother as a kid. But that's where I fail, you see, to really understand my parents, because I've never been to Guatemala, and I've never been to visit my father's country either, so when he says they had tiled floors in every room, and my mother tells me about cattle, I have no choice but to believe them. And if some detail is missing, I just insert it myself, like that cactus that won't go away.

Bad winter. Bad, shitty winter. So when my wife came down the steps that morning in April and said, "It's going to be 68 degrees tomorrow. Let's have a cookout," I don't think I even bothered to take a breath before I said "yes." That's how quickly I said it, because we needed a break. And remember, the baby was only five months old by then, so we were still in that fog, especially Riham, who was nursing. She refused to do any formula, or give her rice cereal—just 100 percent breast. Breast is best. She even pumped it when she needed to be at the hospital with her dad all day, so I could feed it to the munchkin in a bottle. That's my wife—she's pretty determined. She'd read that breast milk is best for babies, and that's what she did. "Look on the can," she told people who questioned our—her—choice. "It says it right there: breast milk is ideal. Would you buy a Honda if the tag said Toyota is better?"

Is that the best line ever, or what? I still laugh when I think of people's expressions. How can you argue with that?

She was hardcore. She even kicked me out of bed for a while, because she worried that I'd roll over on the baby if she brought her to our bed to nurse at night. I'm still pretty heavy, I know. 280—not terrible, but big. Don't forget, I played football in college, you know. The stomach came later. Just two years, I played, then busted my knee. But the UPS job has been good—I'm going on ten years with them. I can lift those boxes like no one else, and every few months they give me a certificate. I keep them all in a drawer in the kitchen, next to the address books and the stamps. Anyway, about a month I spent on the couch while she was nursing the baby, and all I could do was watch TV reruns all night, keeping it so low so the baby wouldn't wake up and I am telling you, it was so low that I had to make up in my head the gaps in the sentences. So when Bill Cosby tells Theo about his schoolwork, you know that one, and at the end he says, "I love you son, and maybe, just maybe . . ." What? But everyone laughs, so I know the Coz delivered a good punch line, but what is it? So I make it up, you know: "Maybe, just maybe, I'll let you live here another year." Or, "Maybe, just maybe, I won't kill you." The Coz kills me, even when I'm making up his lines.

My point here is that it was a rough winter. But by April, the baby was sleeping a little more, Riham lost the blue moons under her eyes, I was back in my own bed, and I'd stopped using my 45-minute lunch break at work to nap in my truck. So when my lady came down our steps, looking so fine in her white nightgown, her hair all curly on her shoulders, wanting to have a family cookout, I just answered, "Yes."

My mother brought empanadas. That's what she brought to every family event. When Riham's father had been in the hospital, with blue lips and his chest sucking in with every breath, like valleys between the hillsides of his ribs, my mother brought tray after tray of empanadas. I told her not to try so hard, that the man is throwing up even water, but my mother is persistent—oh my god, is she persistent. She doesn't care how crazy she looks to other people—she's just stubborn about some things, like she's saying, "I won't give up on you. Look at me here, I won't leave. I won't give up."

My father made *warak dawali* for the cookout. Stuffed grape leaves. He rolls them himself. Yes, I can speak a little—a few Arabic words. *Shukran*—that's thank you. And *marhaba*—that's hello. I can speak more Spanish than Arabic—probably because I was around my mother more than my father.

Riham sent me out that morning to buy charcoal for the grill and hamburger patties and buns, while she made the calls. By 2 p.m., almost everyone was there: my father helped me clean the grill. We hadn't used it since last year, so it was in bad shape. My cousins Lonnie and Jon, and Diego and his wife were there. The little kids insisted we do it picnic-style, so we spread blankets on the grass.

We ate. Everyone said what a good idea it had been for Riham to have a cookout. "Picnic!" the kids yelled every time. "Okay, okay," we shushed them up. Riham looked gorgeous—she put on a red dress, to the calf, that she'd worn before she had the baby, and that made me realize she'd lost the baby weight. She'd said she would, and of course, it happened. Only her face was rounder, her lips as red as her outfit.

We took turns checking on the baby. She woke up around 4 p.m., and Riham went in to nurse her. It was about 4:30, and I was just setting up the volleyball net, when she came back, holding our child.

❧

When I said I spent more time around my mother as a kid, I mean that in every sense. If it weren't for what happened, I probably would still think of him as a mystery. Everyone always thought of my dad as just a shadow in the room. He was next to you all the time, he helped you, but he didn't talk, he didn't engage.

When I was little, it was easier to understand—he was at work all day, and my mom didn't work. Or, as Riham would insist, my mom "chose to raise us at home full-time." Fine. And of course, I don't remember much. Who does? I just know I was happy. All my cousins were raised in the same type of households—dad at work, mom at home. Dads are parents who come home at 6 p.m., with dirty fingernails, and stand in the bathroom, scraping them with a penknife while moms yell at them to change their dirty shirts before sitting at the dinner table. That's how it was. I remember listening to Spanish music on worn-out cassette tapes mom would borrow from her family, and when she really liked one, she'd play it on one boom box and record it on another. And I had to be quiet. Totally quiet. And if a car honked its horn outside, she'd curse: "*Gilipollas!*" and we'd have to start it again. It was torture. Today, I can copy a CD in a second, and back then, Mama would have bought the tapes if she could, but there was always a latest tape that a cousin or friend had brought back from a trip to Guatemala. "Sam Goody don't carry our music," she'd say. "So we do this."

All I remember of dad were weekends, when he was cleaning: wash the car, sweep the front step, wash the windows. He was always crawling up into our little attic, and re-sorting all the stuff—"Do you want this box?" "Sufi, do these skates still fit you?" Always making room, clearing space, for what? I get it now, but I used to be confused when he'd reply, "Only carry in your life what you need. Don't waste what you have." I always assumed it was an immigrant thing, like my buddy Suresh from high school, whose dad stitched socks when they got holes in them and taped up his glasses when they broke. When his mom wanted to buy a new toaster oven—Suresh tells it so funny—it was like a family summit had to be called. Pros? Cons? Could the old toaster be fixed, even though it had almost started two or three fires?

My dad wasn't that extreme. But close. I got all the stories about arriving in Guatemala with twenty bucks and his cousin's address in his pocket. I heard those over and over. The details rarely changed: he wore a blue cotton shirt, he bought a Coca-Cola, the first person who spoke to him was a janitor in the airport who used hand gestures and a lot of pointing to tell him how to get a cab ride. Getting to the US border from there was even harder. It took him four years, but he made it.

He worked longer hours than any dad I ever met, right there on North Avenue in his liquor store. He never let me work with him. I was sixteen when I finally saw the place—imagine seeing my dad taking money and making change from behind a cage—like bars with bulletproof glass. I was only there because I'd gotten my license the month before and mom sent me to give him his wallet—he'd forgotten it at the house. The man actually shooed me away. I was so pissed off, because the couple of guys there, drinking out of bottles in paper bags, started laughing. He came out and yelled at me to get in the car and go home. And that night he and my mom had a bad fight—she was in tears. "How could you send him? Do you have amnesia?" he yelled at her, half in his broken Spanish and half in his broken English. I got his point, and I know he loved me, but I resented him even more.

I've always resented him—that started when I was a kid. Like I said, he was always at work, and I was home with my mom. And it was fine. But I have this memory of a T-ball game, so I must have been five or six. I don't remember the details, but my team shirt was blue and my cap blue too. It was hot, because my neck was dripping with sweat, and my uniform shirt's tag irritated it even more. And I was running and running and landed on home plate. And then I remember two things: my coach hooting like an owl, and my mother screaming, "Go, Sufi, go, Sufi!" It was later, after all the high-fives, after Mama bought ice cream to celebrate, that I realized dad hadn't been there to witness whatever it was I'd done—steal home, hit a grand slam, who knows—and probing my disappointment more deeply, I realize, of course, he hadn't been there for any of my games.

Another one: My confirmation ceremony, seventh grade. I'm wearing a hand-me-down suit from my cousin Diego, and a blue tie. John Adero, a little shit who always poked in people's business, turns in his pew to whisper, "Are your parents divorced?"

"No," I whisper back, and I ask why he said that.

"Your dad's never here. I've never seen him, so—" His sentence is cut off by his frantic, bubbly return wave at someone seated behind me. Probably his mom, and I don't have to turn around to know his father is seated right beside her. And I suddenly felt so angry, but of course, I was really ashamed.

I raked leaves with my dad every Saturday in the fall. Seems like quality time, but not when you're not speaking. He put his head down when we started and only looked me in the eyes when we'd finished three or four hours later. He usually seemed almost surprised to see me, and he'd automatically check his watch, then back at me, like he was asking himself, "Has he been here the whole time?"

I remember once, hearing a Jewish comedian—stand-up stuff—saying that his father embarrassed him because he wore sandals with socks to the mall. It was funny, but I'm thinking, at least his dad took him to the mall. My image of what dads were like came from *Cosby Show* reruns—the joking, but firm father. The "maybe, just maybe . . ." type of dad: a reprimand, softened by a joke.

When I was born, my mom always tells this, he insisted that everyone call him Abu Sufayan, because that's my full name: Sufayan. And Abu Sufayan was an old man in his village that he'd really admired. So one day, while I'm in high school, we're all doing stuff on genealogy in class and I'm moved—yeah, that's right, I'm literally *moved*—to find out why my dad named me after this man. I know nothing about him, and it's such an unusual name, right? When I asked him one day to tell me about him, he just looked over my shoulder, like I wasn't in the room. He stayed like that for so long, and I got so annoyed that I left and never brought it up again. That may be the last time I ever initiated a conversation with him.

"Your papi loves you," mom always said. "Never doubt it." But she could not really understand the problem, she who came from a big family—there are ten of them—where everyone hugs, kisses, where your cousins are your best friends and your crowd, where your parents are always either yelling at you or trying to feed you.

Either way, my point is, it's still communication. I know dad always loved me, that he sat behind his metal and glass cage in a shithole neighborhood from noon to 2 a.m., for me, but the void, the silence is what I think about. He's the one person I could sit in a room with, not speaking at all, for hours and feel like it's completely natural. Maybe not natural. Normal. For us, it was normal.

The joke for a long time was that he might not show up to my wedding. "Maybe he'll just come to the church and then skip out on the reception to go to work," I'd tell mom, and she'd shush me. But he came and did his duty. When he kissed me, three times in the Arab style, his hands slamming on my back like a jackhammer, my mom told me he was so happy that I had to trust her, but I told her it didn't matter, because what mattered was communication. If you love someone and don't show it, don't tell them, does it matter?

"Some people show their love in other ways," she said to me, "and he really adores you." But I thought "adores" was taking it too far, so I laughed, and she didn't want to talk anymore after that.

Riham. Now that girl communicates. Freshman year of college, 1978, and I'm thinking I'm the great man on campus. Got the scholarship to play, and a room in the nice dorms, the new building where every suite has its own bathroom. No running down the hall with your towel to beat the guy next to you. My roommates are all on scholarships too. Awesome guys. Everything is rolling along, until one day, this girl in class, right behind me, says, "I didn't get a paper."

"What?" I turn around, and I'm blown away. Gorgeous, gorgeous—black hair down to her hips. Big brown eyes. But she's low maintenance, I can tell right away. She's got on jeans and sandals, and a keffiyeh around her shoulders, like a warrior.

"I think there's another paper stuck to your copy," and she's impatient, whispering because the professor has already started the lesson on commas or semicolons, or whatever it was. And the girl is right, but I can't make my fingers separate the papers, and so she leans forward and with one slip of her index finger and thumb—long fingers, tanned, no nail polish, no jewelry—she gets her paper and slides back into her seat. And I'm ready to pass out because that black hair just touched my cheek.

But when I try to talk to her after class, she's cold as ice. Later I find out that she's working two jobs to pay her tuition, and my football jersey gave me away as a player. And maybe I said something about being on scholarship that I thought would impress her but actually turned her off. But a bunch of students in the class organize this study session, and she comes to it and she's wearing that *keffiyeh* again. And I try to talk to her about being Arab, except I don't know much, and she looks at me in that way, the way that tells me she's a thinker. And that means that she's not impressed by things that impress other girls easily, so now I've got to get creative.

So I did. No fear. I joined the Arab Students Union, and I showed up at their meeting four weeks later, right before the spring semester began. She's the treasurer, and she's selling these red, white, black and green bracelets, so I fork over five bucks. I can barely hear her say "thank you." During the meeting, they discuss visibility on campus. "We're a small group," says the president, Omar—we're still friends with him; he's got four kids now. Good guy. Anyway,

Omar, who was so skinny back then, he's up there ranting about nobody knows we exist on campus and we need more of a presence. So I put my hand up, and she notices, she stares at me, but I go ahead anyway and tell them that they should link up with some of the other ethnic groups on campus. Have a joint event or a multi-cultural thing with the Korean students or the black students. And then I'm a hero—everyone loves it. I go a step further, because now I really have the girl's attention, and I offer to contact the Latin Students Organization, and I say, because I'm half Latino. They love me even more, and after that meeting, I'm chatting with Omar and she comes up to me, all big-eyed, and says, "I didn't know you were half Latino."

I explain it all, how my father left Palestine when he was seventeen, moved to Guatemala and met my mother, and the whole story.

"How did they get to the United States?" she asks.

I don't want to tell her the whole story: the crossing at night in the back of a truck; the smell of rotting vegetables that still makes my mother throw in the trash any vegetable or fruit that gets overripe in our refrigerator; being dumped in Brownsville, Texas, and not believing that they were still alive. I don't want to share that, not yet, because I don't tell anyone that story. It was drilled into me since I was a little kid, not to mention it to anyone ("The police will come and take me away from you, Sufi," mom used to scare me), although I have a feeling that at some point, if this goes well, I will be telling this girl anything she wants to know.

But then, she asks me next, "Why did your dad leave Palestine?"

And I have to admit that I have no idea.

My father was completely shocked when I told him about Riham. He never imagined his only child would marry an Arab girl, and even though he didn't say it to my mother, he was really happy about that fact. I knew when he met Riham—I saw the charmed look on his face when she said, "*Marhaba*." And when she called him "*Ammo*" respectfully—she hooked him.

"My grandchildren will be full-blooded Arabs," he said, in a bemused voice, at breakfast one day.

"Three-quarters," my mother corrected him, slamming a plate of eggs in front of him, pretending to be mad. He winked at me, and we both laughed, while my mother threatened to poison our omelets. "Full-blooded," she muttered with a smirk on her lips. "He's so happy, huh? A man who's never even gone back himself to see the country he loves." And even though she was kidding, using that fake-anger, my dad got quiet. She kept on joking, and I kept laughing, trying to keep the joke going, encouraged that he'd winked at me and unaware that anything had changed. When I laughed again, he quietly left the room.

⁂

We're all sitting on the blanket. Riham has the baby in her lap. My dad's about to start on his plate of watermelon and stands up. "I need to get a fork," he says.

As I remember it, Riham gets up too. "I'll get it, *Ammo*. I need to change Juju's shirt." I think the baby had been drooling a lot—she must have been teething—and her little one-piece was wet around the collar. It was a green one-piece that said "Angel" on it. Riham didn't really dress her in pink.

"No, I'll get it," my dad insists, and they have that argument Arabs always have, where they're trying to prove how much they respect each other: Riham has the baby on her hip, and trying to pull dad's plate from his hands. I specifically remember Riham saying, "No, I'll take it because it's my fault—I forgot to bring out more forks for dessert."

My dad just settles it by putting his plate down, and taking the baby. He's grinning, and I remember thinking that was nice to see how Riham could actually bring out that side of him. "I'll change her shirt," he says. And that was nice too, because I never really saw my dad be insistent or make himself involved with the baby before.

So he goes inside. Ten minutes later, we hear him screaming. And that's when we all race in.

She'd been on the changing table, and when she fell, the side of her head hit the tiled floor. She wasn't moving, although her eyes were wide open, and her head looked like it had caved in a little above her ear. Diego was on the phone right away. My girl did not make a sound or move the whole time the EMTs were working on her, and a little while later, she closes her eyes and doesn't open them. "Is she okay?" Riham finally screamed. "She is, she is," they assured us, but their faces were grim. "But she lost consciousness." Riham climbed into the ambulance. "I'm gonna book it," the driver told me when I shouted that I would follow. "I'm not waiting for you to catch up." She gave me the name of the hospital and slammed her door; the ambulance pulled away with a sudden jerk, leaving me behind in the driveway with my car keys in my hand, and that's when I started shaking. Until then, I'd been watching the whole scene before me, afraid to move, to breathe, to touch her. All I kept thinking was that I might hurt her more if I moved her the wrong way.

Diego rode with me. My mom stayed behind to take care of my dad, who, I found out later, had passed out in the other bedroom.

Juju was fine. Four days later, when she came home, there were area carpets in every room in the house.

"A moderate concussion," the young female pediatrician told us reassuringly, "although we always worry with such a young infant." They put a tube in her head to reduce the swelling, they said, and her skull had a faint fracture that would take years to heal on its own. Although it may never heal, the pediatrician said in a way that was oddly comforting, despite the meaning of her words. "It seems bad, but in a few years, you won't even remember this."

They told Riham to pump her milk and store it. She fed it to Juju from a little dropper, a quarter-ounce at a time. The nurses assured her that the IV gave Juju what she needed, but she didn't buy it for a second. She just stayed there, every hour, to try again. A quarter-ounce here. An eighth there. The third day, she drank a half-ounce in one sitting, and by the next morning, she took it from the bottle. She was nursing again before she was discharged. When we left, we filled the back of my SUV with all the teddy bears, flower vases, and get-well baskets we'd received. We left the baklava and chocolates for the nurses.

The first night she was home, it was like when she was born again—we didn't sleep all night and kept waking up to check on her, to feel her pulse. Riham finally just slept on the floor next to her crib.

That night, as I lay in our king-sized bed alone, knowing the two females I loved were safe in the next room, I suddenly remembered my dad. Not directly—initially I was thinking about my mother, and then the exhausted train of my thoughts pulled into his station. Because that is what he was in my life: a person I only thought of in connection to someone else, never one in his own right, who deserved recognition.

I wondered how he was doing. My mother had never mentioned him in all her calls to us in the last few days, and I hadn't asked.

I called him the next day. My mother answered, and spent ten minutes asking about Juju, until I nearly forgot why I was even calling. Everything was so easy with my mother: she'd been to the hospital everyday and practically lived there, although I never really felt her presence. Whenever Riham or I needed to leave the room, she appeared out of nowhere: "You go, I will stay with the baby. Don't worry."

"Is dad there?" I asked her. "I want to see how he's doing."

"Oh yes, Papi is here. He will be so happy to talk to you." A full minute goes by, so I know she prepped him for the call. I can imagine what she said, because I'd seen her do it with so many other calls. "Radwan," she'd say, "Radwan, Sufi is on the phone. Come and talk to him. Ask him how the baby is doing."

I know she told him that, because that is exactly what he said. "Sufi, how is Juju doing?"

"She's fine, she came home yesterday."

"Thank God."

"Don't you want to come and see her?"

"No." He paused, then said again, "No, I do not."

I have to admit, hearing that was . . . so forceful, so hard. It was like a confirmation of everything I'd ever felt about my dad. No, I don't really care about you. No, I am not interested in your life. No, I do not want to be involved in what's important to you.

Maybe it was because I hadn't slept the night before—hadn't slept in four days at the hospital, hadn't really had a decent sleep all winter, to be honest.

Maybe that's why I answered the way I did, a way that—mom told me later—made my father burst into tears when he hung up the phone.

"You almost killed her!" I shouted. "And then you don't want to see her? Fine, I don't want you to come near her again. How's that?"

"I'm sorry," he said.

"I don't care!" I screamed. And that's when I hung up the phone.

My stomach felt like it had fallen out of my abdomen and onto the floor. My whole torso felt empty, shaky. I checked on Riham, who was washing the dishes, the water running loudly, which is why she probably didn't hear me yelling. The baby napped in the bouncy seat next to the counter—within Riham's line of vision. Knowing that everything was safe, was okay, in this house of mine, I told my beautiful wife that I needed to go lie down. She turned to me, smiled, and said, "Get some rest, *habibi.* I'll have dinner ready when you wake up."

"Don't let me sleep too long? An hour, maybe."

"Okay, sure," she said, stacking plates on the dish rack. They were the plates we had used that day at our cookout—and as my head sunk into the pillow, I realized that, yes, we had not been home in four days, and that we needed to catch up with things in the house.

But when Riham woke me up, I knew it hadn't been an hour. My head felt heavy, and for a second, I thought I was back in the hospital, sleeping in the blue vinyl recliner that had been my bed for three nights. But then I saw my dresser, felt my quilt, and saw my wife. She looked concerned. "Your father is here," she said. "He looks really upset. Come downstairs."

He was sitting quietly in the living room, his car keys in his hand, his jacket still on, his back to the baby sleeping behind him in the kitchen.

He stood up when he saw me.

I just didn't want there to be a scene, so I said, "Look, I'm sorry. Let's please forget what I said."

He nodded. "Okay. Let's go for a ride."

"What?" I asked. "Where?" I looked at Riham, who seemed alarmed, but my father was already headed for the door.

"Come on." He spoke in a way that—it wasn't authoritative, but it was almost like he was desperate to sound authoritative, and I didn't want to make him realize that I could simply ignore him, go back to bed. It would have been so easy to do that, or to just sit down on my couch and refuse to go.

But I didn't want to hurt him. I've never wanted to hurt him. My outburst on the phone was probably the roughest way I've ever spoken to him. When had I ever had to confront him before, ever, about anything? Even when I was a teenager, all those confrontations that kids have—I'd had them with my mother, not with my father.

"Where are we going?" I asked again, but he was walking down my driveway. So I squeezed Riham's hand and followed him.

We drove in his rusting Toyota Corolla around the neighborhood, in silence, and for a while, I thought that maybe he didn't know where to go. Maybe he'd assumed I wouldn't follow him, and now he needed to make a decision. Eventually, after about ten minutes, I could tell we were actually headed somewhere, and once we past the main stores in the downtown and then, fifteen minutes later, past the train tracks, I knew that there was only one place we could be going: the old Rosario vineyards.

And that is what made me continue to remain quiet. I wanted to see if he was really going to take us there. The Rosario family had owned this vineyard when I was a kid—their son was in my class, and he was forever inviting me to go there on weekends. They had wine tastings, tours, festivals. On holiday weekends, for Mother's Days and Memorial Day weekends, they would invite local bands to play, and people would bring picnic blankets. I used to ask my dad to take us there, to hang out for the weekends. Once I even made the argument that it was a vineyard, where grapes grew, and didn't they have grapevines in Palestine? I mean, this is how little I understood about Palestine—I arrived at that conclusion because, if Palestinians cooked with grape leaves, they must have grapevines, and then they must have vineyards, right? It didn't work—he just looked at me, amused, and said that he had to work, but that I could go with my mother if I wanted. But of course, that wasn't my point. Anyway, when I was in high school, the Rosarios had to finally admit that they weren't making enough money to sustain the business; they closed it down and moved to Arizona, and the place had been shut down since then, the vines running over and the old barn, where they used to have bands and tastings, filled to the window panes with grass and weeds.

But now, here I was, with my father, twenty years after first begging him to take us as a family. I wondered if he even knew it had been shut down—maybe he thought this would be a big reunion for us, to sit together over a glass of wine and finally connect as father and son. I studied his face as we got out of the car; no, he didn't seem surprised. He looked ashen, tired.

"So what's up?" I asked, following him as he walked to the field where the vines grew so thick and were so twisted that the wooden rails that ran up and down the field were not visible.

He didn't answer, but peeked under the leaves. "No grapes," he muttered. "The leaves are too thick—the sun cannot reach the grapes."

"I'm sorry for what I said on the phone," I tried again to restart the conversation. I was starting to feel tired again. We'd left my house an hour ago, and I was sure the baby would be waking up by now, and maybe Riham would be wondering where I was and whether I'd be back in time for dinner.

"I'm sorry I dropped Juju," he said quietly. "I turned around to get something and she rolled right off the table. I should have held her, been more careful."

Before he'd finished, I hurried to say, "It's okay. She is okay now, and I don't want you to be upset." I really didn't. But I added, so he would know: "I just didn't know why you wouldn't come to see her."

He leaned forward, his back turned slightly to me, as if he didn't want to look at me. His palms rested on the twisted vines, his index and middle finger playing with a green leaf as though it were a lock of hair.

"I love her so much, and I love you very much."

"I know."

"I am afraid to love you very much. I always was, because . . . it's like, if I show it and I am happy, then maybe God will take you away from me."

I sensed instinctively, at this point, that I should keep my mouth shut because he was about to gush out something revelatory. Maybe this would be our first real conversation. I followed those instincts and just listened, staring at his feet, his brown work shoes that he wore everywhere, with the thick rubber soles, that looked like old-school Doc Martens. I stared at them hard, afraid to look at his profile so that he wouldn't stop speaking.

"Sufi, when I was twenty years old, back home, I killed a little boy from our village. The neighbor's son. I was out shooting with my friends for rabbits. We did that all the time, and I didn't see him—Demetri. His name was Demetri. I didn't see him playing in the grass—we have tall grass in some parts of the hills back home."

He paused, then quickly said, "It's not an excuse. After they buried him, the boy, his family burned down my father's house, and my father told me to get out of the country. He said that they could reconcile it with the family, but never with me. I had to get out so that the problem would be eliminated.

"He gave me some money, maybe one hundred dollars, everything he had, and the priest in the village helped me to leave. I'm glad I left. I didn't go back. Never. Not when my father died. Or my sister. Not one time. All they knew of me was a check that arrived once a month, with my name on it. And the church got a check once a year, at Easter, from me, to thank them because they helped me be reborn. I was given a new life when I had taken another life."

After a long pause, I worried that he wouldn't speak again, so I pushed the conversation along timidly: "Does mom know?"

"I was honest with her always. She still wanted to marry me. I didn't want children, I told her. And she said okay. You know, our life was too hard. But then we began to hope. We asked questions about how to leave Guatemala. You know that story—I'm sure she has told you most of the details. We got to America and when we finally felt safe, she changed her mind. One child, she said. Before I am too old to become a mother. And I thought, please God, don't give me a son, because I don't deserve it.

"When you were born, I tried to deny my happiness, but it was there. My son." He smiled, a sad smile, but he wasn't looking at me, was staring into the vines. "In my heart. And at the same time, I was afraid.

"I named you Sufayan, so that I would be called Abu Sufayan—that was the name of a man I respected in our village. He saved me the night that they burned down my father's house—he saved all of us, actually. I will never forget him. He was so wise, so reasonable. His sons lived in Guatemala—they gave me a job when I got there and I lived with them for a month until I was okay. They did that for me because he told them to—he said, go find my sons and tell them I sent you. That was it."

"He sounds like . . . like a really . . ." I didn't know what to say.

"He was religious—maybe I thought naming you after him would show to God that I understood what I had done, that it would protect you somehow." He paused. "And then when Juju fell, I thought finally, here it is . . . the curse is revisited upon my son. Through *me.*" He stopped. I thought he was going to start crying, and I held my breath.

But he didn't. Instead, he suddenly thrust both hands deep into the vine and pulled, and he screamed at the top of his lungs. A roar that came from deep within him, filled with—*anguish.* And I felt my own tears climbing up inside my throat, as he stood there, wrestling with the old vines and roaring.

"Dad, stop it, stop," I said weakly. "Come on."

"I should have been dead fifty years ago—they came to kill me that night, and only the old man saved me."

We stayed there for so long, both of us leaning on the vine, and my dad muttering occasionally, and me thinking how I didn't even know him well enough to know the words that would comfort him.

~

My father died of lung cancer, within a year of being diagnosed. It was aggressive. It happened the summer that Juju finished eighth grade, around the time she started insisting that we stop calling her Juju and start calling her Jumana. "It's a more elegant name," she said. "Juju is a baby name." We'd had our other two children by then as well, my boy Alex and little Sophia.

When Alex was born, I'd wanted to name him Radwan, for my father, as our custom dictated (according to Riham). My mother thought he would like that, but my dad forbade it. He cracked down on me like the hand of God and said, under no circumstances was a child to be given his name. And once again, I felt that old anger rise up inside me, that same feeling of rejection, of not being understood. Like I told Riham, it's not like that day at the vineyard changed my relationship with my father. When I told her what happened, what he had confessed to me, she was so moved by it all, and she tried to insist for months after that I move closer to my dad. "This is a major breakthrough," she would tell me. And once in a while, on a quiet Saturday, she would encourage me to call him. "Call him up and tell him you want to take him to the museum," she would say. As smart as she is, she didn't understand that my dad is not a museum kind of father, and besides, while I understood him now, it didn't mean that everything was suddenly okay. He was not suddenly Bill Cosby and I was not suddenly Theo. It took me a while to accept that maybe that is what it was supposed to be.

I spent long hours talking to my mom about what dad had told me. She seemed so relieved that now the burden was off her chest, that someone else knew. "It's been so hard living with that," she told me one afternoon in her kitchen. "It's hard to be married to someone who does not want to be happy, who is waiting to be punished."

The cancer was diagnosed in the autumn, when my mother could no longer ignore his cough and his persistent bouts with bronchitis, when I kept pointing out that his lips were always blue. It's not that she didn't want to take him, but that he refused to go. "They never tell you anything good," he said of the doctors. And they sure didn't. It took about three weeks and several tests before they confirmed the cancer, and they started the most aggressive treatments they could. "Your dad is in relatively good health," one doctor said to me when I took him in for a treatment. I was concerned because of how hard the nausea and the weakness was hitting him. "We think he can withstand it," the doctor said, "and it's his best chance."

When it didn't, he refused anything else. No more IVs dripping into his arm, no more pills, nothing. Even when we knew the pain must be excruciating, he just got still, became quiet, like he was collapsing into himself, didn't complain.

"Take the pills, Radwan," my mother begged. I begged. Even Riham tearfully pleaded him to take the painkillers. We even put Juju up to asking him, thinking he couldn't refuse. But he would just pat us on the hand, the head, to reassure us that he knew what was best.

I knew what he was doing. I understood him a little now, enough to see that he wanted to feel the pain. This was finally the punishment he felt he deserved. And nothing could convince him differently.

But that is when I finally lost it. Only Riham knew that I lost it, because my mother had enough to deal with. Only Riham saw me, that night when I came home after he'd had a really bad night and finally slipped into the coma, when we sent the kids to sleep at their cousin's house. I lay on the couch, my head in her lap, and cried like an infant with colic, like a pain was tearing up my chest and only the screams relieved it. Like I couldn't find the words I needed but wanted someone to just hear me, and to know what I felt.

His funeral was quiet. There were no major speeches. I gave a simple eulogy, just saying that he had been a devoted father who worked hard for his family. After we buried him, we sent the final check—at his request—to the church in his village. A week later, I was sitting in the bleachers, watching Alex play his first T-ball game at the park by our house, wearing his blue uniform shirt and his white stirrup pants. He smacked the ball and ran for third base instead of first, and in between laughing and cheering for him and the other three-year-olds, I suddenly realized that my father had paid over ten thousand dollars in his lifetime to that church. And I hoped that, at some point, he felt that it had been enough.

BEHIND THE PILLARS OF THE ORTHODOX CHURCH

1994

I'm attending Mass again these days. The village is talking. They think Jesus has found me again, caught the wayward lamb. These sheep know nothing except how to be herded, I think, and I feel sorry for them. I left the flock years ago, before some of these lambs were even born, before some of these buildings were even erected in our neighborhood. When this village was just a collection of rough houses, blackened by smoke from wars, the mold growing like fur between the stones, I made a choice and abandoned the church's false comfort, its promise of forever. I threw it out like an old mattress, stained and soiled.

No, I'm not coming to church for faith, or for salvation.

I'm here for love.

So many Arabic poems, song lyrics, equate love with the moon—the roundness of the moon is supposed to reflect the fullness of one's heart. But that image isn't quite right for the way I feel about you. I've been thinking about it these many years, and I'm sure I've finally settled it: the glimpse of a crescent, not a bursting moon, evokes a memory of you. It pulls me down until I collapse into my thoughts, and I see your face, behind a stone pillar, and a few hours pass by like just a couple of minutes, because I'm sitting under that glowing sliver and imagining you beside me, your anguish, "It's so hard here," spoken between sobs.

Last week, the church started collecting money, part of the new priest's plan to raise funds to expand and renovate the church. The idea was different for us, something people liked—"You claim some part of it, and your name or your dedication is put there. You can donate enough to restore a pew, or an icon, or some other part of the interior. Paint the walls, a tile on the floor, a door," they explained, marveling at the new priest's marketing abilities. Maybe he'd get companies to paint slogans on the Virgin Mary's face, others grumbled. Don't give him a shekel, two or three said. He's a thief. You should know better, Miss Salma.

I do know. I've seen his fine silk shirts, his eyes rolling towards every woman in a skirt. How he turns his "Our Father who art in heaven" into a flirtation. But I have another goal, and so I unlock my small iron box that my grandfather once gave me, take out several bills, and walk down to the priest's office. He is a shrewd, performing man, the type who watches you, assesses you, and then adjusts his own face and gestures to suit you. His face is one squat rectangle, his chin flowing down into his neck. Avoiding small talk, I tell him clearly that I want to donate my money to the refurbishing of the pillar at the back entrance.

"We are in need of a new chalice for the Communion . . ."

"I'm interested in the pillar, please."

"Yes, of course," he says, counting the bills. "You are very generous, Sitt Salma, even though God prefers your presence on Sundays to your donation." I note how he nevertheless slips the money into an envelope and writes my name on the front. "And the inscription?"

"What inscription?"

"We told our parishioners that we will inscribe their names or 'in the memory of' a loved one on the item they pay for—so your neighbor, Imm Fareed, has already donated a pew in memory of her parents, so we inscribed their names on it." He shows me a small, bronze rectangle sitting on his desk. "This size. The carving will be done by Abu Salim in Ramallah—very elegant. Very nice."

"Can I think about it?" I ask him.

"Yes. Let me know by next week." He stands up, dismissing me. Maybe there isn't enough money in the envelope. I think about how old Father Alexander, with his shiny bald head, had never wanted me to go. We'd sit for hours in this office—it used to be filled to the ceiling with books, and talk and talk, draining two pots of tea in one sitting. But this new man—he's younger, his head is a thick harvest of black, carefully gelled curls, and he's busy. The books are gone, the surface of his desk holds just a few letters, a lonely pen. And I'm old now, and it's time for me to leave.

"Good bye, Abouna."

"God bless you, Sitt Salma. I will wait to hear from you." He opens the door and shuts it quickly behind me.

On the way out, I linger by the pillar—our pillar—with its pocked, yellow stone, but it's beautiful nonetheless. From here, I am hidden from the view of everyone, except the Virgin's statue at the very top of the dome, who sees all and is in need of repair herself. I can see inside Father's office window as well, and he pushes aside a curtain, and behind it is a lady, who falls into his arms. As they kiss passionately, I shake my head, stunned, and hurry away.

For as long as I can remember, Constantine was treated better than I was. You only knew him as a cute little boy—you never lived with him as I did. It wasn't obvious to most people, but I noticed how my mother plucked the juiciest chunks of meat from the *mansaff* platter for him, how she pressed his school uniform early in the morning, so he could slide his arms and legs through warm fabric and welcome the day, how the new notebooks and pencils were placed into his school satchel, while last year's half-used tablets and pencil stubs sufficed for me. Did he ever understand this difference, this overt way in which he was Jesus and I was expected to soap and wash his feet with my hair? Did he ever sense, deep inside of him, that it was wrong for me, his older sister by eight years, to pack his school satchel at night, to take his soiled plate from the kitchen table to the sink, to wash it, to dry it, to put it away, and then—above all—to ask him if he needed a cup of tea before bed? A prince cannot be a prince without the requisite servants around him, to fan him, to hold up clothing for his nod of approval or his "tsk" of disdain, to ensure that he never feels hungry, cold, or inconvenienced in any way—and to develop a worried knot in the pit of one's stomach if it turns out that he does. The role of the prince is a performance played by many actors, not one independent in his own play, with his own story.

My mother scripted this all in our house. I can see that now. I used to think it was my father, and he certainly acted in it, making sure everyone called him Abu Constantine, and refusing to speak to old Imm Fareed for months after she once mistakenly addressed him as simply "Sufayan" in front of a large group of clan members. They were all gathered at my cousin's wedding, waiting for the family to arrive, and she was passing around a tray of coffee. "*Itfadhal*, Sufayan," and he froze, refused the cup, only accepted it later from the bride's father himself, who prattled on about "our worthy cousin Abu Constantine, our leader." I bet you didn't know that about my father, how absolutely stubborn he could be when he felt that someone had insulted him. I know you didn't know that. If you had, our story would have ended differently.

My parents were thrilled to have a son, of course. I don't blame them. After waiting eight years to get pregnant again, to finally have another baby, my mother accomplished her goal, and she had a son, for which two young goats met their fate, offered as a *nithir* for his birth and health. I remember the days before he was born, how absolutely exhausted my mother looked, how worried my father became, and it was his fear that made him offer that promise to God—the goats' throats slashed cleanly, their blood drained over the steps of the house, their meat donated instead to the local orphanage instead of filling our stomachs. But those worrying days before: I had felt certain that my mother was dying, even though it had been explained to me in simple, careful terms by my grandmother that I would soon have a sibling and that pain was part of the process. The adults around me spoke brazenly, voicing their hope that I would have a baby brother, that my mother's grunts and cries would result in the birth of a boy, pushed out by her efforts in the bed on the second floor bedroom, pulled into the air and the world and life by my grandmother Hilwa. (He was named Constantine, after my mother's father, instead of Jamal, after my father's father. That made people gossip too, the long awaited child who doesn't carry the name.) It wasn't until years later that I wondered how everyone must have felt at my birth, when it may have seemed that all that work and worry had delivered only a girl. That is when I first began to understand my own role in this play.

It was fun to learn how to diaper him, less fun to handle the aftermath, several times a day, of his diapering. I enjoyed learning to spoon small puddles of broth into his tiny mouth, less enjoyable to know that this was my responsibility, that whether he ate or not, and how much, and whether or not he burped effectively afterwards—that these details were my new reality, and that I fretted over them, knotting the hem of my *thowb* as I worried.

Sometimes I felt proud to be my mother's helper, but as Constantine grew older, as he crawled, then walked, then scurried from room to room, I began to despise him. His energies, so adorable and endearing to others, became the force that shaped my days. Do you remember—I told you once—about the day he climbed up on the roof? It was not my fault. He'd watched my grandmother climb those steps several times a week, push the door open, and disappear into the sky. One day, when I had gone into the kitchen to warm up some milk for him, he decided to explore. And it was Imm Fareed's screams—she'd seen, from her perch on her verandah next door, Constantine's head poking around on the roof, running through the hanging sheets and towels that my grandmother had set to dry.

I rushed up there and pulled him down before he splattered his brains on the courtyard below, and I even fashioned a new lock for that door, by driving two nails—one into the door and one into the door frame, and connecting the two with a loop of wire. But when my grandmother and our neighbor recounted and highlighted the drama, spinning it worse and worse, my mother settled upon me: Why had I left him alone? Didn't I know a four-year-old could not be trusted? In her anger, she grabbed the sweater she was knitting for me—a thick, gray, warm yarn and pulled it all out, until it was just a heap of loose noodles. "Roll it up," she screamed. Later she took out her long knitting needles and refashioned it into a hat and mittens for Constantine.

The day Constantine was born, my father stated it clearly: "You will have a brother to defend you, to protect you when I am gone. God has blessed you." That defined for me what relationship I would have with Constantine: he would take grow up and take care of me later, but I would pay for it until then. Of course, that didn't work either: Only a few years ago, in the months before the intifada erupted, my brother dropped to his knees in the *qahwah* one night, after an evening spent smoking *narghile* and drinking *arrak,* his torso twisting with the pain that shot through his left side. He was dead before his wife or the doctor could reach him. His wife took the children back to her village in the Galilee—she hated Tel al-Hilou anyway—and that was when the house became mine, its possessions mine, and all its needs and all its memories—mine. That was when I made these walls my fortress, because I was the only one strong enough to last, to conquer the things that subdued other people. And I removed the wire and loop from the roof door, and I come up on this roof whenever I want, alone, after an evening spent on the book, and watch the moon and remember you.

I'm still bitter, yes; there was the time, when he was ten and I was eighteen, that he came home from school during lunch and I wasn't there to prepare his meal. I'd stayed late in school to finish taking a test, but I rushed back to warm his *maloukhiyyeh*. I was greeted at the door by a flying dish that smashed against the metal doorjamb, right by my ear.

"Costa!" I cried.

"When I come home, I want my food ready!" he bellowed. "I've been waiting and waiting!"

Such a tantrum from a little pest who desperately needed, not an older sister like me, but a new baby to draw attention away from him. How I prayed for my mother to have another baby, even if it meant more work for me. The attention, over the years, had pooled around Constantine, having had no other grate, no holes, to divert it elsewhere. And it had started to mold and to rot his personality in ways that became apparent only on certain occasions—when he was tired, when he was overwhelmed by other issues in his life and unsure of how to channel his frustration. A prince is a performance. He cannot function alone.

My parents wanted more children, but my mother's body would not cooperate, I suppose. She did become pregnant twice after Costa, but the babies were lost early on. I remember the second one very clearly, sitting with the mattress in the morning sun, behind the house so nosy Imm Fareed, with her stripe of gray through her black hair, like the flag of a meddling, foreign nation, wouldn't see, and scrubbing the blood stains out, using alkaline, soap flakes, everything I could. It didn't quite work, which angered my grandmother; the mattress had been part of her dowry from her family, and now it was ruined by four brown patches in the shape of cannons, aimed at one another. The disappointment, the continued failure to have more grandchildren, was all right there, marked permanently on the mattress, which was shoved into a closet and not used again until years later, when the scarcity of the war forced us to depend on everything we had, beautiful or not.

I knew all this, knew that Costa was good inside, but I used my shoulder to wipe my angry tears that afternoon as I swept up shards of white porcelain.

I presented them in a bag to my mother that evening, when she'd returned from the fields with my father and grandparents. "Well, you know he's sensitive. If he's hungry, he lashes out," my mother said tiredly.

"But he almost cut me with it!"

"Try not to upset him. I don't need any problems from either of you."

But at least he introduced us. That was one good thing that Costa did. When I do my duty and put flowers on his grave at Easter, I remind myself that I can be grateful to him for that at least.

It was a quiet day, unlike the days when I usually walked with Constantine to the new school. It looks old now, but you remember it back then—when the Greek nuns first arrived and supervised its construction, how grand and bright it seemed. They had so much money, and the *mukhtar* grumbled that he wished they would donate the money to the existing school, or to the village's food stores, but everyone in Tel al-Hilou secretly loved it. It was a large building, and it rose, stone by stone, between the Orthodox church and the farming supply store that is now the *qahwah,* high up to the sky, rivaling some of the buildings the Israelis were erecting on the next hilltop. What I loved about the new school the most was the arched doors and window frames—I often lingered at the supply store whenever I had an errand for my father so that I could see how they built those arches, layering stone upon stone, shifting angles and such to make sure it was strong, then finally inserting the keystone. The nuns, meanwhile, had corralled part of the Sunday school room to organize their materials until they could move into the school building. So austere they looked in their black veils, their long gold crosses resting on their black-clad bellies, and their snowy, smooth faces.

Constantine was enrolled quickly. Anything that seemed grand or new or special in any way was usually grabbed by my mother on his behalf. Why should he continue to attend the old village school, when a better one was available? The only problem is that it was on the other end of the village, and Costa was not accustomed to walking that far alone. But I was, and so it became one of my duties to escort Costa to school in the morning and to pick him up afterwards. And you had benefited as well—your first job, wasn't it, to stand on the *manarrah* with your whistle to help the children cross safely?

We didn't make eye contact for weeks, although I could see and discern your every movement as Costa and I approached. I couldn't help but notice your thick, curly hair, your straight black brow, your tall frame, your slight limp. I found out later that you'd been born with one leg slightly shorter than the other. You always said goodbye to Constantine at the end of the day, and sometimes if you chatted with him, I would interrogate my brother all the way home.

"I don't know. Ask Baba who he is," Costa snapped at me once.

I'd irritated him and gone too far. If I wanted more information, I would have to secure it myself, from some other source.

I pieced together your identity. Here's what I learned, in the order I learned it: You were twenty-one and worked at the cinema in Ramallah. You were not natively from our village, which is why I didn't recognize you. Your father had moved to Tel al-Hilou from Jerusalem after his shop had been burned during the strikes. Your mother had died of the cholera when you were a baby. Your father was deeply unhappy in our village, even though he couldn't move back to Jerusalem. Maybe the explosive separation from his business, from the East Quarter, and from Damascus Gate and its winding corridors had devastated him. Who could blame him? The area in which he'd grown up, where you could turn down a dingy, dark alley, pass through a door into a room that looked like a palace—those surprises only existed in Jerusalem. Our village is fine, but it's quiet. Even those of us born here grow irritated, annoyed, at hearing the same bit of recycled gossip, at the shame of feeling suddenly excited when someone builds a new well, or a woman wears a new dress—the minutiae is all too apparent to us, and yet there is little else to divert our attention. But maybe, your father was sad because he'd lost his wife—he'd never remarried, people said, and you were an only child.

So we were at a stagnant point—I knew all about you, and you, as you told me later, had discovered as much as you could about me.

And then Constantine tripped one morning, crossing over the *manarrah.*

His scratched knee, his bleeding palms, provided us with the chance to speak—it gave us the reason to address one another directly. How selfish of me, I still think sometimes, that my first thought was not about Costa's safety or his pain, but about whether my hair looked neat and if my breath still gave off the odor of my breakfast, a hurried scoop of the hummus my grandmother hadn't finished.

My first thought was of you, as it still is, even now, when hope is as far away from my grasp as the moon.

"I'm Issam."

"I'm Salma."

In the late spring, the Scouts planned a big parade that year through our village, and they would be joined by the Jerusalem Scouts. I rushed through my chores that morning so I could walk with Costa to the *manarrah,* where the parade would both begin and end. I oiled my hair, brushing it dozens of times until it shone, then pleated it halfway down, let the bottom half fall around my shoulders. My hair was long, like a horse's mane, in those days—strong and thick—and it fell on my shoulders like a blanket when I let it loose. As I walked with Costa, who wore his junior Scout uniform, his khaki shorts and tall white socks, his green kerchief knotted neatly at his collar—it would be some years before he earned his badge—and excitedly bounced beside me, I pinched my cheeks unobtrusively, hoping they'd sprout a blush.

Most people were there, lining up the small road, waving flags and handkerchiefs. "They've reached the school," someone said behind me, and I knew that it would be any minute now that they would march down in front of where we stood, beating their drums and playing their flutes, their feet in leather boots stamping on the ground like a militaristic dabke line.

Costa saw his friends from school and hurried over to where they stood, in the front, right on the street. I stood back, looking for my friends—for Maria, for Rudayna, and my other classmates. I noticed them standing in front of the supply store, and then I saw you—further down, by the large pillar in front of the Orthodox church. You stood patiently, as if waiting to catch my eye, and when I gazed at you, you suddenly winked and disappeared.

I knew where you were going. I knew you'd been looking for a way to speak to me, privately, alone. We'd exchanged hellos and *salaams* since the day Costa fell, when you helped me carry him to the main office for a bandage, even though he was perfectly able to walk on his own. We fussed over him and fretted together, but there was no danger, of course, only opportunity.

You were brilliant, you know—finding time for us to speak alone, in the midst of a crowd—when everyone would be focusing on the parade and their attention diverted. I checked on Costa, made sure he was fine, slipped back behind the store from the west side so that my friends wouldn't see me, and took the small road behind the main street to the church's courtyard. I stood in the courtyard, the sea of white stones washing out before me, leading me to a new shore. I waited to see where you were, and then a pebble skipped next to my feet, and I followed its trajectory back to where you crouched in the shadow of the vestibule.

We only had a few minutes—we both knew that, as we could already hear the crash of the drums in the distance and the cheers and ululations of the people in the street on the other side of the church—and we didn't waste time. You held my hand. I wasn't in the least afraid or worried. The voice that had been drilled into my head by my mother and grandmother, and bored into my consciousness by the snooping glances of neighbors and aunts, the voice that dictated, "Keep your glance down. Obey your parents. Don't shame your family"—that voice had gone suddenly mute. I let you hold my hand in your large, dry ones, though your nails were startlingly smooth and squared and white. I stared down at our fingers, twisted clumsily together, your thumb stroking my knuckle.

"Salma, do you know my intentions?" you asked. "They are honorable."

"Yes."

"I'm twenty-one. I'm going to find better work soon."

I nodded, impatiently. I didn't care for the details.

"May I speak to your father?"

"Yes."

And that was it. You kissed my hand, then paused, as if to see if it were okay, if I would object. A strength, a power I'd never imagined flowed into my spine and I looked up, right into your eyes, and waited. The kiss that descended on my lips was gentle and quick, like a flutter of secret wings. Then a second one, your tongue slid over my lips as if you were tasting me, and I thought I'd lose my breath, until you kissed me deeply, your palms warm on my cheeks.

The crash of the drums subsided and the roars of the crowd dissipated into chatter. I tried to move but I saw your hand slip into your pocket, a flash of metal, a knife aimed at my throat. A kiss, followed by death—is dishonor punished so quickly? I thought instantly, irrationally. But no, you were sawing off a small lock of my hair, twisting it around your fingers, and grinning. Then we both fled, in opposite directions. Costa hadn't even looked for me, was not worried that I had slipped away, and I joined Rudayna and her mother by the *manarrah* where I could chat as well as keep an eye on my brother, who was earnestly asking one of the Scouts if he could bang on his drum. My lips felt swollen, engorged, and I held my fingers over them, sure that everyone would know I was in love. That I was loved.

That night, I watched my parents worriedly. Was Baba in a good mood? Had the crops been good this year? I hadn't paid much attention, as he and my mother discussed these matters on their own, when I wasn't listening. Was he content?

Who would you send to ask for me? Did your father have any relatives, any brothers, or cousins? Could they come from Jerusalem? Looking at my father, and knowing that he would soon find out that I was in love, that I had been kissed, was almost frightening.

What would he think? Should I warn him? Should I give him a hint of what I felt towards you?

I'd never had a good relationship with him. I wished then that my grandfather was well, that he weren't always so ill and in bed and so frail. I could talk to him, could confide in him, and he would help me. I trusted him more than anyone. If you and I had married, had been given half a chance in this life, you would have eventually become jealous of my grandfather, of how I loved him and told him everything. Do you know that the Turks kidnapped him during the first war, that they marched him and other men from the village to Syria and made them fight? My grandfather escaped, but he was hurt, almost dead. A band of gypsies rescued him, and he repaid them by stealing away the sheikh's only daughter! He told me this one night, when we stayed up talking in his room, after I'd brought his medicine and his evening tea.

"I didn't really kidnap her," he said, looking so thin and frail under the white sheets. "She was escaping a bad marriage, and I helped her get away."

"What happened to her?"

"She lived in Jenin, got married to a shopkeeper there. I never saw her again." He smiled then, saying, "I wouldn't want to see her anyway. She was a brave girl—a strong girl. I wouldn't want to see her domesticated, with babies on her hips and paint on her face."

"But women enjoy looking nice . . ."

"Ah! It's like when a cloud covers up the moon. You feel deprived, and it's always a shame."

But his health had failed since the arrival of bad news about Uncle Raed in Guatemala. The telegram briefly described how the cancer had spread to his lungs like mold. I never met my uncles, who'd left for the Americas when I was a newborn. They'd both married—one to an Arab girl, born in Guatemala to Lebanese parents, and Uncle Raed had married a Guatemalan woman who had four children by him. It had always struck me as funny that I had first cousins names Frederico and Enrique, but it was saddening to know that I probably would never meet them.

"They are lost to me," he told me one time, when I sat up with him in his room, rubbing oil into his bad shoulder as I'd done since I was little. His body, once so tall and strong, was now folding in on itself. The flesh clung to his shoulder blades tightly, like dried paper, and the veins in his neck bulged out like worms trying to burrow out.

"How? They will come to visit you. They must be smart, nice children."

"Even if they come, how will I speak to them? How can I talk to them, tell them stories of their father when he was little?"

"Maybe my uncle speaks to them in Arabic. Yes, yes. Surely he's taught them."

He sighed heavily, his chest rattling as he did, a sound that was subtle but so terrible to me to hear. "Your uncles barely write to me. They are busy—this new country has eaten them up, chewed them up, no doubt. They are living in a land of strangers, so maybe they've forgotten that this is their home."

"No, stop. You're just feeling down."

"It's the truth, my gazelle." For a terrible moment, I thought he would cry—that my strong, iron-willed grandfather might weep in front of me. I prayed quickly that we would maintain his composure, and he did. But he added, "It was bad of me—to send them out. But we needed money, and they were good boys. They went, they worked, they have sent me a check every month since they left. And it's been twenty years."

He seemed like he wanted to add something else, but refrained.

But I, the keeper of his secrets, his closest friend, knew it anyway. He was thinking that it wasn't, in the end, when you really thought about it, worth the separation. Now that he was old and his body crumbling, when the simplest task of breathing was painful, now he wanted to travel back to the past and resist the pressue to send them abroad, to say, "No," to stamp his foot down and enforce his policy that a family is only a family if it can survive together in the worst times, when the wells are dry and the clouds completely obscure the full moon and it feels like God has forsaken us. That is when you draw your children close to you, so you can hear their stomachs rumble, when all you can do is keep them warm under your heart.

When I returned from school one day, I saw that my mother was home already. She was boiling water on the stove and digging through the cabinets.

"Your father is having a visitor after dinner tonight, and I don't have any coffee," she muttered, not looking at me fully but from the side of her eyes. Strands of her light brown hair peeked out from underneath her tight red head scarf, and her skin was wet and sweaty. "I need to get in the bath," she said, lowering the heat on the water. "I smell like the horses."

"Who is it?"

She ignored my question, and pulled a few coins from inside her bodice wrap, deep inside her *thowb.* "Go to Abu Raed's shop and buy me two pounds. Two pounds only! And make sure you watch the scale. That scoundrel always tries to rip me off."

My stomach contracted, and I felt that I would be sick as a sandstorm of nerves rumbled up into my throat. It was surely your father, or your uncles. Why else would she need so much coffee?

I hurried to the store and made the purchase, forgetting to watch the scale. When I returned home, my father was there too, washing his face.

"How are you, Baba?" I asked cheerfully, watching his moves carefully.

He studied me. "Do you know Issam, ibn Masoud, the boy who works at the school?" he asked me bluntly.

"I've seen him, because I take Costa every day." I forced my voice to sound calm. "I'll see him now in a few minutes when I go pick up my brother."

"No, you won't. I'll send your mother."

"Why?" I asked too sharply, and he noticed.

"Masoud is coming today to talk to me, he said. What else could he want to talk to me about?'

I remained quiet, as I instinctively sensed I should, to assure him of my modesty, to reassure him that I had never had any inappropriate or indecent or forward interactions with you.

You would have been proud of me. I was an amazing actress in those few moments—even I temporarily believed myself completely naive, a young girl who had never left early to pick up her brother, stolen away behind the pillar for a minute or two for a quick kiss, a nose buried in my neck, a few golden words about the promise of the future, notes passed between nervous hands. He couldn't know you'd kissed me again, many more times, behind the pillar, that your hands had splayed across my stomach, my breasts, frantically caressing me, because we only had five minutes, one minute.. And he couldn't know, could he, that even when my skin tingled through my clothes, I didn't stop you? Just yesterday, you had told me it could come soon, that you'd spoken to your father, and that he'd helped you find work in Jerusalem to make the offer more promising. A large British hotel, where you could earn almost as much in tips as you would in salary, and the work was easy—carrying bags, straightening furniture and rooms, fetching cups of tea. And who knows? Maybe one of those ambassadors or pashas or officials would take a liking to you—God, remember that idea?—and would hire you as his own personal assistant. Would I like to live with you in Jerusalem? Husband and wife? My heart twists to remember how hopeful you were, how far your dreams stretched. That's how these things happen, you said, and it could open the door to travel around the world.

Hard work meant nothing to you; it was a way to move forward, to pull ahead in the race even when the course was constantly shrinking. We both knew nothing of life, but yet you wanted so much out of it. Even now, when I am old, experiencing the same creaking and rattling that plagued my grandfather so long ago, I still feel that the greatest compliment I ever received was given by you, when you selected me to share with you a future that glowed, even when everything else around us was dark.

I remained between the kitchen and the bedroom that evening, although I heard the metal door on the verandah creak and your father's step on the stones. I heard no other voices, just his, and the visit didn't last long.

My stomach began to ache when I realized that my father never called for my mother to serve the coffee.

When the door opened and closed again, and my father appeared in the kitchen, his face red and angry, I asked no questions. Indeed, I didn't need to. My mother asked them all, and I was oddly grateful because I feared that I might burst into tears.

I wonder if your father ever shared the reasons with you, or if he spared your feelings. I heard them over and over, during the weeks that followed.

You were too young.

Your new job was not official yet.

And your father worked for the Jews. "Oh, he denied it," my father said angrily about your father. "He said that it was honest work, doing construction on their homes. And I told him that they are building homes on our land, that hilltop belongs to our village, and if we help them do it, we are ushering in our own disappearance." Your father had protested that he knew many Jews when he'd lived in Jerusalem and they had no ill will. "Then why are they building gates around their buildings? And towers for soldiers?" my father had responded. And there had been no answer.

The few buildings my father was talking about are now an entire city, on the hilltop opposite this one, on which Tel al-Hilou rests. In the last sixty years they have not stopped building, and the fences are now walls, topped with barbed wires and lookout posts around the perimeter, the walls are so high, so they don't have to see us and can pretend we don't exist.

But most of all, and this is what I sensed was the real issue: your father had come alone. How could my father agree to marry off his only daughter, he railed, standing there in the kitchen, his fist coming down on the table, when they send only one man to ask for my hand? "Calm down, *ya* Sufayan," my mother said, consoling him instead of me. "A man of my stature?" he argued. "In my position? Every man with two legs in his tribe should have come with him tonight. I cannot give my daughter to a family that shows me no respect."

My grandmother Hilwa had come in by then, not one to miss any excitement, cracking in her mouth the small seeds she carried in the pocket of her *thowb.* She tossed two or three in her mouth, never interrupting her conversation, and spit out the shells one, two, three back into her palm. She listened for a while, watching me carefully to gauge my reaction, then, perhaps sensing my anxiety, murmured that Masoud's family was mostly in Jerusalem, and possibly they could not cross over to the village because of all the troubles. "When the strikes are on, the soldiers close the roads, my son," she said, still cracking, cracking. "What can he do?"

"No matter," my father replied stubbornly. "He's coming to ask for my daughter, not a barrel of olives."

My grandmother and mother both bestowed on me, just then, a look of total pity. It was the closest I'd ever felt to either of them.

One of my friends in Tel al-Hilou is sixty years younger than I am.

"Why are you doing this?" my young friend Jamil asks me, bouncing his daughter on his lap. His wife Muna spoons some yogurt into their son's mouth, but listens. "This priest is a crook."

I know, I assure him. The donation is personal, and besides, it's for the church.

"What is it for?" he asks stubbornly.

"Remember when I told you once that I can keep secrets?" I tell him playfully. He has the modesty to grin, and his wife blushes. "I have a few of my own."

My mother, since the spring harvest was over and she wasn't needed in the fields so early, took Costa to school every day after that. I remained at home and tried to study for my final graduation examinations, but of course I had trouble focusing on anything. Those days felt long and unending, broken up only by fits of angry crying when I was sure nobody else was around. I was desperate to find a way to communicate with you, but the clouds of my panic were still covering the moon, the way forward in the night. Grandfather had gotten worse, his lungs were filling with water, they said, and so nobody paid much attention to me anyway.

And then one day, when Constantine arrived home, he slipped me a note. "The boy gave me a candy to give this to you. Don't show mama, he made me promise."

I put the note in my pocket and hurried to the only place where I could have some peace: the bathroom, where I locked the metal door and shut myself inside. The note slipped out of my hand once, twice, like a comedy, before I finally seized it, opened it and was able to read the few lines on that small, white square: *I start my new job tomorrow. Try to come to Jerusalem to see me there.* An address.

This request became my new goal. You had clearly defined a mission for me.

It took me a month. Did you wonder? Were you worried? It was true that my father, perhaps realizing that I was now marriageable, had started bringing me around to family gatherings more, telling my mother to be sure my clothes were new. She allowed me to wear lipstick once, to a baptism, and loaned me her good shoes to wear. I had four cousins, all in their twenties, who needed wives, and I was sure that I was intended for one of them. Surely you'd heard about this. Nothing stays a secret for long in our village.

My grandfather, God rest his soul, provided me with the excuse, without even knowing it. The doctor prescribed a special medicine for him, something to help clear the water out of his lungs, so we wouldn't have to keep pressing his back, hurting him even as we tried to help him move the water out. My father worried about going himself. The British were stopping a lot of the men on the roads, detaining them, questioning them, sometimes for days. But my grandmother could go, and they decided I would escort her—surely the sight of an old woman with her teenaged granddaughter would elicit no suspicion. We would get the medicine and return right away. It would take no more than several hours.

I was determined that it would take longer.

The journey was long, and we reached Damascus Gate in the late afternoon. Our car, in which rode two other people from the next village, had been stopped twice. The soldiers, in their bright uniforms with tall hats, pink skin and sharp accents, ordered us out and checked the car thoroughly. What was our business? When would we return? The driver spoke English and I knew a bit as well, and so we answered them. We made it through, and I spent the rest of the ride wondering how I would see you. This was my third time in Jerusalem. We'd been here for two weddings and I'd once come with my grandmother for a women's march, long ago.

It was loud and dirty, but filled with the most interesting people. Men sat in their shops, smoking fat cigarettes, women hurried around me, their heels cracked and dry in brown sandals, children chased a bony cat down a small alley, a trio of nuns in their black cloaks passed on my left. One of them had a patch of black hair on her chin. The other had green eyes and a mole on her cheek. A bearded sheik whose thick brown glasses clung to the tip of his mountainous nose was chatting with a newspaper seller. Two white women and one white man, all wearing khaki pants and sturdy boots, wide-brimmed hats on their heads, stood on the corner watching me and everyone else. I moved on.

The pharmacy was in the Old City, and it took some time to find it. In the meantime, we passed by so many shops and stores, and the goods were like nothing that could be found in either the village or in Ramallah: carpets, silver tea sets, jewelry.

That's how I began—"Teta, look at these shoes. Wouldn't my mother love a new pair?" or "Look at this *qamis*—Constantine's is getting so small. His arms stick out of the cuffs!" We didn't buy much—we had just enough for the travel and the medicine and some extra for an emergency. But while she was busy looking at fabrics, I asked an old hajj, in a whisper, where I could find your hotel. He told me how to get there, and added, "You'll see it easily, my daughter. It's magnificent."

At the pharmacy, the *saidalee* told us it would take an hour or two to mix up the chemicals. "This is not a common prescription," he said briskly. "Come back at three o'clock."

Thoroughly annoyed, Teta berated me for wasting time. "We could have come earlier, and by now he could have almost finished. We won't get home before dinner now."

"Let's walk, Teta."

"I'm tired."

"Just a short while. How often do we come here?" Besides wanting to see you, I also wanted to absorb the smells, the sights, the sounds around me. I felt like a small decoration in a huge tapestry of ornate designs, colors and patterns unfurling all around me. I go there a lot more now, of course, but I still feel that way, like I'm a leaf floating along on a powerful river.

We walked, and I watched the street signs until I saw it: King David Street. I knew Teta couldn't read and so would have no idea what I was planning. We walked and walked, until I was sure she was tired. But I wouldn't stop until I saw it—the hotel. The hajj had been right: the pink-hued stone rose up before me, a flat, rectangle of brightness, seven or eight stories high. The courtyard in front of surely had been designed for a king and queen, and the throng of men and boys in clean, pressed uniforms scurrying around busily, made me feel like an intruder. You were here somewhere, part of this busy world, this place permeated by an atmosphere of official business. Cars were parked all around—I had, indeed, never seen so many new and shiny ones in all my life, doors were slamming. Nobody was shouting, just murmuring, all was quiet and calm.

I found a small coffee shop in which women were sitting a block or so away, and I suggested to my sweating Teta that we rest here.

"Thank God! I need to eat something," she muttered, lowering her heavy body into a rickety chair. I sat beside her and we were approached by a young boy, who said nothing, just waited quietly.

"Two *shais,* no sugar," I said. "And one *manouche,* with *zaatar.*"

"For you, child?" my grandmother asked me, using the end of her scarf to wipe her forehead.

"No, Teta, I am not hungry. Just thirsty."

I waited until her food arrived to enact my drama. "My purse! Teta, my purse! I must have left it in the shoe store, just a block away." Had I said the pharmacy, which was now several streets back, she would have insisted on coming with me, but just a short walk away? And she was hungry—it was an easy choice.

"Come right back! I hope you find it, so we don't have to tell your mother how careless you've been!" But even as I was leaving, she was biting into her *manouche,* and testing the tea with her lips to check how hot it was. I was almost afraid at how easily the lies slipped out of my mouth.

Had you already seen me walking by? Maybe. I never found out. All I knew is that when I did approach the courtyard again, from the front of the hotel, there you were, standing by the stone-walled gate. I waited on the other side of the street, tucking myself away behind the quilts that hung from a street vendor's shop. You hurried across the street and grabbed my hand.

"I can't believe it!" I'll never forget that look of surprise, and of pride, on your face. "How did you manage it?"

"My grandmother is in the women's *qahwah* down the street."

Then it became awkward for a moment or two. I wanted to apologize for my father, to explain everything in a way that wouldn't hurt your feelings.

"Are you okay?" you asked.

"No." I was honest only because we had so little time. I was aware of your co-workers across the street looking at us, and I felt suddenly ashamed. One large fellow, with frizzy black hair and a red suit that hugged his torso like a corset, stared openly at us. Who would they think I was? A loose girl? Should my grandmother stroll by right now, it would be a disaster.

All you said was this: "How long can you wait?"

"Wait?"

"I'm saving a lot of money already," you said. "I wish I could show you inside this hotel—it's like a palace. The Ethiopian emperor was here last week—" your voice grew excited—"and he tipped me as much as I make in three days of working. Like it was nothing. You cannot believe it."

"I will wait."

"It cannot be too long," you promised. "Your father will surely rethink it when I come with a better offer, with a better future."

"You know . . ."

"Yes? Tell me."

I wanted to make sure I said this to you, and to make sure you understood it. "You know that, for me, it is not important. These are—they are formalities that, for my father—"

You smiled. You understood.

"I knew we were alike, Salma."

"I'm sorry for all the problems."

"I will do whatever your father requires. And if he still says no, I will make sure I am a millionaire and come again and again until he cannot deny me."

You made me feel so relaxed at that moment, relieved. All this planning, this secrecy for just a few moments together, it was worth it. I knew I would come again as soon as I could, and risk it any time.

"We're like the two shells of an almond, right?" You kissed my hand. "Connected. In the middle is the future."

"The future," I echoed.

The new priest offers his hello to me today on the street. He is sitting in the *qahwah,* which I don't like. I don't like a man with a collar to be sitting amid the gossip, to be gambling, exchanging news and storming about politics.

This is why I must finish the book, I think, nodding and hurrying past.

Three years ago, I started this project. And it has filled my time, given my days a structure, my awakening a purpose. Otherwise, I would slip into my dreams, believe I was really seeing your face everywhere.

Three years ago, when I retired from the UNRWA, my colleagues threw me a little party. I'd known most of them for three decades, traveled with them to camps in Gaza and even Lebanon, sweated with them in cement-roofed school rooms, painted over graffiti on refugee camp walls, waited with them at checkpoints, presenting papers while mastering a look of control and nonchalance, as if it didn't really matter to us if we were turned away.

Most of them were women, as we'd quickly realized that the women could get through more easily than the men. So we went first and most frequently. But one of them was a man, Mourad, who had been with us for ten years as a volunteer, not a paid staffer. Mourad was a retired schoolteacher from near Jericho. "Either I work, or I shrivel up and wait to die," he joked often, and his easy smile made us all like him.

At the retirement party, for which Layla had purchased a tray of *kunafeh* from Nablus and for which our upper-school students had prepared and served fresh coffee, Mourad asked me now what I would be doing.

I tried to avoid this conversation, because the truth was that I did not know. I knew he was writing a book, about which he always spoke, and so to change the subject, I asked him for an update. "It's halfway completed," he said jovially, rubbing his palms together. "My friend is a lawyer in Ramallah, and he is working on one, and he's asked to see some of my research and my methods."

"What is this for?" asked Layla.

"My village book. Surely you know I'm writing one," he told her.

"Everyone knows, *ya* Mourad! Except Mr. Reagan—did you send him a telegram about it?" called Huda from the other end of the room, sending everyone into a titter.

"Well," he said, pretending to be offended, "when your grandchildren know nothing about their culture, you can tell them you thought it would be a waste of time to record it!" Then, sensing that our conversation had ended, he walked back to the table for another square of hot *kunafeh.*

But it made me think. Of course—all those stories I'd heard from my grandparents, and the fact that our village was changing every day, every minute—people leaving for America, for Jordan, for Europe—a village book would record this history for everyone to know. I thought over the idea in those two weeks after the retirement, when I suddenly woke up in my grandfather's home, the chatter of my nieces and nephews on the floor below rising up through the stone walls, and realized that I had nowhere to go.

Could I do it? I started by making a list of all the people in our own family, starting with Abu Hanna ibn Sufayan, my ancestor about whom I knew nothing except that he had died in 1856. I sketched out a rough family tree in my notebook, then remembered what Mourad had said one day about his hunt for photographs to assign a face to a name. I pulled out all the photo boxes that we had in the house, including the ones stored in the closet in Constantine's level below.

Because I had no system with which to work, I devised one as I went along, still unsure if there was a way to pull this information into a book. I coded the pictures, using a light pencil mark, on the back—*alif, beh, teh, theh*—and so on, until I had exhausted the alphabet. Then I thought to add our family's last name, and a number as well, so that the picture of Abu Hanna ibn Sufayan became labeled as "Sufayan, *alif,* 1." I made a list of all the names, and ascribed birth and death dates as well as I could, checking occasionally with my cousins, and next to each name, I wrote the code of the picture, if I had one.

Then I went to the Catholic church, and later to the Orthodox church, and checked their records to see if what I had was accurate. The priests knew nothing about it—the ladies who helped in the office, who were my friends and former schoolmates, showed me a table and brought me cups of tea and huge crates of files. When I'd finished each day, they said, "*Ya'atiki al afiyeh,*" and we spent some moments chatting about their families and grandchildren. They often paused before relating a story about a grandson's antics at school, or something funny a granddaughter had said, paused as if to check that it would bring me no pain. Me, the sole classmate of sixty years ago, who had passed all her tests and yet never married, despite several offers for my hand. Of course, I couldn't marry, but they didn't know. They thought it was my choice, that I was stubborn. I knew that they felt something was wrong with me, but since I'd adopted the role of everyone's friendly aunt, the lady who always had some candy in her pocket for the kids, the one who arrived early to every party, baptism, wedding, to help roll *warak dawali,* to arrange plates of food, and the one who stayed late to clean up—they'd felt at ease. Perhaps they sensed that I'd found a part for myself in the performance, even if I had no lines to recite, even if I just blended with the scenery, and that made them feel better. I'm glad that they did.

Before I quite realized it, four weeks—one month—had passed doing this work. And I loved it.

And so I moved on to the next home, to my neighbor, Imm Fareed, to start recording what I could of her family. Her white wave shining in her Umm Kulthoum–like updo, she sat for hours telling me everything, pausing indulgently as I scribbled. Her nephew had a good camera, and he came with me to photograph some of the older buildings and to take pictures of people for whom I had no pictures.

And my work proceeded from there, house to house, mosque to church, generation to generation, slowly collecting facts, using them to assemble stories and the details of people's lives. I started to see our village, Tel al-Hilou, as a repository of dreams, some achieved, some refined, but many lost and snatched away. And my new role was to collect them in one place.

I saw you once more, and I exploited Imm Fareed to do so. She was to go on a very important social call in Jerusalem, and I suggested that I could go with her to stock up on grandfather's medicine. It was agreed to—"Anything for dear Abu Sufayan," said our neighbor—and we left early in the morning in a *servees.* Imm Fareed, with her black leather pumps and armor-like purse, worried me—no frail grandmother was she. She could outmarch the Irgun, but I suspected I could depend on her love of chatter. And I was right. We sat in her friend's salon, ensconced on Parisian-style chairs, or *chaises,* as her friend insisted; she was an Armenian woman who spoke French, and Italian, and a smattering of Russian, and Imm Fareed was trying to enlist her help to get her son a job in her husband's factory. "He's quite clever, top in his class," began Imm Fareed, which I knew was a lie, because Fareed was my schoolmate and an imbecile, and besides, the top student in our class at that time was actually me. At that point, I murmured that I'd be back soon and slipped out. I never went to the pharmacy, no time, but almost ran back to King David Street, getting lost once in a winding back street but thankfully finding my way. I recited the rosary the whole time, getting through four decades in those ten minutes. You were loading a heavy trunk into the boot of a large black car, and when you saw me, you held up a finger and hurried inside. A minute later, you came out and crossed the street, whispering that you had an hour. Maybe more. And then you were pulling me down a snaking alley, up the back stairs above a bakery—I smelled the sweet bread—and to a small room. There was a thin mat on the floor, and a bowl on a table, and a nail in the wall that held up a black hat.

No windows anywhere. We never hesitated, not when you pulled my *thowb* over my head, when your mustache scratched my bare throat, not even later, when the pain daggered through me. Afterwards, you kept saying, "I'm sorry," and I made you stop apologizing. "I've just missed you," you said, your voice hoarse and thick with tears that didn't fall.

"What is it?" I whispered, like a mother, cradling you to my chest. You'd become so thin, and even though it was my first and last time stroking the warm skin of a man's back, even I knew your bones weren't supposed to feel so sharp.

"It's so hard here. I wish you were with me, all the time," you replied so softly I could barely hear you. We held each other, feeling so in love but so sorry for ourselves. I cried when I had to go, when the hour was up, and you leaned down and kissed me once on each eyelid and made me promise to come again. "Do whatever you must." I hobbled back to the Armenian woman's apartment, sinking my sore body down into her plush *chaise,* and drank a fresh cup of tea. Imm Fareed barely noticed me, but her elegant friend watched me carefully, as if she were looking right into my heart.

Later in the *servees,* when Imm Fareed asked about the medicine, I mumbled that the *saidalee* didn't have the chemicals he needed to mix them. "No matter," she replied. "We'll come again next month. You're a good companion."

A few weeks later, I had just emerged, nervous, from my school examinations when I heard people talking on the street, and joined the crowd. Rudaynah told me that the British headquarters had been bombed in Jerusalem.

I didn't understand it right away. How stupid I used to be.

I was worried about something else, you see—I'd missed my cycle that month, and I knew what had happened. When I'd first started my period at the age of eleven, my mother had handed me a cloth napkin, then squeezed my earlobe between her rough fingers. "This means you can dishonor us. Keep your legs closed until you leave this house as a bride, do you understand?" And I'd nodded, my eyes bubbling with tears because I was sure my ear would come off.

I was consumed with my own secret, and so I did not worry about the news from Jerusalem. These attacks had happened before, usually by underground groups. But by evening, I knew it was the worst possible news, when the wind carried a new wave of information: that your father was in mourning for his son, who'd just started working at the hotel a few months earlier. And I realized the hotel *was* the headquarters, and I almost climbed to the roof and threw myself off.

Ninety-one dead, and you were one of them. Many of the people who died were passersby on the street. I could have been one of them, had I been able to meet you that day, had Imm Fareed decided to visit her friend.

They couldn't find your body, and so you were presumed dead. Even now, when I am in Jerusalem regularly to do research for my book, whenever I pass by the hotel, I pause before it and wonder if your body is somehow in the earth below, in the soil that nourishes the trees, floating in the air, dust that colors the old buildings all around. I pause beside the store where we once hid, partially shielded by billowing quilts; the store is now a sweet shop, where baskets of chocolates are decorated in gold paper and wrapped with rhinestone-studded ribbons—baskets intended for weddings and bar mitzvahs.

There was no body, and so there was no funeral. But on the fortieth day, your father held a service for you at the church. My whole family attended, because you were being portrayed as a martyr, a hero, massacred by the Zionists. Your mass would be a patriotic spectacle. "I don't feel well," I said, "and someone has to stay with my grandfather." My parents agreed.

As soon as they had gone, when I saw them from my window—

grandmother, my parents and Constantine—on the far hill, I checked on grandfather. He was sleeping, and I knew this was my only chance. I dug into my mother's green basket until I found her knitting needles, heated one on the stove, then locked myself in the storage closet. I pulled the old mattress from the back shelf, put it on the floor, spread an old towel on it and removed my long underwear. The first jab was exploratory, the second was so painful that I screamed and froze, listening to see whether I'd woken grandfather. When it was still quiet, I shoved my rosary between my teeth and knelt again. The final stabs were so painful, that when the blood poured out like a tipped jar, I bit down so hard that the links broke, scattering beads down onto the bloody mattress and across the floor. After almost an hour, a clump of tissue slipped out and I scooped it up and saved it. Weakly, I removed the towel, hauled the mattress back into the closet, hiding it behind boxes. I burned the towel. When my family returned, I was feverish and my mother sent me to bed, warning me to stay away from Constantine. A few days later, when the bleeding had stopped and my fever had passed, I walked to the cemetery and buried the baby and the broken rosary beads in a little hole in the earth.

I changed after that.

When mother ordered me to do something, I took my time. No more rushing, no more worrying. I ignored Constantine often. Even my father didn't intimidate me.

All four of my cousins ended up asking for me. All four. And I refused every single one of them.

By the fourth one, my father was livid. He slapped me, and I continued to stare him in the eye. I told him I would not eat anything else and kill myself that way if he forced me. And I didn't eat for six days, just slept; I would rise to sip water, then sink back into bed. They were sure I'd die and join my grandfather, who didn't live more than four months after the bombing. I'd been too mired in my own grief to even mourn my grandfather properly. I wore black for him, but I was really wearing it for you, for our baby.

My grandmother intervened finally and demanded that we eliminate all the tension in the house. "She will find someone eventually. What girl doesn't want to be married?" They nodded and agreed, acceding to the wisdom of her words.

This morning I re-entered the pastor's office and handed him a paper with my inscription.

"In memory of Issam al-Saleemi?"

"That's correct."

"Who is that? I don't know any of the Saleemi family?"

"Issam lived here long ago, and he died in 1946. He was not originally from our village."

"Aah, well, that is why we need your book, Sitt Salma. To educate newcomers like me. But I don't know if I can include the name of someone who is not from our village originally."

I walk over to the heavy curtains, and deliberately step on the red shoe peeping out from beneath it. A whimper escapes from behind the curtain, and the priest's face is pale. I smile at him. "I'm sure you won't have a problem with it, will you?"

I leave before he can say anything else. I don't have to answer anyone, anything.

There is no one left. Your father died and your uncle and two aunts came to claim his body and bury him in Jerusalem. I never met anyone else from your clan, nor did they ever return.

But you will be remembered. I will carve out a space for you, a space that was sacred to us, and I will honor it. Dreams cannot dissipate as easily as flesh and ash in the air.

Your name will be out in the open, for all to see, as clearly and vividly as the moon that shines most brightly when the sky is completely black. And when I sit here in the left pew, I can gaze out the window of the Dormition and see the obelisk I have dedicated to you. The sheep look at me and remark on my faith, and I mock them in my mind.

They see the glory of God in the highest.

I see your hopeful eyes, your excited smile, beckoning from behind a pillar. That memory belongs only to me. Trust in that.

VILLAGE GOSSIP
The View from the *Qahwah*

1996

The new priest was from Lebanon, by way of Syria, everyone said. "Divorced," they added, but this was shared in a whisper, which made us in the *qahwah* smile—silly, really. Divorce? It was nothing these days. Our village had seen so many changes. Even Emad ibn Waleed had married a divorced woman and fled to America with her. Last year, the interim priest, The Most Reverend Father Marcus Haddad, had been caught having an affair with his wife's younger sister. His wife had left, gone back to her family in Tiberias, and taken the three children with her. Months ago, Imm Fareed, the mayor's wife and reigning president of the Orthodox Ladies' Society for twenty-four years, had heard from a knowledgeable source that Father Marcus had entered a rehabilitation center in Jerusalem, run by the Israelis, for alcohol addiction. "Honor," she'd said mournfully every time she'd repeated the information. "Nobody values it anymore."

When people married, they still handed out candied almonds in batches of five or seven—maybe nine if they wanted to show off—always a number that was indivisible. So for some older women, like Imm Fareed, like Elaina Shammas, that nice widow, such tales of marital breakability still astounded them; they'd grown up in the days when your husband could blacken your cheekbone, your temple, and you still had no hope of ending it, and the church would turn you away if you tried, tell you that what God has joined must never be severed. But then again, everything was changing: just like the borders, always contracting, collapsing in on us.

One day, we watched Elaina's daughter Samar walk to her mother's house. She went every day, but today was different. It was the day that the new priest started wreaking havoc on our village. The rest of the story we filled in from our wives. That's how it is inside the *qahwah.* One of us has a scrap of information, he shares it, and ten others add to it, based on what their wives, their aunts, their sisters know.

That day, Samar walked, holding her son's small hand as they passed Abu Raed's grocery store and the *qahwah,* though only two of us were out smoking, too early still, as the younger crowd would arrive in the late afternoon when their work in the olive groves, the candle factory, the mechanic shop, would end for the day. Samar looked good, and she walked confidently. She was sure these daily walks had helped her shed the last six kilos of baby weight, and her hair was smooth, her legs long and firm, her fingernails sculpted and polished. The tumult of having a newborn in the house was over—Fares slept for eight hours a night now, her in-laws had stopped coming over all the time, and her husband's hand had begun slipping over her thighs under the covers, in the dark, again. She was almost content.

Fares stumbled in a small pothole, his thick legs shooting out to the side, and fell on one knee. She scooped him up quickly and started laughing loudly. "Isn't that funny, Fares? You're silly!" and he looked confused for a moment—hovering between pain and joy—and then joined in the apparently funny joke. A few minutes later, he squirmed to be put down again. The beauty of three-year-olds, Samar thought, was how quickly they forgot about pain. They weren't old enough yet to blame God, fate, the government for all their problems.

Her mother Elaina lived on the upper floor of the house, while Samar's brother had moved his wife and their daughter to the spacious lower level. "As long as I have a kitchen, I'll be fine," Samar's mother had said, and so they'd installed a small kitchenette in a corner of one of the bedrooms, and moved the old kitchen table, the one Samar and her brother had spent their school days writing their homework on, next to the large window that opened on the balcony. That it faced east and she could drink her coffee while watching the sun rise over the hill, beyond the blue dome of the Orthodox church, topped by the statue of the Virgin, was happiness to Elaina. Her son, living below, and her daughter, living a kilometer away, saw her smile more often, which she'd stopped doing after her husband died during the war, and they assumed all was well.

Elaina, of course, like any good village mother, was doing her best to affect happiness, for her children's sake. When everyone married, she'd planned to live on her own, to rent one of the small apartments being built on the square. But her son, who'd gotten it into his head too seriously that he was the new man of the house, showed his stubbornness. Elaina had shrunk into herself when she heard him say, for the first time, that he would never allow his mother to live alone. What if a soldier broke in? What if she got sick? People could start rumors. But she'd been living alone since the war, hadn't she? Elaina repressed her instinct to slap him as if he were still five years old, and instead cursed the well-intentioned fellow villagers who'd spent years pumping up her fatherless boy into a little tyrant. They'd ruined him. Samar had remained the same, her sweet, tranquil daughter, although she'd insisted at only seventeen years old on marrying. "There's a war, Mama!" she'd begged, as if that were a reason, but Elaina understood: there's no time to wait and think. All the young men were rushing off to America faster than before, draining the village of its testosterone. The only puddles of it gathered at the *qahwah,* where we spent our time clacking black and white chips on the *tawla* board. There was a virtual attack on what young men were left in Tel al-Hilou, and even the most unpromising boy, even if he had a limp mustache, even if he couldn't sit straight on a horse, could still attract smiles from several pretty girls. Samar's husband was handsome, at least, but he was one of these young ones who'd regressed to the old-fashioned values. He wanted Samar at home, and she started wearing long skirts and long-sleeved shirts, even in the summer. Her mother began wondering if she'd see her daughter one day sporting a shackle on her ankle.

Samar, of course, knew nothing of her mother's concerns. She found it strange that her husband always wanted to know where she was going, but she told him what he wanted to hear. Now, she walked past her brother's kitchen window, where she heard her sister-in-law yelling at one of the kids to turn off the water, for Christ's sake, and pulled Fares up the wide front step, inlaid with white and blue tiles that spelled out *Ahlan wa Sahlan.* The left side of the rectangle had cracked soon after father had been carried out. The crack had swallowed too much water, which had iced that winter, lengthening the split until all the tiles her father had once carefully cemented threatened to separate from the left side of the block. Her father had created the mosaic after a trip to Cyprus, where he saw the same concept on other people's entrances and thought it would please his pretty wife.

Using her own key to enter the apartment, Samar called out to her mother, then opened the window to the balcony. She pushed the table close to it, blocking any opportunity for Fares to climb out and plummet down to the courtyard. Until her mother's face would freeze later that year, and she would begin to imagine her mother in old age, this—Fares falling down to the courtyard below—was her most nagging fear. Rula Hassan had fallen from her balcony twenty-five years ago, and died, and Khaled Ibrahim had done it only two years ago and had to be schooled at home because he'd not been right in the head since, repeating himself over and over, giggling to himself at nothing at all. If only people would prevent these things, Samar thought, reflecting with satisfaction on all the precautions she'd taken in her own home: insisting that the wide metal door to the useless well always be bolted, locks screwed into the door leading to the roof, and a bar drilled into the ledge of their own small balcony, just in case Fares did slip out of her line of vision.

"Where are you, mother?" she called now, putting a small kettle on one of the convenience stove's two eyes. "I'm starting the coffee."

"One minute, *habibti,*" the reply floated in from the bedroom, the only other room upstairs besides the bathroom. Samar's mother received formal guests, on the rare occasion they came, downstairs in her son's apartment, as Samar's sister-in-law had created a formal sitting salon by installing some Japanese furniture in the large sunroom. But other informal visits, such as Samar's, or those of the Ladies' Society members, who often met in Elaina's apartment to plan bake sales or write invitations or roll grape leaves for everyone's salvation—those usually took place in the sunny kitchen, with coffee and conversation. Once, Rudaina al-Qudsi, the treasurer of the Society, had reported to her husband as they lay reading in bed, after a big meal of *kefta* with *tahine,* that she planned to convert their grown son's room—he was in America now, and probably wouldn't return until he was ready to get married—into a private receiving room of her own. When her husband grunted and said the salon would serve that purpose just as well, she, who'd always been envious of Elaina, closed her book, turned over, and spent the rest of the night and week wondering when he would do her the favor of passing away.

Samar had stirred in the sugar and brought the coffee to a boil before her mother had emerged from her bedroom. Fares, who had opened the box of toys his grandmother reserved just for him under the pantry, walked over, planted a quick kiss on her cheek before diving back into his private chest. Elaina sat at the table, looking puzzled, then got up again—as if just remembering she had a guest—and put a plate of butter biscuits for Fares. "Sorry. Your grandmother's distracted this morning."

"Nothing is wrong, *inshallah*?" Samar poured the coffee into small cups, set them on the table.

"This new priest—he's driving us all crazy."

Samar had seen him only twice, since she didn't go to church a much as her mother would have preferred. But her husband worked six days a week, and Sunday mornings, he liked to relax in bed, to play with Fares and enjoy a late breakfast. She hated the chaos of getting up early, bathing and dressing Fares, sitting through a long liturgy. And you could never just leave right after Mass—the coffee hour, with its socializing, opining, gossiping, was almost mandatory. Sometimes, it felt like the only reason to go. She hadn't told her mother, for example, that she thought the priest dragged out most of the liturgical hymns, elongating the "alleluias" until her eardrum threatened to burst, that he spoke with a grandiosity that annoyed her, or that she thought he'd been extra solicitous of her husband's attention when he learned that his brother was the rich American who regularly donated to the village. Even though, as a girl, she had dutifully attended Mass, these days she didn't protest when her husband pulled her back into bed.

"Well, I've been in this church my whole life. I was baptized there!" Elaina exclaimed, as if that said it all.

Samar swallowed a bit of bread. "What's he doing now?"

"He's trying to change the Ladies' Society, to make us a group of women who just throw parties," she said, stroking Fares' head as he loped to the table, refilling his plate with more biscuits. (When Fares was a grown man, with his own children in America, one day he'd enter a new Arab-owned grocery store in Boston and find a paper-wrapped packet of those biscuits, and memories of mornings in his grandmother's kitchen would seize him so powerfully that he'd buy the whole shelf, take them home to his daughters, who would disappoint him by insisting that Oreos were better.) Elaina thought her grandson, with his curly hair, looked so much like her own son at that age, and she usually marveled at genetic magic, how one trait could be passed down wholly to another—the twitch of an eyebrow, a lone dimple. But this morning, even Fares couldn't distract her from her thoughts, her annoyance. "He wants to give us a calendar of parties, and each one should be a fundraiser. That would be best for him. 'Best for him!' I told Imm Fareed—what on earth? He wants to eliminate all our political work. She agreed, but you know how some of these people are, *ya binti.* The priest is close to God, so *khulas.* Finished. No more questions." Elaina had no tolerance for people who mingled superstition with Christianity, who hung a crucifix in their home next to a blue stone to ward away the evil eye. Christ had come to save us from our pagan, backwards ways, and here were people forgetting the essence of their faith. The priest was just a man, not a demi-god who had a special connection to God, or who could order a plague on their heads.

"I mean, I don't see . . ." Samar poured herself a cup of coffee, and rinsed her plate in the sink. "Every priest has his own way." She thought about Father Marcus, who had indeed changed everything about their mass, even eliminated the children's sermon. The children should be able to understand the regular sermon and be enlightened, he'd argued, but everyone knew he was just too lazy to write a second sermon every week, to worry about props and little jokes to interest the range of age groups. He forgot about Arabic even, switching to French whenever a tourist was in attendance, so only two out of two hundred people understood anything at all and the rest spent the hour wondering who in the crowd was the foreigner, scanning the pews for the blonde head among the black ones.

But the Ladies' Society, with Imm Fareed and her mighty forces, had changed that: they'd petitioned the priest and then the bishop to restore the children's sermons. Father Marcus had obeyed, but still they were watered-down and shallow. "Like grape leaves stuffed only with rice, no meat," Elaina had said to her friends, at which they'd all laughed and remarked on Elaina's ability to always say the thing accurately. Elaina had, in fact, become the spiritual leader among the ladies her age, the daring one, the one who signed petitions, attended rallies in Ramallah, organized fundraisers. Her widowhood was like a kind of freedom, the way spinsterhood had allowed Miss Salma, the old UNRWA worker, to do anything she liked. That lady had lived alone in her home, driven her own car, earned her own money—she'd been content and kind and smart, writing her book. She'd died alone. After two days of nobody seeing her, the mayor and some *shebab* had broken down the door of her grandfather's house and found her smiling sweetly, softly, in her bed.

"At the meeting yesterday, we tried to talk about the elections," Elaina said now. "So he arrives, wearing his shiny leather shoes and his gold rings—I never saw a priest wear so much gold—and tells us that there will be no more elections. He will appoint a new president and treasurer next month! Imagine!" She pressed her fingers to her temple, as if a migraine had suddenly attacked her nerves. "Imm Fareed? Furious. Because you know why? He's basically telling her that she has done a terrible job for the last twenty-four years."

"So why do you even have elections, if you're always appointing the same people?" Samar asked, smiling. But the look that settled over her mother's face erased her smile quickly.

"There is a process, and it should always be respected," her mother said grimly. "Do we all kill each other because the Israelis are killing us? No, there is always the way, the right way, something should be done."

"So Imm Fareed is Arafat," Samar joked.

Elaina didn't laugh or smile. Her annoyance stunned Samar, but she didn't try to slide over the awkwardness and move to a new subject. That would be too false, and she knew better than that. Her mother was the shrine of courtesy and custom, inviting someone who waved from the street in for coffee, though she knew they'd decline, because it was a hospitable and kind gesture. But she was never false. When Samar had asked, that night so many years ago, when the bombs were falling and her cousins carried them all to the caves, when she'd asked where Father had gone, Elaina had patted her hand in the back of the truck, huddled among the rest of their family, the blast of gun shots breaking the night's tense silence. "He stayed behind to defend the house."

"Will he be okay?"

Her mother's simple answer: "I'm afraid . . . no, I'm afraid not."

Samar had been fourteen years old, and despite the chill that settled over her heart, there was, below it, in the depths where coldness could not creep, a warm security that her mother would always be honest with her, about everything. On the night before her wedding to Jibril, Samar's mother had given her the talk. Samar had been impatient, because she knew the mechanics, how the thing was done. What she wanted to know was whether or not it hurt as badly as her newly married friends claimed it did. "Yes, it hurts. Like someone is stabbing you. But, later, if he is gentle, it also feels nice." There it was.

Samar walked home an hour later with Fares beside her, having elicited a promise from her mother that she'd stop over for dinner. Samar's mother- and father-in-law were both out of town, visiting their daughter for a week in Ramallah. "It'll be just you and me and Jibril." Her mother and mother-in-law got along well, but it just wasn't comfortable. Even Jibril was different when his parents were home, more formal, he wouldn't even hold her hand or kiss her cheek, and often, especially lately, he would criticize her in small ways with his mother in the room, about the house paperwork being unfinished, about why Fares wasn't eating fruits the way he should, and why she spent so much time during the week out of the house. That she was usually visiting her mother, not waitressing at the *qahwah,* didn't matter.

As they passed the *qahwah,* Fares waved to our table. "Hello, Mr. Fares!" we called out. "Come play a round with us."

"I was actually going to get some things from your store, Abu Raed," Samar called, remaining on the road, even though Fares tugged at her arm. That rascal always walked away from his shop and came to sit with us, telling people to just leave the money on the counter.

True to his nature, he told Samar, "The door is open, my daughter." We laughed as he pulled up a stool for the boy, who scrambled up and grabbed at the dice.

Samar crossed the road and entered the dark, narrow shop. It hadn't changed in years, not since she was a girl and had pulled father in to buy her a chocolate and toffee mound or a square of powdered Turkish delight. She would make something simple tonight, and she pulled some bags of lentils from the shelf, scooped some long rice into a bag from the open burlap sack on the floor. Meat was too expensive, on Jibril's salary alone, and she hadn't been to the butcher shop in over a month. When the next check came from his brother in California, she'd make *mansaff,* she thought.

Budgeting like this was frustrating. But his wife would not work, insisted Jibril, who'd developed a stubborn streak as soon as Fares was just a bulge of her stomach. And so she'd said goodbye to her co-workers at the bank in Ramallah, promising to keep in touch with them after she'd had the baby. She counted out thirty shekels for Abu Raed, left them on the counter, scribbling a note in his ledger with a dull pencil she'd found on the cement floor. She thought of all her pretty work clothes, the long skirts and blazers, the soft sweaters and cardigan sets—now, she only wore them on the rare Sunday that they made a social call, spending the rest of her time in her jeans and sandals. Years later, when her father-in-law would die suddenly of a heart attack, she would go to America with Jibril and Fares, and there she'd realize that her pretty clothes were hopelessly outdated, and she'd use the weekly coupon in the Sears circular to slowly rebuild a new wardrobe, buying one item at a time at 40 percent off, until she had a neat row of airy, lovely things in her closet.

After she'd fetched a gleeful Fares, who'd been allowed to win two games in a row by wide margins, and had put him in bed for a nap, she washed the lentils and put them in her mother-in-law's stainless steel pot. Then she sat at the table to smoke a cigarette until they boiled. She cracked the window to let out the smell of smoke, because Jibril disapproved of that too. Where had she met such a man with such outdated ideas? He brought home his check every Saturday from the factory and showed it to her like an unearthed treasure, as if she should admire it and clap wildly and forget that her own check used to be almost as much and that they could eat meat twice a week. Jibril's mother, who often smoked cigarettes with her daughter-in-law by the kitchen window, had complained to her son privately that he should let Samar return to work. "She walks around here like a ghost, and she misses dressing up and having time to herself," she'd told her son in a momentary rare alliance with Samar. "I can watch Fares all day—my schedule is empty." But nothing changed his mind. He was a *man*, a man, and a man did not let his wife go out and work outside of her home. Samar's mother-in-law complained to her husband more than once that their worldly son had shriveled up into a husband of the old days. "Why did he insist on marrying an educated girl if he won't benefit from her education?" they asked themselves, for it was a fact that Samar's paycheck would have helped them too, and they wouldn't have to ask for so much from their eldest son, whom they hadn't seen in years, swallowed up, as he was, by California. They were convinced that one day, a really terrible earthquake would strike the American west coat, and neither George Bush nor his son would be able to stop California from separating cleanly from the mainland and floating away into the Pacific, carrying Rafah further and further away from them. The Mossad would have engineered the whole thing, of course. Abu Rafah promised his wife that he'd speak to Jibril about his old-fashioned ways, but he never did. Once, he'd planned to, during a drive out to Ramallah for a rally, but Jibril, anticipating his father's purpose, started speaking about how the occupation made a man feel like less than a man and wonder how many households these days depended on their women. His father, unsure of how to handle anything emotional or psychological, did what he always did: he started cursing the bastard Arab dictators and Ariel Sharon the devil.

Samar knew nothing of this aborted conversation, over a year ago now. She inhaled and blew out her smoke artfully, thinking her precise rings of white smoke were wasted on an audience of pots and pans.

By the time Fares woke, the *majadarah* was ready, only the onions left to fry, and Jibril newly arrived home, telling her about the foreman who claimed to be related to King Hussein. "He's nuts, for sure," Jibril sighed, still disbelieving this man, whose pants always sagged around the crack of his ass, who needed a belt as no human being before him ever did, could be promoted over him. "When is your mother—," but he was interrupted by the soft rap on the door. He opened it and kissed Elaina warmly three times on her cheek, his hand pulling her in every time, and saying over and over, *"Ahlan wa sahlan."* Samar laughed to see him, and thought how ridiculous it was that her mother should be kissed more often than Samar herself in this house. But Jibril had always been fond of her mother, and she felt grateful for this. It was as if, even during their school days when he would walk her home after class, or volunteer to help tutor the children in Sunday school, when she knew at one, irreversible moment, that she would marry him when she was old enough—always her mother had been there in the background, offering Jibril an encouraging benevolent smile, inviting him in for tea. At Elaina's funeral, just a few months from now, Jibril would argue with his brother-in-law over who would deliver the eulogy, and he would win and make everyone weep with the generosity of his words. For another three generations, we would say in the *qahwah,* after any mother-in-law joke had been told, that Jibril ibn Musa would have never thought it funny, the lucky bastard.

"But what is wrong?" he asked Elaina now, pulling Fares off his grandmother. The child had pounced on her like a clumsy cheetah, digging greedily in her pockets for a lollipop or sour chew.

"I have nothing," she protested, apologetically. "I left before I remembered." When his face crumpled, his father promised him an ice cream after dinner.

"Poor child," she muttered. "His grandmother's mind is as empty as her pockets."

"The new priest," Samar explained to Jibril, as her mother sat at the dining room table. She was indeed in a strange mood, forgetting to ask about his parents, his sister, his brothers in America, thus parting the curtain on the very real fact that she knew all the details anyway from Samar. "He's driving all the ladies crazy."

"Do you know what he told us, that bastard?" she raged. Samar and Jibril startled, and Jibril ushered Fares out of the kitchen, down the hall to his bedroom. "Mariam Khalifeh and I met with him, about his interference, and he yelled at us to never question his judgment. And then he said—he actually said—'Watch yourself with me. You'll die soon, and I'll refuse to bury you in sacred ground.' To two widows he said this!" Samar almost dropped the plates she was setting on the table, and Jibril muttered at what an unrefined beast the man must be.

"You know, I've heard gossip about him," said Jibril slowly. "Who knows if it's true, though?" Jibril felt gossip was a woman's domain, as we all did, even though we sometimes indulged in it.

"Tell me," Elaina commanded, sitting up pertly, eagerly, like a student before her favorite teacher.

Jibril and Samar laughed, but Elaina waited, eyes patient but hungry. "He was, before here, in Syria," he began.

"Yes, yes, and before that in Lebanon."

"So why such a big move, in only four years?"

"His divorce?"

"And why the divorce?" Jibril thought he would protract the moment but then seeing his poor mother-in-law, this woman for whom church was everything, he showed mercy. "I heard his wife divorced him in Lebanon for having an affair. The church apparently had a beautiful, young secretary who helped out part-time."

"So they sent him to Syria?" Elaina looked like Fares when he'd successfully linked together two puzzle pieces, the bright smile, the eager search for the next piece.

"And there . . ." Jibril was delighted now, Samar could tell, as he scooped large ladles of *majadarah* onto everyone's plates. "There, he met another young woman, a Damascene, who may be expecting his baby this summer."

Samar, who was frying the onions, almost burned her fingers. "Jibril!" But he shrugged, adding, "That's what I heard."

"Do you have proof?" Elaina asked, like a detective. "Who told you this?"

"Yacoub, ibn Wail."

"And who told him? He doesn't come to church."

"I have no clue."

"Ask him tomorrow." Elaina stuck her fork eagerly into the mound of rice and lentils, forgetting to wait for the onions. She planned to call an emergency meeting in her kitchen the next day.

"I can't believe he spoke that way to your mother," Jibril told Samar later that night in bed, after the dishes had been washed, the table wiped, the coffee drunk, and Fares dropped sleepily into his bed. "I may go talk to him myself."

"Yes, do," Samar urged him. She thought of her mother, alone in her bedroom next to the kitchen, praying her rosary in confusion before she slept. She didn't realize that Elaina was mapping out her strategy.

The Ladies' Society held a covert meeting in Samar's mother's kitchen the next evening, and Samar attended, despite Jibril's grumbling, and watched her mother in amazement. Elaina seemed so powerful. By that point, Jibril had followed the chain of gossip from Yacoub ibn Wail, who'd heard it from Saleem Malek, the local pharmacist, to the wife of his brother, who had a nephew in the seminary. "She says," Jibril told his mother-in-law, "that her nephew absolutely confirmed it. He doesn't want his name mentioned, but yes, there is a girl in Syria pregnant by this priest."

"So they did get rid of him there?"

"They housed him in the seminary for two weeks while they decided how to proceed. The archbishop eventually decided to give him another chance, because he needed to fill the vacancy here after Father Marcus and his issues."

Elaina shared the information—leaving out the source, although she dropped the information that the news was legitimate as it came from someone in the priesthood—with the eight women sitting in her kitchen. Two of them—including al-Qudsi's wife, Rudaina—had heard it before, though not in so much detail, and so they were just as scandalized as the rest. And it wasn't even an instance where they all were scandalized but secretly—they'd never admit it to anyone else—enjoyed the adrenaline; no, now they were horrified that a priest—a priest!—would behave so sinfully.

"Tomorrow is Friday," said Elaina, "so what shall we do before Sunday?"

A community petition was suggested and agreed upon, and the next day Samar took Fares to the small library building and asked to use the typewriter. She paid one shekel for three sheets of paper, and typed the same sentence at the top of each: "We the undersigned, as members of Theotokos Orthodox Church of the village of Tel al-Hilou, Palestine, request that Father John be required to make his past history clear to our parish, and if deemed as necessary, be removed and replaced with a more morally fit member of the blessed and noble clergy."

Under each sentence, she carefully typed several lines by using the "dash" key repeatedly, sending Mrs. Farah, the elderly and obese librarian, an apologetic look as the clatter caused her to raise her eyebrows as a reprimand.

"What are you working on, Samar?" the mountainous lady asked, leaning forward on the counter to cover up the old machine with a plastic drape, her enormous stomach pressing into the worn wood thickness of the counter. She rested one plump hand, three of five fingers adorned with yellow-gold rings, on Fares' head. "Were you helping mommy?" But he was buried in a book of Barney the purple dinosaur stories, where someone had written the Arabic translation carefully in permanent blue marker below the English text. "Can you read?" she suddenly asked the boy.

"Yes, pretty well," Samar replied for him. "He knew all his letters by the time he was two, and now he can read simple words."

"And he's?"

"Just four."

"Well done, my dear." They watched his absorbed, attentive face for a while, then smiled at one another. "So. What is this?"

"A petition. For my mother."

"About? The refugees?"

Samar wondered for a moment if she should be quiet, but she assumed that Mrs. Farah was a long-time friend of her family. "It's about the priest."

"Father John? What's the problem with him?"

Samar could not know it, of course, but Mrs. Farah attended church stubbornly and sat in the second pew—Elaina explained all this to her later, angrily—and watched the priest as though he were the burning bush speaking to Moses. She had also increased her pledge, against her husband's wishes, from 1,000 to 2,000 shekels a year, and two weeks earlier, when the priest had asked for volunteers to make holy bread for the month of April, she had raised her hand immediately. And why not?, she'd thought. She'd never been too involved in the church's activities before, but lately her husband worked more hours at his butcher shop, and her two sons were always busy with their studies, plotting a way to get to America. The library opened from 7 a.m. to 2 p.m. only, and only five days a week—it was nothing compared to the Ramallah branch, just two small rooms in the old Radwan farmhouse after it had been rebuilt, shared with the post office and the mayor's quarters. What life did this village offer? she'd begun to wonder, and had come to look forward to Father John's visits to her home for coffee at 3 p.m. once a week, relating stories about the beaches of Lebanon. He'd told her that she reminded him of those elegant Lebanese women—"You always look very well . . . 'put together,'" he'd said once. He'd even complimented her home décor and her taste in fashion. A man who understood her—a rarity. She'd even renewed her confessions, something she'd done only as a girl, but now she went once a week and knelt with difficulty before him and told him everything. Thus, Mrs. Farah was keenly interested in Elaina's petition and asked Samar to see it. "Are they going to ask everyone to sign?" she asked incredulously.

"Yes, I'm sure," Samar responded, becoming distracted by Fares, who was getting fussy, so that the look of betrayal on Mrs. Farah's face was lost to her. She finally turned back to the librarian and said gently, "I think I have to exit the premises, *ya tante.*" She took back the papers and left.

Mrs. Farah's body was heavier than an IDF tank, but her tongue could dart more quickly than all the feet of the members of the Ladies' Society. The next day, during mass, Father John attacked. He'd practiced this all night and had even had an erection thinking about how this would be the moment when he'd finally assert his absolute authority over these old busybodies. "My brothers and sisters," he declared, "I have a sad announcement to make. There is an agent of the devil in this church, among us."

Nobody spoke, neither the altar boys holding censers on either side of Father, nor the rows of parishioners in their pews, nor Mrs. Farah, who sat placidly beside her husband, furtively chewing the holy bread she'd already received in her mouth.

The village gossip network nearly collapsed like an old aqueduct from the flow of information it sustained over the next few hours.

Samar's mother-in-law insisted that a group of ladies, including Elaina, come to her house to sit and relax. When Samar arrived, the whole story was retold between sips of coffee. After his declaration, Elaina explained in a breathless, gaspy voice, Father had given a sermon that had clearly targeted her and the other ladies. "Be careful," he'd warned the stunned parishioners. "Be careful, because sometimes Satan works through a familiar face. And be careful of what you sign your name to, because these papers are intended to destroy our church." After the mass, Elaina said, eleven of the thirty people who'd already signed the petition approached her and insisted that their names be removed.

"Someone told him," Elaina said. "And he scared everyone else to death."

"Not everyone," Jibril's father pointed out, to show the poor lady some solidarity. But truth be told, even he had become wary of the situation that seemed to be developing right at his kitchen table. He'd served the church as an altar boy when he was young, and had briefly considered becoming a deacon after he'd married. If Elaina was going to become an outcast, he didn't want to be close to it, and he told his wife later, in bed, not to encourage anyone to battle the priest. "He's insane for sure," he told her, "but I want no part of this." His wife began to lose respect for him starting that night, even though she said nothing.

Before Elaina walked home, though, Jibril asked her if he should go speak to Father on her behalf. "Let's get this settled now. Your son and I will go together, so he knows you have men to stand behind you." But she turned down the offer, because she understood human nature and could already see her daughter's father-in-law receding quietly within himself, withdrawing from the conversation, and she didn't want to cause problems for Samar. Abu Rafah had always been a follower—her husband used to say so, how many years ago now?—not willing to step forward. He wasn't with the other men that night the Israelis raided the village—he'd hidden in the caves with the rest of them, claiming his back was acting up again. Not that she blamed him, even now. If she could have convinced her husband not to go, wouldn't she have done it? Who was the loser here, she who was married to a martyr, or Jibril's mother, who still had a husband to defend her and share stories with her in their old age? Elaina missed her husband more than ever, as he would have settled the matter by visiting the priest—he feared no one—and cracking his jaw.

As Elaina walked home that night, she passed the church and

paused before it, to make the sign of the cross, as was her habit. But her right hand moved slowly from her forehead to the center of her chest, side to side—and then dropped tiredly. The statue of the Virgin stood at the pinnacle of the white stone edifice, still pock-marked by bullets. The parishioners had voted not to repair it, to leave it as a symbol of what they had endured. Even now, the tourists from France, Germany, and Switzerland, who passed through their village on their Holy Land tours or as part of their pilgrimages, photographed this damaged lady, pulling out their slim digital cameras to snap her image.

Elaina continued walking home. She was sixty years old. She felt even older. Her daughter was married, her son was married—one child each so far. More blessings hopefully in the future. Was she up for a fight with this priest, who had arrived and attacked their quiet life?

Leave us be, she wanted to tell him. We have bigger problems than you.

Behind her, the Virgin glowed, its white stone a sharp contrast to the black night, small shadows pooling in the crevices left by the long bullets of terrible guns.

❧

The village simmered, like a bubbling volcano, for weeks about the news of an agent of Satan living amongst them, potentially in the disguise of Elaina Khoury. Mr. al-Qudsi, who had also stayed behind in Tel al-Hilou that night of the raid, long ago, but had been missed by the bullets, was furious and strode angrily to the pastor's residence, a large new house behind the church building. "Her husband was my best man," he said angrily, not caring that the olive-skinned, thickly bearded young man before him wore a priests' collar. "She's a good woman, and now people are gossiping about her."

"Remember what I said about the devil," the priest said, speaking almost in a whisper. "He works in quiet but surprising ways. He lurks everywhere, waiting to catch you."

"That is ridiculous." Al-Qudsi's chest heaved deeply from his brisk walk. "She has the kindest heart in this village."

The priest leaned forward over his desk. "I am God's messenger," he said simply, not blinking. "She is obstructing the path of others to me. God cannot tolerate such tampering with salvation."

Mr. al-Qudsi concluded, as others had, that the man was insane and when he returned home, he drank a cup of tea to gather his scattered thoughts, then urged her to call Elaina immediately. By Tuesday morning, we all knew of the conversation. More fuel poured on the flames. Mrs. Farah, entertaining four ladies in her salon on Wednesday afternoon, served *baklawa* on her new, gold-trimmed dessert plates and said she felt that anyone who took up a petition against the priest was committing a sin. "It's a crime against the church," she said simply, fluffing her hair with her meaty hands and their blood-red nails. "You really should come to church more regularly, to hear his sermons. His voice!" she told Mrs. Radwan. "Don't you think," she said, turning to Mrs. Toufic, "that they're wonderful? That his voice is heavenly?" The voluminous hostess had no way of knowing that, last month, after the slim and curvy Mrs. Toufic has raised herself from her knees after her own confession held in the back of the small chapel, that the priest had placed his hand on her waist and kissed her fully on the mouth, sliding his tongue expertly across the top row of her teeth. As he pressed her closer to his black robe, he whispered of his need for her, of how a man could only deny his body for so long for the sake of his soul, and how God knew and understood this. "Yes, his sermons are enlightening," Mrs. Toufic replied now to her hostess, thinking that she'd been back to confession so often since that first kiss, that she wore thigh-high stockings to make things easier. "It's terrible what Elaina and these older women are doing." The others agreed that they should be ashamed and that perhaps they should all join the Ladies' Society to wrest control away from the older women, an idea that pleased Mrs. Farah, who liked to consider herself one of the younger ladies.

Elaina wrote letters and did her research quietly; she continued to attend mass and Samar went with her, leaving Fares with Jibril for those two hours. She met her mother every Sunday morning for three months in the lobby, beside a large icon of Jesus Christ trimmed in gold, his elongated face and droopy eyes sad and fore-boding. They sat together, mother and daughter, in the middle row of pews, while everyone around them filtered to the altar for com-munion, and waited quietly during sermons that seemed to revolve around the priest himself and his divine mission. Coffee hour was like the Red Sea, as people parted to two sides of the small room: those who supported the priest and those who were suspicious.

In July, the priest announced that the Ladies Society was being terminated. A new society, the Parish Ladies' Committee, was to replace it, and its President was Mrs. Farah and its treasurer was Mrs. Toufic. Only women in good standing in the church could join with his approval. War had been officially declared.

Elaina was ready.

She wrote a letter to the bishop, explaining that the priest was blasphemous, and including a letter from the consulate in Syria, her prized proof, attesting that Father John had been expelled from the country by order of his employer, the St. George Orthodox Basilica, and his visa revoked. She also included a list of eighty signatures of the petition. What she did not mention was that as many people had refused to sign it, and she had detected both fear and annoyance in their eyes as they turned her down. "Maybe you should go to confession," one of her old friends had suggested kindly, and in that way, had closed the subject. She mailed the letter and waited for justice.

A letter was delivered to Elaina two weeks later, on a Saturday afternoon. The altar boy who delivered it knocked first on her daughter-in-law's door downstairs and was directed to go up the stairs on the side of the building. He almost tripped on the cracked mosaic welcome, knocked several times, but when he got no reply, slipped the letter under the door as the priest had instructed. Elaina stepped out of the bath thirty minutes later and saw the letter. According to what we heard, she opened the door to air out the apartment, the wind blowing on her wet hair, while she read it. Her daughter-in-law hurried upstairs, leaving the baby wailing in the crib, when she heard the screams.

Samar spent the rest of the week in her mother's apartment, leaving only to check on Fares at home, massaging her mother's face, the left side of which had frozen in place, the mouth twisted at a bizarre angle. "*Lefhit hawa,*" the doctor had pronounced. "It may return to normal and relax, or . . ." Elaina only admitted Samar to the apartment, allowing no one else to see her, and filled her daughter's ears with angry words, spewed with drool that dripped down her chin, at what the priest had done, what he had actually had had the nerve, God help him, to do. The letter itself, meanwhile, was circulating throughout the village, taken up by Imm Fareed and Mrs. al-Qudsi, who were surprised to see that half the people were furious, but the other half seemed to think that the tragedy had confirmed the priest's divine power. (Many years later, while sitting in a *servees* to attend Catholic mass in Ramallah, Imm Fareed would recount the story of Elaina to another lady, and she would remark that it was curious how quickly and easily Father had divided them all up, "like straining the tea through the *musfai,*" she added, "and my friend, God rest her soul, she and I fell to the bottom.") Mrs. al-Qudsi and Imm Fareed continued their persuasive door-to-door campaigns, baking *baklawa,* paying visits and showing the awful, unthinkable letter.

"Just listen," Samar said to her mother-in-law one night, when she'd arrived home late again to find Fares bathed and put to sleep. Jibril's mother had kept dinner warm and prepared two cigarettes.

> "*Miss Elaina Khoury* [not even "Mrs."!, you see, to acknowledge she was once married], *Due to your recent actions, perpetrated as an attack on the spiritual leadership of the Very Reverend Father John, in the last five months, our divinely-inspired Pastor requests that you not return to his church* [*his* church, the bastard!]. *He respectfully insists that you not set foot on church property or be present at any church function or event, unless you make a full confession of your sins and renounce Satan.*"

"Signed by?" her mother-in-law asked.

"The pastor-idiot, son of a devil himself, and the bishop," Samar replied. "The bishop—the one she asked for help!" She folded the paper back up and returning it to her purse.

Her mother-in-law passed her a cigarette. "The bishop is a fool as well." She thought of the time when he, a man who yearned to be five feet tall, with a nose like a rotten potato, came to Tel al-Hilou preaching that "we Palestinian Christians should reach out a hand in peace," all while Jenin was being bombed and razed! She flung her hand in irritation, as if brushing away a fly. "These men in power—they're all the same. Covering for one another."

They smoked quietly for a while, listening to Fares whimper in his sleep.

"You should see her face. Like a mask," Samar muttered. "She can barely eat—it's like feeding Fares when he was a baby." She didn't realize it—how could she? She wasn't a doctor—that her mother had actually suffered a minor stroke. She put out her stub in an empty plate, then carried it to the trashcan. "My father's been dead for fourteen years. The church is her life. Why take it away from her?"

As they prepared for bed that night, Samar's mother-in-law decided she would put her name on any paper asked of her in support of Elaina, and she would tell her husband she expected the same of him.

The doctor in Tel al-Hilou, who was not really a doctor but a pharmacist with a degree from Baghdad who thought highly of himself, told Samar that she needed a specific medication that she could get from Jerusalem. "They are muscle relaxers and will help ease the tension in her face." Samar reported this to her brother and suggested he go that day to get it. "But the checkpoints are up now," he complained. "It's safer for a woman to get through than a man."

Samar, who felt at this point that the whole world was abandoning her and her mother, left her brother's apartment on the lower level of the house without another word. "Don't be mad!" he called after her. She returned to her house and picked up her son, telling her mother-in-law that she'd be back in a few hours.

"It's not safe to go to Jerusalem. There's a new checkpoint up."

"They won't bother me. I have Fares. How dangerous do I look?"

But four hours later, when the soldier tapped on the window of the *servees,* it was Samar he wanted. At that moment, she felt she would explode. They'd been sitting in a warm car, for three hours, crawling along to get to this moment, to this arbitrary line in the dust drawn by a cluster of soldiers. Fares had fallen asleep, thank goodness. Another twenty yards, and she would be in Jerusalem, and she would have her mother's medicine. She lifted Fares' head off her lap so she could dig through her purse. She pulled out her ID card and passed it to the driver, who handed it to the soldier. He studied it, then looked at her, then studied it again, and looked at her again.

"Come out," he ordered.

"What? Why?" she burst out, lowering her own window. The other passengers tried to shush her—"Just do it, don't make a problem for yourself," they cautioned, and sighing heavily, she did. The lady in a brown *abaya* and hijab next to her shifted Fares' head to her own lap, and Samar opened her door and stepped out.

"Why you go to Jerusalem?" the soldier asked in broken Arabic.

"To get medicine for my mother," she replied pointedly in Hebrew.

"No pharmacies in Ramallah?"

"Of course I tried that, but only the one on Jaffa Road has this medicine."

"And what is wrong with your mother?" He crossed his arms over his chest, his rifle dangling provocatively from his shoulder strap.

He was an older man, maybe her father-in-law's age, and Samar wondered why he was still in the military at this age. Didn't they usually send their youngest men to the West Bank to handle the Palestinians?

From the car, she heard Fares' whimpering. He was awake. "Listen," she said, trying a softer approach. "I just need to get these pills and . . ."

"What is the specific condition your mother has?"

"What?"

"Her diagnosis?"

"Are you a doctor, goddamn you?!" she screamed, stepping closer to him. There was a shout from the car, and then she saw the soldier's fist come around, felt it crash into her cheek. Samar flew back against the *servees,* sprawled across the hood. In her head, she heard Fares screaming but wasn't sure if she were imagining it or not. She looked through the windshield, saw the occupants staring at her in horror, saw the driver, Abu Muhammad, trying to get out of the car.

"Stay in your car! Stay in your car!" the soldier shouted at him in Arabic.

"She's hurt! Maybe you broke her jaw!" Abu Muhammad yelled back.

The other soldiers were now gathered around them. A younger one pulled Samar off the hood and inspected her face. "Get back in the car, and don't make any problems for us today." He opened the door for her.

She nodded, clutching her face, holding it with both hands as though it would come apart, tasting the blood inside her mouth, surging between her teeth. Inside the *servees,* Fares was sobbing inconsolably, and he buried his head again in Samar's lap. One of the older men in the back row quietly took off his white headscarf and passed it to Samar, who pressed it to her cheek.

"Are we okay?" the driver asked everyone.

"Let's keep going?" asked the lady in a trembling voice, looking at Samar.

Samar couldn't speak, but she nodded, and the *servees* lurched forward, kicking up dust as it entered Jerusalem.

Samar, a few weeks later, put in an application at the new visitor's center opened by the convent, selling olive oil, embroidered coin purses and pillow cases, and Miss Salma's history book. When she was offered the job, three days a week, for six hours a day, she arranged to leave Fares with her mother-in-law. She explained her new schedule to Jibril that evening in the same tone as the woman who announced the evening news on the satellite news.

"I don't want you to work," he said brusquely.

"That's fine," she said dismissively, rubbing lotion on her still-bruised cheek, then added that she'd look for full-time work when Fares started school, as though she'd not heard his protest. And she walked out of the bedroom to collect the dry laundry off the clothes line. She was done talking about it.

Samar's face healed after another week, and Elaina's face healed two months later, just slipped back into place one day, her muscles once again retreating to the center. She lifted it up to Samar, waiting patiently as her daughter inspected every line, every curve with her fingers.

"It feels numb."

"I guess that's normal, but I'll call the doctor this afternoon. Thank God for your well-being, mother."

They had an hour or two, quietly in the kitchen, and they spent it sitting at the table, clasping hands.

"On your way home, tell Deema and your brother that I'll see them now." She touched her cheek tenderly, with her fingertips, and made the sign of the cross. "Now that I look like a human being again."

"Imm Fareed wants to see you too. And all your friends."

"Yes." Elaina rested her good cheek on her palm.

"They're causing quite a stir, still. All of Tel al-Hilou knows what happened."

Her mother remained quiet.

"He has mental problems, that son-of-a-devil," Samar said, surprised to hear how fluidly she cursed these days. She's never seen her mother look so lifeless, and it terrified her.

"Mother?"

"They won't stand with me," Elaina said. She'd spent these two months feeling terrified, and she knew what people thought: God had struck her with this malady because of her sins. It was a convincing story. Samar's father-in-law surely believed it. Even the small number of people left who supported her were surely spooked—she knew, she knew how people thought.

"This is why I miss your father," she told Samar now, and got up to make coffee. After Samar had left, she waited for the expected visit from her son and daughter-in-law, and after they'd gone, after she'd held the baby and smiled and pretended all was well and that no sinful priest would rock her, she lay in bed, reciting the entire rosary for herself, her daughter, and the Virgin who stood alone and battered, unmended, on top of a cold building in the center of the village. A month later, when a second stroke attacked her brain, while she slept, she didn't survive it. Samar and Fares found her the next morning, and her hand was clutching the rosary so tightly that they had to bury her with it.

CHRISTMAS IN PALESTINE

1998

The morning that their marriage began to change wasn't different, or at least, it didn't start differently. When her alarm rang at six, Adlah, already awake, tapped it off after the first trill. Ken snored gently beside her, his cheek warm and sweaty against his pillow, some of his gray curls damp against his eyelids. She pulled the quilt off him, leaving only the cool sheet to cover his long, thick body. All their sheets and bedding had to be 100 percent cotton, and she'd learned to read labels carefully. No rayon, no polyester. His average body temperature was 98.9, and that extra three-tenths of a degree meant that their air conditioning was turned on by late April, and that Adlah never packed away her sweaters for the winter. As she slid out of their large, white bed, she suddenly recalled the time she'd naively suggested a Bermuda vacation, and the pained expression that had overwhelmed his face. He looked now like a giant, slumbering on a cloud, his large shoulders hunched up to his neck—such a broad back, like he could carry the world if only she asked.

The bathroom's floor tiles were cold, like the floors back home, and she thought about home as she began her ritual: she stood by the window, lined up all the vials, the three syringes, the pills. Then, before she began—plucking a layer of skin beneath her belly button, plunging the syringe through the foam at the top of the vial to swallow up the meds, the very liquid that made her feel, on a good day, that she was unraveling—before all that, she paused. A sweet nurse had advised her once to breathe, to fill her lungs with oxygen, to think of something calming and peaceful. "Focus on something positive," she'd said quietly, her eyes wrinkled up in earnest sympathy. "It's not science, but I don't know . . . I think it helps." The view from the window overlooked the large maple in the backyard, its reddening leaves hanging on desperately to their branches, defying the uncaring November wind. She gazed at it, then over at the horizon, where the Hudson glittered in the morning light. She focused on a buoy in the middle point of the river, on how it bobbed, tilted and righted itself, over and over, bracing the thrust and tug of the choppy water. She inhaled deeply, smelling the cool air slipping in through the window, exhaled, steady, steady.

"*Yallah,*" she mumbled. Now: wash hands, swab belly with alcohol, pinch skin, then the plunge—wait for it, ah, the initial sting of the tiny needle. Then the second. The third one, in her thigh. A baby aspirin, swallowed without water. Then the suppository, the tiny yellow capsule filled with progesterone, inserted deeply inside of her. At last, the escape into the reprieve of a hot, relaxing shower, where she tried hard to avoid thoughts of victimhood, while the water splashed down on her tie-dyed stomach, all purple and blue bruises from months of such mornings. When she emerged, rubbing her hair and neck with a towel, she heard Ken's voice chattering in low tones on his cell phone. So early that it must be his contacts in India or Japan. "The contracts need to be rewritten to reflect that liability," she heard him say, and she grinned in the mirror as she combed her hair. If she didn't know for a fact that, on the other side of the door, her husband lay in bed wearing only his boxer shorts, his large feet sticking out from the cotton sheets, she would have assumed from the crispness of his voice that he was sitting in his 46th floor office, in his leather chair, wearing one of his Brooks Brothers suits and tapping his chin patiently with one of his Mont Blancs.

She slipped quietly out of the bathroom, out of the bedroom, to the kitchen to brew coffee. As she waited for the dripping to stop, she organized her work papers, which were scattered on the kitchen table, before he had a chance to see them and complain. He'd gone to bed before her, and she'd spent those late hours finishing two cases. Since the treatments had started, when she first realized it wasn't going to be as easy as it seemed in soap operas, she'd cut her work down to part-time: Ken had begged her to quit altogether. Her days were spent tramping all over the city, in Queens and the Bronx mostly, checking in on the foster children who'd been recently placed, translating between Arabic, Spanish and English for the families and her colleagues. Parking, looking for house numbers, avoiding roving eyes in the streets, then sitting at her desk and typing up her reports—it was exhausting. But she'd never once missed a shot, a blood draw, a pill. She was handling it. Ken would often frown as soon as he saw her at their occasional lunches, or when she came home in the evenings later than him, looking wrung out. "This can't be helping," he'd said one night as they lay in bed, having just completed their "homework," as one elderly nurse had called it. So comical, to be schooled on sex by a woman whose breasts hung down to her waist and whose hair shone like a fat, gray pearl.

When the first treatment failed, then the second, Ken had started to worry even more vocally. But even part-time, the work was too good to pass up. People in New York always needed Spanish translators, and more and more, they needed Arabic as well. Requests rolled in as the word spread. Once, there was a lawyer, who'd asked for her services during a trial—the client was facing charges of laundering money through his pizzeria, and he needed someone to review all the Arabic scribblings on various notes, contracts, and receipts, that filled six cardboard crates. A local newspaper affiliate often needed extra help sifting through the headlines in Arabic newspapers and on satellite news programs. The state's social work department had wanted someone to translate its lengthy application for foster care services. "You've become a successful freelancer," Ken had told her admiringly in the past. When she signed up to take a Hebrew class at the community college, he thought it a fine idea. Now, however, he just frowned disapprovingly when he saw her briefcase, an eruption of papers and files. But work was work. She hated saying no—maybe that was the mentality of immigrants, to balk at the ridiculousness of turning down good money; an opportunity to earn eight hundred dollars in two weeks for mere paperwork, not for hard, physical labor, seemed like you were almost taking advantage of someone. When you'd experienced true hunger, "stress" was intangible.

As the coffee perked, she set out his New York Giants mug and poured some milk into it. The buzzing of her phone startled her—she darted back into the bedroom to mute it, mouthing "sorry" to Ken, who'd been trying to reach for it himself while carrying on in his unruffled tone.

The number was listed as "unavailable" and she hurried to answer it in the kitchen, assuming it was Amira.

"Adlah Muneer Miltner?" asked an English-accented male voice, mangling her first and middle names.

"Yes?"

"Hello! Yes. I'm Peter Larner, calling from the London Institute of Near East Studies. I'm the resident Near East archaeologist, specializing in the twelfth century."

As he rattled on, his voice rapid and loud, Adlah couldn't help but think that she was desperate for a cup of coffee herself, and started to pity herself, which she often did these days because caffeine had been on the "no" list during fertility treatments. So were wine, cigarettes, shrimp, running, jogging, and lifting anything heavier than a milk gallon. Ken often muttered that her briefcase counted, once asked the doctor to have a talk with her, which had caused a major argument during their drive home. The self-pity rose up slowly from her ankles, above her thighs, and over her heart—and then she usually hovered above it, treading for a few days in a dark mood, until something distracted her and the tide ebbed.

But now, the words "Tel al-Hilou" caught attention, and she interrupted her caller quite rudely, to ask him to repeat what he'd said.

"It's the village in the West Bank, Israel—"

"Palestine."

"Yes. Of course. One hundred percent. And so I've understood from Anna Orsini that you hail from that town." She remained quiet and listened carefully, and was able to piece together that he'd just explained that his graduate assistant knew Anna, her old graduate school friend. "So we wanted to enquire about your availability. It's the first attempt to dig in this valley, so we want to build ties, in case we're there for some time, you see."

It became clear, as she asked more questions, that his team wanted her to fly to the West Bank to serve as their guide, translator and connection to the townspeople—all in one. They'd already processed paperwork with the Israeli military and the Palestinian Authority: "Now is the time for phase two," he kept saying. Ken strolled into the kitchen, in his green boxers, looking for his coffee. He looked puzzled as he rewarmed his mug in the microwave, listening to her "Mhms" and "Yes's," and she didn't try to give him a clue, just winked at him when the microwave dinged. She didn't want questions, and she could tell he was annoyed as he finally walked back into the bedroom, sipping from his mug that was shaped like a football helmet.

The call, the offer—everything was sudden. She should have felt jarred, hesitant, and so she wondered why she felt so clear-minded about it. "If I accept, I can't leave until after the 20th," she said, the smell of roasted coffee in her nostrils, her mind filled with images of a hillside in Tel al-Hilou. They were all tangible—an orange. A dusty road. A wave from a balcony. She craved it. "There's an appointment I can't miss."

⁂

The 18th was their eight-year wedding anniversary, and they ate dinner at the small French place in Midtown where he'd proposed. It used to be their annual tradition, but they'd not dined there in some time, and Adlah could see that the décor was changed—new, sparkly chandeliers and long curtains, but she didn't mention it to Ken. He was too angry, and had barely spoken to her on the drive over. He'd spent the last two weeks sulking, since she told him about the assignment. Strangely—and it scared her—she didn't care. It was too tiring to muster up some indignation or mount a counter-argument. Now, as they sat and sipped their drinks—he had some Pinot Grigio and she sparkling water—he barely looked at her, just hunched over his menu.

"It's almost like you're not trying," he said finally.

"I am." She felt sick at how he was beginning. "In 45 minutes, I have to go to the bathroom for the 7 p.m. injection."

"I know."

"Christ, Ken."

"But this trip—you don't need to do this."

She didn't answer, not sure how to explain it to him. For two years, her life had been consumed by this thing. Two years of solid failure. Everything on hold, don't change the house, don't buy new furniture, keep the same car. Their lives were frozen in place, awaiting a blue line on a white stick, the symbol of success. Her arms, her stomach were blue from needle marks. And when her father died eighteen months ago, she didn't go because they'd just done an embryo transfer. It had made her sick, to grieve alone—here in New York, while everyone back home comforted each other. She'd consoled herself with the idea that, if it were a boy, she's name him Muneer, and Ken agreed easily, trying to help her deal with the injustice of it. She'd even convinced herself that her father would bless her from heaven, and make things right, make that cycle "the one." And, like a cruel prank, it hadn't worked.

"I'm not leaving till after the transfer on Thursday."

"Flying can't be good—"

"There's no proof of that."

After their plates were slid onto their table and their drinks refreshed, when they'd eaten in near-silence, she ordered a glass of wine, her eyes locked on Ken, daring him to oppose it. He sighed and raised his glass, clinking it gently against hers. The stem looked so fragile, like an icicle in his large hands.

"Happy anniversary," he said softly. "I love you," he added, and the words stung her because he sighed as he spoke them, like it was an exertion of effort.

Tears sprang to her eyes, and without even taking a sip, she stood and picked up her purse.

"Well—what's . . . what is it?"

"Seven o'clock. I'll be right back." She walked quickly to the restroom, sliding between tables of couples too engrossed in one another to notice her.

Later that night, she retreated to the small office on the third floor of their house. Ken had gone straight to bed, having given up on the evening. She finished some paperwork: Two more cases—

two children to be placed before she left—and she wrote up her summaries rapidly but with care. At one in the morning, she called her stepmother, Amira, in Tel al-Hilou—she was just waking up—and told her she'd be visiting.

"It's for my work—I'm doing some onsite translation."

"How long?"

"At least a month. Maybe more."

"Your husband?"

"No, he won't be coming."

"Ah." Amira paused. "Well, I hope to meet him one day. And maybe you'll be able to stay for Christmas. The house is empty, you know."

"*Inshallah.*" She asked her stepmother how things were, if she'd had any recent trouble with the soldiers. How much did bread cost? Were there new checkpoints?

"Sometimes, yes. Sometimes, no." Amira sounded weary. "They wear you down because you never know what will happen. If I go to Ramallah, do I need half an hour? The whole day? I'm getting too old for this guessing."

Amira tried to reassure her. "I can't wait to see you, and spend some real time with you."

"*Ahlan wa sahlan,*" Amira said, her voice full of life. "I'll start counting the days, my darling."

The village hadn't changed very much, she thought as she rode in the backseat of the servees. Entering the village from the south road, she saw some fine new houses, palaces dotting the hillside, hewn of rose-colored stone. But everything else felt and looked as she remembered: dusty roads, patches of green thorny bushes, free-falling views of the horizon that startled you at every curve in the road.

Her colleagues sat behind her, absorbed in their paperwork and chatting about protocol, protocol, deadlines, rustling paper for emphasis. During the flight, they'd spoken with her a bit. "We're so lucky, aren't we? That you're from Tel al-Hilou," Peter had gushed from his seat. They sat, a group of four, in the business-class section, doubles facing each other. "It's a good omen for our research."

"Of course, we're also paying you well," said Christopher wittily, drawing a frown from the noble Peter, but a snort from the usually quiet and irritated Moira, the third member of their team.

"Be nice," Adlah chided sweetly, "or I might mis-translate something for you." Peter practically applauded and even Moira nodded appreciatively.

Now, as they bumped along the south road, Adlah felt quite alone. His wrist hooking the wheel, the driver smoked a cigarette and listened to Umm Kulthoum's "Inta Omri" on his cassette player. A crucifix, a rosary and a blue glass evil eye trinket dangled from his rearview mirror. Adlah remembered what Amira always said: "The crucifix is enough to protect you. We don't need to add the evil eye too—that's a pagan relic." She'd never allowed the *kaf* or the evil eye in their home, urging her Christian and Muslim friends not to hang it. Adlah thought back to her own large and stylish house on the Hudson, where almost nothing sacred hung, not a crucifix, not a *kaf.* Only a small plaque of the Virgin, above the living room door, because it had been a wedding present, mailed from the Ramallah post office, from Amira.

"Whose homes are these?" she asked the driver, leaning forward. His hair was spiky and gray, cut unevenly behind his ears, and she suspected he'd performed the trimming service himself with a rough pair of shears.

"Madame?" he replied with a start, meeting her gaze in the mirror. He reached out to lower the radio. "Es-coos me?"

"These new homes?" she repeated, in Arabic this time. "To whom do they belong?"

"Your Arabic—it's perfect!" he complimented her, ignoring her question. He hadn't heard her because, at the airport, only one taxi had the special license to travel to the West Bank and they'd been shuttled into it by a middleman, who'd instructed the driver, "Ramallah."

"I'm from Tel al-Hilou, actually. I was last here about ten years ago."

"Which family, my sister?" He was eager and curious now, shutting off the music completely.

"I'm the daughter of Muneer al-Ghalani."

"Ah! *Allah yerhamo,*" he offered his condolences. "How did they treat you at the airport?" he asked in a low, intense voice, as if he would turn the car around this instant if she reported that the Israelis at Ben Gurion had troubled her.

"No problems at all," she lied. "*Allah khaleek, ya rab.* Are you also from Tel al-Hilou?"

No, he was from a nearby village, but he knew all the residents of Tel al-Hilou, and he began grandly ticking off their names on his fingers: "Abu Nadeem, Abu Hanna and his brothers, I know the whole Sufayan tribe, I know . . ." Suddenly he paused. "Are you Muneer's daughter from his first wife or from Madame Amira?"

She bristled at his roughly-posed question; it was intrusive, reminding her of how much of an American she'd become. Her New York sensibility shrank from showing an abundance of curiosity, but she reminded herself that the man was just making conversation. "My mother was Lina, his first wife. She died in—"

"In '66, right before the war, no?"

"That's right. I'm her eldest."

"Your mother—*Allah yerhamha*—was from the north, no?"

"From Jenin."

"Right, right," he said, nodding as if to confirm her story. "I didn't know her—I was too young—but your stepmother! She is amazing! She hid a lot of the *shebab* in '87, and one time she saved my brother's life."

"How?"

"Well, he'd been throwing stones, and the soldiers came looking. When they spotted him from a window—the idiot!—they dragged him out and were ready to take him."

"But she threw herself on top of him," Adlah finished, recognizing it.

"And? And?" He waited for a second before adding, "and claimed he was her own son! They kicked her once or twice, goddamn their souls to hell, but then they just let it go. She wouldn't let go of him—she had her arms locked around his neck. He thought if the Israelis didn't break his neck, she would!" He laughed in a merry, carefree way, slapping his palm on the wheel.

Adlah giggled too, despite herself. She had been away during that time, but she'd heard about this incident, had listened to her father complain worriedly that one day the Israelis would come and haul his young wife off to jail if she kept involving herself in the troubles.

They sat silently, content, for several minutes, then the driver recalled her original question. "Those homes back there on the hill—they belong to some of the exiles who came back in '93, after Abu Ammar sold his dignity to the Israelis," he said with a charming laugh. "They wanted a fresh start. It brought a lot of business here—the builders and their lot were happy for the work, but it's drying up now."

"Are they gone now?"

"America called them back, and they obeyed. And why not? The Authority taxes us like crazy—building, income, business, everything. They are making it very hard to be patriotic." His words were grim, but his tone light. "Abu Ammar had his show, he shook hands with his friend and tried to make America love him. They still hate him, and so we're losing. Everything changes, nothing changes." The taxi floated down the hill, further into the valley and towards the center of town. Adlah realized that her initial impression, that Tel al-Hilou had changed little, was quite wrong. Street lights stood tall and dignified, like sentries, along the main road, and a traffic light guided cars at the only large intersection, in front of the *qahwah* and the grocery store. There were paved sidewalks now, and a covered sitting area in front of the post office, proclaiming itself a waiting area for the *servees.*

"What a difference!" she muttered in some astonishment.

"One of those exiles, the owner of a few of those homes—he did most of this. He has a clothes factory, and he tried opening a branch here, but Abu Ammar taxed him 50 percent of his profits! Can you believe it? And the Israelis kept denying him a building code anyway." He sighed irritably. "See? Everything changes, nothing changes."

They spent the rest of the drive in silence, listening to the chatter of the scientists behind them. Adlah was tired—it had been a long flight, all of it spent missing Ken. She'd spoken lovingly of him to the nervous, elderly woman who sat besides her. Her hazel eyes, round and red, had been blinking nervously, and she took deep shuddering breaths, praying loudly during takeoff. "My husband once told me he had a fear of airplanes," Adlah said to distract and comfort her, "so when he was seventeen, he took sky-diving lessons." The woman listened raptly to the story, and Adlah soon launched into another story of how she and Ken met, in a coffee shop in New York where she corrected him when he asked for a Turkish coffee. "I interrupted him, you see, and he didn't seem to mind, but the waitress did. I said, 'Actually, it's Arabic coffee.'"

"Oh!"

"Yes, it is," Adlah said. "And I told the waitress that the menu should probably be changed to reflect that, and she gave me a rude answer—"

"Why? What did she say?"

"I don't recall exactly, but I stormed out of there and said I'd never be back."

"And your husband?" The veins in the woman's hand bulged like worms under the think, blue-mottled flesh, and her fingers trembled as they hovered near her lips.

"He followed me out! And took me to dinner."

"Oh!" gushed the old woman. "How wonderful. I love a romantic story." She had a tale of her own, of her parents, who had barely survived a Russian pogrom in the 1920s, but were separated. Like leaves blown by a gust of wind, they drifted away but found each other in a pharmacy in Tel Aviv. "My mother said she knew him right away. But he needed some prodding. Isn't that always the way? We women—we never forget, do we? Even when we should."

She remembered what she'd said to the woman on the plane: "Anyway, my husband still hates to fly, though. He does as much work as he can over the phone—the last time he flew anywhere was about six years ago. " They laughed about how old fears are stubborn and how old habits die hard.

In the taxi, Adlah began to worry, for the first time, that maybe she'd made a bad choice in coming home. What had come over her, leaving in the middle of a cycle? Ken had dropped her at the airport, had held her in one of his all-encasing hugs, but she'd been unable to really look at him, had hurried it all along, because she was on a schedule, had to check in, find the gate, get situated. Besides his anger had been palpable, and her nonchalance still shocked her—when had she ever not cared about his feelings? Not tried to make it right when he was upset, even apologizing just to repair the mood, to restart the conversation. But this was not something she could fix—he wanted a baby, she wanted a baby, and her body was not complying.

When they arrived at the hotel, the driver got out and opened her door. "Welcome home, sister."

❧

The small hotel in Ramallah was part of a French chain. Adlah's room was cozy and warmly decorated, in olive green and tan accents. The room was small, but the bed was large and soft. The sole indication that the occupant was in the Middle East was the small, framed square of Palestinian embroidery hanging on the wall.

She lay down on top of the green coverlet and tried to figure out the room's telephone system. So the West Bank had its own phone company now—she felt amazed by this fact alone. She pulled her purse toward her, searched for one of the many calling cards she'd purchased at the airport. She dialed the code, then entered the lengthy pin, only to realize she hadn't successfully dialed out of the hotel's internal system. It took three more efforts until she finally heard Ken's gravelly voice on the other end.

"I'm here," she said in a bright voice.

"Honey? Oh good." He sounded rushed. "How many hours are you ahead?"

"Six, I think. It's eight o'clock here."

"Okay, I will call you back, or you call me back in twenty minutes?"

"Yes, sure." She hung up, feeling startled.

Now, in the hotel room, she wished he were with her. She wanted him at the airport with her when the soldiers in white gloves unearthed her carefully packed bags, opened her Follistim pen and questioned her—"Hormones for what?"—and she feared they would dump her progesterone in the trash. *Oh you want to make more Palestinians?* she'd imagined them saying in their minds. *We'll see about that.* Ken, had he been with her, would have calmly and authoritatively told them that they couldn't treat an American like this. But she didn't have Ken's height, or his deep voice, or his white skin, and so she'd remained passive, worry eating away her insides, until someone took pity on her, decided to give her what she wanted. Her pills were returned, and they gave her time alone to repack, and then three hours after the other passengers had passed through, she passed through the line. "How long is your stay?" the customs agent had asked her routinely, but she'd been asked this now a hundred times, by the soldiers, by her husband, by Amira.

"About one month."

He nodded, lifted his hand, but she stopped him. "I don't want my passport stamped." He shrugged. And fuck you, she wanted to add. Fuck you all.

Now, in the room, she unpacked the disheveled contents of her suitcase, and hung all the clothes. She read through some background documents, waiting until 10 p.m. to insert her progesterone supplement. The embryo transfer had taken place just a few days before. Four embryos this time—the doctors were going for broke—and the progesterone would support growth, if indeed, one had attached. She called Ken twice between 8 and 10 p.m, but she couldn't get through. The front desk insisted that the phone system was working well. At 10:30, her room phone rang, but it was just Peter, letting her know they'd agreed to breakfast together in the restaurant at 7:00 a.m. "Your first duty will be to help us decipher the menu," he joked, and she wanted to grumpily point out that surely the hotel staff spoke English, if not a half-dozen other languages. She called Amira and promised to visit soon. "I'm only a few miles away. Don't make me wait too long," and Adlah said she wouldn't. She forgot to try Ken again, and fell into a restless, agitated sleep, filled with worry and images of herself falling, down, down, into a long well, but never hitting the icy water at the bottom.

Within the first week, Adlah acclimated herself to Peter's grueling schedule. They met at 7 a.m. for breakfast, climbed in the servees at 8 a.m., and arrived at the dig site by 8:45. Christopher and Moira complained that Ramallah was only twenty minutes away from the site, but Adlah reminded them that the checkpoint was usually the hold-up. The soldiers inspected her American passport every time, flipping through it carefully. "I've had to wait all day sometimes," one driver told them once, perhaps annoyed by the scientists' complaints. "What do they know about inconvenience?" he later grumbled to Adlah in Arabic. "I once watched a man deliver his own child right there on the road. They were okay, God is merciful." He snorted. "Come live my life. It's all one big delay."

The first day was spent meeting the local crew, at the site of the old Roman fortress. Only two walls remained, shaping an L, and a large brass crucifix had been hammered into the stone. Inside the crevices of the old stones, they found burned candle stumps and sheets of verse ripped from old Bibles and prayer books. "Dedications," Adlah explained to Moira, who was shining a flashlight inside the walls, where spurts of rough grass grew like mold. "We used to come here as kids every winter with our father, to pray."

"For what?"

For the war to end. For a good harvest. For my mother's soul.

"Lots of things. Mostly for good health."

"Oh," Moira said, looking unimpressed. "So, listen. Woman to woman. Are we going to be asked to veil or any of that? Because I'm not okay with that."

"Who asked you to veil?" Adlah asked, startled.

"Nobody. But I'm just saying—" She waved her hand around, as if the concern should be immediately understood.

"You'll be fine." Feeling raw and rattled, Adlah hurried away.

The rest of the day was spent translating for the crew, and later, measuring the lands and studying the plans. "We need to dig underneath the ruins, while not compromising the structure," Adlah translated. "We have to move slowly and carefully." Peter stood beside her, nodding cheerily, his cheeks ruddy, his forehead slick, in the heat.

"What are they looking for, my sister?" asked the crew's leader, Abu Ali, a leathery-faced older man with thick white hair and black brows. "What do they think is under there? We've lived here all our lives and never suspected anything."

Adlah wasn't sure how much Peter wanted her to explain. When she demurred, another man turned to the others and joked, "They're going to make the desert bloom again, show us what we don't know." The others snickered, and Adlah felt compelled to add, "They seem to think that the Crusaders used this fort as a hiding place for certain things—weapons, gold. Allah only knows. They've found caches in other places not far from here."

"That's right. Two years ago, if I remember," chimed in one of the crew, as she'd earned their attention again. "In the Galilee—they found saddles and swords buried under an old convent."

"Who dug it? Not Arabs," asked Abu Ali.

"Europeans dug it," the fellow answered, then challenged his white-haired chief. "Why not Arabs? We cannot do it?"

"No!" protested the older man. "We can, of course, but Abu Ammar won't let us keep whatever we find!" The other men burst into a fresh bout of laughter. Finally, as the laughs faded, the leader raised his eyes to the skies and sighed. "Do I know anything?" he muttered dramatically. "All this history and treasure beneath my feet—let them take it all but let me live here in peace."

"Yes! Yes!" the other men cheered, but Abu Ali watched Adlah, waiting for her reaction. She grinned at him, doing her best to charm him because she sensed that his support would make the whole task run more smoothly. Seeming appeased, he turned away and gave his team their instructions.

She went that night to her old home to see Amira. As she stepped out of the *servees* in front of the large, white stone house, she saw her stepmother's form sitting on the verandah, and she felt a flash of nervousness. She'd been gone for ten years—that was unforgivable. She worried about facing Amira, but it was simple: a strong hug, kisses on both cheeks, and a "welcome home." The older woman's face was still smooth, although there were lines etched around her mouth. She was only thirteen years or so older than Adlah, so young when she'd married Muneer. An act of sacrifice, everyone had said. And yet, she seemed so much older—while Adlah was wearing her tall Aldo boots, with the polished brown leather, and her hair was colored and cut in a stylish angle across her brows, Amira wore one of her light housedresses, like a clean, worn handkerchief, and her hair was more gray than black, her face unadorned and colorless.

The house hadn't changed much—the same velour sofas, the Lebanese marble that covered the floors gleamed throughout the house, their indoor skating rink when they were kids, when their father had started to laugh again. Amira had made them happy again. More than any of her siblings, only Adlah remembered the dark months when her father had locked himself in the bedroom and sobbed convulsively, while she stood by the closed door and shoved her younger brothers away. The only thing new, she noted, as she sat down on the couch, was his portrait hanging on the wall, his *hatta* pure white, his mustache and brows pure black.

"It's beautiful," she told her stepmother. "It really captures him."

"We'll go later tonight, you and I, to pour coffee on his grave."

They did, walking the half-mile to the cemetery arm in arm, and there they sang all the old songs and Adlah wept and so did Amira and it felt good. Some of her tension and misery drained out of her and into the ground, to her father. Take it, she told him. I can't handle all of it. She knew, as she and Amira walked back together and waited for a *servees* bound for Ramallah, that her stepmother wanted desperately to know why she'd missed the funeral. Who would not come home to see her own father buried? But Amira wouldn't ask, and Adlah was thankful that she'd been raised by this quiet woman, who didn't pester and nag. Amira was good at being patient, at waiting. Maybe that was why her father had finally found peace.

The next day, Adlah and Peter, along with Moira, spent only a few minutes at the site before driving to an appointment at the mayor's house. His home was small, not very elaborate, as it was one of the older homes in the village. The furnishings were old, and the rugs on the cement floor worn thin.

"Ahlan wa sahlan," he greeted them. A short man, bald, with plastic glasses, he nevertheless had an authoritative air that made them obey when he pointed at the leather sofas with their worn cushions, rubbed free of their brown color. In fact, the large sofa on which she sat reminded Adlah of a spotted brown cow, with patches of tan on the seat and armrests, and she suppressed a smile.

"Something is humorous, Madame?" the mayor asked quickly in stilted English.

"Your eye always was sharp, Mr. Samir," she said in a soft voice. "But I see you don't remember me?" she asked, switching to Arabic for the last question.

He frowned, but seemed pleased to solve the puzzle she presented to him. "Please indulge me, Madame."

"You taught my brother Issa during his high school year. He finished the *tawjihi* only because of you." She turned to her colleagues and spoke in English. "I'm not surprised Mr. Samir is the mayor now. When I was growing up here, he was one of the most well-respected teachers in Tel al-Hilou. And the most feared."

"You are not Muneer's girl, are you?"

"I am!" A bolt of satisfaction ran through her, and she felt unexplainably thrilled to be recognized, to still be known.

"Adlah?"

"Yes, sir!"

He clapped his hands and came over to her, kissing her cheeks roughly. "A million welcomes, young lady," he said loudly, while Peter watched with a big smile and Moira rubbed her palms together, unimpressed.

She was re-introduced to his wife, who wore a blue housedress and had a patch of white flour on her forearm. Mrs. Samir served them tea and headed right back to the kitchen, too busy to notice the disdainful look of Moira. Adlah wondered if she should tell Moira that Mrs. Samir had once famously smacked a Ramallah boy in the *servees* for harassing a pretty college girl beside him. Would that make her feel better?

Peter prompted Adlah to start the meeting. Adlah began outlining the crew's mission, and was about to detail their requests of the mayor when he halted her politely. "Let's save this part of the conversation until my friend joins us. He should be here soon."

"Your friend?"

"Yes. I told him you'd be coming at 9:30."

"It's 10:30 now," she pointed out gently.

He shrugged. "More tea?"

When he stepped into the kitchen to request his wife brew more tea, Adlah explained the delay. Peter, who usually seemed unflinchingly cheerful, exhaled loudly in irritation while Moira launched into a full-scale complaint. "I need to be back at the dig by noon to meet with the recorders. Tell him we need to talk now."

"He won't. Plus we don't want to be rude if he's invited his friend."

"We don't even know who his friend is! We were supposed to be in and out. This wasn't supposed to be a social visit to catch up on the good old days."

"I can leave now and let you talk to him," she said angrily. She felt herself unraveling, as though Moira were an annoying bird, pecking away and pulling at the loose strings of her thoughts.

Moira huffed and rolled her eyes, then ran her long, bony fingers through her short red hair. "This is ridiculous. You could simply tell the man we're on a tight schedule."

"And he could just tell us to leave his village. Nothing would make a Palestinian mayor more popular," Adlah replied, and put her smile back on when Mr. Samir returned.

At 11:45, a knock on the door interrupted Mr. Samir's reminiscing with Adlah. He'd recounted his school-teaching days with her, pausing occasionally to let her translate for Peter, who seemed genuinely interested and even chimed in a few thoughts, and Moira, who didn't bother to hide her boredom. She started, however, at the sharp rapping on the metal door and sat up straighter, muttering "finally" and they could hear the enthusiastic welcomes of Mr. Samir, then a tall, black-haired man in a crisp white shirt and pleated gray trousers followed him into the room. His eyes were a light brown, under thick black eyebrows, and a deep cleft parted his shadowed chin like a dark fruit.

"May I introduce Mr. Rafah, a businessman from America and wonderful benefactor of our town?" Mr. Samir pointed to Peter and Moira, who shook his hand dutifully, then at Adlah. "Rafah, this is Adlah Miltner. She grew up here—*bint* Muneer, and the stepdaughter of Madame Amira. Perhaps you two remember each other as children? Rafah was also one of my students, long ago," he said to Adlah.

"Not that long ago!" protested Rafah with a laugh. Then he leaned forward and clasped her hand, saying nothing but looking down at her intently as if trying to remember. Adlah was startled that a shiver rippled up her back as the light eyes peered into her own. It must be the damned meds, she thought, making her hyper-sensitive to every touch and sensation.

"I don't remember you," he said finally, in Arabic, "although I certainly know your family. You have a brother in Dubai, no?"

"Yes, he's the youngest."

"A fine man."

"Thank you."

"You live in America?"

"Yes, I left for graduate school in 1982," she offered. "Before the intifada." Amira's good friend, an elderly Greek nun, had miraculously secured Adlah a scholarship in Connecticut, and within two weeks, Adlah was packed and flying over the Atlantic, terrified but excited.

"And I left long before that," he said, releasing her hand as if satisfied that the puzzle had been solved. "So that explains it." He sat down and gratefully accepted the cup of tea Mr. Samir's wife placed in his hands. He held the saucer easily in his left palm, securing the tiny cup with his thumb and index finger as he brought it to his lips. In his right hand, he twirled the beads of a red and gold *masbahah.*

"How is the dig going?" he asked Peter and Moira in perfect English, startling Adlah by the way he got immediately to the point.

"It . . . it hasn't started," Peter replied. "Your English is excellent, sir."

"It should be," he dismissed the compliment. "I lived in America for thirty years." He sipped his tea again. "Wonderful tea, Mrs. Samir," he called to the lady, who had disappeared into the kitchen again.

"The mint is from our garden, Rafah," she called back gaily.

"God bless your hands."

"And yours."

"So?" he turned to Peter. "What are the requests?"

"Excuse me," Moira began, her voice annoyed. "Are you the deputy mayor or something?"

"Mr. Samir asked me to be here, much in the way that I assume you've both asked Madame Adlah here"—he nodded toward her—"to be with you. Let's get on?"

Peter made his requests in full, listing a need to find a local caterer to bring a daily lunch and coffee twice a day; the need for a house to be used for a rest room and a rest area for the members of the dig; the confirmation of how deeply they could dig before requesting further approval, and other details. Rafah gazed directly at Peter, never wavering, although he translated for Mr. Samir at several points. Adlah sat mutely, watching the exchange.

"Very good," Rafah said. Leaning forward, he added, "And these are our requests: you will provide rent, on a weekly basis for the use of the house. You will hire, among your crew, young men who are residents of the village; at least 50 percent of any additional crew should be residents of Tel al-Hilou." He spoke briskly, and cocked his head to the side. "You will also hire three local youths as errand boys, or 'gophers' as you may call them, to be paid on a daily basis. I will send over three boys I know today, from among a group that just lost their jobs at the water department. And no work to be required of people on either Christian or Muslim holidays. Agreed?"

"Well," Peter said, glancing at Moira, who shrugged. "I suppose that works. We agree. One hundred percent."

"One more thing: there are a few good restaurants here in the village. Once or twice a week, rather than returning to dine in Ramallah, it would . . . how to say? . . . behoove you to eat here, to make yourselves visible to the people of this village."

"Sure," Peter said, nodding amiably. "That is a wonderful suggestion. Much appreciated indeed."

"We even have a small hotel here, so if it's not too far beneath your standards"—he glanced derisively at Moira's cropped pants and pink linen shirt—"you might think about staying right here and not in Ramallah. Keep it in mind."

He stood up, and so did they. "We must be leaving," Moira said. "I'm late for my appointment."

"I'll drive you to the ruins," Rafah said grandly. "It'll take a long time to wait for a *servees.* It's past 1 p.m."

"Don't I know it?" Moira muttered, but Peter quickly accepted the offer. They all thanked Mr. Samir, who had remained mute for the past twenty minutes, but now wished them well and grandly invited them to come over anytime. They all walked outside to see a silver Mercedes parked before the house.

"I'll walk," Adlah said suddenly. "It'll take me but a half hour, and I need to stretch." She walked down the stone steps to the street.

"Nonsense," Rafah said in Arabic, opening the front door of his car, waiting for her. "Get in, Madame. The mid-day sun is too hot. Don't you remember it?"

Sensing that he would insist and make a fuss, she silently climbed in. "We'll be there in five minutes," Rafah said, and as he drove, he pointed, like a tour guide, to several buildings they passed. "I bought that strip last year . . . I'm about to put an offer on that storefront there . . ." Adlah said nothing, but felt that he wanted her to speak.

"You must have done very well in America," Peter said dependably, softening the silence.

"Not too badly. I spent thirty years there, wondering how quickly I could afford to come back home."

"Now that you're here?" Peter gently inquired, perhaps struck by the taller man's pensive tone. Rafah didn't respond, but pulled into the site at that moment.

"Here we are." He left the engine idling, climbed out and walked around to open Adlah's door. "Better than walking, no?" he asked, reaching down his hand.

Irritated, Adlah climbed out without his help. "Thank you." She turned to follow Peter and Moira.

"Madame!" Rafah summoned her, and she turned back to face him. "Why are you annoyed with me?" he asked in Arabic.

"I'm . . ." For a half-second, she intended fully on responding as she would to someone back in New York who had annoyed her: the time she told the bus driver that he was a "combleet jerk" for taking her to the wrong stop, or the time she told her old office mate that she needed to take her personal calls to her ex outside because it was too disruptive. In America, she'd created a bold, new Adlah, a woman who spoke freely. But now her inner Arab girl, *bint* Muneer, came out, wanted to please and diffuse any tension, the girl who had remained quiet at the airport while the soldiers with guns dumped out her makeup bag. "I'm not annoyed," she responded.

"You are." He stepped closer. "Mr. Samir just wanted another set of ears with him. He's not totally comfortable in English."

"That's why I was there, to be the translator." Her voice sounded more prim than she wanted it to. "But you rendered me useless. Everyone forgot I was in the room." She started to turn away. "It doesn't matter. I need to get back to work."

"You're wrong, Madame."

"Excuse me?" When she turned again, she almost gasped to see how close to her he stood. "What did you say?"

His light eyes shined down into hers. "I certainly didn't forget you were in the room."

She stepped back uncertainly. "Have a good day, Mr. Rafah." She walked as steadily as she could to the site, where Christopher waved frantically for her help in talking to the crewmen. When she looked back several minutes later, the silver Mercedes was gone.

Friday was her first day off, since most of the crew were Muslim, and Adlah decided to skip breakfast and sleep in. Her legs felt glued to the bed, her head cemented in the plush hotel pillow. Her arms were even too tired to reach for the remote control to at least watch the morning news, to catch the sound of CNN with Arabic dubbing or to find al-Jazeera. Or did the Authority block the broadcasting of certain stations? She didn't remember. It had been a rough four days—and she'd felt like she lived in a dark box, knowing only the company of Peter, Christopher and Moira. She smiled as she thought of Moira's red hair caked in damp brown dirt, after she'd fallen into a small ditch on the outskirts of the dig site. A steady stream of curses had poured from her lips as she'd swung one muscular leg up over the edge to lift herself out. The crewmembers hurried to help her pulling on her lean, tanned arms until she was standing on the ground again. "What was the Madame saying?" Abu Ali had asked Adlah, but she'd grinned at the older man and replied, "I'd better not soil your ears with that language, my brother!" He'd raised his chin up to the sky and bellowed in laughter: "Thank you for protecting my innocence."

"Such is my duty." Then she'd walked over to placate Peter, who stood nervously watching Moira as she marched to the north road. "She's probably heading to the rental house to wash up."

Peter pulled off his canvas hat and twisted it in his hands. Adlah noticed a tremor in his palms. "She's prickly, but she's very good at her job, so that's it. I'm lucky she joined this dig."

"She'll be fine. I'm sure you're all anxious for results. Moira's just more . . . ah . . . vocal about it."

He smiled broadly for the first time, in Adlah's presence. His green eyes almost glowed, and his teeth—chipped, but white—gleamed. "I'm glad you're here, Adlah. One hundred percent. I have a good feeling about this dig. It's my life's work, you know. Unless I find what I hope to find, I doubt I'll get more funding or any grant money to keep investigating." His words were uttered casually, but Adlah suddenly understood his perpetual anxiety.

She spent the rest of the day in bed, reading, thinking about Peter, whose life came down to this moment, to whatever he could unearth from the ruins. She thought about Ken and wondered what he was doing, if he was thinking about her. She wished she had an ultrasound machine, to be able to see what was happening inside her. Her body was traitorously quiet—no fluttering, no twinges, no clues at all. Were they embedding? Were cells dividing? Today was November 29th. She needed eleven more days to know. At 6 p.m., she got up and put in her progesterone, then showered and dressed. She was starving. Ken would disapprove.

Adlah walked out of the hotel and down the street, to a *shawarmah* stand. She bought a sandwich, with extra pickles, and ate it as she ambled along. She heard the chatter of people around her, returned the smiles of the vendors. A young man leered at her, but he was quickly berated by his two companions, and Adlah moved on quickly. A scent came to her: her father's brand of cigarettes. She felt so happy, so calm. Something else: safe. She returned to her room at 10 p.m. and slept deeply.

On Monday night, she left the dig site and went right to Amira's for dinner. She arrived, knocked her dusty boots against the marble threshold, and noticed her stepmother's disapproval. Clucking her tongue, Amira disappeared into her bedroom. "Come here," she called out to Adlah, who was still standing in the salon. Adlah walked down the hallway to the back bedroom, her father's and Amira's, where she saw a towel and a large housedress in pale pink laid out for her on the bed. "You cannot sit on my furniture like that. Shower and dress while I finish the salad."

Adlah didn't bother to argue or protest. She simply started to undress. As she pulled off her canvas pants and t-shirt, however, she was startled by Amira rushing back through the door. The older woman held a bar of soap in her hand, but she didn't speak as she gazed at her nearly naked step-daughter. Adlah rolled her eyes. Amira's own eyes were locked on Adlah's stomach, which was black and blue, a web of bruises from badly aimed needles. The web rose from the top of her panties and climbed over her belly button. Amira's eyes slowly moved to Adlah's arms, to her inner elbows, where the purple bruises from blood draws over the past few months had gradually yellowed.

"Thanks for the soap," Adlah said, breaking the silence gently, taking the yellow, oily cake from her stepmother's limp hand. "I'll be just ten minutes."

Amira pulled away from the door, back into the hallway. Adlah walked into the adjoining shower, a small luxury Amira had installed years ago. When the water was warm, she climbed in and hurriedly soaped and rinsed. She also washed her panties and bra by hand and hung them on the metal curtain rod, as she and her sisters had always done. "Get a chore done while you wash and save me some work," Amira had been fond of muttering. As she rinsed her hair, Adlah's mind wandered to a thought she'd often pondered in the past: how had Amria, at such a young age, become a mother to so many children overnight? Including Issa, who was a newborn? Her marriage had come not long after Adlah's mother's death. Had she really loved Adlah's father? Truly? Growing up, Adlah never noticed anything awry between them. Amira had even had a baby of her own, Yusuf, who was in Dubai now, to study. Surely, surely, Amira and her father had grown to love each other. They'd certainly been affectionate—they danced together at weddings, they walked hand-in-hand to church on Sundays, she served him tea every night and when Muneer got older and his back and leg pains set in, Adlah often observed a nightly ritual: after dinner, Muneer sat on the balcony, with his tea and cigarette, while Amira wrapped his feet in a moist towel, steeped in hot water and peppermint leaves, then she'd massage warm oil into his skin, between his toes, around his ankles until he'd sigh and mutter, "Bless your hands. Bless your heart."

Adlah shut off the water and wrapped the thin, worn towel around her. Everything in this house was like this towel—Amira never threw anything away. As she dressed in the houserobe, Adlah glanced around. There was the same handwoven rug on the floor, the same pink doilies covering the dresser, the same mirrored cosmetics tray holding Amira's treasured bottle of Chanel No. 5 and her pot of kohl, her small tin of brown hair pins and her wooden hairbrush. The quilt on the bed was the same one—pink with gray flowers—given to Amira as a wedding gift by one of her sisters. Life was so hard here, Adlah knew, and that was why she herself had abandoned it. But there was something alluring about the simplicity—she missed the unhurried lifestyle, the absence of pressure to update, refine, keep in touch with fashion. Just to *be*—just to use what you had—was deeply satisfying. And there was always time for a chat, to boil a small kettle of tea. Here, the hours, the minutes, did not own you.

In the kitchen, she found Amira sitting quietly at the table, which was set with two plates and several plates of food—*warak,* hummus, stacks of warm loaves. She thanked Amira and ate, taking care to show much gusto even though her stomach roiled. "You made so much," she said. "As usual."

"You haven't been home in ten years. I get your checks every month and wish I could see your face instead and now you're here. Should I serve you leftovers, or take you to a coffee shop for a sandwich?"

"I miss your cooking."

"I missed you," Amira said, her voice growing intensely, unsettlingly warm as her eyes fixed on her stepdaughter. "You missed your father's funeral. You're covered with bruises. What's happening to you?"

Adlah covered her face with her hands.

"Tell me."

Adlah sat on the edge of her bed in the hotel, trying to dial Ken. The sixth time was successful, and she listened to his deep voice, its natural gruffness, unable to respond at first. "Hello?" it came again, louder.

"Ken, it's me."

"Darling . . ." His voice lapsed instantly into gentleness. "How are you?"

"Okay," she replied, her voice suddenly trembling. Her throat felt raw. She stood up and paced as far as the spiral telephone cord would allow, like an anxious pet on a leash.

"You sure?"

"Yes, yes."

"Your period didn't start, right?" he asked hesitantly.

"No. There's still another week."

"You have some tests with you, right?"

"Oh, only about five or six," she said lightly, offering him a soft laugh. Why did she do this? Always slide into silly humor, not allowing the conversation to become awkward? She was still *bint* Muneer, still deathly afraid of awkwardness.

"And you're not exhausting yourself?"

"I'm being careful . . ."

"Okay."

"Yes."

"I'm sorry we fought before you left." He cleared his throat. "I just worried."

"This is the first time I've really spoken to you all week—"

"I sent an email."

"I know. But talked . . . we haven't talked. I've called every day since I've been here . . ."

"Okay, calm down."

"Dammit, don't tell me to calm down!" Suddenly her tears flowed, fast and freely, and her breath came in ragged gasps.

"Okay, okay . . ."

She accepted that, his way of calling for a truce, a time out. "I'll call you later, okay? Nine p.m. your time."

"I'll be waiting. And email me the hotel's phone number."

"It's in the book by the coffee maker. I put it there before I left. And emailing is kind of complicated here," she said carefully, feeling a dull ache behind her eyes.

"Right, okay."

"Bye." She hung up and walked slowly to the bathroom to wash her face. It was ten o'clock and the breakfast had ended half an hour ago. She studied her pale skin, the emerging wrinkles at the corners of her eyes, the oily strip that was her nose, her chapped lips. Hadn't she read that oily skin was a sign of very early pregnancy? Someone had written that on one of the fertility list-servs she'd subscribed to. Pineapple—someone had also said eating pineapple helped with implantation. She'd scoffed at that bit of information during the last two cycles, but those two cycles had failed. But now, it gave her something to do.

Renewed by a feeling of purpose, Adlah put on her walking shoes and a red, wide-brimmed hat and left her room. In the lobby, she saw Moira and Christopher walking toward the main exit.

"Where are you headed?" Christopher asked.

"Just out for a walk. To meet an old friend," she added hurriedly, in case they asked her for help in translating for cab drivers or for shopping at the bazaar.

Their deflated expressions told her she'd been correct. She waved bye cheerily and pushed herself out of the large, brass-plated door.

The street was busy, and she ambled along, following the curling sidewalks past bookshops, the cinema, music stalls, and endless cafes. Finally, at the open market, she tracked down one elderly man whom the other vendors claimed sold pineapple. But he spread his hands apologetically. "I can only get a few a week. My cousin smuggles them in for me. But the Dollar Grocery carries them."

"Fresh?"

"No! Canned." He seemed genuinely sad about this fact. "Do you know what I want?" he asked, leaning closer suddenly, his eyes squinting intensely.

"No, tell me," she replied, amused and curious, taking in his stained *hatta,* his faded *abaya,* and his stubbled chin. His breath smelled like stale cigarette smoke.

"A kiwi. Before I die, I want to bite into a kiwi and know what it tastes like." He grabbed her wrist. "Did you ever taste one?"

"Come on, come on," murmured the vendor in the next stall, leaning over and gently unclasping the old man's hand. "Leave the sister alone. She's never tried one either."

"Olives are sour and hard." The old man sighed wistfully, addressing the produce lined up in the bin before him as if they were members of an audience. "We love olives because the oranges are all gone."

"He gives everyone the same speech, my sister," said the other vendor, smiling ruefully as he wiped his brow with the end of his *keffiyeh.* "God go with you." She thanked him and pulled herself away, wishing them both a good day although the old man was still lecturing his rows of yellow squash and didn't seem to hear her. Trying to shake off the somber mood that settled around her, she walked quickly in the direction of the grocery store, where she found that a can of sliced pineapples cost nine shekels, or three dollars, which shocked her. "They're hard to get," the owner, a stout woman with a bristly chin said. There were only two cans on the shelf, so she bought them both, as well as a can opener that cost only two shekels. As she paid at the cash register—a scuffed wooden desk with a metal box and a calculator—she looked up at the open door and saw a pair of light eyes fixed on her.

Rafah leaned against the street pole, on which were plastered several posters, overlapping each other, each screaming for attention: "Fatah wants your support!" or "The Nadi's new teen center—now open!" or "All music cassettes—Egyptian, Lebanese, Maghrebi—80% off!" She walked to the door, holding her plastic bag, her black purse slung over her shoulder.

"Madame Adlah, *sabah al-kheir.*"

"*Sabah al-noor.*"

"Where are you headed? Need a ride?" He pointed nonchalantly across the street, and she saw his silver car parked illegally in front of a driveway. It took up space on the street, and a rusty red Toyota Celica maneuvered around it carefully to get past.

"I'm fine, but thank you."

"I'll walk with you."

"Don't you need to move your car?"

He looked at it, as if unsure of her point. "Why?"

"It's blocking the street. And the driveway."

"They never ticket me." She suddenly glimpsed what it meant to have money in the occupied West Bank: you imported designer clothing for yourself, you parked your distinctive car anywhere you found a space, knowing the police wouldn't dare fine you, you dined and lunched with mayors and ministers and made yourself invaluable to them all. Rafah, she could see, had left America, where he was a man, and returned here where he was The Only Man.

"You may not be inconvenienced with a ticket, but surely other drivers will have to find another way to get down the street?" she pointed out, glad, somehow, to have found something wrong about him. An imperfection, a mislaid stitch.

But he grinned and called into the window of a music stall next to the grocery. "Ahmed? *Habibi*? A favor."

A handsome young man, with a mustache that looked penciled-on, stuck his head out of the stall. "Rafah! *Itfadal.*"

"My car is across the street. Move it for me when a better place opens up, *habibi.*"

"*Wa'lay himak,*" Ahmed said, nodding and accepting the keys, tossing them casually on a counter behind him.

"God bless you and keep you."

Ahmed waved his hand, as if embarrassed by the thanks, then turned his attention to a clique of young girls looking at Amr Diab tapes.

"Madame, shall we?" Rafah asked, holding out his hand. She wasn't sure what he wanted—surely he didn't think she was going to hold his hand?—but then he reached gently and plucked the plastic bag from her fingers.

"Oh. Thank you."

"You can thank me by telling me about yourself." He peered down at her.

"Why?" she asked, suddenly wondering if he were an Israeli spy, a plant who kept tabs on everybody and everything. Maybe that was why he enjoyed everyone's eagerness to please him. And why he had so much money. "Tell *me* about *your*self," she responded, refusing to smile when he chuckled. "I want to know."

"How far are we walking?"

"To the end of the road."

"It's a long one, or have you forgotten Jaffa Road?" She didn't answer, so he acquiesced. "*Maashi* . . . I'm from Tel al-Hilou, originally. Like you. I have a younger brother. He still lives in the village, with his wife and son. I was a teenager in '67, and afterwards, because I was the oldest, my parents booted me out to make money. I was the sacrificial lamb."

"Where did you go?"

"Egypt first. Later I ended up in America. I started a business, and thank God for his goodness and mercy, here I am. Trying to come around full circle. I am literally back to the beginning."

"What kind of business did you start? Some kind of clothing store, I heard?" People pushed past them, and the street was busy and loud.

"A factory. I patented a new blend of material—like rayon, but softer—and the manufacturers liked it. It washes well and keeps its color, and its shape, unlike cotton. I learned about material, you see," he began enthusiastically, leaning down and hunching forward as he spoke, so that his lips hovered over her ear, "while in Egypt. Their cotton is the best in the world, but they don't experiment with blends, you see. Cotton feels good, but it shrinks, it fades, it wrinkles. These are problems, yes? I worked in the mills, surrounded by it, watching how they wove it—from fiber to fabric—I learned it all. And, in America, I figured out a way to improve it. And to produce it cheaply."

As he continued talking, Adlah's suspicion that he was a spy faded until she began to feel ashamed of the thought at all. As he spoke, she learned that the houses he'd built on the hills above Tel al-Hilou were for family members—he'd given his brother a house when he'd married, and one to his mother who still lived there. "She hates it, I think," he quipped. "She'd rather be back in our two-room house next door to the church, so she can keep tabs on who attends mass and so everyone can tell her good morning." One house had been made into an orphanage and another had been donated to the village as a meeting center, a library and office space and housing for government documents.

"That land—your homes are built on them. It's your land?"

He nodded. "Most of it inherited. I bought the adjacent pieces so that there would be a clear and secure perimeter. I don't want what happened to the other hill to happen to my hill."

"The settlement?"

"It's huge," he said, nodding grimly. "And I don't want them to ever think they can build another one close by. If the land ownership is solid, under one name, it's harder for them to confiscate."

"They can take it anyway." She thought about the south hill, where they'd been building since she was a girl. There had been riots back then, and a few men shot by the settlers, a classmate's uncle took six bullets to the stomach and lived. Six rubber capsules, each the size of a finger, but inside, her classmate had reported, was a metal ball. "We peeled it like a banana," she'd blabbered, enjoying her brief playground fame. Lawsuits filed, cases submitted to the military courts. Nothing.

"Maybe." He seemed unconcerned, but maybe that was a show for her benefit. "But why make it easy?"

They reached a taxi stop and Adlah realized they were at the entrance to the city. The sun was centered in the sky and blazing, and she felt exhausted. "I'm going to take a cab back to my hotel," she said, reaching for her bag. "Thank you for—"

"No, no!" He pulled it back from her grasp. "Not until I buy you lunch." He steered her up another street until they saw a French-style eatery with a picture of the Eiffel Tower on its sign. "This place," he decided.

Adlah didn't want to argue. She was tired and besides it felt good to walk into an establishment with a man like Rafah, and watch everyone's face light up, to see waiters scurry to give him the best table up on the second level, to have the owner sit with them and personally have him recommend the entrees, to have her glass of juice eternally full. As they ate, they talked and Adlah realized that Rafah had been inquiring about her: he knew of her mother's death, how she'd been raised by Amira, how she'd left for the United States long ago.

"Are you happy to be back?"

She shrugged. "I came back before. To visit. But this is the first time in several years. Once the assignment ends, I'll be leaving again. Or maybe even sooner."

"What are you going back to?" he asked, his voice edgy. "A job? Your children?"

"I have no children," she replied slowly. "But I am married."

"Yes, I heard that," he responded, as if it were no more than a detail dropped in a catch-up conversation with an off-again, on-again friend. Oh, you have a Volvo? A condo at the beach now? A husband too? "An American?"

"Well, yes." He didn't seem impressed, as if a marriage without children, and to an American, wasn't permanent or real, or maybe that was just her imagination. She offered up a quick prayer, as she often did these days, begging for the embryo to be lodged in her uterine wall snugly, for it to be already growing, replicating cells at a steady rate. She wanted to graduate from being a Couple, to being a Family. Everything would start to be right again, if only this could happen. They could exit Purgatory. She'd told Amira everything, and her stepmother solemnly vowed to pray for her, and Adlah couldn't help but feel that God would favor her wish more kindly if Amira were an advocate.

"You?" she asked, turning it around.

"What?"

"Are *you* married?"

"Well, I am in the opposite situation," he said. "I have a son, back in San Diego. But I'm not married."

"Oh."

"I'm not ashamed of it," he said almost sharply.

"You shouldn't be."

"I know." He looked around the second floor. They were alone, and he reached lazily for another piece of bread from the basket between them. "Back here, it's a blight on my name."

"I doubt there could ever be a blight on your name," she said gently. "Everyone here adores you."

He waved his hand dismissively. "His mother and I dated when I was in my early thirties. I didn't want to marry her for various reasons, but I do love my son. His name is Adam," he added, smiling. "He lived with me during the summers when he was a child. He'll be starting college this fall at the state university. Since I've been back, I talk to him every day. He calls me 'his best buddy.'" The phrase—an American one, a log suddenly bobbing up in a river of Arabic—made them both laugh. Adlah couldn't help but think to herself that Rafah had a deep and rich laugh, and a handsome face, when he smiled.

He retrieved his car eventually by calling Ahmed, who sent a fourteen-year-old messenger boy to drive it over. Rafah, in turn, slipped the boy a note before delivering him back to the office building where he worked. He drove Adlah back to her hotel. "I'll walk you in?" he said, ready to park, but Adlah waved her hand.

"No, thank you."

"Okay, I won't," he said quickly. "I enjoyed our talk." He turned on a tone of warmth in his voice, switched it on so suddenly that Adlah felt he was about to say something secretive, private. As she thanked him again and reached for her plastic bag, on the console between them, she looked down at his lap and saw the unmistakable rigidness there, a bulge pressing upward against the pleats of his gray trousers. She said goodbye, slammed the car door behind her, and fled inside.

Later, as she sat on the tub's edge, soaking her tired feet in hot water and greedily eating pineapple slices, she realized that she'd forgotten completely to call Ken.

Work progressed steadily at the site, although it was clear to Adlah that the construction team did not think much of the notion that anything was buried under the ruins. "What if it caves in?" their leader fretted openly to Adlah. "Does the *frangi* have the right to destroy our history because he has an idea?" Adlah often felt trapped, stuck between the increasing questions and Peter's genuine attempts to work in a collaborative way with the team. She saw how, when lunch arrived daily, he walked over to the pack of men, arranging his meal on the rocks beside them, nodding at their animated conversation as though he understood. Moira and Christopher lunched by themselves, like a pair of quiet birds abandoning the flock. Adlah began to wonder, as the days slipped by, whether or not they were having an affair. She didn't know if either one was married, but she realized that, once back at the hotel, they sat at the bar for a while instead of heading to their rooms, as she did, directly for a bath. Of course, she realized, they must be waiting to go off together unseen. One of them—or both—must be married, the thought persisted, or else why the secrets?

She usually took her lunch alone, in the western corner of the ruins, where people placed their candles and offered prayers. In one wide crevice, she could see one bundle of candles that looked ancient—the wax cracked and broken, sheets ripped from the Bible lodged between them, charred. The candles looked like they'd been sitting in the wall for decades—grass had sprouted between some of them. One day, she pushed her face as far as she could to see more—to her astonishment, the opening was deeper than she'd imagined, stretching back almost to the outer wall. One section caught her eye—it looked like a small cave, filled with dozens and dozens of the same type of candle: pale blue wax with a gold-colored base. She saw a gray corner of a sheet and reached in. She pulled it loose slowly, worried that it might crumble. She saw some letters and parts of words—"-tri" and "-essed"—and more. Who had been praying here, lighting candles and offering chants up to the Virgin, so steadily and for so long? She guessed that there were twenty or thirty years worth of devotions here, all using the same blue candles.

"Hello, Madame," came a male voice, and she thought at first it must be Rafah. But it was Abu Ali, who'd sought her out more and more upon learning that Amira was her stepmother. "A fine and noble lady," he'd said.

"*Kifak?*" she greeted him now.

"What have you found?" He took the small paper gingerly in his large hands. "Interesting."

"Seems like a regular worshiper." She explained her curiosity, her wonder at this blue cluster of devotion.

"I don't know all the people of this village, and I only know of the more recent deaths and illnesses." He peered at her face. "You're intrigued, no? Cheer up." He added brightly, "Your wonderful stepmother can tell you anything you need."

"That's right," Adlah said and smiled. She took out her notebook from her bag and pressed the paper into it.

"Madame?" Abu Jamil said reproachfully. "I'm not a Christian, but still . . . Is it a good idea to remove an offering someone has made?"

Like a naughty child, she grinned bashfully and replaced it.

That night, Ken answered on the first ring of her third attempt. She was quiet, listened to what was happening with his work, new plans, new project. Then he quieted down himself.

"You still there?" she asked.

"How are you, really?"

"I'm okay."

"Nothing yet?"

"No."

"Isn't there anywhere you can get a blood test?" he asked slowly. "Won't it be soon?"

"The 30th. I should know then."

"'Know' how?"

"I mean, it would show up." She felt irritated. All she wanted to do was sleep. She'd dined with Amira again, but she'd stayed later than expected.

"I miss you, honey," he said after a pause. "I'm worried about you."

"I miss you too." She said these words routinely, without feeling them. "I'm sorry," she said, again out of habit.

"Why? For what?" he said, sounding alarmed.

"For all this . . . trouble." Because my body should be able, she thought, to make a baby without a dozen needles. I should be able to make a dozen babies without one needle. I should have to take meds to stop my body from making babies, because that is what my body is supposed to do.

"Are you taking care of yourself?" he asked gently, and somehow, it was the wrong thing to say, like a reproach, a reminder that it was all up to her to get this done.

"Yes. But let me go. I'm so tired." Their goodnights were quick, mumbled words, and then Adlah fell into a fitful sleep, imagining an ancient castle, lit by blue candles, being invaded by soldiers with massive swords, who ate up all the inhabitants alive.

At the site the next day, Amira sat in the shade, translating some documents for Peter into English. Now that there was a rhythm to the work routine, she was needed less and less and she felt rather like a toy that had been opened, celebrated, admired and now sat on the shelf to anchor cobwebs for some enterprising spider. Peter was her spider, sliding her documents, snippets of articles—small things and tasks—to occupy her, insisting that he needed the information for his reports.

"How long will you be here?" she asked him this morning. "I mean, what's the outlook?"

"We'll know for sure once we start to actually dig. Now we're still skimming the surface, surveying and might do an underground scan. That might last some time."

"I just need to know for myself. We never discussed when my availability would expire."

Peter peered at her. "Expire?" he grinned.

She giggled, and the bright sound made him laugh as well. "You've hired a very gloomy translator."

"Oh . . . I'd say you're one of the happier elements of this trip," he said, indicating Moira with a slight nod. She stood by the eastern wall, arguing with Christopher vehemently. The younger man was measuring some stones and steadfastly ignoring her. "He's smarter than I was."

"Peter?"

A wave of regret, of sadness, passed over Peter's face. "He doesn't take her seriously."

Adlah suddenly understood: Moira had broken Peter's heart once. She saw, as she looked at Peter, his light hair flopped over his forehead, his skin blotchy with heat patches, a red heat blister snaking up his neck—she saw that he was a man capable of great passion, who could easily lose his heart over a pretty smile or a silky voice in his ear.

"Are you alright, Peter?"

He shrugged. "Yes, yes! One hundred percent." He began strolling to the shade. "Now . . . your schedule? What are your limits?"

"It's possible that I may have to return in a couple of weeks," she explained carefully, "but I may also be able to stay longer. I'm not sure yet."

"I see," he said, and she could tell that he didn't see at all. "Well, if you're able, we'd love to have you stay until at least March."

"The whole winter then?" It was December already.

"They're mild winters, of course. By the time we're clear, we could dig by early February."

"The winters here are actually bitter cold, Peter." She remembered, as a kid, huddling with her brothers and sisters under the thick, goat-hair blankets, vying for a spot close to the *soaba,* her father stalking through the house with scraps of cloth, stuffing them under doors, around window frames, wherever he felt a draft, quietly sliding his hand along the stone walls as if checking for a pulse.

As she sat now, staring at a single line—"The last known Crusade battalion to pass through Tel al-Hilou was a French battalion, in approximately 1294"—she couldn't think of the structure to use for "the last known" . . . suddenly, a sharp longing began gnawing at her insides, a need to stay here in the village, whether she worked for Peter or not. She *wanted* to be here in the winter, when the scent of Amira's baking bread awoke her, to last through it and to witness the spring, Demeter come to seize her daughter, when the purple flowers dotted the valley and the lemons sprouted on the trees. She wanted to stay, to remember that the fruits here were sweet indeed.

"Madame?" came a gentle voice, interrupting her nostalgia. "Can I steal you from your work for a while?"

It was Rafah, with his light eyes.

"*Sabah al-kheir,* Rafah."

"*Sabah al-noor,*" he said, squatting beside her. "I was hoping you'd come see the new library with me. Tell me what you think."

Peter waved her off when she said she was leaving, but they were delayed when the crew caught sight of Rafah. He stood among them, insisting on shaking dusty hands, inquiring after the health of Awad's mother, and after Hassan's son, who'd been in college in Germany now for over three months—how were his studies? He should contact Rafah when he graduated, when he started looking for a job. Did he have a lovely German girlfriend yet? And that elicited laughs from them all. "*Yallah, ya shabab,*" Rafah finally said. "I'm showing Madame Adlah the library today."

"*Allah ma'akum,*" Hassan said, still pleased that Rafah had remembered his son.

"Everyone really does adore you," said Adlah, climbing into the car before he could open the door for her. "When Mr. Samir retires, they'll elect you *mukhtar.*"

"Unless I'm careful," he laughed. "The Authority doesn't care for me much. Neither do the Israelis. And the priest cannot stand to see my face."

"Well, they can eat dirt," she blurted out in English.

He slammed the steering wheel with his palm and laughed. "Yes, they can!" He steered the car carefully out of the site and turned onto the road. "You make me miss the US sometimes."

They drove in silence, up the hill, past the *qahwah,* which seemed to her to be the one structure that hadn't changed in ten years. The men still sat outside on woven stool seats that threatened to unravel under the heavy pressure of their thighs. They smoked, pushing their cigarette stubs into overflowing, sooty plates before lighting another or snapping their fingers for more coffee or tea. This was a place where a man felt like a man, where a raised eyebrow or a snap of the fingers sent a waiter scurrying, where a demand was satiated quickly. The tiny demitasse cups, their designs long rubbed off, now plain, looked strange in their thick, long fingers. These were the fingers, the leathery faces of farming men, she suddenly thought, men like her father, who rode horses everywhere and drank milk freshly squeezed from a goat, not from a plastic jug. The man beside her now, driving a sleek silver car was a new entity—modern, worldly, fresh, but a real man, a popular one, nonetheless. One who could speak eloquently to any woman, but also shoot a rifle like any man. How definitions had changed.

Amira had practically gushed about Rafah, telling her what everyone else had revealed: he was generous, progressive. He had such big plans for Tel al-Hilou, trying to help people find jobs. No, to create jobs—that's how ambitious he was. He could do it, because of the new agreement. Hadn't Mr. Clinton smiled at Arafat on the big lawn, and promised things would change soon? Any day now, when the plans for Rafah's factory were approved, he would hire scores of men. He'd promised Amira and the other ladies he'd hire women as well, giving special preference to widows and unmarried girls who lived at home with elderly parents, of which there were a lot in Tel al-Hilou. He was the only one who'd challenged the new priest, the one causing all the trouble, and could possibly urge the archdiocese to have him replaced.

Yes, he was the future, and he was a good man. And Adlah could still feel the warm touch of his hand on her elbow.

They pulled up in front of the library, a small, squat building with a rounded entrance. As they entered, she could see that while it looked shallow, it was very large inside. There were shelves of books along all the walls, while the open areas featured clusters of tables with computers, a printing and copy station, and another cluster of individual work desks with lamps. "There is a meeting room in the back," he said, pointing. "And a courtyard." He held her elbow as he guided her towards the door on the far left. The door opened to a central, cobbled space, filled with newly planted small trees, wooden benches, and café style tables.

"How lovely!" she said. "My father's house has a courtyard like this."

"So did my parents' old home. That's where my mother would let us play while she did her work—we were safe there, inside."

"Inside, but outside at the same time." She finished her thought with a laugh.

"Right!" He waved at one of the librarians through the glass door. She had just noticed him. "We need to expand the book holdings, but that will have to wait until there are more funds."

"You are really putting a lot of money into this village, aren't you?"

"Not so much," he said. "I like to be here, even though it's . . ."

"It's hard to come back," she guessed, and he nodded. Of course it was, and she knew it. It felt strange to see old women and old men whom she'd idolized or feared as a child, but she now pitied. A few days ago, she told Rafah, she'd seen elderly Imm Fareed, whose tongue Amira had feared. For years, before leaving the house, Amira would check and double-check Adlah and her sisters: Were their collars buttoned over their necks? Was their makeup natural and not garish? Were their skirts at their calves? Collarbones, cleavage and knees were all *haram* to show, according to Amira, and she'd stuck to that rule to protect their reputations from such women. When Adlah had arrived in America, she'd seen that this was her chance, and she stood in a dressing room at Macy's, wearing a denim skirt that barely covered her thighs. She could walk down the street, with naked legs, and nobody cared or even bothered to look.

She asked Rafah to drive her back to the hotel, and on the way, they passed another small building. Children played on a wooden playset in an enclosed gated area in the back. "That's the new orphanage. The nuns from the church manage it."

"How many children are there now?"

"I think six or seven."

She sighed, feeling an ache in her chest, the same ache that had prevented her, these past few years, from accepting invitations to baby showers and even weddings, because every Arab wedding was about wishing for children: She could read it in the eyes of new mothers-in-law as they looked at their sons' young wives, and in the smile of proud fathers as they accepted congratulations. It turned Adlah's stomach and, within two years, she and Ken had effectively socially isolated themselves from the Arab community in New York. "Don't you miss seeing people you know?" Ken had asked once.

"Not really," she'd replied, and he had not mentioned it again, had let her handle the little RSVP cards and the sending of gifts and the invention of endless excuses. Prior engagements, late meetings, out of town, all to save her sanity.

She asked Rafah now to drive her instead to the hotel in Ramallah, rather than wait for a *servees.* "Of course," he said. "It gives me an extra twenty minutes to talk to you." But she didn't feel like talking much, only wanted to curl up in her bed, which the maids would have done up by now, and sleep; the room would be clean and orderly and neat, and she'd be able to close her eyes and retreat from the thoughts of Ken and babies and wedding nights. She sat quietly during the ride, suddenly wondering what it would be like to be in bed with Rafah. He was not as tall or as big as Ken, but he had broad shoulders and she could imagine wrapping her arms around them. The vision of him nestling his face in her neck was so clear to her that she sat up straight suddenly to shake it out of her mind—God, this medicine was really making her unhinged. When they arrived, she let herself out of the car in front of the hotel. He asked worriedly if she were alright. "Yes, yes, yes," was her reply. "Just tired."

After her nap, she felt energized and it was only six in the evening. She sat on the toilet, planning her evening: she'd grab a *shawarmah* sandwich from the corner place, then walk to the movie theater to see what the 8 p.m. show was.

She stood and wiped herself, and saw it right away: a smear of pink on the white tissue.

It was over.

She washed her hands, dug a sanitary napkin out of her purse, and stuck it to her panties. She felt oddly, crazily relieved. There was no more waiting, hoping. No more anxiety—only a bright, clear answer. God, the universe, the Virgin had all agreed: no. Then she dropped into bed, made a cave under the quilt, and put the television on to prevent herself from thinking any more. A movie with Adil Imam was mid-way through, and she left it on, hoping to lighten her mood, but now it seemed like the actor was mocking her with his exaggerated expressions, the bugged eyes and the arched brows. Years ago, when she was still in denial, she'd often hang onto hope, having read articles about faint spotting being an early sign of pregnancy. She'd only accepted the truth when her flow began in full force, soaking through napkin after napkin. She didn't believe in those hopes anymore, and even wondered how she could have been so naïve, so stupid.

Night sneaked up on Ramallah, and the sky darkened, and Adlah slept, the only noise in the room the hum and buzz of their Arabic voices on the television.

A week later, the shops in Ramallah shuttered their windows and doors for Eid al-Fitr. Knowing that Tel al-Hilou, with its large Christian neighborhood, would be still operating, she headed out to call a *servees*. "None are running today, Madame," said the young woman behind the desk apologetically. She always insisted on speaking in English, even though she knew that Adlah, who'd been there now for three weeks, was fluent in Arabic. "I'll call one for you, but it may take up to an hour."

Adlah stood there, tempted to just go back to bed. She surveyed the hotel lobby, which had been decorated at one end with a small, green tree, festooned with red and gold bows, a large, glittery plastic star nestled at the top. A shimmery red cloth swathed the base of the tree. Christmas would be here in just a few days. She wondered if she should take Amira and spend it in Bethlehem, pray at the church of the Nativity as they'd done a few times when she was young and the checkpoints were eased.

"Madame?" asked the woman. "I actually have a few phone messages for you, here. You didn't pick them up. One of them is several days—"

"I know. Yes. Your colleagues told me." They were from Ken, and she didn't want to see them. She'd emailed him the news last week. Now, she was completely unable to bring herself to call him, to hear his voice try hard to soothe her. She was beyond that now.

She asked the woman if she could use the phone to dial a local number. "Please, *itfadali*," the woman replied, handing over the black, flat phone across the counter. Adlah stared at it, wanting some privacy, but found that she didn't care. She pulled a slip of paper from her wallet, and dialed the number scribbled on it in dark blue ink. When he answered, Rafah's "hello" was cheerful and energetic.

"I'm glad it's not too early to call," she said in a low voice.

"Adlah!" His tone was warm, pleased. "What are you doing? The site is closed today, no?"

"I wanted to come to the village for the day. Everything here is closed."

"Let me come for you. I'll meet you in half an hour, *inshallah*, depending on the mood of the soldiers at the checkpoint."

"Use your charm," she advised him, consciously flirting.

"Even my charm wilts at the sight of an AK," he returned jovially. "But if the soldier there got lucky last night and he's happy, I shouldn't get held up."

She laughed aloud, getting more and more used to his bawdy humor. "I'll be here."

"Thank God for that."

She handed the phone back to the woman, who tried to press the stack of messages into her other hand. Reluctantly, not wanting to appear rude, because the girl was just being efficient after all and doing her job, she took them, along with Rafah's phone number, back in her purse. She felt guilty, she knew Ken would be worried, but as she stepped outside, wanting a short walk until Rafah arrived, Adlah decided not to worry about it. Her email to Ken had been curt—"Bad news. My period started. Am staying here for at least two more months. Need time away to think. Love you and sorry."—and she hadn't checked for responses. Even if she wanted to email him today, the internet café was closed for the Eid.

As she ambled back to the hotel, Rafah's car pulled up along the curb.

"Good morning to the sunshine," he greeted her with his charming smile. "I hope you'll spend the day with me, and not just use my car as a *servees*?"

"I have some work to do in town."

He sighed dramatically. "You Americans—all you care about is work."

"And what were *you* doing awake so early today?"

"Working, of course."

He drove her through the center of Tel al-Hilou, where she saw red and gold holiday bows ornamenting the new street lamps, and a tall, regal Christmas tree in the center of the *manarrah*. They stopped at the small house, beside the Orthodox church, where the old statue of the Virgin Mary stood, battered, at the top.

"There's my next project," he said, lifting his chin.

"Replace it?"

"No, not a replacement. Just to fix her—I'm talking to a stone mason in Jericho."

Adlah felt pleased by his answer, and that he somehow understood that a new statue wouldn't be the same. Those pockmarks—

they'd been on the Virgin for as long as Adlah could remember—they meant something and they shouldn't be spackled and buffed away.

She asked him to take her to the Records Office, where she got out of the car, resisting his questions. Inside sat old Mr. Awad, reading his newspaper, a stack of books beside him—*Diwan al-Mutanabbi,* Ghassan al-Kanafani's *Three Men in the Sun,* Aristotle's *Poetics,* the last a battered copy, its cover creased and worn.

"Ya'tik al 'afiyeh," Adlah greeted the man, and he smiled, showing his yellow but sturdy teeth, and pushing his slim, wire-rimmed glasses up on his nose. There were the usual greetings, and the warmth of his voice when he realized she was *bint* Muneer, and Adlah began to see that she loved being identified in that way. "I need help tracking down a death certificate," she said clearly, winning the full attention of both Mr. Awad and a startled Rafah.

"Who?" they both asked.

"I don't know exactly." She recounted what she knew. Amira had told her that the blue candles came from a French convent in Nazareth and that the Qudsi family had relatives there. "Someone from that family, who must have died in the early 1930s, before the second world war, well before 1948." She explained that the candles were found in the oldest part of the ruins.

"If there's one candle for every year that's passed, I've counted at least sixty candles," she added.

"Fascinating," Mr. Awad muttered, and Rafah winked at her as they watched the old man hurry over to a small file cabinet. The mystery clearly absorbed him, and his hands, soft and worn and pale, fluttered over files of papers like long feathery wings, swooping down occasionally to snatch a paper like a juicy worm. "I know a lot of people in that family, but most of them—maybe all of them—are in Europe now. Amsterdam. Or maybe Holland?" he waved at a bottle of fruit punch sitting on a side table. "Help yourselves. I need a minute here." He turned his back.

They sat down on a small couch, but neither reached for the tropical flavored punch, or for the scratched-up smudged glasses stacked beside it. Adlah thought of all the pineapple she'd eaten in the last two weeks and felt sick.

"I didn't know you solve mysteries in your spare time," Rafah said. "You are quite an interesting woman."

Adlah shrugged, wanting to tell him the truth, that she needed a distraction. She wished Ken had understood that her work was a balm, not a thorn. She'd spent the last few years, feeling guilty about working, as if that were the reason she wasn't getting pregnant. No, no, she knew now. Work was good, always had been. She wasn't a mother because the gods had voted against her. Not everyone can be a mother, and she had to accept that. Just as Amira, who never wanted children, had been handed a ready-made family. Why did women think they had choices? Like her real mother, who wasn't destined to be a mother for long. "Someone was lighting candles for sixty years," she said simply to Rafah. "That's amazing. What devotion. It intrigued me."

He touched her. Out of the corner of her eye, she watched his index finger slowly trace a line, gently, down from her elbow to her wrist. An ache warmed her belly, and she tried to gulp without doing so loudly, watching his finger draw circles on the back of her hand.

"What are you doing?" she whispered.

"I am intrigued too," he said quietly.

"Here's what I found!" called Mr. Awad, turning back, triumphant. While Rafah barely reacted, Adlah launched herself off the couch and hurried over to the desk. He settled a stack of papers before her. "Four deaths in the family between 1929 and 1938, but here"—he tapped proudly on one of the sheets—"I'm thinking this may be the one."

"I remember when I was a child, that Demetri Qudsi—he was just a couple of years older than me, you see—he was shot. In the chest—killed him in minutes. It was an accident. Radwan ibn Salim did it. There was a whole riot—*that* I do remember—and they burned down Abu Radwan's farmhouse and chased the man out of town."

"Where did he go?"

"To South America, I think. I'm not sure." He continued and now Rafah stood up and moved over to them, bending down to examine the papers. His hair curled on the nape of his neck, and a soft light triangle crept down under the collar of his white shirt. Adlah wanted to trace that line, to see if she could make him react as he'd caused her to react, almost in revenge, but she forced herself to turn her attention back to Mr. Awad. "So it fits, you see? His mother was from Nazareth, and you say, according to *your* stepmother—"

"Those candles are from Nazareth. She's sure of that."

"And she died a few years ago, so that's why there are no recent devotions."

"If we want to know more, then what?" Rafah inquired.

"Well, let's think now," he said, squinting and pushing his glasses back up on his nose. "Abu Ilyas is about ninety now—he would remember. Imm Fareed is over ninety, about ninety-five, I think. She has a sharp memory, that one, and she loves to talk—"

"Thank you so much, Mr. Awad. I think I'm settled—I'm sure you're right and this is the one." She remembered the fragment "-tri" on the charred Bible paper. This was him. She copied his full name, "Demetri Qudsi" into her notebook. "Born March 8, 1928. Died May 12, 1936." Dead at only eight years old, she thought, feeling sick inside. How could a mother stand it, to see a child play one day, eat his dinner, laugh in her arms, and then witness him lying in a box, being carried away? And sometimes the village could be so heartless, telling a woman to sing at her son's funeral, since she wouldn't sing at his wedding—did they make Demetri's mother do that? Or had that started only during the intifada, when the world and all its traditions had become inverted?

She thanked Mr. Awad for his help, then faced Rafah, who straightened up and was looking down at her. His chest was wide and solid, his white sleeves rolled up over his muscled forearms. She had to look away.

"Where to?" he asked.

"If you don't mind . . ."

"I'm at your service."

"The cemetery then." She wanted to find him; maybe that, she thought, would finally satisfy her curiosity, give her some rest.

He shuddered, but agreed. "But we have to eat something first. There's a place on the way."

"I'm not really hungry."

"I am," he said, starting his car. "You're going to occupy me all morning and then deny me a proper meal?"

"God forbid," she said laughing.

"You should be hungry too. It's almost 11." He turned onto a small road, then steered the car carefully up one of the western hills. "George has good sandwiches, and excellent coffee."

"I've never been to his place."

"You'll love it." They were the only customers and stout George, who wheezed as he bustled about, as though he'd just arrived, waved them to a small table in the garden. "Take your time," Rafah urged him, even though the smell of his grill firing up made Adlah's stomach growl. The garden area had a stone floor, and a vine-blanketed trellis provided shade.

"These vines are still alive," Rafah said, standing by one in the corner. "But see? Their leaves are starting to go brown." He held out his hand to her. "Come here. You can see the church from here."

She moved over, but didn't take his hand. But when he quickly looped his arm around her waist and pulled her into his chest, she didn't step away. His lips were parted, his mouth eagerly dipping into hers, his hands massaging her shoulder blades as they kissed. She wanted to wrap her arms around his neck, but they were trapped against his waist.

"Why are you so sad?" he murmured, releasing her slightly, although his arms stayed in place around her. He pressed gentle kisses on her cheek and forehead. "You never smile. I want to know why." When she didn't respond, instead pressed her fingers to her raw lips, he pulled her in again, cradling her head in his chest. He smelled so good, and he was so warm, that she let herself be snuggled and closed her eyes. It felt so good to just rest, to let him take care of her. His hand traced her spine gently, and she had an urge to unbutton his shirt, to touch his bare skin and see how warm it really was.

They parted when they heard George stirring in the kitchen, then his footsteps clicking on the stone floor. He brought drinks and some small platters of *labaneh* and hummus, and a pile of warm bread. They ate *shawarmah* sandwiches, and while Rafah urged her to relax and have some coffee too, she demurred. "Let's go, if you don't mind," she asked quietly. It was already mid-day and she didn't know how long it would take her to find the grave.

Rafah took coffee in a thermos, promising George he'd return it as he paid the bill. The Christian cemetery was not far, behind the church. The statue of the Virgin seemed to watch them as they walked across the large field, covered in white stones. "Let's start with the oldest-looking stones," she suggested, remembering that each family had its own plot and that if they found one Qudsi, they'd find the boy.

They split up and searched from either end, and after half an hour, Rafah called out to her. She hurried over—there was a gray stone, with the name of Muna Qudsi carved on it. Demetri was around here, then. She looked feverishly—the Arabic script on many of the stones was clumsy, boxy-looking and worn. Rafah found another Demetri, but the dates were wrong—it must have been a younger cousin or relative. Finally, tucked behind two larger stones, Adlah found it: a flat gray stone, half-sunk into the earth. The script on the stone read, "May His Memory Be Eternal! Demetri Qudsi, Martyred May 1936."

She sat down beside the stone, while Rafah stood behind her. He poured the coffee into the plastic lid of the thermos and tried to hand it to her, but she waved it off. She suddenly wanted him to go away, to leave her alone with this stone, with the remains of this child whose mother had loved him so. She imagined him as a tall, lanky boy, with a curly head of black hair, impish eyes, and a beautiful smile. Her arms slid around her knees, and she lowered her head and closed her eyes.

"Adlah, please drink. You don't look well."

"I'm okay."

"What's next?" he asked, his voice sounding nervous. "I'm ready for the next phase of the mystery."

Adlah didn't answer him. The mystery was over, she thought, tears sliding down her cheeks, her breath coming in gasps. It was over, the solution reached, and still no satisfaction. Suddenly, she was overwhelmed, it had finally become too much, and sobs shook her shoulders. She heard Rafah's sharp gasp, then felt him kneel behind her and encase her with his arms. "What is it, Adlah? You must tell me."

She didn't answer, could barely catch her breath, but he kept repeating, "Tell me. Please, tell me." Eventually, he became quiet, holding her securely until the tears receded and the wave of grief retracted. She half-sat, half-lay, in his arms, sniffling.

"Where now?" he asked. "Where do you want to go?"

She sat up and pushed her thick hair back from her damp cheeks. On an impulse, she poured all the coffee from the thermos onto the grave, then stood up. "I want you to take me home."

⁂

She moved her luggage and papers out of the hotel that afternoon, leaving her forwarding information. The first few days with Amira were cozy and sweet—they stayed up talking until late at night, wearing their housedresses and soft slippers, munching on apple slices and watermelon seeds. The teapot seemed to never cease working during those days. Rafah stopped by once, but Adlah asked Amira to send him away, to say that she had a headache. She made a choice. She would write him a letter soon, to explain everything, but right now, all she wanted was to be cradled, coddled, and held—but by a mother, not by a man.

One afternoon, she did leave the house, to visit Imm Fareed. Amira wanted to send her some Christmas cookies. "She lives alone," was all Amira said. "I hope people check on me when I'm that old and alone." The lady was sitting on her balcony, as she did every day, getting some sun despite her ninety years. Her hair was completely white, like a halo around her head.

"Sit, sit," she said, patting the cushion beside her. On the wall behind her hung pictures of her children, her late husband, and a wooden crucifix. "How's my American friend?"

"I'm only recently American, my dear lady," Adlah replied.

"Have your friends torn up our shrine yet?"

"I hope not. I've left the project."

"Oh?" The possibility of gossip, of new information, was still tantalizing to the old lady. "Let's hear it."

But Adlah switched the topic to that of the child Demetri. She told Imm Fareed about the blue candles, the shrine. A look of pain swept over the old woman's face.

"Enough, enough. That was a bad time," she said, waving her hand. "Go in and make us some tea."

Adlah wanted to push the subject, but she obeyed, because people still obeyed Imm Fareed. She found the teapot, the loose tea, and two cups in the cabinet and while the water boiled, she glanced around the kitchen. The walls were crumbling, the plaster chipping in every corner, big holes where nails used to be. She saw a picture of Yasir Arafat set on the table, the glass cracked, and realized that it must have fallen off the wall.

"Here you go," she said, setting a cup on the small table in front of Imm Fareed. "Nice and hot."

"They ruined his family, you know." Imm Fareed's voice was dreamy, soft. "It was terrible. They burned down the house, the barn, everything that night."

Startled, Adlah let her continue.

"We thought it was about honor. A life for a life." The old lady turned on Adlah, who suddenly noticed that her eyes were covered with a film and looked glassy. "But I'll tell you. In the end, it wasn't worth it."

The next night, Adlah asked Amira about her mother. Amira shared some stories: Lida as she arrived as a bride in the village, Lida as she was joyously pregnant with Adlah, Lida as she walked the children to school, with baby Fares on her hip, Lida dancing at Amira's sister's wedding. "Hold on," she said, jumping up suddenly and going into her bedroom. She returned holding a box, and from it she pulled a heavy, gold bracelet—a circlet of linked coins.

"Are these liras? They're all different," she said, examining them under the lamp.

"These are all very old, obviously. This was your great-grandmother's bracelet, and Lida used to wear it a lot. She would have given it to you on your wedding, so . . ."

She slipped it around Adlah's slim wrist. "It's a little big, no? Maybe we can remove one of the coins."

"No," Adlah replied firmly. "I don't want to change anything."

"Well." Amira slid the bar through the old-fashioned clasp. "There you are. *Mabrouk.*"

"It's so heavy."

"Your great-grandmother was a Bedouin girl . . . but she somehow ended up in Jenin and had a lot of children. "

"Thank you."

"It's from your mother, not me. She was strong, and you are strong like her."

But Adlah still wasn't sure.

Two days before Christmas, a telegram arrived from Ken: "Taking a plane from NYC to Tel Aviv. Please send me a car in the am. Let's do this together." And so she made another choice.

Amira asked her to translate it for her, and she did. "He seems like a good man," she said simply.

He was a good man, of course, and Adlah couldn't deny a sense of guilt—she really had locked him out of her hurt for a while now. But would he really understand how she felt, unearthed and rootless, like the old barren women of the Bible? Children rooted you, they put you into the earth and settled you, gave your life a purpose. She didn't want to hear easy solutions about adoption. She knew it worked—she'd helped children in New York to be placed in happy homes. She'd grown up with another mother, and it was all well. But this hurt had to be eased through, contemplated, grasped firmly, first before she thought about anything else.

She watched as, over the course of the day, Amira bustled around the house, cleaning and preparing for Ken's arrival. The butcher delivered slabs of lamb, and beans of hummus soaked in a pot of water on the counter. "He's not the king of Jordan," she called out to her stepmother at one point.

"But he is your husband, and we should still treat him like a king," Amira tossed back, as she swept her way, back and forth, down the hallway.

Adlah went into the bedroom, sat down on the plain pink coverlet and realized Ken would be sleeping here with her tonight. She also saw that he would barely fit—the bed was small, not made for a man with a six-foot-four-inch frame. His shoulder span was probably as wide as the bed itself. He'd be terribly uncomfortable.

But he'd handle it. She smiled to herself. Yes, he would. Ken would probably just wake up, hot and sweaty in the morning, and when she asked how he slept, he would smile and say, in his gravelly morning voice, "Oh, not too bad." Maybe she would take him, when he came, to the site. He would surely want to see Peter's work, and study the plans and hear about the project, but maybe she would take him to the devotional site, to the quieter end of the ruins, and show him the crevice filled with candles. Maybe she would light one and insert it, and offer up a prayer for a child lost long ago, and the one newly lost, and ask the Virgin Mary for some peace.

ACKNOWLEDGMENTS

"Abu Sufayan" was first published in a different form in *Mizna: A Journal of Arab American Literature*, Fall 2011. An excerpt from "The Well" was published in *Banipal*, special issue on Arab American Writers, Summer 2010. "Intifada Love Story" was first published in *Sukoon Magazine*, Spring 2014. "The Fall" was named second runner-up in the Maureen Egan Writers Exchange Award, sponsored by *Poets & Writers Magazine*, 2012. The competition was judged by Elizabeth Nunez. "The Fall" was also a finalist in the Solstice Literary Magazine awards; it was published in the Summer 2014 issue of *Solstice*.

ABOUT THE AUTHOR

SUSAN MUADDI DARRAJ is associate professor of English at Harford Community College in Bel Air, Maryland. Her first book of fiction, *The Inheritance of Exile,* was published in 2007. In 2011 it was translated into Arabic by the U.S. State Department's prestigious Arabic Book Program. Her writing has appeared in numerous anthologies, magazines, and journals. She lives in Baltimore, Maryland, with her husband and their three children.